'You're Miss Ly

This was the mat... frivolity and sprea... neighbourhood? H... could have prepared him... reminded him irresistibly of a small kitten confronted by a large predator. Panicked, out-weighed and cornered, but fighting nonethe-less. He had an insane urge to kiss away the anger that had her deliciously curved mouth set in a firm line.

Until he remembered that her uncle was poss-ibly the most promising candidate for the role of traitor.

And she'd been armed. . .

Julia Byrne lives in Australia with her husband, daughter and two overgrown cats. She started her working career as a secretary, taught ballroom dancing after several successful years as a competitor, and presently works part-time in the history department of a Melbourne university. She enjoys reading, tapestry and playing mah-jong.

Recent titles by the same author:

MY ENEMY, MY LOVE
GENTLE CONQUEROR
MISTRESS OF HER FATE

RAVENSDENE'S BRIDE

Julia Byrne

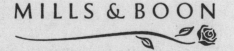

All the characters in this book have no existence outside the imagination of the author, and have no relation whatsoever to anyone bearing the same name or names. They are not even distantly inspired by any individual known or unknown to the author, and all the incidents are pure invention.

MILLS & BOON, the Rose Device and LEGACY OF LOVE are trademarks of the publisher. Harlequin Mills & Boon Limited, Eton House, 18–24 Paradise Road, Richmond, Surrey TW9 1SR

© Julia Byrne 1996

ISBN 0 263 79755 4

Set in 10 on 11 pt Linotron Times 04-9608-90069

Typeset in Great Britain by CentraCet, Cambridge Printed in Great Britain by BPC Paperbacks Ltd

CHAPTER ONE

HE WAS living in a state of siege. There was no other word for it. And no one at Comberford Place seemed to have the least idea of how to deal with such a sorry situation.

Nicholas Everard Dalton, 5th Earl of Ravensdene, glared at the door of the breakfast parlour as it closed behind his late grandfather's butler. This was the third time in as many days that he had been obliged to inform Winwick that unknown females were not to be ushered into his presence, regardless of such heart-rending tales of woe as their favourite puppy escaping onto the grounds through the open gates, the feeling that they were being followed by villainous—but invisible—persons that had come upon them just outside the gates, and, not five minutes ago, a painfully turned ankle, also just outside his gates.

Soon he wouldn't be able to get *through* the gates for the females staging accidents there.

'It's no use sitting there scowling at the door, Nick, old boy.'

The only other occupant of the breakfast parlour, a fair-haired gentleman who was steadily eating his way through a breakfast of gargantuan proportions, looked up to wave an admonitory fork at him. 'It's not poor old Winwick's fault he's a soft touch. Probably never had occasion to deal with predatory women before. Don't suppose your grandfather was hunted right and left when he was alive.'

Nick shifted his lowering gaze to the other end of the table. 'Stow it, Dev.'

A friend of long-standing, Viscount Devenham had

no trouble in ignoring this terse piece of advice. He grinned. 'Do you think Miss Smisby, or whatever her name was, will consent to being conveyed home in ignominious defeat?'

'If she declines my offer of a carriage, she can limp home for all I care.'

Devenham winced. 'Amazing what a man can get away with when he's suddenly become so dashed eligible,' he observed with patently false gloom.

'I would have done the same thing before I came into the title,' Nick retorted dryly. But a wry smile tugged at his lips. 'Besides, I'm no more eligible than you are.'

The Viscount shook his head. 'Not the same. According to m'sisters, I have superior address, but you have an air of danger about you.' The fork was brandished again for emphasis. 'Fatal to females.'

Fatal to my investigation if I don't put a stop to it, Nick thought grimly. But Dev's remarks had touched another nerve. He looked down the table at his friend's pleasant, open countenance and smiling blue eyes, and his own smile faded.

They had both experienced the destruction of war, but Dev had come through it almost unchanged, he realised. His friend's war had been fought across the impersonal distance of battlefields, whereas his own had taken place in the secret, twilight world of the spy. A world where you watched your opponent's eyes as his life snuffed out. A world where you had to be harder and faster than anyone else if you wanted to survive. A world where the line between right and wrong was sometimes very indistinct.

With a swift stab of memory he recalled the proud, young lieutenant who had left England over a decade ago with his new bride and his high minded notions of honour and glory, and found himself comparing the image with the lean face that had stared back at him from his shaving mirror that morning. There had been no trace then of youth or idealism in the cold, green eyes set beneath frowning black brows, nothing soft in the grim, unsmiling line of his mouth, and, not for the first time in recent months, he wondered precisely what it was he had become—and if he could live with the answer.

'Of course the real problem is your mother,' Devenham went on, apparently sensing nothing amiss. He picked up the coffee pot and poured himself another cup with the air of a man needing sustenance. 'I know you were bored with sorting out the mess your brother made of Ravensdene Hall, but inviting her ladyship to accompany us to Comberford was the action of a desperate man. Now that she's put off her black gloves she's had us out to some party or another just about every night, and look at the result—husband-hunting harpies calling on us before we've even swallowed our breakfasts.'

Despite his own annoyance at the situation, Nick had to laugh. 'A hideous prospect, to be sure. But in fact I didn't invite my dear mama, Dev. She invited herself. Perhaps I should have refused her.'

The Viscount looked shocked. 'Good God, no! You couldn't do that. Girlhood home. Hasn't seen the place for years, I daresay.' He paused for a moment, then added rather too casually, 'Didn't know your mother had asked to accompany you. Thought all this gadding about you've been encouraging her to do might mean you're contemplating marrying again.'

A slight narrowing of his friend's eyes was the only intimation Devenham had that this remark wasn't entirely welcome. 'Perfectly reasonable assumption,' he murmured apologetically. 'Know Marianne's death knocked you for six, old fellow, but now you've come into the title... Well, duty and all that. And since you've been perfectly willing to escort her ladyship to every

social event in Sussex, she probably thinks you're
hunting for a wife.'

A rather tense silence seemed to hang in the air, then
Nick stretched his long legs out, crossed one ankle over
the other and contemplated the toe of one highly-
polished Hessian. 'Not quite,' he said at last. 'Actually I
thought my mother's presence might give more cre-
dence to my cover. You see, Dev, I am hunting.' He
looked up, his gaze steady on his friend's face. 'For a
pair of traitors.'

The Viscount promptly choked on a mouthful of
coffee. 'Damn it, Nick,' he wheezed when he could
speak. 'You ought to be more careful what you throw at
a man. Hunting for a pair of traitors? *Here*?'

'One here; the other in town.'

'Good God!' Forgetting such mundane matters as
breakfast, Devenham stared back at him. 'You're *not*
funning. Who. . .? What . . .?'

'"What?" is the easy part. For several years, it seems,
information has been passed from the Foreign Office to
the continent by someone in this part of Sussex. One of
their agents was put onto it two years ago when the leak
was discovered and he eventually found where and how
the information entered France and backtracked from
there. He ended up on the beach a couple of miles away
and hit a dead end.'

'And then?'

'And then nothing. The idiots pulled their man off the
case when Napoleon abdicated and was sent to Elba last
year.'

Devenham groaned. 'Don't tell me. Now they're
panicking because Boney's running amok again. What a
damnable situation, Nick. There's nothing to say the
fellow at this end is still working from here, but you
can't ignore the possibility. The Frogs would give
anything to know Wellington's movements.'

'A situation I may be able to turn to our advantage,

although one would think a man who has evaded detection for years would see through any amount of traps set for him.'

'You're here to spring a trap? For whom? Do you suspect anyone in particular?'

Nick shrugged. 'Sir Jasper Lynley interests me, but he isn't the only gentleman retired from active service who still has contacts in London.'

'Something a touch smokey about the Lynleys,' agreed the Viscount, nodding sagely. 'Don't know about Sir Jasper, but whenever Miss Lynley's name is mentioned everyone clams up. And yet all she seems to do is spread good works or some such spinsterish thing. Sounds pretty harmless.'

'I daresay, but I would like to know more. Unfortunately, Sir Jasper apparently discovered a pressing need to remove himself from the area just prior to our arrival.'

'Would he suspect anything?' Devenham asked doubtfully. 'I mean, you inherited Comberford Place from your grandfather a couple of years ago. Perfectly good reason to be here now you've had to sell out, and—'

He broke off suddenly as Nick held up a hand in warning. Two seconds later the door of the breakfast parlour was opened by a footman and the Dowager Lady Ravensdene floated into the room.

'Remind me to ask you how your hearing got to be so dashed acute,' Devenham murmured in a frustrated undertone as both men rose to their feet. 'Your mother never makes a sound.'

The comment was perfectly justified. Hermione, Countess of Ravensdene, was an ethereal creature whose slender, blonde beauty had made her an accredited Toast in the days of her youth. The tresses, at present covered by a cap of Brussels lace, were now more silver than gold, but her deep blue eyes still held a soulful expression that, together with her fragile appearance and soft voice, never failed to assure her of the most assiduous attention.

The fact that she had managed to present her lord with four strapping sons, all of whom had inherited the tall, athletic physique, black hair and green eyes that characterised the male members of the Dalton family, was, according to the *ton*, nothing short of a miracle. Only the most discerning sensed that, beneath the delicate, pastel-shaded silks and gauzes with which her ladyship draped her willowy form, there was a backbone of pure steel.

Her son was definitely one of the discerning. Fixing his parent with a considering eye, Nick drew a chair out for her. 'Good morning, ma'am. You're astir unusually early. Have you come to take breakfast with us?'

Her ladyship shuddered delicately. 'How can you, Nicholas? You know I take only a cup of weak tea before noon. Good morning, Barney.' The Dowager's gaze fell to the slices of ham still reposing on his lordship's plate. She closed her eyes momentarily and sank into the chair her son was holding for her as though in dire need of its support.

'Shall I ring for Winwick to bring you some tea, then, ma'am?' enquired Devenham, casting a rueful look at Ravensdene.

'Thank you, Barney, but my maid always brings my tea to my room. Besides, Winwick appears to be involved in a most extraordinary argument with someone on the front doorstep. I cannot imagine what it is about.'

'Miss Smisby,' supplied the Viscount helpfully, resuming his seat. 'Haven't met her. Thought she could throw herself in Nick's way, but Winwick is heading her off at the crossroads.'

The Dowager appeared slightly confused. 'Heading her off at the crossroads?'

'Never mind,' Nick interposed sternly. 'Mama, I'm afraid you will have to endure the sight of the breakfast table until Winwick has rid us of our morning caller.'

'If she lays eyes on you, we'll be in the suds,' Devenham explained, apparently feeling that this terse remark needed some clarification. 'Use you to scrape an acquaintance with Nick.'

'Oh, no,' she murmured vaguely. 'A scarlet-and-puce striped walking dress. Not suitable at all.'

'Not suitable for what, may one ask, Mama?'

'Why, for paying morning calls, dearest. What did you think? And speaking of calls, I came to ask if you would be so kind as to escort me to the Wribbonhalls'. Augusta and I are going into Eastbourne to shop, and it seemed foolish for her to fetch me when it means going out of her way. After we depart, you could take Miss Wribbonhall for a drive about the countryside. I am sure she would be happy to point out all the changes that have occurred since you were last in Sussex. She has the most obliging nature.'

Nick exchanged one brief glance with Devenham. 'Unfortunately, mine is not so obliging,' he stated in the bluntest of tones. 'In case you have forgotten, ma'am, I am here to bring some sort of order to the Place—which necessitates my being upon the premises occasionally. That does not mean, however, that your own pleasures have to be curtailed. The carriages are all at your disposal, and you may take as many footmen with you as you like if you feel the need for an escort, but—'

Recognising the ominous signs of danger as the Dowager leaned back in her chair and withdrew a bottle of smelling-salts from her reticule, he forcibly bit back the rest of his lecture.

'Really, Nicholas, there is no need to speak so roughly to your poor mother. Or to loom over me in that odiously threatening manner. Naturally I don't expect you to accompany me everywhere. Although, I must say that, until now, you seem to have been perfectly happy to do so.'

'Getting a bit much,' confided Devenham, observing the way his friend's lips compressed and hastening into the breach. 'Nick's been out of society a long time. Not used to falling over females every time he sets foot out of doors. Why, only yesterday we were waylaid by a bunch of giggling girls on horseback, challenging us to a race. And take the chit who decided to faint in his arms at the Langdons' soirée last night. All a put up job. Can't blame him for feeling a trifle hunted and going to earth.'

Her ladyship revived with unexpected vigour. 'Never have I been so mortified in my entire life as I was upon that occasion,' she declared, gazing reproachfully up at her son. 'I do not hesitate to inform you, Ravensdene, that your behaviour was atrocious. How could you step back in that callous way and let Miss Sherington crash to the floor?'

'Because the little fool was shamming it,' growled Nick.

Devenham started to laugh. 'I should say so. Never seen a female recover her senses so fast in my life.'

In the face of this conspiracy of male heartlessness, the Dowager abandoned scolding for her usual dulcet tones. 'Well, the provocation to teach Miss Sherington a lesson was certainly great,' she conceded. 'However, most young ladies, I am happy to say, are more modestly behaved. I am sure Miss Wribbonhall, for one, would never—'

'Now, look, Mama, before you go any further, let me make it quite clear that—'

Once again Devenham hurried to avert a threatened relapse. 'Be happy to escort your ladyship to the Wribbonhalls' this morning,' he intervened, smiling winningly. 'That is, if you don't object to cutting a dash in a sporting vehicle for a few miles, ma'am. Been teaching Miss Wribbonhall to drive a high-perch phaeton, you know.'

Lady Ravensdene bestowed a seraphic smile upon him and gave him to understand that she was still quite capable of cutting dashes. 'Dear Barney,' she murmured. 'Always so obliging.' She rose from her chair and, after patting Ravensdene's arm in an absent-minded way which nevertheless managed to convey noble forgiveness, drifted towards the door.

Nick stepped past her to open it. 'Dev will be with you in a moment, Mama,' he said, shutting it firmly behind her. He turned to the Viscount. 'If ever a female has matchmaking on her mind,' he stated grimly, 'it's my mother. Bloody hell!'

'Yes, well, I hate to break this to you, Nick, but she isn't the only one. Look at the past week, not to mention the female who dropped her basket at your feet in the middle of the village the other day. If it continues like this, the next thing you know they'll be armed and dangerous. What the devil are you going to do?'

Nick leaned back against the door and folded his arms across his chest. 'Recruit you to distract my mother,' he returned, smiling evilly.

The Viscount put his head in his hands. 'I knew you invited me down here for more than the occasional game of chess,' he groaned. 'I'm to be fobbed off with your mother. You, I suppose, are about to have the pleasure of interrogating some dark, suspicious character.'

'I don't think the vicar quite falls into that category, but, yes, I do intend to speak to him today. He may be the one person in the county who can tell me about the Lynleys.'

'Not if you roll him up the way you just did me,' said Devenham dolefully. He stuck his fork in a slice of ham and shook his head. 'Not subtle, Nick. Definitely not subtle. You'll have to use more delicacy with the vicar if you're going to interrogate him about the neighbours.'

But later that day, when Nick caught up with the Reverend Butterlow in the small garden surrounding Comberford vicarage, he was forced to admit that delicate interrogation was not his strong suit. The trouble was, he reflected wryly, he was more used to holding a knife at his quarry's throat while he asked his questions. It might not be delicate, but at least it got results.

Reminding himself that he was now a civilian, and was obliged to act in a correspondingly civil manner, he tried again to extract some information about his nearest neighbour.

'So the owner of the Grange moved here nine years ago. You are well acquainted with him, no doubt.'

'Sir Jasper Lynley, my lord? Yes, I know him well. And his niece, Miss Sarah.' The vicar interrupted a close examination of his precious roses to beam up at his visitor. 'A most capable girl. Most capable. Feels just as she ought on subjects of a more serious nature. Not one given over to the constant pursuit of frivolity, if you take my meaning, dear sir.'

Nick inclined his head as though in agreement, while he wondered why it was that the Reverend Butterlow's mind, like that of everyone else with whom he had conversed on the subject, seemed incapable of running along more than one track—that of Sir Jasper Lynley's niece. Since it was highly unlikely that such a paragon of virtue was employed as a spy for Napoleon in her spare time, he didn't need to hear anymore about the good works of Miss Sarah Lynley.

Her uncle was another matter.

'I haven't made Sir Jasper's acquaintance as yet, although his land marches with mine. He's staying, at present, in Tunbridge Wells, I believe.'

'Left the day before your lordship's arrival three weeks ago,' confirmed the vicar, bending to tug at a weed that had had the temerity to show itself in the middle of a garden bed. 'But I saw Sir Jasper's carriage pass through the village yesterday evening, my lord. I daresay, if the journey has not proved too much for his constitution, he will invite you to call on him. Seldom goes out himself, but likes to be upon amiable terms with his neighbours. How many times have I heard him say—?'

'They live retired?' Nick cut the vicar off with ruthless despatch. 'That must be somewhat restricting for a young lady.' *And very helpful to a man selling secrets to the French*.

'Oh, Miss Lynley is not in the first blush of youth,' Butterlow informed him. Then added rather hastily, 'But not an antidote, as the saying goes. No, no. She was always a pretty child, and the sweetest, happiest nature—'

But at that point the chatty little vicar broke off of his own accord, his smile vanishing as he shook his head, quite as though Miss Lynley's sweet, happy nature was a matter for the deepest sorrow.

Nick ground his teeth together to prevent the emission of a curse totally unsuited to the hallowed ears of his auditor. He had had enough. This was the last straw.

It was bad enough that no one could stick to the subject of Sir Jasper without digressing to that gentleman's niece, but if one more person began a panegyric on Miss Lynley's sterling qualities, only to break it off with a shake of the head, a melancholy sigh or any other equally lachrymose expression, he wouldn't be answerable for the consequences.

Fortunately for the cordial relations that had always existed between the vicarage and the occupants of Comberford Place, the Reverend Butterlow's housekeeper appeared at that moment with the announce-

ment that another caller was waiting in the parlour. Nick
managed to wind up his conversation with the vicar and
depart with mutual expressions of goodwill. But by the
time he had indulged himself with a gallop across the
Downs that took him to within sight of the Sussex coast,
and was on his way back to the Place, questions about
the Lynleys were again nagging at his brain.

Was Sir Jasper the harmless old invalid he was
depicted to be, or was he the traitor Nick had been sent
here to apprehend? And if Sir Jasper was exactly what
he seemed, what was it about his niece that had
everyone commiserating with her situation? There must
be something. Butterlow was not the only person whose
remarks had been irritatingly mysterious. His grandfather's ancient groom, now living in a snug cottage on
the estate, had started it on the very day Nick had
arrived.

'Neighbours, my lord?' Peake had said in answer to
his query. 'Well, there's the Fishbournes. You'll remember them from the days you spent here as a boy. Good,
solid country folk. And to the south there's Sir Jasper
Lynley and his niece, Miss Sarah. A godsend she is, my
lord, a proper godsend. What I would've done without
her this past winter when the rheumatism got so bad, I
can't tell you. And the number of times she pops in to
the cottage to see how the wife goes on —'

Then he'd stopped and heaved a sigh that had seemed
to come from his very boots.

His elderly housekeeper had been next. 'The dearest,
sweetest girl that ever walked the earth, my lord. Why,
when my Becky's youngest got herself into wrong
company, if you take my meaning, M'lord, Miss Lynley
took the girl in and found her respectable work, and
never a word of blame. But 'twas only to be expected, I
suppose, when you consider —'

And on that tantalising note, Mrs Winwick had shut
her lips tight and become alarmingly formal.

The same thing had happened, with sundry variations, whenever Miss Lynley's name had cropped up. And as he and Dev had been towed about the neighbourhood in his mother's wake, it had cropped up with annoying regularity. He had thought he might finally have an answer when he'd returned the Fishbournes' formal visit earlier this afternoon. Waving away his spouse's offer of tea, Lord Fishbourne had become quite locquacious over a glass of wine.

'I hear Jasper Lynley is back, my lord. His land lies between your southern boundary and the coast, as you probably know by now. Sound chap. Ex-military like yourself. Lives with his niece. Sensible gal. Make some man a damn fine wife, if it wasn't for—' And he'd stopped dead.

At that point Nick had felt his patience disintegrate rather drastically. 'What?' he'd demanded baldly.

But Lord Fishbourne had encountered a gimlet-eyed look from his wife.

'Oh...um...nothing, really, my lord. Females, you know. No making head nor tail of 'em. Girl's taken a notion to remain single. But a very nice little rider. And speaking of riding, do you want to hear what that stupid young cub of Marsham's has done now?'

And the conversation had taken an abrupt turn to the iniquities of the local youngsters.

Nick stared frowningly ahead between his horse's ears and wondered if he was making too much of the fact that, while everyone appeared perfectly happy to gossip at length about their neighbours, whenever the Lynleys were mentioned he met a stone wall within seconds.

It was his misfortune, he decided irritably, that just when he had his hands full with the burden of Ravensdene Hall and the title that went with it, following the unexpected death of his childless elder brother a year ago, his erstwhile superiors had decided that a visit of inspection to his Sussex estate was the perfect cover

and had persuaded him to pick up where their last
agent—since then mysteriously deceased—had left off.

Not that he'd needed much persuasion. Though busy
with the responsibilities of a position he'd never
expected to inherit, he'd been conscious of an increasing
restlessness within himself, a sense of something missing
in his life. He didn't want to think that the missing
element was the feeling of living constantly on the edge
of danger. Because if it was. . .

He frowned, considering. If it was, then he had left it
too late to sell out. And far too late to question what it
was he had become.

A gust of wind whipped through the woods, carrying
the scent of rain and causing the branches overhead to
rustle and sway violently. Nick glanced up, distracted
from his suddenly grim thoughts. He could barely see
the sky through the dense foliage, but the rapidly fading
light was all the warning he needed. There was a storm
coming. One of the easterlies that periodically lashed
this part of the coast.

Pushing his questions aside for the moment, he
loosened the reins a fraction and nudged the powerful
black horse he was riding to a faster pace.

The wind swooped down from the east just as Sarah
reached the top of the steps leading up from the beach.
It snatched at the skirts of her old cherry-red pelisse,
tangling them about her legs, and fought for possession
of her plain chip hat. Below her, the sea began to whip
itself into a white-crested fury.

'Stupid,' she muttered, as a brief splatter of rain
brushed her face. Why hadn't she kept an eye on the
weather?

Clutching her heavy reticule with one hand and
clamping the other over her bonnet, she scurried across
the exposed cliff top towards the shelter of the woods.
Once beneath the trees there was some respite from the

wind, but the light was dim. It wasn't an improvement in her circumstances.

Sarah hesitated, eyeing the narrow, inhospitable-looking path in front of her, and wondered what perverse fate had decreed that there should be a storm on the very day she had mustered the courage to walk alone through the woods after eight years of avoiding the exercise. If wind and rain were to be her reward for trying to be more courageous then she would rather have saved herself the trouble.

In the next breath she told herself not to be so foolish. So what if the stunted bushes on either side of the path looked like crouching, misshapen creatures lying in wait for her? She knew they were only bushes. And the eerie moans above her head were merely caused by branches rubbing together. She was perfectly safe. What was more, she could find her way through these woods if there was no daylight at all. And if she walked very fast she might even beat the rain.

She would *not* run.

A low branch smacked her smartly on the arm as she plunged forward, nearly causing her to drop her reticule Sarah clutched it with both hands, cursing both the branch and her pounding heart. Perhaps she shouldn't have tried to be courageous all the way to the beach. A turn around the rose garden would have been sufficient.

On the other hand, she hadn't had the annoyance of a groom dogging her footsteps and telling her to 'Watch out for that tree, Miss Sarah', or 'Go slow on them steps now, Miss Sarah, they weren't meant for the use of ladies.'

A giggle bubbled up as she remembered the stunned looks on the faces of her well-wishers at the Grange when she had declared her intention of walking unaccompanied to the beach that afternoon. She had caused as much consternation as if she had announced that she was going to catch the stage-coach to London to join the Circus at Astley's Amphitheatre.

Then as another violent gust of wind buffeted her, the tiny sound of amusement faded. Other memories began crowding into her mind. Memories that never quite went away. Memories of the day Amy had died.

Scarcely noticing that she had done so, Sarah quickened her pace until she was almost running, as though trying to outpace the invisible ghost at her heels. She didn't want to remember Amy in these woods. She only thought of her sister when she was safely at home, surrounded by warmth and lights and people.

But warmth and lights and people were at least ten minutes away. And the memories kept coming, taking shape in her mind even as she fought against remembering; for it had been a day like this. . .almost exactly like this. The fading light that kept her gaze fixed on the ground immediately in front of her. . .the swaying trees, branches creaking in the wind. . .the scent of rain. . .the distant, sullen mutter of thunder. . .

She could almost feel Amy beside her. Amy the Beauty. Amy the wilful, the flirtatious, the reckless one, telling her to stop dawdling or they'd be caught in the storm. It had been here on this very path. She had laughed and told her sister that a few drops of rain wouldn't hurt them, that Amy was only concerned about ruining her new muslin dress.

And then just ahead, just where the path crossed a narrow ride, she had glimpsed movement and—

Sarah looked up and screamed.

Out of the wind-torn shadows before her, rising from the very ground at her feet came a creature of horror, a towering black demon, its gaping mouth emitting a shriek that was a hideous echo of her own. She tried to recoil, to slow her headlong pace, but it was too late. The apparition was upon her. She couldn't stop. Couldn't even draw breath to scream again.

Then the black monster was wrenched violently away to the side. Hooves thudded to the ground bare inches away and a blistering curse scorched her ears.

'Oh, dear God!' Sarah stumbled to the side of the path, almost sobbing with relief. She put a shaking hand to the nearest tree and almost collapsed against it. 'It's only a horse.'

A second later she saw the rider.

He seemed to loom even larger and more menacing than the horse, a giant black shadow against the lighter shadows cast by the surrounding trees, his face an indistinct blur in the gloom. He reined the horse around, bringing the frightened animal under control by sheer muscular force, then began to dismount.

No!

He hadn't heard her. The cold fingers of fear clutching at her throat stopped her voice. Sarah backed away, cannoning into another tree as she pulled frantically at the strings of her reticule.

It was a stupid place to keep a pistol, she thought crazily, as her fingers closed around the weapon. The wretched thing weighed a ton, but she managed to level it, hoping the horseman couldn't see how wildly her hand was shaking. 'Don't move!' she cried, the words emerging thin and high. 'Don't move or I'll shoot!'

The rider went utterly still. So, incredibly, did the horse, the two figures seeming to blend with one another as if she was looking at a vision of an ancient centaur. Then—

'This,' he ground out in a furious voice, 'has gone far enough.'

CHAPTER TWO

IT WASN'T the voice of her nightmares.

Sarah sagged limply against the tree trunk at her back, overwhelming relief flooding through her. The voice was deep, rough-edged, and savage with anger, but she had never heard it before.

It was also, unmistakeably, the voice of a gentleman.

'Oh, dear,' she murmured. She blinked several times, trying to think. Now what? Here she was backed up against a tree, holding an unknown man at gunpoint, and she didn't know what to do next. She would gladly have sunk into the ground, but that didn't seem to be an option.

'What's the matter?' the stranger demanded. 'Not quite sure how to go about it?'

Sarah had been thinking of lowering the pistol. Now it seemed like a good idea to keep it where it was. 'Go about what?' she asked cautiously.

'Blackmail, I imagine, Madam Footpad.'

'*Footpad*!' He thought she was a footpad? *Were* there lady footpads?

Sarah shook her head. It didn't matter. She had to extricate herself from what promised to be an extremely awkward, not to say disastrous, situation. 'I think there's been a small mistake,' she began.

He didn't let her get any further. 'Oh, I can assure you there's no mistake,' the dark voice purred. 'You do have the right victim. I *am* Ravensdene.'

'Ravensdene?'

Good heavens! She knew Ravensdene. At least she knew *of* him. He was old Lord Comberford's heir and their nearest neighbour and—

22

'Oh, dear,' Sarah said again. The hand holding the pistol wavered and fell to her side.

An instant later she was slammed back against the tree with a force and speed that didn't even give her time to gasp. Her legs were immobilised between two hard thighs, long, powerful fingers wrapped around her throat, forcing her chin up, and the hand holding her pistol went completely numb under the bone-crushing grip on her wrist. His voice spoke in her ear, the tone so cold and merciless that every muscle in her body turned liquid with fear.

'Never lower a pistol,' he advised softly, 'until you're quite sure you won't lose the advantage.'

She couldn't answer. She simply couldn't speak. Terror paralysed her voice as surely as the hand about her throat. He was huge; his weight brutal, crushing, as he held her pinned to the tree. Sarah squeezed her eyes shut, struggling against the sickening, helpless panic sweeping over her. Had it been like this for Amy? Oh, dear God, *Amy*...

Her fear hit him first. He had, in fact, intended to give the little hussy the fright of her life. What he hadn't expected was that the soft flesh beneath his hand would go ice-cold with shock, or that she would turn so white he could see the blood wash out of her face even in the dim light, could see the damp sheen of fear on her brow where her bonnet had been pushed aside.

Nick knew all about fear. He'd seen it in men before a battle; he'd even used it, made a weapon of it. But he'd never seen such stark, mindless terror in a woman. This was more than alarm at suddenly losing the upper hand. She was in the grip of real panic, almost senseless with it.

The thought shook him—badly. And, shaken, he felt the softness. And the trembling. Sensations shot through him that were violently at odds with the anger still simmering in his veins. Desire, sharp and swift and

hot, but more than that; a need to gentle, to reassure, to
cradle.

God! What was wrong with him? Six months out of
the field and he was in danger of forgetting one of the
basic rules for survival.

Releasing the unknown's wrist, he pried the pistol
from her clenched fingers and examined it briefly. It was
loaded.

'Damned little fool.' Muttering beneath his breath,
Nick pocketed the weapon before shifting his hands to
her arms to hold her upright while he eased his weight
from her. She stayed where she was, scarcely seeming to
breathe, her lashes dark crescents against the pallor of
her cheeks.

'Damned little fool,' he snarled, suddenly furious that
she had made him use such force against her. 'What the
bloody hell did you think you were doing?'

The rough question jolted Sarah back into the present, burying the hideous clamour of screams and harsh
curses echoing inside her head beneath the sounds of
here and now. Gradually the sounds became distinct,
separate; the wild drumming of her heartbeat, the
sibilant rustle of leaves above her, a deep male voice she
didn't recognise.

'All right.' The voice was softer now, more controlled.
The hands wrapped around her arms flexed, but not in
any cruel way. 'It's all right. I'm not going to hurt you.
Do you hear me? You're safe.'

She knew that. Somewhere in the confusion of her
mind was the knowledge that she wasn't hurt. But. . .

She was angry, Sarah realised with a jarring sense of
shock. Furious! Rage was welling up inside her with a
force that made her want to scream aloud with the
pressure of it. Why should this happen to her? *Why?*
What had she done? For years—*years!*—she had been
afraid of her own shadow, haunted by the memory of
violence, hovered over, protected, stifled. And just when

she had tried to be brave, just when she had steeled herself to take the first shaky steps towards facing her fear, *this* had to happen. It wasn't fair. It simply wasn't fair!

Her eyes snapped open to glare straight up at the face of her captor.

'Better now?' he asked quietly.

'If I am, it's no thanks to you,' Sarah flung at him, then promptly fell silent as an instant impression of darkness and power hit her like a blow. Darkness that had nothing to do with the midnight shade of his hair and his shadowed eyes. Power that was more than physical strength, more than a strong masculine jaw and a hard, sharply etched mouth that looked utterly, indomitably, ruthless.

Sarah shivered, suddenly grateful that she couldn't see him clearly, that the daylight seeping through the trees behind him left his upper face in shadow. Had she been foolish enough to lash out at him because he was the Earl of Ravensdene and a member of polite society and thus safe? She peered at the hard face above her and knew that Ravensdene was capable of exactly the kind of brutality she had armed herself against. Tough-looking rather than handsome, he made her think of a predator, fierce, savage and dangerous. He belonged in a jungle, in a dark, deadly jungle.

'You won't get away with this,' she warned, her voice husky and trembling with the strange mixture of fear and rage still roiling inside her.

'I should be saying that,' he retorted. 'But we'll sort out that little detail later. Who are you?'

'Sarah Lynley. Not that it's any of your—'

'*What*?' She was freed so abruptly she would have stumbled if not for the tree at her back. Ravensdene stared at her as if she had just produced another pistol.

'*You're* Miss Lynley?'

'Yes,' she stormed. 'And if you've quite finished

assaulting me, my lord, you may remove yourself from my uncle's land. Immediately!'

Nick didn't even listen to the order. He was too busy trying to reconcile the tiny spitfire confronting him with his mental image of Sir Jasper Lynley's spinster niece.

This was the mature woman who shunned frivolity and spread good works all over the neighbourhood? He rapidly reviewed all the conversations he had had about Miss Sarah Lynley and decided that none of them had prepared him for the reality of dark, wildly tousled ringlets and huge long-lashed eyes set in an exquisite face that, at present, combined feminine delicacy and fierce determination in equal measure.

She reminded him irresistibly of a small kitten confronted by a large predator. Panicked, outweighed and cornered, but fighting nonetheless. The impression was heightened by the faint tilt at the outer corners of her eyes. Eyes, he decided, that, heated with fury, were the warmest shade of amber he had ever seen.

His gaze slid swiftly over the rest of her, noting that the prevailing fashion for high-waisted garments suited her slender figure to perfection. Her pelisse was rucked up at the side, exposing one neatly-turned ankle and a small foot encased in a suede half-boot. Beneath her bonnet, which had been pushed to a haphazard angle, her sable-brown tresses were liberally adorned with leaves and twigs. He had an insane urge to brush them away, to thrust his fingers into those thick curls, turn her face up to his and kiss away the anger that had her deliciously curved mouth set in a firm line.

Until he remembered that her uncle was possibly the most promising candidate for the role of traitor.

And she'd been armed.

His eyes narrowed abruptly on her face. 'Do you always make a point of confronting strangers with a pistol, Miss Lynley?'

'Of course not,' Sarah muttered. She had just discovered that long tense silences were not conducive to maintaining outrage. That intent stare was horribly intimidating. So was his question. Especially when she thought about the various and disastrous consequences of aiming loaded pistols at strangers who turned out to be neighbours. 'You gave me a fright because it was getting dark and I wasn't expecting to meet anyone.'

'I gave you a fright so you whip out a pistol? Good God!'

'I was only being cautious.' She shifted uncomfortably.

'Cautious! You think it cautious to wave a loaded pistol at anyone you happen to meet?'

'I didn't just *happen* to meet you. You nearly ran me down! You had no business to be riding so fast through these woods, and in fact,' she added, grasping at the first frail straw to occur to her, 'if you hadn't been trespassing in the first place, my lord, none of this would have happened.'

'I understand Sir Jasper Lynley allows this bridle-path to be used as a right-of-way to the village,' he retorted instantly. 'However, you may correct me if I'm wrong.'

'Well, no, but. . .'

'In that case, Miss Lynley, I am at a loss to understand why your uncle allows you to walk about unattended when you appear to be of an extremely nervous disposition.'

She flinched. 'I am not—'

'Or is he unaware of the situation? Such freedom would not be permitted in London.'

'This isn't London,' Sarah muttered. She lifted her chin. 'And my uncle is perfectly well aware that I walk about unaccompanied on our own land. There is nothing improper in that.'

When he raised one black brow, she bit her lip. The accusation hovering in the air of the impropriety of brandishing loaded pistols at all and sundry was almost visible. Words of apology began floating about in her mind. Perhaps that would placate him.

'In that respect, Miss Lynley, if in no other, I am obliged to admit you are right,' he owned tersely. 'In which case I suppose I should count myself fortunate that my head is still attached to my shoulders.'

The words of apology vanished. In her opinion, sarcasm did not deserve an apology. Besides, a rather horrible reaction was setting in. If she stayed here much longer she was going to collapse.

'Yes, well. . .' She took an experimental step to the side, hoping her trembling legs would support her long enough for her to escape before she made a bigger fool of herself. Her reticule knocked against her knee with the movement. There was a faint clunk.

Ravensdene's gaze narrowed even more menacingly than before. 'Not so fast,' he ordered. He reached out and plucked the bag from her nerveless fingers. 'Let's see what else you have in this handy little receptacle.'

Before she could utter one word of protest, he upended the reticule and shook it. The contents fell to the ground and shattered.

'What the — ?'

'Shells,' Sarah informed him righteously.

'Shells?' He stared at her as if she'd lost her wits.

'Yes. You know—' she waved a hand furiously towards the beach '—shells. I happen to collect them. And now look what you've done! A particularly fine specimen of—'

'You drew a pistol on me for a handful of shells?' he demanded incredulously. 'What the devil did you think I was going to do? Steal them?'

Sarah glared up at him. She had forgotten all about escape. The perverse sense of satisfaction filling her that it was now Ravensdene who was in the wrong was too revivifying to abandon.

'Why would you want to do that?' she demanded.

'They're in a thousand pieces. And I can assure you, my lord, that it will take a more delicate touch than you possess to piece them back together again.'

That sardonic eyebrow shot up again. His voice went very soft. Very soft and very interested. 'Would it?' he murmured.

Sarah had a sudden desire to take several steps back. Unfortunately, the tree behind her showed no inclination to move out of her way.

'Anyone who smashes people into trees after frightening them out of their wits does not have a delicate touch,' she informed him, trying to rally her wits. 'And as if that is not enough, you've killed all my shells.'

She looked pointedly at the shattered wreckage at her feet, wondering if the words sounded as idiotic to Ravensdene as they did to her. So much for rallied wits. Then she heard an odd sound. Her head came up. Surely that hadn't been—a laugh?

There *was* a faint difference in the set of his mouth, she thought bemusedly. Somehow his lower lip looked. . .fuller. Softer. The sight sent the most peculiar tingles through her.

'Once again, Miss Lynley, I am forced to agree with you,' he acknowledged, the merest hint of a tremor in his voice. 'If it is any consolation, however, the sight of you with that pistol aimed at my head had a rather unnerving effect on my wits, as well.'

Sarah's gaze flew upward. For the first time she wished she could see the expression in his eyes. Would it match the faint gentling of his mouth? The subtle change in his voice? More tingles shivered through her. Very strange tingles. It was definitely time to put an end to this whole ghastly encounter.

Before she could decide on the best method of removing herself, preferably instantly, from Ravensdene's vicinity, however, he stepped forward a pace, reached for her hand and slipped the strings of her reticule over her wrist. He seemed to take a great deal of care over the exact placement of the ribbons, then his fingers closed around hers.

'I hope that under those circumstances you will accept my apologies for frightening you out of your wits, smashing you into a tree and slaying all your shells,' he murmured.

'I. . .um. . .' She was completely unable to think of anything more intelligent to say. All her awareness was focused on the size and strength of the large hand that was enveloping hers and the utterly astonishing gentleness of his hold. How could his grip edge towards brutal one moment, and then. . .and then. . .become almost *protective*?

'I accept your apology,' she managed at last, dragging her hand from Ravensdene's warm clasp and clutching her reticule to her breast as if she feared he might try to snatch it back at any moment. 'Good day, my lord.'

There was a bend in the path only a few steps away. Sarah forced herself to start walking. Head high, she managed to maintain a dignified pace until she was out of sight. Then she gave in to her instincts. Picking up her skirts, she clamped a hand over her bonnet, broke into a run and fled home as if every dark spectre she had ever imagined was at her heels.

Nick was left staring at the empty path in front of him and wondering if he'd suddenly gone soft in the head. He couldn't believe he'd let her get away with it. One minute his would-be assassin had been almost senseless with fear, the next she had treated him to the cutting edge of her tongue, and finally she'd left him with. . .

What? No apology. No explanation. Just threaten to shoot him over a bag of seashells and then saunter off with a 'Good day, my lord.'

No wonder everyone was so damned mysterious about the woman! Now he knew what was wrong with her. She was mad. Insane! A prime candidate for Bedlam!

And the most intriguing little creature he had ever met.

A searing wave of heat hit him as he recalled in sudden, excruciating detail how Miss Sarah Lynley had felt crushed against him from shoulder to thigh. Soft. Incredibly soft. And fragile. He'd almost torn his hand from her wrist in case the delicate bones had snapped beneath his fingers.

Which would really have left him without a head on his shoulders, Nick concluded disgustedly. She would probably have shot him then and there.

But even that grim thought couldn't prevent his fingers curling into his palm as though he still held that delicate feminine softness within his grasp. Nor had desire been the only emotion that she'd aroused in him. She had fought back fear and defied him with the kind of gallant courage he'd seen in men about to charge a battery of cannon.

And once, just for one infinitesimal second when he'd accused her of possessing an overly nervous disposition, there had been such a look of pain in her eyes that he'd felt something stir deep inside himself. Something he hadn't felt for a long, long time.

Beside him, his horse snorted, nudging his arm as if reminding him of the rapidly worsening weather. The movement shifted the gun in his pocket and Nick reached for the weapon, testing the aim and balance before laying it across his palm. For some reason, the sight of the weapon made him recall something else about Miss Sarah Lynley.

She had made him laugh.

He regarded the slim, deadly looking pistol for a moment, then lifted his gaze to the point where Sarah had vanished. A faint smile edged his mouth. A smile that would have caused the battle-hardened guerillas he had once commanded to tread very cautiously around him indeed.

'I'll let you go this time, Miss Lynley,' he murmured. 'But you are going to tell me why you held me up. Very, very soon.'

'*You held him up*?'

The stunned question reverberated around the elegant drawing room at Wribbonhall Lacy as though the walls themselves had spoken. Even the blue and gold brocade curtains seemed to quiver with shock.

Sarah turned from her contemplation of the sheltered courtyard garden beyond the long windows and nodded confirmation. Horrified comprehension was dawning in Miss Julia Wribbonhall's soft grey eyes, but clearly she was still struggling to absorb the tale she had just heard.

'You held up Lord Ravensdene?'

Sarah nodded again.

'You held up the *Earl of Ravensdene*? With a *pistol*? Sarah. . .?'

'I know. He had trouble with the idea, too.'

Julia sank onto a convenient sofa, distractedly brushing away a blonde curl that had strayed over her shoulder. 'I can understand why,' she said faintly. 'He must have thought you were out of your senses. And you say he still has Sir Jasper's pistol? Oh, Sarah! What are you going to do?'

'Get it back before Ravensdene goes to Uncle Jasper. But don't ask me how. I haven't thought of a plan yet.'

'Before Ravensdene goes to Sir Jasper? Good heavens!'

'I wish you would not repeat everything I say, Julia,' Sarah commanded sternly, beginning to pace up and down in front of the windows. 'It is not at all helpful.'

'How can I think of anything helpful with you whizzing about like that?' Julia retorted with spirit. 'Come here and sit down. I swear my head is spinning.'

Sarah obliged, seating herself on a matching gold brocade sofa on the other side of the fireplace. She kicked a fold of her green velvet riding habit out from under one small foot and gazed hopefully at her friend.

'Do you suppose. . .?' Julia leaned forward, frowning intently. 'Do you suppose, if you were to explain about Amy—?'

She was cut off by a laugh that wobbled desperately in the middle. 'What do you suggest I tell him, Julia? My lord, the reason I held you up was because my sister and I were set upon at that very spot and she was assaulted and murdered while I did nothing to help her, so I've avoided the woods ever since unless I'm with someone, and since I was unaccompanied for the first time in eight years yesterday, you happened to be unfortunate enough—'

The rapid spate of words at last dried up. Sarah swallowed hard, fighting back tears. 'Can you imagine what he'd think? That I am positively unbalanced.'

'You know it wasn't like that,' Julia reproached gently. 'You couldn't have helped Amy, so there would be no need to say anything about that part of it. For goodness' sake, Sarah, you were knocked unconscious.'

Sarah stared unseeingly at her hands. 'Not quite,' she whispered. 'I knew. . . I could hear. . .'

'Oh, Sarah, I'm sorry.' Springing up from her seat in a flurry of white muslin skirts, Julia rushed across the small space between them to fling her arms around her friend. 'I'm so sorry. This is all my fault. I should never have reminded you.'

'Hush, it's all right.' Sarah returned the embrace, blinking rapidly until her control was restored. 'I can always go to Comberford Place and demand that Ravensdene give my pistol back,' she said bracingly. 'I can hardly make a worse impression than I already have. Not that I care what he thinks of me,' she added hastily.

'But poor Uncle Jasper would collapse from mortification if he ever found out.'

Julia's eyes grew round at this display of courage but before she could comment, the door opened.

'Sarah, dear child, welcome.' Lady Wribbonhall, a plump, still pretty matron as fair-complexioned as her daughter, crossed the room to enfold Sarah in a scented, blue-silken embrace. 'How is Sir Jasper after your sojourn in Tunbridge Wells? I know Dr Salcott considered that taking the waters would prove beneficial enough to offset the disadvantages of the journey. I trust it was so?'

'I'm afraid Uncle Jasper drank very little of the waters, ma'am,' Sarah responded with a rueful smile. She resumed her seat, exchanging a speaking glance with Julia as ·Lady Wribbonhall disposed herself comfortably on the opposite sofa. 'In fact, after the first swallow he refused to take another drop.'

Julia giggled. 'And you were stuck there for three weeks with all those elderly invalids! Why didn't you return earlier?'

'In this instance Uncle Jasper had another reason for going in the first place,' Sarah muttered somewhat grimly. 'He thought some poor, lonely old gentleman would be misguided enough to offer for me.'

'No doubt with your welfare in mind, Sarah,' Lady Wribbonhall reproved, frowning as her daughter went off into peals of laughter. 'Perhaps he thought an older man might suit you.'

Sarah sighed. She did not feel in the least inclined to share her friend's mirth. 'I know, ma'am. In fact, it is because of Uncle Jasper that I came to see you today. I have a favour to ask of you, if it should not prove to be too much trouble.'

Lady Wribbonhall leaned over and patted her hand. 'You know you have only to ask, dear child. It is to do with Sir Jasper's health, I collect.'

'Not quite, ma'am.' Sarah took a deep breath. 'But you are right about Uncle Jasper being concerned about me...about my future to be precise. I had no idea... that is, I thought he had accepted...'

'That you don't wish to be married?' Lady Wribbonhall concluded for her. 'You were only four-teen when you made that decision, Sarah, and still very...hurt.'

Sarah knêw 'hurt' was not the word Lady Wribbonhall had been about to utter. 'Hurt' didn't begin to describe what everyone had thought of her eight years ago.

Extremely disturbed. A severe shock to the brain. Must be kept very quiet. The doctor's verdict had been whispered from manor to hall. From village to farm.

'Yes, well, when I twitted Uncle Jasper about his plans for me—only joking him, you understand—he confessed how worried he's been since that bad spell he suffered at Christmas. And I know he was thinking of what will happen after he...after he dies.'

Lady Wribbonhall nodded. 'Very sensible,' she approved. 'I don't mean to sound harsh, Sarah, but Sir Jasper would be most remiss not to be thinking of your future, especially as his health is now so frail.'

'Yes, I can understand that, Mama,' put in Julia, frowning thoughtfully. 'But surely he will provide for Sarah.'

Sarah shook her head. 'I won't be destitute, of course, but everything is entailed on my cousin, Alfred. Uncle Jasper explained it to me. What is left over would not be sufficient to set up my own establishment, which means I'd have to engage in some respectable employment, or make my home with Alfred and his wife.'

'Alfred and Charlotte? You'd be turned into a drudge,' stated Julia, not mincing matters. 'And an unpaid one at that.'

Sarah spoke before Lady Wribbonhall could reprove

her daughter for this brutally honest appraisal of the situation.

'What I've come to ask, dear ma'am, is if you would be so good as to chaperon me whenever we're invited to the same social events. Only until you go to London for the Season, of course. I—'

'My dear child, as if you need to ask. I will be delighted to see you go about in society a little more.' A warm smile spread over Lady Wribbonhall's face. 'You know I have always said you may call upon me at any time. As for the Season—with half the *ton* in Brussels at present, we have decided to remain in Sussex for several more weeks. One or two little country gatherings will be just the thing to accustom you to society.'

'Strictly speaking, Mama, our little country gatherings are not so little these days.' Julia gave Sarah's hand a surreptitious squeeze. 'In fact, I was about to tell Sarah about the exciting new arrivals in our midst when you came in.'

'I expect you have already heard about Lord Ravensdene, if you've been home for a day, my dear,' Lady Wribbonhall said with a wry smile. 'The neighbourhood is in such an uproar that you never did see. One would think the Regent had come amongst us.'

'Mama, how can you speak so?' demanded Julia. 'When you and Lady Ravensdene have become as thick as thieves. I didn't know you were even acquainted with her until recently.'

'Lady Ravensdene?' Sarah's eyes widened.

'Hermione Ravensdene and I have been acquainted for years,' responded Lady Wribbonhall placidly. 'She was presented a few seasons ahead of me, but was kind enough to come to my assistance one night at Almack's when her partner put his foot on the hem of my gown. When I married and came to live in Sussex our friendship was kept up mainly through the occasional letter, your papa having no taste for town life. And when *you* made your come-out, my love, she was in black gloves for her husband, and then for George, her eldest son, so you have never met her until now.'

'Then you also know the present Lord Ravensdene,' murmured Sarah. She wondered why she had felt so strange when Julia had mentioned the existence of a Lady Ravensdene. And why she felt even more peculiar now that she realised the lady in question was the Earl's mother and not his wife.

'We've met, of course,' Lady Wribbonhall agreed. 'But I doubt if anyone, with the possible exception of Lord Devenham, can claim to *know* Ravensdene. There is a certain reserve, a coldness one might say, that is extremely daunting, and quite unlike the rest of his family.'

'I daresay it may be caused by his years in the army,' offered Julia, clearly hoping to allay any alarm Sarah might feel at having to confront a cold, daunting Ravensdene and demand the return of her pistol.

'It is far more likely to be caused by all the caps that are being set at him, my love,' responded Lady Wribbonhall dryly. 'For all the good it will do them.'

'Why is that, ma'am? Does Ravensdene not wish to be married?'

'As to that, I cannot say.' Her ladyship reached out to tug at the bell-pull hanging beside the fireplace. 'He certainly had no objections to the married state twelve years ago, for he wed Marianne Moreton before she was scarce out of the schoolroom and carried her off to Sicily where he was posted. Quite in the teeth of her parents' misgivings, I might add, not to mention his own family's doubts. But he wouldn't settle for a betrothal. It was marriage or nothing and, as he was perfectly eligible, the Moretons eventually capitulated.'

'Well—' Julia looked doubtful '—it sounds very romantic, but I don't think I'd like Ravensdene to be pursuing me so relentlessly. Was she happy with him, Mama?'

'I should think Marianne was very happy,' Lady Wribbonhall replied. 'Remember, my love, that ten or twelve years makes a difference in a man. Ravensdene was still a boy himself at the time, had scarce attained his majority, and Marianne was exceptionally lovely, and quite angelic so I've been told. I imagine she saw a side to him that others might not.'

Sarah shivered inwardly as an image of darkness and power returned to her mind. 'What happened to her, ma'am?'

'There was an accident only a year after their marriage. It was very tragic. They were still living on the continent, but I remember how shocked everyone was to hear the news. Marianne was expecting a child and had some sort of fall. Both she and the baby died.'

'Oh, how terrible!' exclaimed Julia. 'No wonder Ravensdene is so cold and intimidating. It must have been dreadful for him to lose his wife and child like that.'

Sarah didn't comment. For some reason the knowledge that Ravensdene had known tragedy just as she had, that he had grieved for his wife to the extent of never remarrying, both fascinated and frightened her. She remembered the swiftness of his attack, the devastating strength with which he'd disarmed her and shivered again. She hadn't even seen him move. She couldn't believe she had stayed there in the woods and argued with him. The very thought of what might have happened made her blood run cold.

The sound of voices intruded and she glanced up to see that Lady Wribbonhall's butler had answered her summons.

'And see that a message is conveyed to Sir Jasper immediately, Humby, that Miss Lynley will be spending the day here and that she will be attending our party this evening. Naturally we will see her safely home. In fact, I had better write him a note if you would be so good as to sharpen a pen for me. One of the grooms can deliver it when he returns Miss Lynley's horse.'

'Returns my horse? But, ma'am...I don't think...' Feeling as if the ground had suddenly been cut from under her feet, Sarah glanced down at her riding habit. A party? She wasn't ready for a party! 'I haven't got anything to wear,' she finally wailed, falling back on the age-old feminine excuse. 'And I can't spend so much time away from Uncle Jasper—'

'Nonsense, my dear.' Clearly, since her new charge was already in her clutches, Lady Wribbonhall was not about to let her escape. 'If Sir Jasper is as concerned about your future as you say, you can best set his mind at rest by contracting a respectable alliance, which I gather is your purpose in entering society. And what better place to start than a small gathering of friends, most of whom you already know. As for a gown, I am sure we will find something in Julia's wardrobe that will suit you admirably. This isn't a ball, you know, although there will be music if enough young couples wish to dance.'

'*Dance*?'

Lady Wribbonhall swept over this alarmed interjection. 'Now, let me see. There is an Assembly at Eastbourne next week which we should attend, and the Sheringtons are giving a waltzing party— We will have to go shopping as soon as possible. And a visit to my dressmaker must be arranged. Julia, take Sarah upstairs so she may choose a gown for tonight, while I make some plans.'

Sarah found herself swept out of the room before she could voice another protest. They passed Humby bearing notepaper and a selection of quills on a salver. Obviously, a protest on the grounds of leaving her uncle to his own devices would be useless. Besides, she knew

Uncle Jasper would be positively delirious with joy that she was going to a party.

'I have just the gown for you, Sarah,' Julia confided as she prodded her unwilling guest up the stairs. 'I've never worn it because Mama thought it should have an over-dress of white gauze or some such thing, but thank goodness you are two-and-twenty and need not feel obliged to wear white all the time. The jonquil silk will look charming with your colouring, and if we can prevail upon Mama to lend you her gold-spangled shawl you will outshine every lady present.'

'I don't want to outshine anyone,' Sarah muttered rebelliously, but without much expectation of being attended to. Julia was as carried away with plans as Lady Wribbonhall. Somehow she had to regain control of the situation. If she was constantly attending social functions under Lady Wribbonhall's aegis, people would naturally assume one thing—which fitted in with her plans up to a point. But beyond that point, how was she to let Uncle Jasper think she was on the look-out for a husband, while making sure every other male in society knew she wasn't?

Nor could she confide her true reason for going into society to Lady Wribbonhall. She was quite sure her ladyship would not be receptive to the idea of her making contacts for the express purpose of hiring herself out as a governess or housekeeper at some later date.

'This is going to be such fun.' Julia's voice bubbled over with excitement as she threw open the door to her bedchamber. 'Mama was right, you know, Sarah. There won't be many strangers here tonight. Why, you even know Lord Ravensdene.'

'Wonderful.' Sarah balked on the threshold and glared at her friend. 'I can ask him to return my pistol. That should enliven the evening considerably.'

'That pistol is not a matter for ill-timed jests,' Julia

said severely, pushing Sarah through the doorway and
heading straight for her wardrobe.

She then ruined the entire effect of this stern rebuke,
however, when she emerged from the closet a moment
later, yellow silk spilling over her arms and laughter in
her eyes. 'But I have to confess, Sarah, I would have
given anything to have seen Ravensdene's face when
you aimed that pistol at him yesterday.'

Sarah plumped herself cross-legged on Julia's bed,
propped her chin in her hands and resigned herself to
the inevitable.

CHAPTER THREE

SEVERAL hours later Sarah was wishing she hadn't been quite so resigned. So far the only ray of light on her horizon was that Ravensdene had not yet put in an appearance. Aside from that, however, she had had to endure an endless line of people exclaiming at seeing her in tones that would have led the uninitiated to suppose she had been incarcerated in a dungeon for years, and at the same time had had to deflect a good deal of curiosity, albeit politely veiled.

And Julia had reverted to scolding.

'Sarah, will you stop pulling at that gown. You look delightful.' She glanced down at her own gown of white sarsenet, its scalloped hem caught up with knots of sapphire ribbon, and added with deeply feminine satisfaction, 'We both do.'

'I should have worn the shawl.' Sarah twitched the tiny puffed sleeves of jonquil silk higher on her shoulders. The adjustment merely caused the bodice to gape. Even the row of gold and white silk roses bordering the neckline didn't make her feel more comfortable. Sighing, she pushed the sleeves down again. 'Really, Julia, how did your mama come to countenance such a low-cut bodice? I feel positively naked.'

'If you were naked people would be staring. Do you see anyone staring?'

Sarah glanced cautiously around at the groups of chattering guests. The first thing she saw had her clutching her friend's arm. 'Oh, no! Julia, it's him!'

'Who?'

'*Who*?' Sarah's voice soared to a hastily stifled squeak. 'What do you mean "who"?' She turned incredulous eyes on her friend and saw her gaze fixed on the entrance to the drawing-room. 'You're looking straight at him.'

Julia's gaze shifted fractionally. 'Oh! You mean Ravensdene. He must have come with Lord Devenham.' And to Sarah's utter amazement, she blushed.

She had never seen Julia blush in her life. Stunned, she looked back at the doorway, momentarily diverted from the unnerving prospect of meeting Ravensdene again.

The gentleman standing next to the Earl and conversing easily with his hostess was possessed of a pleasant countenance and average build. His fair hair was cut short in the military fashion and he was dressed with quiet propriety in black evening clothes. Sarah could not see anything about him that would cause a female to blush. She was perfectly happy to go on studying him, however. Because it was preferable to looking at the tall, black-haired nemesis beside him.

'I take it that is the friend who knows Ravensdene better than anyone,' she murmured.

Julia nodded. 'Yes. Viscount Devenham. Actually, we've come to know him quite well. In fact—' she paused and faint colour tinted her cheeks again '—he's been teaching me to drive his phaeton.'

'Drive his *phaeton*? You hate driving! You can't even drive a gig!'

'Yes, well, that was when Papa was teaching me, and if you only knew how impatient he used to become merely because the stupid horse would go through a garden bed, or if I chipped the paint on the gates. But Lord Devenham is everything that is kind and patient.'

'Kind and patient,' repeated Sarah weakly. All of a sudden she felt very odd. As if the world had shifted in some indefinable way. As if Julia, though three years younger, had somehow stepped past her, to discover something that was beyond her comprehension. How could that happen in just three weeks?

She glanced back at the group by the doorway, telling herself it was her overwrought mind at work, only to have that and every other thought fly right out of her head as her gaze met Ravensdene's with an impact that shook her all the way to her toes. He was looking at her as if she was the only person in the room. As if he would look straight into her soul and discover all her secrets.

Then before she could recover from the shock of his intent gaze, he detached himself and Lord Devenham from the group around Lady Wribbonhall and came striding across the room towards her.

Sarah's mouth went dry. In the brightly lit drawing-room he looked even taller than she remembered. Bigger. Darker. But it was not the threat of his size that had her heart pounding as he approached. It was the way he moved. She had been right about the jungle, Sarah thought. He moved like a large hunting cat; lithe, powerful, intent on his prey. And this time there was nowhere to flee.

'Good evening, Miss Wribbonhall. I see you have quite recovered from our narrow escape yesterday.'

The cheerful voice wrenched Sarah back to an awareness of her public surroundings. She took a step closer to Julia and tried to control the urge to grab at her friend's hand.

'Oh, yes,' Julia was saying gaily. 'Though it is most ungallant of you, sir, to remind me that I nearly sent us into the ditch when I have been telling my friend, Miss Lynley, how my driving has improved out of sight. Oh, Sarah, I don't believe you have met Lord Ravensdene and Viscount Devenham. Gentlemen, Miss Lynley.'

Both men bowed. Beneath an exchange of polite pleasantries, Sarah could only marvel at her friend's aplomb. While her own mind was still in a turmoil, Julia, with a neat turn of phrase and a blithe pose of ignorance, had left it to Sarah to acknowledge any prior encounter with Ravensdene.

Not that she was going to acknowledge any such thing. Indeed, she hadn't dared raise her eyes above the level of either gentleman's exquisitely tied cravat.

She was just hoping that Lord Devenham's apparent ignorance of the situation was as genuine as Julia's was false, when he offered his arm to her friend.

'I see they are forming a set in the next room, Miss Wribbonhall,' he said. 'Will you do me the honour?'

Julia's poise promptly deserted her. 'Well, I—' She sent Sarah a frantic, questioning glance.

'I advise you to accept, Miss Wribbonhall,' Ravensdene said gently. 'Dev was a member of Wellington's staff, you know, and considers himself, quite erroneously of course, to be the master of any number of intricate steps. You can't have him making a cake of himself in your parents' drawing-room.'

'Well, of all the dashed insults!' exclaimed the Viscount. 'See if we don't take the shine out of every-one.' And taking advantage of Julia's confusion, he whisked her into the upper half of the drawing-room where a string quartet was preparing to play.

Sarah was left marooned with Ravensdene on an island of silence amid the sea of conversation going on around them.

'Your little friend did that rather well for an amateur,' he murmured, far too softly for anyone near them to hear. 'But I should warn you, Miss Lynley, that Dev and I have had a great deal of experience in strategy.'

Sarah gasped and looked up. And promptly forgot what she was going to say.

Ravensdene was looking down at her, his face as hard as she remembered it. Hard and lean, with sharply-chiselled cheekbones, a straight aristocratic nose and twin lines bracketing the firm, cleanly etched mouth. All that, she recalled. It was his eyes that startled her into

silence. Though framed by thick black lashes, they
weren't dark as she had expected, but a clear, crystalline
green, as cold and brilliant as winter sunlight on an
emerald sea.

And like the sea, she thought with a small shiver of
awareness, the glittering surface hid depths that could
prove dangerous.

'You mean you planned—' she began faintly.

'I'm afraid so,' he answered. And then the cool
intelligence gleaming in those ice-green eyes warmed
with amusement. 'A risk, I know, but it seemed fairly
safe to approach you. That piece of nonsense you have
on your wrist isn't large enough to hold a pistol.'

Sarah's mouth opened. Nothing came out. Clamping
her lips shut again, she glanced around at her very
respectable neighbours and almost choked on a giggle.
It was partly caused by nerves, she knew, but the picture
conjured up of herself holding Ravensdene at pistol
point in the middle of a party was suddenly too much.
Laughter bubbled over and escaped in a delighted
gurgle of sound that had his eyes narrowing briefly.

'Oh, it is a great deal too bad of you to remind me of
such an embarrassing situation, my lord,' she
reproached, laughter still dancing in her eyes as she
gazed up at him more naturally. 'How was I to know you
would turn out to be Uncle Jasper's neighbour?'

Nick's mouth quirked. The little devil had turned the
tables on him very nicely, he thought wryly. Disarming
him with her mirth. He wondered how amused she'd
feel if he followed his baser instincts and put his mouth
to the pulse he could see fluttering in her throat.

'Most disobliging of me,' he agreed instead. 'But as
my mother will be only too happy to inform you, Miss
Lynley, I am disobliging.'

'Oh, no. I don't think you are at all,' she said,
surprising him again. 'I am sure most gentlemen would
have gone straight to my uncle to complain of my

hoydenish behaviour, or whatever word they might have put on it.' The animated little face upturned to his was suddenly very serious. 'I am glad you did not,' she confided. 'Uncle Jasper's health is rather fragile at present, and I don't wish to cause him any concern.'

'Very commendable,' Nick returned. He saw the almost imperceptible renewal of tension in her body at his dry tone and smiled down at her. 'We do, however, have unfinished business to attend to, Miss Lynley. Would you prefer to discuss it here, although I should warn you that we may attract unwanted attention, or shall we join Miss Wribbonhall and Lord Devenham?'

The tentative poise Sarah had been gathering about her shattered in an instant. 'What?' she stammered.

'Would you like to dance?'

Dance! With *him*? 'No!'

Oh, good heavens! Had she lost her manners along with her wits? What if someone had heard her? 'I. . .that is. . . I don't dance, my lord.'

He didn't even hesitate. 'In that case, let us take a turn in the courtyard, Miss Lynley. I see the windows are open and several people seem to be finding this room as oppressively warm as you are.'

'It. . .it is particularly close in here,' Sarah managed, and laid the barest tips of her gloved fingers on the arm he offered her.

One dark brow lifted fractionally, but, to her everlasting relief, Ravensdene had no opportunity to comment on her obvious discomfort at even that light contact. Their progress across the room was constantly hindered by those guests who had not had an opportunity earlier of remarking on how delightful she looked, and how happy they were to see her.

Sarah answered automatically, glad of the few minutes' respite in which to pull herself together. Her nervousness at being alone with Ravensdene was quite irrational. There were plenty of people admiring Lady

Wribbonhall's courtyard garden. All she had to do was remain calm, and politely ask for the return of her pistol. There was no need to be thrown into a panic over that.

'Why do I have the impression that your appearance here tonight is something quite out of the ordinary?' Ravensdene demanded as he eventually drew her through the long windows opening onto the courtyard.

Since he chose that moment to take her hand and tuck it firmly beneath his arm, Sarah barely heard the question.

'I...don't go into society very much,' she finally stammered. How was she supposed to answer questions when all her senses were being overwhelmed by the male heat and power beneath her fingers, when she knew that beneath Ravensdene's formal clothes and cool, polite manner he was capable of exploding into violent action when he was pushed too far?

The memory had Sarah quaking inwardly. She had escaped him once, but now she was in a trap of her own making; not even the presence of several other guests in the garden calmed her nerves. Ravensdene was taking her as far away from them as propriety allowed. By the time they reached a small marble bench set beneath a hedge of greenery, her heart was beating so hard she could scarce hear anything else.

'Dear me.' Ravensdene halted at the bench and looked up at the topiary in front of them. 'Is that supposed to be a mermaid, do you think?' Then he looked down at her and his voice changed. 'Stop it,' he ordered softly.

'I beg your pardon?' Her voice was no more than a whisper.

'I brought you out here to discuss the return of a certain object, Miss Lynley, not to exact whatever dramatic revenge your overly vivid imagination is conjuring up.

He pressed her gently down onto the bench as he spoke and seated himself beside her. Sarah edged further away at once, but Ravensdene's curt tone had stung her pride. Her imagination really had run amok. She took a deep breath and felt the cool air clear her head a little. The garden seemed to come into sharper focus, the lanterns in the trees casting a soft glow over the flower-bordered paths and strolling guests.

Now if only she could banish a lingering vision of a large black panther cutting his intended prey from a herd of brightly coloured, exotic creatures, she might recover her usual calm, sensible manner.

'You were right, my lord. It is much more pleasant out here. But we should conclude our business before anyone remarks on the length of time we spend conversing. After all, we have only just been introduced.'

His mouth curved slightly. 'I am glad you didn't claim to have only just met me, Miss Lynley. You would seem to have a fine appreciation for the exact truth.'

'Well. . .'

'That alone makes you a rarity,' he murmured before she could enter a caveat in the interests of self-preservation. 'But you appear to be a most unusual female in other ways, too. You don't dance. You don't go into society in the normal way of things. I am forced to conclude, therefore, that you ventured forth tonight for the sole purpose of regaining your. . .er, property.'

'Well, actually, the pistol is not precisely mine,' she confided, relief at his ready understanding loosening her tongue. 'My uncle has a collection of firearms, you see, and I. . .*borrowed* one. Just in case. I mean, I was on the beach. And one cannot be too careful, can one? We used to have smugglers in this area, you know.'

He raised an eyebrow.

'Yes. Smugglers are very dangerous persons, my lord. And I was by myself. Collecting shells,' she tacked on in case he might be wondering why she had ventured to the beach alone.

'Ah, yes. The slaughtered shells.' The faint smile

reached his eyes. 'A most perilous expedition. I can see why you would feel the need to arm yourself, Miss Lynley. I can also see the impending peril confronting you should your uncle discover that one of his pistols is missing.'

Sarah glared at him suspiciously, then decided to ignore Ravensdene's descent into levity in favour of forming a plan. She nodded. 'All too likely, I'm afraid. Uncle Jasper's collection is quite extensive and he likes to reminisce over it from time to time. In fact, quite often,' she concluded gloomily.

'Obviously there is no time to lose. Be assured, Miss Lynley, that I will call upon Sir Jasper tomorrow and contrive to slip the pistol to you without anyone noticing. I hope.'

'You *hope*?' She glared at him again. 'Don't you know?'

In the light from a nearby lantern, she could see the gleam in his eyes. 'I see you have no comprehension of the delicacy of such an operation, Miss Lynley. One must consider every aspect of the situation. For instance, would it be preferable to pass the pistol to you as we shake hands? But what would you do with it in full view of your uncle? Or perhaps I could stuff it beneath a sofa cushion for you to retrieve later. However, if your uncle were to wave me to a chair without a cushion we would be forced to think of something else. And even if that small setback could be overcome, there is always the possibility of some unsuspecting person sitting upon the cushion and setting the pistol off before you have a chance to—'

'Oh, stop!' Sarah almost bounced with the force of her impatience. 'You are not taking this seriously, my lord. You know perfectly well that it is Uncle Jasper's place to call on you, or leave cards, since you are newly come to Comberford and have never met him.'

Ravensdene merely smiled. 'But I have met you, Miss Lynley.'

Sarah only just managed not to fall off the bench in shock. Even the thought of her uncle's reaction—not to mention the reaction of everyone else in the neighbour-hood—to the Earl of Ravensdene calling on her after one brief meeting at a party, and before he had been properly introduced to her guardian, was enough to overset every faculty.

The suspicion that Ravensdene knew precisely what he was doing and why, prevented any such frivolous feminine weakness.

'I am glad to be able to provide your lordship with an evening's entertainment,' she informed him tartly. 'No doubt you consider that I deserve it after giving you such a fright yesterday. However, I assure you that you were never in any danger. I am an excellent shot.'

He just looked at her. 'An excellent shot.'

'Yes.' She suddenly remembered Ravensdene's assessment of her truthfulness and hoped the muted light in the garden hid the blush creeping into her cheeks. She had never fired a gun in her life. But on the other hand, how difficult could it be? You just aimed the thing and pulled the trigger.

One look at the Earl's expression, however, convinced Sarah that he would not subscribe to this simple philosophy. In fact he continued to regard her as if he was examining some strange and hitherto undiscovered form of life.

'Do you know, Miss Lynley, I believe I did you an injustice before. You are not merely rare or unusual. You are unique.'

This time he succeeded in robbing her of breath. Her lungs constricted and her heart began beating in a light, rapid rhythm that reminded her of the fluttering of butterfly wings. The butterflies seemed to be migrating to her stomach. 'I do not know what you are talking

about, my lord,' she said with distressingly less forceful-
ness than she'd intended.

'No, I can see you do not,' he murmured. 'That is part
of your singularity, Miss Lynley. And—' he paused and
a crooked, unexpectedly appealing smile curved his
hard mouth '—if I explained it to you, I would sound
like a veritable coxcomb. Suffice it to say that a lady of
less character might not be so nice as to object to a man
calling on her before he had obtained an introduction to
her nearest male relative.'

'Character has nothing to do with it,' Sarah muttered,
unnervingly aware that her eyes were fixed on the
softened line of his mouth. She wrenched her gaze
upward. 'I do not wish to be the subject of gossip. It may
not make any difference to you, being a. . .a. . .'

'Gentleman?'

Her brows met in a severe frown. 'That was not the
word I was searching for,' she enunciated with great
precision. 'If you were a proper gentleman, sir, you
would not sit there making idiotic suggestions when I
may be faced with disaster at any moment. You claim to
be the expert in strategy. Think of something!'

He could think of any number of things, Nick
reflected ruefully. And none of them had anything to do
with pistols, stolen information or traitors. Having
succeeded in making Miss Sarah Lynley forget her
nervousness, he was becoming fascinated by the imperious little creature who had taken her place.

And yet he sensed that her instinct to flee was never
far from the surface. There was a soft, almost vulnerable
curve to her mouth that contrasted intriguingly with the
delicate feminine strength in her firm little chin. And
though her amber eyes mirrored annoyance, he knew
that if he touched her he would feel the tension
quivering within her slender body.

The image had him setting his teeth against a sharp
stab of desire. He forced it back, suppressing an urge to

reach out and run his fingers down the fragile line of her throat to the gentle upper swell of her breasts nestling in a row of silken flowers; to find out if she was as soft as she had felt yesterday. He was here for a purpose, damn it. And that purpose was to gain an entrée into Sir Jasper Lynley's home. One social step at a time.

'I am trying to think of something, Miss Lynley,' he told her, more brusquely than he intended. 'However, our options are severely limited. If I am not to call upon your uncle, and if the risk of discovery is probable before he calls upon me, then we shall have to meet somewhere else.'

'Do you mean. . .at another party?' Sarah quailed at the thought. This was not turning out to be as simple as she had supposed. And her own brain was very little help. It seemed to be far too occupied with trying to fathom Ravensdene's quick changes of mood than in thinking of ways out of her predicament.

'Where precisely is my pistol, sir?' she demanded, as if the answer might solve everything.

He stared down at her rather thoughtfully. 'Locked in the desk in my library, Miss Lynley. Were you going to suggest that we meet there?'

'Good heavens, no! Of course not!'

'We could, however, meet again in the woods.'

The suggestion was so smoothly delivered that for a moment Sarah simply stared at him. Then an unnerving memory of herself, Ravensdene and woods took hold of her mind. She swallowed and gripped the edge of the bench while her thoughts scurried to and fro in search of an alternative. There was none.

'When?' she managed to whisper.

'I will be inspecting a farm several miles away in the morning,' he answered, still watching her closely. 'Shall we say three o'clock, Miss Lynley? At the same place?'

She nodded, her senses slowly going numb. That was probably a good thing. If she couldn't feel anything. . .

'Miss Lynley.' He waited until she raised dazed eyes to his. 'The last thing I wish to do is cause you distress,' he said very softly. 'And it would be plain to the meanest intelligence that you are extremely reluctant to meet me in such a clandestine manner. Why not ask your friend, Miss Wribbonhall, to accompany you? She knows what happened.'

'She does?' Sarah struggled to collect her scattered wits. 'I. . . I mean. . .how do you know that?'

'She was watching me earlier as if I was about to sprout horns and a tail.' He didn't add that the expression had been shared by several other people who had encountered him in the past under less than salubrious circumstances. 'And,' he continued, 'I think she knows why it happened.'

Now Sarah couldn't speak at all. Ravensdene held her shocked gaze for a moment, then reached out and covered her hand with one of his. The warmth of his touch startled her, making her aware of how chilled she had become.

'Miss Lynley, you did not arm yourself yesterday against smugglers, real or imagined. Apart from anything else, smugglers seldom operate in broad daylight, a fact which I am sure you know well. If you are in any kind of trouble—'

'No!' She tried to pull her hand free. 'It's nothing. . . whatever you're thinking. . .it's not. . .'

'You're afraid of something,' he persisted, overcoming her attempt to escape with terrifying ease. 'And you were afraid yesterday. Panic-stricken, in fact. That's why you were hurrying. Was it something you saw? On the beach? In the wood?'

She shook her head frantically. Why was he asking these questions? Why wouldn't he let her go?

'There was something,' he said, and the absolute certainty in his voice sent a convulsive shudder through her. 'Tell me.'

'I'm sorry,' she said in a stifled voice. 'I'm afraid that is not possible.' She felt the colour seep out of her face and trembled, knowing her words had been an admission of sorts but helpless against his stronger will. She wished she could look away from the intense green of Ravensdene's eyes—heaven only knew what he could see in her own—but his gaze held hers captive.

'Are you sure?' he asked quite gently. 'I might imagine something far worse than the truth.'

'No,' she whispered. 'You couldn't. Nothing could be worse than the truth.'

She turned away at last, blindly, trying to rise, instinctively seeking the lights and warmth she needed to replace the dark chill of her memories, only to be stopped as Ravensdene's hand tightened around hers.

'Wait,' he said softly. 'You can't go back inside like this. You're as white as a ghost, and trembling as if you'd just seen—'

A sudden burst of talk and laughter interrupted him as several young couples came through the french doors into the courtyard, all seeming to be chattering at once. The rather voluptuous red-head leading the fray spotted them immediately and waved.

'Sophie Sherington,' Sarah whispered. 'Oh. . .'

'Yes, a feather-brained ninnyhammer. Leave her to me.' Still holding her hand, Ravensdene stood, drawing her up beside him but half-shielding her from the crowd while she struggled to retrieve what was left of her composure.

'Sarah, dear,' trilled Miss Sherington, reaching them at last and smiling sweetly. 'You sly creature. I had no idea you knew Lord Ravensdene so well. Here I thought you such a retiring miss, but you have been sitting outside chatting with him for the longest time. Oh, good evening, my lord.'

'Miss Sherington,' acknowledged Ravensdene.

Despite her still shattered senses, Sarah's eyes

widened at the ice in his voice. Without any warning whatsoever, he was the chilling, ruthless stranger who had terrified her yesterday. Then his long fingers squeezed hers gently and he released her.

'No doubt you also are in need of some cooler air,' he continued with a smile that frosted over at the edges. 'As I recall, your senses are somewhat susceptible to overheated drawing-rooms.'

Miss Sherington's fair complexion took on a hue that clashed hideously with her red tresses and amber gown.

'Jupiter, yes.' Her escort, a callow young gentleman who was apparently oblivious to his partner's discomfort, nodded owlishly. 'Wouldn't want you swooning again, Sophie. Dashed uncomfortable situation. Not but what she's right, Sarah. You shouldn't be—'

He encountered Ravensdene's frigid stare and blanched visibly.

'Don't be such a goose, Harry.' Feeling as if *she* could swoon with very little assistance, Sarah stepped forward. Her legs were shaking and her voice sounded rather far away, but she could not stand by and let young Mr Marsham, whom she had known since he was in short-coats, be annihilated. And from the look on the Earl's face, Harry Marsham's annihilation was imminent.

'Surely you remember that when Lord Comberford became too ill to venture out, he and Uncle Jasper continued their chess matches using me as their proxy. I swear I wore a path between Comberford Place and the Grange. Lord Ravensdene wished to thank me, and naturally asked to hear more of his grandfather. They were very close when he was a boy. Isn't that so, my lord?' She looked up at Ravensdene in silent appeal.

The cold glitter of his eyes was hidden, shadowed by half-lowered lashes as he gazed down at her. For a moment Sarah thought he was going to ignore her plea, then he inclined his head slightly. 'Yes, Miss Lynley,' he murmured, his voice a deep, dark purr. 'As a matter of fact, we were.'

She smiled shakily.

He did not return her smile but glanced away at once, using his impressive height to look over the heads of their stunned audience as if the small crowd did not exist. 'Are you ready to return to the drawing-room, Miss Lynley? I see Lady Wribbonhall signalling to us. Shall I take you to her?'

'Oh, yes. Thank you.' Aiming a vague, meaningless smile in the general direction of her friends, Sarah took the arm he offered her as if it was a life-line. For once the strength in him was welcome. Not a threat but a haven; something to cling to while they approached the lights and chatter of the bright drawing-room.

How could that be? she wondered, confused. Ravensdene might have been compliant a moment ago, but he still frightened her. The daunting steel of the forearm beneath her fingers should have been enough to make her run as fast and as far from him as she could. And yet. . .when she pictured herself doing that, she saw herself halting, and looking back. Even, heaven help her, being drawn back.

She must have taken leave of her senses! He was male, therefore unpredictable. He was larger and more powerful than her, therefore dangerous. And if Julia could not accompany her tomorrow, she would have to face him again without any defences at all.

A second later that fact was brought home to her in no uncertain terms. As Lady Wribbonhall's kind face appeared in her line of vision, Ravensdene bowed and left her—but not before he had murmured for her ears alone, 'Until tomorrow, Miss Lynley.'

CHAPTER FOUR

SHE was doing the right thing, Sarah told herself for
about the fiftieth time that morning as she turned her
mount onto the narrow path that branched off the main
road just before it reached the charming little village of
Comberford.

Knowing her rider's destination, the chestnut mare
responded eagerly, trotting briskly along the laneway
that was bordered on one side by the high stone wall
surrounding the gardens of Comberford Place, and on
the other by a hedge dividing the lane from cultivated
fields. Several hundred yards further on, the path veered
westward at a pair of wooden gates to eventually
disappear somewhere in the grassy folds of the Downs,
but Sarah had no interest in the magnificent vistas to be
seen in that direction.

She reined in her horse and dismounted to open the
gates, then, being country-bred, carefully shut them
behind her. The mare danced with impatience as Sarah
climbed onto the second bar of the gate to mount again.

'You might as well calm down, Honey,' she warned,
regaining her saddle with some difficulty. 'No one is
expecting us, so there won't be any treats for you today.'

Honey merely snorted in disbelief and set off along
the faint track that skirted the fields of the home farm
before her mistress had given her the office to start.

Sarah sighed and let her horse have her head. Life
was very uncomplicated for those of the equine persuasion, she mused. The track ended at the stableyard
where such delicacies as apples never failed to materialise. Honey apparently saw no reason to believe that
today was going to be any different.

Not that she herself wanted to dawdle. Sarah frowned as she ran through the plan she had devised after discovering that Julia was engaged elsewhere this afternoon, and again assured herself that she was doing the right thing. Retrieving her pistol from Ravensdene's library was a good deal safer than meeting the Earl in the woods. And probably a good deal easier as well.

In fact, the circumstances could hardly be better. As the guests had been leaving last night, she had overheard Lord Devenham arranging another driving lesson with Julia for this morning, while Ravensdene's delightfully vague mother had said she would visit Lady Wribbonhall at the same time to gossip about the party. As for Ravensdene himself, she knew he was out inspecting farms. The only people she expected to encounter, therefore, were the servants, and they were accustomed to her comings and goings.

Of course the senior members of Ravensdene's staff might think it a little odd that she would call at the servants' entrance with a fresh pot of salve for Mrs Winwick's bunions while the family was in residence, but they would very likely dismiss it as force of habit. After all, in the months prior to old Lord Comberford's death and during the two years since, she had been a regular visitor to Mrs Winwick's sitting-room.

She even had a ready excuse if anyone caught her sneaking into the library. And she would leave a note for Ravensdene. He would probably be very grateful to be saved from a third encounter with a female whose nerves and brain turned to mush whenever she was in his presence.

Sarah nodded. Yes, her plan covered every aspect of the situation. She was doing the right thing. Certain persons who would remain nameless might think her cowardly—and it was true that she had been dreading her next meeting with Ravensdene—but she didn't care what he thought. *She* knew the truth. It had not been dread alone that had kept her awake half the night, planning, but a faint, whispering sense of anticipation. It had scared her witless.

She was definitely doing the right thing.

'My God, it's true.' Devenham looked at the pistol held casually in his friend's hand then collapsed onto the nearest chair and started to laugh. Again.

Raising his eyes towards the library ceiling, Nick propped himself against his desk and waited for the paroxysms to subside. It was not the first time he had been obliged to do so. Since regaling Devenham with the story of his initial encounter with Miss Sarah Lynley, the Viscount, between bouts of disbelief, had been doubled over with laughter for a good ten minutes.

'If you've quite finished cackling like a maniac,' he said when Devenham finally sat up and mopped his streaming eyes, 'we can get on with discussing the situation.'

'Sorry, old boy.' Devenham grinned unrepentantly. 'Couldn't help it. I know I said the next female chasing after you would be armed and dangerous, but I didn't expect it to actually happen.'

Nick felt a reluctant smile tug at his own mouth. 'Believe me, Dev, if I thought it was that simple you could laugh yourself silly, with my compliments. But it's not.' He glanced down at the pistol and frowned thoughtfully. 'It most definitely is not that simple. Miss Lynley did not know who I was two days ago when she brandished this gun in my face, and last night I received the distinct impression that she would have preferred to remain in that ignorant state of mind.'

'So the lady isn't joining the ranks of females falling over you.' Devenham chuckled. 'You ought to be grateful. Pretty little thing,' he added judiciously. 'Shame she's so timid. Although if she pulled a pistol on you. . .'

'Precisely.'

'Good God!' The Viscount's jaw dropped. Suddenly he was completely sober. 'Surely you don't think... A *woman*?'

Nick shook his head. 'You're going too fast, Dev. I don't suspect Miss Lynley of being a spy, but I think she knows something. Perhaps she's known it for some time, or maybe she stumbled onto something the other day, which would explain why she was going full-tilt along that path from the beach.'

'There was a storm coming,' Devenham reminded him.

'She didn't arm herself with this against thunder and rain,' Nick said quietly. He tossed the pistol gently into the air before straightening and returning it to the half-open drawer in his desk.

Devenham watched him lock the drawer and pocket the key. 'Lynley is supposed to be a recluse, but you're going to contrive a meeting with him using his niece, aren't you?'

'Using her or anyone else who'll oblige me,' Nick returned. He glanced at his friend. 'Including the Wribbonhalls if I have to.'

'God, Nick, you don't have to say that as if you're warning me. Whoever is selling information to the French has to be stopped.' He paused, frowning. 'If Lynley is your man, though, it'll cause the devil of a scandal.'

'And an innocent girl will be hurt. At the very least she'll feel used. Probably others will also. Is that what you're thinking, Dev?'

'Hard not to think it,' Devenham said shortly. 'It's the truth.'

Nick met the Viscount's frowning gaze for a moment, then turned and walked over to the window. He propped one broad shoulder against the wall, shoved his hands into the pockets of his riding coat and stared out at the view of the lake and the home-wood.

'Yes, it's the truth,' he admitted. 'But you see, Dev, I can be very. . .discreet.' His mouth twisted. 'It's a rather particular talent of mine .'

In the hazy reflection in the glass he saw Devenham rise swiftly to his feet and knew his friend had picked up the faint trace of bitterness in his tone. Before the Viscount could speak, however, the door opened to admit Winwick.

'Excuse me, my lord, but Lord Devenham's phaeton is at the door and Holcot has instructed me to inform his lordship that the greys are, er, damned nasty devils to hold, begging your lordship's pardon. He wishes to know if he should take them for a turn along the carriageway.'

'Good God!' The Viscount strode forward, seized the hat and gloves he had thrown carelessly onto the desk earlier, and headed towards the door. 'Not unless he wants a broken neck. Thanks, Winwick, I'd forgotten the time. Tell Holcot I'm coming, would you? Her ladyship, too. Can't keep your mother waiting, Nick. I'm taking her to the Wribbonhalls'. I'll convey your thanks for the party last night.' He reached the open doorway and stopped to look back. 'And don't think this conversation is finished because I have to dash off,' he warned.

'You're allowing Miss Wribbonhall to drive your greys?' Nick queried politely, ignoring the rest.

'Are you mad? Of course not. She only thinks she is.'

'Indeed? That must be an interesting method of teaching a lady to drive.'

Taking hold of the door handle, the Viscount prepared to depart. 'It is,' he said, and grinned. 'You ought to try it some day.'

Nick was still smiling as he turned back to the view beyond the window. For some reason Dev's suggestion held a definite appeal. He was just wondering whether

Miss Lynley had ever driven a high-perch phaeton when, far to the left, he glimpsed movement. It was brief, nothing more than a flash of colour among the trees, but to senses honed by years of danger it was enough. His eyes narrowed on the spot where he thought the flash of chestnut would come again. When it did he smiled in satisfaction. It was always gratifying to have one's suspicions confirmed.

He stood there for a moment, thinking rapidly, then strode over to the fireplace and reached for the bell-pull to summon Winwick back into the room.

Sarah couldn't understand it. There was no one around. The Place appeared to be deserted.

True, there had been plenty of bustle in the stable-yard, with grooms and stableboys tending their high-strung charges, but since she had left Honey with a young undergroom and stepped into the small entryway serving the kitchen wing, she had not encountered a single soul. It was all very odd.

On the other hand, she mused, as she slipped into the vacant dining-room at the far end of the passage connecting the kitchens and the main wing of the house, perhaps she should be grateful. She could complete her errand in peace, and then look into the kitchen on her way out as if she'd just come in. Surely the chef and his minions would be present. She would leave a message and the pot of salve for Mrs Winwick and make good her escape. Simple.

Sarah closed the dining-room door behind her and spared a quick glance at the charming view of lawn, lake and woods to be had from the two bay windows in this corner of the Place. She was really very fortunate, she told herself again. Comberford Place being built in the shape of a U, all the rooms along the south wing opened into each other: dining-room, breakfast parlour, draw-

ing-room, library. There was no need to go into the hall,
even if everybody did seem to have vanished.

Less than a minute later she reached her goal.
Sunlight streamed through the long windows at the far
end of the library, illuminating the big mahogany desk
that stood there. The rest of the room was furnished
with comfort in mind, from the thick flower-patterned
carpet to the commodious chairs and sofas grouped
about the fireplace, above which hung a portrait of the
late Lord Comberford.

The black and white marble chess table, its pieces set
out as if the absent players were in the middle of a game,
caught her eye as she sped down the long, book-lined
room, but Sarah didn't pause until she reached the
window alcove. Her story of a lost glove, possibly
mislaid weeks ago when she had last visited Mrs
Winwick and had found the housekeeper in the library,
would do to explain her presence. It would hardly be
reason enough to be rifling through Ravensdene's desk.
She would have to be quick.

A qualm shook her as she realised just what she was
about to do. Then she thought of the alternative. Taking
a resolute step forward, she bent to tug gently at the
middle drawer of the desk.

It was locked, of course. Ravensdene had said as
much last night. But that was not a problem. Fate was
still on her side. She had not exaggerated last night when
she had mentioned her many visits to Lord Comberford.
The elderly baron had become quite fond of her. She
had even penned the odd letter for him. She knew
exactly where the keys to the drawers were kept.

Steadying herself with one hand, Sarah leaned forward and reached for the ornate silver quill-holder on
the far side of the desk.

'I'm afraid I neglected to tell you, Miss Lynley, that
my habits are rather different to my grandfathers. I keep
my keys upon my person.'

A most unladylike shriek echoed through the library before the last words were out. Sarah jerked upright as if she'd been seized by the neck of her riding habit. She collided with the chair behind her, staggered forward again and ricocheted off the edge of the desk to land in a dishevelled heap, this time *in* the chair. Clutching both its arms she watched, frozen with shock, as Ravensdene rose slowly from a high-backed chair near the fireplace and paced down the room towards her.

He came to a halt on the other side of the desk, tilted his head slightly and raised an eyebrow in silent enquiry.

The barely suppressed amusement gleaming in his eyes had Sarah wishing she had her hands around his throat rather than the chair arms. Stunned by this hitherto unsuspected propensity for violence in herself, she uttered the first words that sprang to her lips.

'Are you out of your mind?' she yelped. 'How dare you give me such a fright when you're not supposed to be here!'

His lips twitched. 'My apologies, Miss Lynley. However, you may have noticed that I, er, live here.'

'That's no excuse!' she raged. Then, as he burst out laughing, she moaned and sank back in the chair, one hand over her closed eyes. What on earth had made her say such a thing? What was the man doing to her?

The discreet creak of expensive leather had her eyes flying open again. She peered out from under her hand to find that Ravensdene had drawn another chair up to the desk and was sitting down.

'Are you going to have a fit of the vapours?' he enquired, regarding her with great interest.

Sarah lowered her hand immediately. 'No, I am not! But if I was it would be all your fault.' She suddenly realised how ridiculous she must look sitting there behind the huge desk while Ravensdene occupied a visitor's chair. Not that he seemed to be conscious of the absurdity of the situation. In fact he looked as if he was prepared to spend the entire day right where he was.

She scowled at him suspiciously. 'Why are you sitting down?'

He merely smiled in answer and stretched his legs out. As one transfixed, Sarah watched him settle back in a lazy masculine sprawl that made her heart start to pound. She had a strong urge to spring to her feet, except that such a move would make Ravensdene feel obliged to stand also, and she wasn't sure she could cope with him looming over her.

Even sitting he looked far too big and dangerous. The panther at his ease, she thought, shuddering. Relaxed, but alert and powerful.

'I think you and I should have a little talk, Miss Lynley, don't you?'

'Talk?' Sarah tried to moisten suddenly dry lips. 'What about?'

Ravensdene's gaze lowered to watch the small, betraying movement of her tongue, then lifted again. All traces of humour had vanished from the gem-like green eyes gazing into hers, to be replaced by a rather disturbing gravity, and behind it, for a fleeting second, something more intense, and infinitely more disturbing.

'Would it have been so very terrible to have met me in the woods?' he asked quietly.

Sarah groped frantically for a response that wouldn't require any complicated explanations. 'It was. . .it would have been. . .quite improper for me to do so, my lord.'

He raised a brow. 'And stealing into a gentleman's house without so much as a maid to lend you countenance, is not?'

'I intended to meet Mrs Winwick,' she muttered, feeling extremely put upon. 'But I should have known it was too good to be true when I didn't see anyone at all.' Anxious to get off the subject of her improper behaviour, she scowled even more ferociously. 'Which reminds me, sir. What have you done with everybody?'

He eyed her for a moment, then gave a short, rueful laugh. 'You must indeed consider me to be a dangerous character, Miss Lynley, if you believe I can cause an entire houseful of servants to disappear. Would it set your mind at rest to know they are in the west wing, cleaning?'

'*All* of them?'

'I'm afraid so. My mother intends to entertain shortly, you see, and she seems to be set on a larger gathering than can be accommodated in the family wing. I put Winwick onto the task of preparing the state drawing-rooms this morning.'

'Oh.' She mulled that over for a few seconds before seizing on his other iniquity. 'You were supposed to be inspecting farms.'

'And so I did.' He smiled. 'Wasn't it fortunate that the property was in such excellent condition that I could return in plenty of time to meet you?'

'Fortunate for whom?' Sarah muttered, trying to ignore the odd little shivers coursing through her at the sight of his smile.

At her disgruntled tone the smile broadened into a grin of such blatant male wickedness that she blinked. For an instant she had a sudden unnerving vision of the boy Lady Wribbonhall had described yesterday; of how he must have looked before personal loss and war had carved the twin lines bracketing his mouth and hardened the devilish light in his eyes into glittering green ice.

And yet she had seen the ice melt last night, she remembered, feeling strangely shaken. More than once.

'There is no need to be so nervous, Miss Lynley,' he said, his voice lowering again. 'I am fully aware of the reason you came here this morning.'

Sarah wondered if he thought that dark, purring tone was soothing. She could have told him it wasn't. Shivers ran up and down her spine every time he used it. 'It's just that. . .and then there was. . .'

'Perfectly understandable.'

'Yes, well, it would have been most improper,' she mumbled, feeling like an idiot.

'Most. And since your reputation may be at stake the longer you remain here, Miss Lynley, the sooner we are on our way the better.' He fished a key out of his pocket and tossed it across the desk. 'Here. Catch.'

Her eyes widened in surprise a split second before she managed to loosen her grip on the chair and catch the key. Sending him a look of uncertainty, she fitted the key to the lock and opened the drawer. Ravensdene looked on in silence as she removed the pistol and, without so much as glancing at it, stuffed it into the reticule dangling from her wrist. Taking a deep breath, she rose to her feet.

'Thank you, my lord. I am very gr—' She stopped dead, her eyes going wide again with alarm as he rose also. 'What do you mean, *we* can be on our way?'

He indicated her reticule. 'Surely it is obvious, Miss Lynley. When a young lady feels the need to arm herself with a lethal weapon merely to ride about unescorted, it is the duty of any gentleman worthy of the name to offer his protection.'

'But—'

'Besides—' he walked around the desk and took her arm in a light clasp '—in the interests of public safety, I really must insist on accompanying you. . .'

'*Public safety*! Just what do you think I—?'

'Oh, don't worry about the proprieties,' he continued, ushering her through the adjoining rooms as if her spluttered protest had not been uttered. 'You can go out the way you came in and I'll meet you as though by chance in the laneway. No one need ever know you ventured further than Mrs Winwick's parlour.'

'But—'

'And so you feel quite safe during our ride, I'll have my groom, Figgins, accompany us. At a discreet distance, of course.'

Before Sarah could open her mouth to suggest that Figgins' escort would be quite sufficient, Nick opened the dining-room door, pushed her gently into the room and shut the door again on her bewildered countenance.

He leaned back against the wooden panels, feeling as though he'd had a rather narrow escape. As if his quarry had almost got away from him. He frowned at the thought. He wasn't hunting Sarah, damn it. It was her uncle he had to investigate. Why did he keep forgetting that?

Pushing away from the door, he strode determinedly across the breakfast parlour and out into the hall, more than a little annoyed with himself. The only question remaining unanswered about Miss Sarah Lynley was why she had felt obliged to defend herself in such a drastic fashion on her own land. But did he have an answer? No, he did not. Because for some ridiculous reason he had found himself reluctant to push her just now, reluctant to say anything that might end their strange, almost private, relationship.

He slammed the front door behind him with rather more force than was strictly necessary. He was definitely losing his edge. This was not the time to be distracted by a woman, no matter how intriguing he found her. For one thing, Sarah was not a candidate for a brief seduction. And for another, whatever else she might be, he had no illusions that he would find her politely waiting for him in the lane. If he didn't get to the stables in the next two minutes, she would be more than halfway home before he caught up with her.

It was no use blinking at the facts, Sarah mused gloomily as the rugged Sussex coastline came into view. She had been outwitted and outmanoeuvred by an expert in strategy.

Of course, he had received some unexpected assistance from her horse, she remembered, bending a fulminating look upon the chestnut fiend she was riding. No sooner had they reached the laneway than Honey had objected strenuously to returning home after a mere two-mile ride. Several minutes later, Ravensdene had found her involved in a most undignified tussle with her suddenly recalcitrant mount, and when he had suggested they shake the fidgets out of their horses by taking a long roundabout route to the Grange which included the scenic path along the cliffs, her mare had taken off as if she'd understood every word, and before her mistress could think of an excuse to refuse.

If she hadn't been such an experienced rider, Sarah fumed silently, she would have found herself left in an ignominious heap in the middle of the road while Honey galloped off after Ravensdene's black stallion.

She stole a glance at her escort and had to admit that the huge horse suited him. Both males were big, dark and powerful. Both were capable of making any sensible female think twice about approaching them. She was forced to the conclusion, therefore, that her horse had no sense at all.

'Behave yourself, Honey,' she admonished in a muttered undertone as the mare frisked closer to Ravensdene's mount, flicking her heels out in what Sarah considered to be a decidedly flirtatious manner.

The Earl turned to smile at her as he slowed the black to a walk. 'Honey?'

A tide of hot colour flooded Sarah's cheeks. 'Short for Honeycomb,' she elaborated hastily. Really, when he'd said 'Honey' in that dark, purring tone, her insides had threatened to melt to a similar consistency.

'She is certainly the right colour,' Ravensdene observed, running an expert eye over the mare's points just as if he hadn't managed to addle her wits. 'And you appear to have excellent hands, Miss Lynley. I suspect you ride regularly.'

'Oh. . .yes.' Deciding after a moment to take this unobjectionable remark at face value, Sarah launched into a monologue on the advantages of riding this particular path. 'Especially along here. I love to watch the sea. It's so changeable. Serene one day and the next like a playful child with the sunshine dancing on the water as it is now. But I like it best when it's wild, and the waves are hurling themselves against the cliffs as though daring the land to break them.'

'Which the land does,' he murmured.

Carried away by her descriptions, she scarcely noticed the amused interest in his eyes as he watched her. 'Yes, but the sea wins in the end, doesn't it?'

He smiled at the triumph in her voice. 'A lesson in patience over resistance, Miss Lynley,' he acknowledged softly.

She was promptly struck dumb again.

'However, I doubt if the crews manning the ships out there share your love of wild seas,' he added smoothly.

'Er. . .no.' Carefully avoiding his gaze, she looked out across the sea roads named for the Sussex Downs. Scenery and the weather, she told herself grimly. Two very innocuous topics of conversation. There was no need to suspect some deep, hidden meaning in Ravensdene's every other remark. 'We do get some dreadful weather here,' she continued with rather determined chattiness. 'I remember when a troop ship was nearly driven onto the rocks not far from this spot. But unless we grow wings and fly, ships are our only means of crossing the Channel.'

'Oh, I don't know. Were you aware that several years ago there were plans for a tunnel to be built beneath the sea?'

'A tunnel! Beneath the Channel?'

'Yes. It was all going to be very elaborate: underground staging posts for changes of horses, air shafts sunk from mid-Channel islands, and the whole lit by candles in the finest chandeliers.'

'Good heavens! Whose idea was that?'

'I'm not sure. Napoleon was very enamoured of the plan, however. Needless to say, the English government was not.'

Sarah looked across the sunlit expanse and shivered. 'One can hardly blame them,' she said. 'I, for one, would rather take my chances with the weather than go burrowing beneath the earth. Or the sea in this case.'

'I agree with you, but one day in the future it may not be such an impractical alternative for negotiating a very treacherous stretch of water. I remember my grandfather telling my brothers and I about a terrible gale that blew up in the year his father was born, when hundreds of ships were caught in the Downs and destroyed.'

'I was very fond of your grandfather,' Sarah mused. 'Lord Comberford was very kind to me.' She remembered the way Ravensdene had backed up her explanation for the amount of time they had spent together at the Wribbonhalls' party, and retreated hastily to safer waters, 'And I do believe he told me that same story.'

He laughed softly. 'I must confess it was one of our favourite tales. Especially the part about the local fishermen launching their boats in the teeth of all danger to rescue the sailors who were struggling towards the shore.'

'They still do so, whenever the need arises.'

'Yes. I suspect that was the reason my grandfather was rather lenient when some of those same fishermen turned to the occasional spot of smuggling,' he said dryly. 'Despite his being a Justice of the Peace.'

'You don't approve of such leniency?' she asked, momentarily forgetting that she, herself, had supposedly been armed against such dangerous persons as free-traders.

Ravensdene shrugged. 'I can understand how a man with a family to feed could be tempted to trade in harmless commodities, Miss Lynley, but sometimes more than brandy or lace is conveyed across the Channel.' As they turned their horses inland towards a wider path than the one Sarah had taken two days ago, he looked at her rather intently. 'Sometimes information is traded.'

'Oh. You mean. . .about the war?'

'Yes.'

'It's hard to believe anyone would do that.' She glanced away, suddenly uncomfortable with the conversation and aware of the narrow-eyed gaze with which Ravensdene was studying her, of a strange tension in him, as though he was waiting for her to say more.

In the distance the sun glinted off the rail at the top of the steps she had mounted with such haste two days ago, and, unbidden, her mind began retracing the path through the woods to the spot where she had first encountered Ravensdene. And perhaps it was the talk of smugglers, or maybe the sudden, unaccountable grimness about his mouth, but all at once she recalled the initial words he had spoken that afternoon.

'Was that what you meant the other day?' she asked, turning back to him impulsively. 'Did you think I was a smuggler? Is that what had gone far enough?' It would be rather reassuring if he had meant that, she thought, without quite knowing why.

But to her amazement, he appeared momentarily disconcerted, as if he had not expected such a response. Then that wicked male grin flashed out again, and the impression was gone.

'Miss Lynley, I have a confession to make,' he began. 'I'm afraid I was guilty of judging you by the standards of some of the other ladies in this area. To tell you the

truth—' his smile turned rueful '—and at the risk of
sounding insufferably puffed-up with my own consequence, I have been living under siege. Miss Smisby was
the last one—a sprained ankle. During the two days
preceding that, we had lost puppies, invisible footpads—
Well, I won't bore you with the rest, but, believe me, an
armed and dangerous female was the next logical step.
At least, according to Lord Devenham, who, by the by,
thinks the whole situation is absolutely hilarious.'

Sarah couldn't contain herself any longer. The dis-
gusted note in his voice as he finished the tale was too
much. She leaned over Honey's withers and burst out
laughing. And if there was more than a little relief in her
amusement, she ignored the fact.

'My lord, I forgive you instantly,' she gasped when
she recovered. 'It sounds to me as if the Miss Smisbys
have been trying to scrape an acquaintance with you.'
She looked up at him and nearly choked on another
gurgle of laughter when she saw Ravensdene staring at
her with a kind of horrified fascination.

'Good God! Do you mean there's more than one Miss
Smisby?'

'Three,' she managed, trying to control herself.
'They're really very good-natured girls, you know.
Very. . .enthusiastic.'

'Good God!' he said again.

'Yes. The sprained ankle sounds like Leopoldina, and
the puppy—'

'*Leopoldina*?'

Sarah succumbed to another fit of the giggles. 'I'm
afraid Mrs Smisby indulged herself in choosing unusual
names for her daughters,' she explained kindly.
'Averilla probably imagined the footpads—she is rather
prone to melodrama, you see—and the puppy must
belong to Euphemia. She is extremely fond of animals,
which is not very appropriate really, because she was
named for a martyr who was consumed by wild beasts.'

'I suppose it is too much to hope that the dog will eventually grow large enough to—?'

'Oh, no! You must not say it, my lord.' Sarah clapped a hand over her mouth to stifle her laughter. 'Poor Mrs Smisby is forever trying to instil notions of propriety into her offspring, with little success, unfortunately. She herself is quite respectable, you know. She is the widow of a gentleman who owned a manufactory somewhere in the north, and after his death she sold the business and decided to move to a genteel neighbourhood in the country.'

'Aha! Trying to marry them into the squirearchy.'

'Not an unreasonable ambition given her wealth,' Sarah reproved him, trying to look properly severe. 'And one cannot blame her for wishing to establish her daughters creditably.'

'Believe me, Miss Lynley, I have no argument with that. Mrs Smisby may aim as high as Almack's if she likes, so long as she keeps those girls away from Comberford Place.'

'I'm sure it must have been very annoying for you,' she said soothingly. 'But now that you've been settled at Comberford for several weeks, I daresay all the excitement over your arrival will calm down.'

'You're an expert in these matters?'

'Of course not.' She levelled her brows at him. 'To be quite blunt, sir, I have no understanding at all as to why so many girls behave in such a peculiar fashion. Anyone would think marriage to some man, who in many cases is little more than a stranger, is the only way of life available to an intelligent female.'

'From that remark, I deduce that you have not gone hunting at Almack's, yourself, Miss Lynley.'

Sarah shuddered. 'Never!'

'You have no hankering for a London season?'

'I am perfectly happy in the country, my lord.'

'And the, er, joys of wedlock hold no appeal for you?'

'That very word is a masterly description of what a woman can expect of marriage,' she informed him tartly. 'Locked away, at the mercy of some man, for the term of her natural life.'

'Hmm. Don't you think that *you* are becoming rather melodramatic, Miss Lynley?' he queried gently.

Sarah blushed and looked away, suddenly aware of what she was saying. Heavens, what was the matter with her? She couldn't remember when she'd last lost control like that in front of a man. Probably not for eight years. She thought back over the last few minutes and frowned again.

'But I don't quite understand,' she said, prudently ignoring his last remark. 'How would holding you up with a pistol force you into marriage? If that was indeed what you assumed I was intending the other day.'

He smiled faintly. 'Miss Lynley, it is plain to see that you have no idea of the lengths to which some people will go to have their way. We were quite alone in the woods. Once the opportunity had presented itself, all you would have had to do was disarrange your clothing, accuse me of luring you to a clandestine meeting and trying to seduce you or worse, and then run screaming to your uncle that you'd been compromised. He would have stormed over to Comberford Place, probably armed with a shotgun, to demand that I marry you.'

Sarah had only heard one thing. 'Or worse?' she whispered.

He looked straight into her eyes. 'It would not be the first time, Miss Lynley, that a woman has acquired a husband, or otherwise extricated herself from trouble, by accusing a man of raping her.'

CHAPTER FIVE

SHE couldn't move. She couldn't even breathe. She sat rigid in the saddle, staring blindly at Ravensdene, while heat swept over her in a sickening, suffocating wave that blurred her vision and threatened her senses. Her lips parted, she tried to drag in some air, but every ragged gasp seemed to catch in her throat, choking her. An instant later she was shivering as violently as if she'd been plunged into a pool of ice-water. Then the heat returned. Terrified she was going to be sick, she clenched her teeth together.

'Miss Lynley! Sarah!' Ravensdene's hand shot out and closed over hers. He pulled both horses to a halt, dropped her reins and without any hesitation at all, passed his arm around her waist.

Just in time Sarah sensed his intention of lifting her out of the saddle and onto his own horse. She regained her powers of movement in a hurry. 'No! Let me go!'

'I will when you're better,' he said, with a calmness that contrasted sharply with her frantic efforts to escape his touch. 'Be still now. You know I'm not going to hurt you. We're not even alone. Figgins will be coming up with us at any moment.'

He was right. Sarah obeyed, ceasing her struggles as the knowledge that Ravensdene was merely supporting her seeped into her consciousness. But even as her body went limp in his hold, her mind seemed to lurch into action, setting words and images swirling about in her head in a dizzying, bewildering jumble. She could still hardly breathe, let alone speak, but somehow the words were spilling out.

'How *could* you? How could you say that? No woman

would ever. . . It is men who. . . Do you think a man has never done *that*. . .in order to acquire a *wife*?'

'Hush,' he murmured. 'Don't try to talk.' He pressed her head gently against his shoulder with his free hand, removing her hat as he did so.

And she let him. How could she do that, Sarah wondered dazedly? He had said a terrible thing. Made an unforgivable accusation, and she could only rest limply against him and feel the warm strength of his body wrap her around, sheltering her.

'That's it.' The deep velvety purr washed over her shattered nerves like a caress. 'Take a deep breath. You're going to be all right. Ah, Figgins.' The tone of his voice changed and Sarah felt him look around. 'Miss Lynley has been overtaken by an unfortunate bout of dizziness. Ride on ahead and warn them, would you?'

'No.' Quite unaware that her hand was clutching Ravensdene's lapel for support, Sarah raised her head. 'I don't want to worry Uncle Jasper. I'm much better now. Quite well, and—'

'You're as white as a sheet,' Ravensdene muttered, glancing down at her. But he didn't insist on his order being carried out, merely gestured slightly to his groom.

The man nodded. 'There's a gate up ahead that opens into the field behind the Grange stables,' he said. 'I'll wait there, me lord.'

Sarah watched him go, eyes wide with surprise. 'How did he know that?' she asked.

'I don't know. Perhaps he takes this path occasionally when he exercises my horses.'

'But this is private prop—'

'It doesn't matter,' he cut in impatiently. 'Sarah—'

The sound of her name brought the world crashing back with a resounding thud. Sarah found herself staring in stunned astonishment first at Ravensdene, then at her hand clasped tightly around his lapel. At the same time she became intensely aware of the solid pressure of his arm around her, and the way she was all but nestled against him. The last time they had been this close she had felt the crushing imprint of his body against hers for hours afterwards.

The memory had her unlocking her fingers and wrenching out of his hold with a violence that almost sent her toppling from the saddle.

The horses, who had both been standing obediently motionless until that moment, flung up their heads in startled reaction to her sudden movement. Honey pranced sideways, wickering nervously, while Ravensdene's black reared up sharply and nearly went over on his hocks.

He was brought under control immediately. Ravensdene reined the stallion in close again and caught Honey's bridle, steadying the little mare. 'Are you all right?' he rapped out.

Feeling like an idiot, Sarah snapped back just as sharply. 'Of course I am.'

She wasn't anything of the sort. She felt horribly weak, her insides quaking madly and her hands barely able to grip the reins. She would have given anything to have been able to ride away, but the effort of keeping her seat had taken every ounce of strength she had left.

'I'm sorry I barked at you like that,' Ravensdene said in a milder tone. 'I was concerned about your ability to hold your horse in your present fragile state of health.' He released the bridle and handed her hat to her. Its bright green plume had been sadly squashed during his tussle with his horse, and Sarah realised he had managed to control the huge beast with only one hand and the power of his thighs. The knowledge stirred up another unnerving memory of his strength. She jammed the hat down on her ruffled curls and glared at him.

'My health is not the issue here,' she retorted. 'It is my. . .my sense of propriety that is outraged, my lord. How dare you make such a contemptible accusation?'

His brows snapped together. 'I wasn't accusing you, for God's sake!'

'I realise that, and am happy to know that you don't believe me to have any designs on your. . .your. . .'

'Yes, you don't have to search for a socially acceptable euphemism, Miss Lynley. After this encounter, I am quite sure my lack of delicacy has given you an ineradicable distaste of me. I can only apologise. Your understanding of my situation, and your questions, led me to believe you would prefer a candid answer.'

Sarah gasped. 'That was no candid answer, sir. You traduced the entire female sex!'

He reached out and captured her wildly gesturing hand. 'No,' he said. 'I didn't. And I agree with you that there are men who have used force to acquire a wife. But I was speaking of the type of manipulative female that you, fortunately, know nothing about.'

When she tried to tug her hand free, his fingers tightened and he looked directly into her eyes. All at once his voice was very low, very soft, and wholly serious. 'Miss Lynley, when you asked me for an explanation I had no thought of distressing you so cruelly. I see I was appallingly blunt. Please forgive me.'

'I. . .' She couldn't go on. She couldn't speak. The utter sincerity in his voice shook her unbearably. She had the most absurd desire to burst into tears, and at the same time wanted to go on railing at him for the dreadful things he had said. Both reactions were so horribly unlike her usual self that for several nerve-racking seconds she felt as if every faculty was suspended.

'I can't believe we're having this conversation,' she finally managed, bewilderment clear in her voice.

'I'm not surprised,' he muttered. 'Since our rather singular meeting, I seem to have spent a great deal of time upsetting you and then apologising.' He released her hand and indicated the path. 'Shall we ride on, Miss

Lynley? I daresay you wish to gain the privacy of your home as soon as possible.'

Again she couldn't answer but merely allowed him to set a sedate pace towards the open fields of the Grange. Honey, as though sensing her mistress's distraction, kept to the steady walk without argument.

Sarah was feeling anything but steady. As well as all the other emotions roiling around inside her, she was now coping with a hefty dose of guilt. She risked a quick glance at Ravensdene, riding stern-faced alongside her, and was painfully conscious that she hadn't accepted his apology, nor barely even acknowledged it.

'I can see where you might have received a...a mistaken impression of me, my lord,' she got out, keeping her gaze fixed on a point between Honey's chestnut ears. Swallowing the lump in her throat, she added valiantly, 'You must think me quite unbalanced.'

'No,' he said curtly. 'I don't.' Gallant under fire, thrown into panic by close proximity to him, and utterly free of feminine wiles, Nick added silently, but not unbalanced.

Nor was the mystery surrounding Sarah going to be solved today. Already he felt as if he'd been pulling wings off butterflies. Whatever terrible secret it was that caused her to go from delightfully natural and amusing one moment, to the verge of panic the next, she had endured enough for one day. He couldn't probe any further.

Besides, it was becoming perfectly obvious that her fear arose from some incident that had nothing to do with spying. Or smugglers. He didn't need to be a genius to see the way she flinched from any close physical contact. With any man, or just with him? he wondered grimly, remembering their first stormy encounter. And then he wondered why he should suddenly feel so savage about the matter. It was none of his business; he already had enough to worry about.

So why was he unable to leave well enough alone? he asked himself wryly. Why was it so difficult to wait until the warm, red-brick walls of Sarah's home came into view and he could see Figgins waiting for them before he felt he could turn to her and ask, 'Has it?'

As he hoped, the cryptic question at least aroused her feminine curiosity.

'Has what?' she asked in a very subdued voice.

'Has my lack of finesse given you an ineradicable distaste of me?'

She should say yes, Sarah thought. Say yes and be done with it. Now that she had her pistol back, there was no reason for her to speak to Ravensdene again, apart from the usual polite acknowledgement when she saw him in public.

But she couldn't bring herself to do it. She couldn't bring herself to be so cruel when he had been so understanding. He had been kind last night also. And the other day, even when furiously angry, he hadn't hurt her.

'You do not lack finesse, my lord,' she said before she lost her courage. 'And—' she kept her gaze resolutely forward '—I do not have a distaste of you.'

'Thank you, Miss Lynley. May I presume, then, that you will still present me to your uncle? I should very much like to meet him.'

'It was my intention, my lord.'

'Again, thank you. I shall not stay long, I assure you.'

'I believe twenty minutes to be the correct length for a first visit, my lord.'

Nick set his teeth and persevered. 'Then I will endeavour to redeem myself by keeping your uncle occupied while you return his pistol to its proper place.'

She sent him a very swift, very shy glance from beneath her lashes that had him forcibly suppressing a violent urge to take her in his arms and shield her from whatever spectre was haunting her. Fortunately, before he could do anything so calculated to chase her away for good, she nudged her mare into a canter that quickly brought them up to Figgins and the gate leading to the stableyard.

Neither of them said another word until they had dismounted and Sarah had led him along a path bordered by garden beds to the main entrance of the neat, square Georgian house. They rounded the corner in time to see a tall, white-haired gentleman descending the portico steps with the aid of a cane. He glanced up and smiled.

'Sarah, my dear,' he said gently, holding out a thin, frail hand. 'I've been wondering where you were.'

'Oh, Uncle Jasper, I'm sorry. Am I very late?' Sarah hurried forward with an alacrity that had Nick clenching his fists in silent self-reproach at her eagerness to leave his side. She took her uncle's outstretched hand and stood on tip-toe to kiss his wrinkled cheek. Clearly, whatever nightmare she feared was not here, and it struck him again that although she was afraid—of men? Of *something*—he had never seen her completely give in to it. She had always managed to rally herself and recover.

'It was all Honey's fault,' she was saying now, with a droll look that Nick knew had to be forced. 'She simply would *not* return home before she'd had her gallop along the cliffs, and then what should happen but that Lord Ravensdene must come upon me losing the argument. However, he very kindly offered his assistance, and I knew you would wish to thank him, so. . .'

Before this breathless speech was over, Sir Jasper had released Sarah's hand and was turning to greet his visitor. Nick found himself meeting a kindly, blue-eyed gaze that for all Lynley's age was still surprisingly shrewd.

'So, you're old Comberford's grandson, my lord,' he said in his soft voice. 'I am very happy to meet you. I had formed the intention of calling on you in a day or two, you know, and am much obliged to you for saving me a trip in that rattletrap of a carriage Sarah insists that I use. But I hope in assisting her you did not have to go out of your way?'

'How do you do, sir?' Nick returned the handshake, instinctively softening both grip and voice. Most people, he reflected, would respond that way to the old man's gentle, curiously old-world air. 'No, I'm not out of my way at all. Miss Lynley exaggerates. I merely escorted her home.'

'Well, I am grateful to you, sir. To tell you the truth, I cannot like this notion she has taken into her head to start walking or riding alone. And now we see what has come of it.'

'Now, Uncle Jasper, I told you—'

'Yes, yes, my dear.' He patted her cheek. 'I daresay I am sadly behind the times, but there it is. You will have to indulge an old man who worries about you.'

She dimpled at him. 'Dearest Uncle Jasper, there is not the least need, I assure you. But I'm sorry to have made you fret. What is to be done? Shall I lose our next match?'

'Cheeky puss.' He chuckled. 'You see how it is, my lord. Little did I think it would come to this when I introduced Sarah to a chessboard. But what are we doing standing about in this wind? Come in, my lord, come in. Your grandfather told me you are no mean chess player yourself. Learned it from him, I expect. Perhaps you will give me the pleasure of a game one day?'

'I'm afraid you will find me sadly out of practise, sir, but I would be happy to oblige you.' Nick reached out to hand Sarah up the steps, frowning slightly at the almost imperceptible tremor that shook her the moment his fingers closed around her arm.

He saw her glance quickly at her uncle, but Sir Jasper

was busy with the careful placement of his cane and hadn't noticed anything amiss. Still chatting away in happy ignorance of any undercurrents, he led the way into a small, well-lit hall. Doors led off it on either side and, opposite the front door, a narrow but elegant staircase rose to the upper floors.

As soon as they were inside, Sarah extracted herself from his hold and gathered up the skirts of her riding habit, obviously preparing to flee at the first opportunity.

'Yes, off you go, my dear,' Sir Jasper approved, waving a vague hand towards the upper reaches. 'No doubt you will be wishing to change your gown. This way, my lord. Let me show you the state of play your grandfather left me in. Never got to finish our last game, you know. Sarah offered to take Jonathan's place, but that wouldn't do. The little minx always wins. No respect for her elders at all.'

'Don't believe a word of it, my lord.' Sarah turned to him with a carefully polite smile. 'Uncle Jasper gives no quarter.'

Sir Jasper beamed modestly.

'Indeed?' Fully aware that she was trying to make an unobtrusive retreat towards the stairs without any further contact, Nick stepped into her path and held out his hand. 'In that case I shall count on your good advice, Miss Lynley, to avoid any pitfalls your uncle has in store for me.'

She hesitated a moment then placed her hand lightly in his, her colour rising as his fingers enveloped hers. 'Good day, my lord,' she managed to utter in a very formal, very small voice. 'Thank you for your assistance earlier.'

Nick released her, stunned to discover that for the first time in his life it was difficult to keep his mind on social conventions that should have been second nature. Quite simply, he did not want to let her go with this constraint between them. He watched her ascend the stairs and he knew, as surely as if she had admitted it aloud, that she was fiercely resisting the urge to run.

She would not run, Sarah told herself as she mounted the stairs. She would not run and she would not look back. She would keep her eyes straight ahead until she got to her room. She would not even peek. She would *not*—

He was standing where they had parted, one hand resting on the newel post, the other clenched at his side, looking up at her. Sarah felt her steps slow. Her gaze was caught, held captive. It was as if he had been waiting for her to turn, to glance back. She stopped, her hand gripping the bannister, waiting also. . .

And then he smiled. A crooked smile of such wry understanding that her heart stopped in mid-beat. Time stopped, stood still. And to her utter astonishment she felt her own lips part and curve in an answering smile. A shy, hesitant, fugitive smile, but still a smile, that perhaps held everything she wanted to say, and could not. Gratitude, tentative friendship, the beginnings of trust, reassurance.

Reassurance?

The smile was wiped off her face in a flash. Sarah whirled about and fled up the stairs and into her room with nary a thought for what her uncle might think of such peculiar behaviour. Far from stopping, her heart was now racing like a panicked deer. Reassurance! What on earth had put *that* idea into her head? She had never in her entire life seen anyone who looked less in need of reassurance than the Earl of Ravensdene.

If anyone needed comforting and reassurance, it was her. Because she was very much afraid that she was taking leave of her senses. Ravensdene scared her. Of course he did. That was absolutely indisputable. He was a man. She was frightened of him. Of his strength, his size, the compelling force he seemed able to command at will. And yet there was gentleness in him, in his voice, his touch, in that last long look they had exchanged. It disturbed her. Terribly.

And she didn't know why.

'Very easy on the eyes, the little lady, me lord.'

Nick shifted his frowning gaze from the road in front of him to his henchman's inquisitive face. They had left the Grange five minutes ago; he knew from long acquaintance that five minutes was about the limit of Figgins' silence when he had something to say.

'Very,' he agreed repressively. 'She also happens to be intelligent, Figgins, so mind what you say in her hearing.'

'Aye, sir.' The groom thought this over and added, 'Not that we'll need to slum the place from the outside anymore now that you've met the lady's uncle.'

'*Slum* the place? I won't ask where you picked up that thieves' cant.'

'No need, sir. Probably the same places you've been in your time, sir.'

A reluctant grin tugged at Nick's mouth. 'Very likely,' he said. 'You know, Figgins, this is getting damned complicated.'

'Never known a job o' yours that weren't,' Figgins remarked with laconic understatement. 'If you'll pardon the liberty, me lord, what did you think of the old gentleman?'

Nick narrowed his eyes thoughtfully. 'That's what's so damned complicated, Figgins. He *is* old. Older than I would have expected an uncle of Miss Lynley's to be. He must be close to eighty, more my grandfather's generation.'

'Well, he weren't much more than a likely prospect,' Figgins observed, apparently feeling the need to offer some consolation. 'Funny how everyone talks about the

Grange folk, though. . . Well, they *don't* talk about 'em. That's what's strange.'

'No doubt. However, from this moment on, Figgins, you also will maintain a like silence on the subject of Miss Lynley and her uncle. At least while we search further afield.'

An expression of resigned suffering appeared on Figgin's rough-hewn countenance. 'I'm to stay friendly-like with every fisherman up and down this blasted coast,' he said, as if reciting a standing order. 'And here I was thinking after we left France that I'd never have to set foot in a boat again. Give me a horse every time.'

Nick grimaced faintly. 'Console yourself with the reflection that you'd feel even more out of place in a drawing-room. I'm the one who'll have to observe my neighbours a little more closely than I have been doing.'

'Ah, well, 'tis probably for the best.' Figgins cast a shrewd, sidelong glance at his master. 'If the little lady's gettin' her hooks into yer lordship, things could get a mite lively.'

There was a frozen silence.

'How long have you been with me, Figgins?' Nick asked at last in a very soft voice.

The groom pursed his lips and looked cautious. 'Er. . . about eight years, me lord.'

'Ah, yes. I remember the occasion of our meeting. You saved me from a rather nasty encounter with a knife.'

'Never did approve of coves stabbing people in the back,' muttered Figgins.

Nick's voice became even softer. 'A sentiment I applaud. However, if you wish to remain in your present post for as long as another eight seconds, you will not again refer to Miss Lynley as "the little lady" nor that she has her hooks into anyone.'

'Aye, me lord.'

'And while we're on the subject,' he added as Figgins

looked uncharacteristically crestfallen, 'you ought to know me better. Women do not get their hooks into me.'

'No, sir.' Figgins revived somewhat. 'Well, not those kind of hooks, anyroad. I ain't forgetting that hussy three years back who thought she had you caught good and proper. Tried to get information out of you and ended up flat on her back telling *you* what we wanted to know.' He chuckled. 'Sang like a bird, she did.'

'Thank you, Figgins. I hadn't forgotten. Perhaps you could contrive to do so, however.'

'If you say so, me lord. But you was always very cool with the ladies. Very cool. Talk of the troop, it were.'

Having had the last word to say on the subject, Figgins finally subsided and the ride back to Comberford Place was accomplished in silence, leaving Nick to the contemplation, not of the task he'd been set, but of a certain small female who seemed to have the knack of arousing some very primitive emotions in him.

Desire he could understand, even if he couldn't so easily dismiss it; not only was Sarah uncommonly pretty, there was both humour and an innocent, enquiring intelligence in those soft amber eyes that was appealing in its very rarity. But beautiful women had come and gone before in his life without disturbing his concentration. They had occupied their place, usually very briefly, and he had parted from them without regret.

Simple physical attraction, therefore, did not explain the quite disproportionate sense of relief he felt at the possibility that Sarah's courtly, frail uncle might be precisely what he seemed. It didn't explain the near-savage rage he felt every time she flinched from his touch.

And it didn't explain the sudden sharp need he had experienced to have her run to him, and not to her uncle, for protection, to fold her in his arms and keep her safe. Once again she had reached a part of him he thought had been closed off forever, and he was discovering, much to his surprise, that the steel walls he had constructed years ago were being shaken to their very foundations.

By an elusive slip of a girl so fragile he could have broken her two days ago without even meaning to.

'Oh, dear, why did we not bring a footman with us to carry some of these parcels? How on earth are we ever going to manage? We shall have to return to the inn and then set out again. Sarah, do you have that russet cambric walking dress wrapped up safely? And where is my new pelisse?'

Talking non-stop, Lady Wribbonhall emerged from her dressmaker's establishment onto the busy street and began counting packages, to the vast inconvenience of several passers-by.

'Oh, Mama, do stop worrying. Sarah and I can manage perfectly, and we have only the haberdashery to visit now.' With a good deal of dexterous juggling, Julia transferred the strings of several bandboxes to one hand and relieved her flustered parent of yet another.

'Yes, but there are so many things still to purchase. Silk stockings, gloves, dancing slippers, ribbons. I think some knots of cherry ribbon will be just the thing to set off the cambric, Sarah. And we positively must return to Celine's for that russet and ecru bonnet to wear with it. Oh, dear. Why cannot things be in the same shop? It would make everything so much easier.'

'Dearest ma'am, there is not the least need for you to be running all over Eastbourne for a particular bonnet,' Sarah ventured. 'I am sure I already have a score of hats and gowns for every possible occasion. You must be exhausted, and—'

'Exhausted?' Lady Wribbonhall looked at her charge in the liveliest astonishment. 'When there are clothes to be bought? Never, dear child. Come! The haberdashery!'

Lady Wribbonhall might as well have said 'Charge!' Plunging into the crowd, she set off down the street like a velvet-clad ship of the line, accompanied by two small frigates. Sarah could only marvel at her ladyship's stamina.

On the other hand, such constant activity was at least keeping her mind from the contemplation of a certain exchange of smiles that had been haunting her dreams for the past couple of days.

'Two pairs of dancing slippers, I think,' Lady Wribbonhall decreed, as if they had just been discussing the subject.

Sarah blinked away yet another mental image of glittering green eyes and a hard mouth that could curve without warning into a crooked, heart-shaking smile, and tried to drum up some interest in the current conversation.

'Two, ma'am? But—'

'At least two, my dear. There is the Assembly tomorrow night and ever since the invitations went out for the Sherington's waltzing party next month, every-one is determined to give a ball of their own. Which reminds me. I have been meaning to warn you, my love, on no account must you dance more than twice with the same gentleman, and should anyone solicit your hand for the waltz—'

'I have *no* intention of waltzing,' Sarah broke in with more haste than grace. She flushed and tried to soften the abrupt interjection. 'I remember when you warned Julia that she must not waltz before she had been approved by the Patronesses at Almack's, dear ma'am. Besides, I truly don't wish to find myself in such an intimate situation with any strange gentlemen.'

'Well, I don't think you will meet anyone precisely *strange*,' mused Lady Wribbonhall, completely missing

Sarah's meaning. 'The Assemblies are quite well-conducted, you know, and when performed correctly, the waltz is a most charming dance. However, there are several young officers quartered in the town who perhaps may not be counted upon to keep the line, and you may be sure those dreadful Smisby girls will turn the whole evening into a romp.'

'Mama, be assured that Sarah and I shall sit virtuously on the sidelines,' promised Julia with a mischievous smile.

'Nonsense, my love,' Lady Wribbonhall declared, responding to this sally with all the comfortable assurance of one who knows her charges will not suffer the fate of less attractive damsels. She turned the corner onto another street, causing a gentlemen in a buff-coloured coat to dodge hastily to one side to avoid a flying bandbox, and continued with her lecture. 'I was only advising Sarah to exercise discretion in the case of the waltz. But if there is any gentleman with whom you do not feel comfortable, Sarah dear, you need not feel obliged to dance with him. Which leads me to another point. It is an unfortunate fact that some men do not know how to accept a refusal gracefully. If that should happen, you have merely to say your card is full.'

'Thank you, ma'am,' returned Sarah with real gratitude.

'Well, I am not usually an advocate of falsehood, but sometimes it is a lady's only recourse. I recall a gentleman at a ball many years ago who kept insisting that I dance with him, although he did not know his left foot from his right. He simply would not take "no" for an answer.'

'I know precisely what you mean, ma'am,' Sarah agreed with a rueful smile. 'I met a very similar gentleman at Tunbridge Wells who had accompanied his invalid parent, but who spent more time trying to persuade me to go driving with him, or take a turn about the town, than he did with his mama. I am sure she considered me to be a most unscrupulous female, out to ensnare her precious child, but for my part I was heartily glad of her presence.'

'Oh, dear. You did not consider him to be at all eligible, my love?'

'Not at all,' responded Sarah, dashing Lady Wribbonhall's hopes for a possible suitor. 'And to top off his very unfortunate manner, he looked just like a frog. He even wore a green coat.'

'Well, rest assured that you are unlikely to be pestered by any frogs while you under *my*— But here we are. Gracious! What a press of people. Why must everyone choose to shop here at once? How will we ever...?' Lady Wribbonhall subsided once more into flustered incoherence as she forged a path through the doorway and into the crowded haberdashery.

'Now, Mama, there is no need to fuss. We will just have to separate.'

'But—'

Julia took command. 'Sarah, you will have to try on dancing slippers, so you had best wait for a chair to become available. Mama, you are in charge of purchasing ribbons, and I shall buy gloves and silk stockings. We shall meet back here by the door as soon as we are able.'

Lady Wribbonhall acquiescing to this sensible arrangement, they each went their separate ways. Not without some difficulty, Sarah acknowledged as she was beaten to the only vacant chair in the immediate vicinity by a stout lady in purple grosgrain. The lady settled herself triumphantly on her perch and straightened her turban which was dipping drunkenly over one eye after her dash through the crowd.

Sarah retired from the lists to a tiny space near one wall and considered the possibility of lacing up slippers while balancing on one foot and while her hands were

full of parcels. That was if she managed to attract the
notice of one of the clerks who were scurrying back and
forth behind the counters like so many ants.

Around her all was bustle and confusion. Nearby, two
ladies were arguing loudly over the selection of a
cashmere shawl, while their respective offspring were
busily employed in emptying the contents of a large
glass buttonjar onto the floor. Several buttons had
already been crunched underfoot, much to the delight
of the small miscreants.

She was just beginning to wonder if her old evening
slippers would survive several parties and balls, when
she noticed another lady who looked as hot and tired
and uncomfortable as she did. Like the two patrons who
had by now all but buried their attendant clerk beneath
a pile of discarded cashmere shawls, her fellow sufferer
also had a little boy with her. Unlike his contemporaries,
however, the child had hold of his mother's hand and
was looking up at her with an anxious expression on his
round, cherubic face.

Sarah smiled in sympathy. The poor little fellow
probably thought he was going to end up like the
buttons. She glanced up to see if the mother had noticed
anything amiss with her offspring and suddenly understood the reason for the boy's concern. The lady was
now as pale as she had been flushed a second ago, and
even as Sarah watched, she swayed and put out her free
hand.

Sarah sprang forward, narrowly avoiding a collision
with a passing clerk and grasped the lady's arm. 'Forgive
me, ma'am,' she said quickly as the lady turned a pair of
startled blue eyes on her. 'I couldn't help but notice that
you are unwell. There is a chair over here. I am sure that
lady in purple won't object to—'

'Oh, no. Please.' Shaking her head, the lady
straightened and took a deep breath. 'Please don't

disturb her. I am not ill. It is just so hot in here, and when one has been standing forever. . .'

'It is a wonder we are not all laid out upon the floor,' Sarah finished with a smile.

'Yes, indeed.' The lady smiled back at her and seemed to recover a little of her colour. 'What we females will put up with for a new shipment of India muslin.'

'Is that what has caused such a crowd? Good heavens! We shall be here all day. Are you alone, ma'am? Can I—?'

'Of course my mama is not alone,' piped up a small voice from the vicinity of her knees. 'She has me.'

'And I am sure she could not wish for a better escort,' Sarah responded instantly, smiling down at the indignant face upturned to her. 'Do you think, sir, that if I make a path for us, you will be able to guide your mama outside?'

The cherub nodded and puffed out his small nankeen-covered chest.

'Oh, please, dear ma'am. Giles and I can manage. There is not the least need—'

'Nonsense. I shall be glad to leave this place myself.' Sarah bent to retrieve the bandbox she had dropped when she had leapt to the rescue and indicated the door. 'Come, Master Giles, follow me.'

'My name is really Master Giles Beresford,' the cherub announced importantly once they found themselves safely out on the street again. 'And my mama is Mrs Major William Beresford.'

'How very clever of you to introduce us,' Sarah said, charmed by the little boy's quaint manners. 'My name is Miss Sarah Lynley. How do you do?'

'As you can see, Miss Lynley, Giles does very much better than his mama,' Mrs Beresford answered ruefully, as her son solemnly shook hands with his new acquaintance. 'Thank you. You are very kind. It was foolish of me to wait in such a horrid crush in my present situation, but the fresh air will soon put me to rights, I assure you.'

'Oh. Yes. Of course.' Feeling remarkably foolish herself for not noticing what should have been patently obvious from the start, even in the confines of the crowded shop, Sarah struggled to hide her shocked reaction. She didn't even know why she was shocked. Mrs Beresford was certainly not the first lady she had encountered who was expecting an interesting event.

As the lady concerned bent to straighten Master Beresford's small coat, Sarah studied her more closely, startled again to discover that Mrs Beresford appeared to be only a year or two older than herself. She was a pretty girl, with large blue eyes, a tiny rosebud of a mouth, and an exquisitely fair complexion that was set off by a wealth of red-gold hair. She also looked as if the interesting event was going to take place in a matter of weeks, not months.

'Er, should you not be sitting down, Mrs Beresford?' she asked diffidently. 'There is a bench over there near the gardens, or perhaps your carriage. . .'

'Oh, we walked.' Mrs Beresford straighted and smiled. 'And my name is Lydia. I know we have never met, but I am sure I have seen you in the town before. Forgive me, but you are so pretty, I couldn't help but remember you.'

Sarah blushed, hardly knowing how to reply to this forthright speech. 'You are staying in Eastbourne?' she asked.

'Yes, my husband has taken lodgings for us only a block or two away. He is on leave for a while, until his wounds heal—' A shadow crossed her face briefly and was banished. 'But we must not detain you further. The bench will be the perfect place to wait for him. He is to meet us at this corner, you know, after he has seen his doctor.'

'I see,' Sarah murmured somewhat awkwardly. 'Your. . .that is, Major Beresford's wound was serious?'

'Yes.' Lydia Beresford glanced quickly at Giles, but the little boy's attention had been drawn to a dashing phaeton and pair being tooled along the other side of the street, and he was no longer listening to the conversation. 'Poor William was in a French hospital in the most appalling conditions for months,' she explained in a low voice. 'He was eventually exchanged with other prisoners of war, but it was almost a year before he began to regain his health.'

'I'm sorry. You must have been very anxious.'

In the face of the grim memories still lingering in Mrs Beresford's fine eyes, Sarah felt her remark to be utterly meaningless. She could have bitten her tongue. But what else could she have said? Any dutiful wife would have been concerned for the health of a wounded husband. Why then did she sense that, in the Beresford's situation, duty had very little to do with it?

'Dreadfully anxious,' Lydia Beresford agreed. 'But,' she added, brightening, 'that is all behind us now. William is improving every day, and in the summer Giles will have a little playmate. Which reminds me. I fear I did not thank you properly for your kindness, Miss Lynley. It was very good of you to come to my assistance. But what of yourself? Are *you* alone? May we escort you somewhere when William—?'

'No, no,' Sarah interrupted hastily. 'My friends are still in the haberdashery. I am to meet them here, so you see I am not put out in the least.'

Lydia smiled again in her friendly fashion. 'Oh, I am so glad. Well, we must let you return to your shopping. Do you ever attend the Assemblies here? Not that either William or I are in any condition to *dance*,' she tacked on drolly, 'but the suppers are very good, and there are cards. Perhaps we shall meet again. Come,

Giles, dearest. Make your bow to Miss Lynley and then you may give me your arm across the road.'

Feeling somewhat responsible for the little family, Sarah waited until they had crossed to the other side and Giles had seated his mama on the bench outside the entrance to the gardens. She waved farewell and had half-turned to brave the hazards of the haberdashery again, when a tall gentleman in hussar's uniform strode around the corner. Even from a distance and with the noise of the traffic, Sarah could hear Giles's shrill cry of 'Papa! Papa!'

The little boy rushed forward to be swept up in his father's arms and carried back to the bench. Sarah could see him talking nineteen to the dozen and knew he was relating the tale of their adventure. Suddenly unable to move, she stayed where she was, all thought of Lady Wribbonhall, Julia and shopping gone from her mind.

It was like watching a play, she thought vaguely. But this was real. The look of tender concern on Major Beresford's lined but handsome face as he bent over his wife, was real. The expression of love, wholly returned, shining in her eyes, was real.

They exchanged a few words and she saw the Major shake his head and smile. Lydia laughed up at him and he took her hand and kissed it. Sarah knew what they were saying as surely as if she was standing right beside them. Knew that he was chiding his wife, but gently, and that she was reassuring him that nothing was wrong.

Then he put Giles back on his feet, drew Lydia up beside him and they all turned towards the gardens, and just for an instant Sarah saw the expression on the Major's face as he gazed down at his wife unbeknownst to her. Adoration, total and unwavering, was there, plain to see.

She looked away, shaken and embarrassed, feeling as if she had intruded on something very private, and then, unwillingly fascinated, unable to resist, she looked back.

They had entered the gardens, young Giles running ahead and leaping into the air with childish exuberance every few steps. Without stopping to think, drawn by a compulsion beyond reason, Sarah glanced up and down the street, crossed over when the way was clear and followed the Beresfords through the gate.

She didn't hurry. She might have been moving in a strange sort of daze, but she retained enough wit to know that she would look very foolish if she was caught.

The Beresfords didn't hurry either, but strolled along, pausing now and then to admire an early spring bloom or a tree bursting into blossom, while Giles ran all over the place, returning every so often to show his parents some new treasure he had found on the grass. There was an odd familiarity about the scene, but she had no memories of any similar outings with her own family.

She puzzled over the small point for a few seconds before the answer came to her with stunning clarity. The Major walked with a slight limp and his tall frame was thinner than it should have been, evidence of a long illness, but he moved with the same controlled power she had seen in Ravensdene. Beside him, Lydia looked small and dainty, and yet she had entrusted herself to her much larger husband, had borne him a child and was carrying another.

Sarah stopped dead in the middle of the path. It was as well she did so, because a second later the Beresfords stopped also. The Major passed his arm about Lydia's waist, leaned closer and said something to her that made her smile. She stood on tip-toe and brushed her lips across his, only to have them captured in a swift response. Then, as if recollecting their public surroundings, the Major broke the embrace, turned his wife's steps towards a gate in the distance and called to Giles.

Frozen where she stood, Sarah watched the Beresfords leave the gardens and vanish from sight, the memory of their brief kiss imprinted on her mind as if etched there.

Eventually, without really being conscious of moving, she started to walk again. Time passed. She tried to reason, to sort out the jumbled images in her mind, but the only thing she knew with any certainty was that a world that had once seemed very familiar to her was now very, very different.

And so were her surroundings.

'Oh, no!' Sarah stopped short and looked around her in dismay. She was still in the gardens, but in her abstraction she had wandered far off the path and was in some sort of leafy glade, surrounded by rhododendron bushes. It was pretty enough, but the bushes were too tall for her to see very far. Somewhere in the distance she could hear voices, but they came to her on the wind and she couldn't tell from which direction.

'Oh, you *idiot*!' Wheeling about, she began to retrace her path, castigating herself every step of the way. For some reason the sound of her own voice was comforting, even if she was running through every synonym for fool that occurred to her. She had just reached mooncalf and was about to go on to numskull when a faint sound behind her pulled her up short.

She glanced back at the glade. There was nothing there of course. But even as she turned to start walking again, she felt the hair at her nape stir ever so slightly. The feeling that she was being watched swept over her like the brushing of icy fingers across her flesh.

Sarah's stomach clenched in a spasm of fear. She fought it back at once. This was ridiculous. She was taking her recent folly to new heights. Mouth set in a determined line she turned again to confront whoever was there.

No one. Except an increasing awareness of a presence. Invisible, but there.

It was enough. Fleeing from nothing might be silly,

but since there was no one around to see her foolishness, she didn't care. Sarah broke into a run. In seconds she was clear of the bushes and on a wide, curving path that did not look in the least familiar. It didn't matter. Picking up speed, she raced along the path, went hurtling around the corner and ran straight into the Earl of Ravensdene.

CHAPTER SIX

'OH! MY LORD!'

Sara scarcely had time to recognise the other victim of the collision before she found herself locked in an embrace that threatened to crush her ribs.

At her startled exclamation he released her as if she had burned him. 'Miss Lynley! What in God's name are you doing alone in these gardens? Are you insensible to the dangers in such a situation?'

As a first reaction from a gallant rescuer, this thundered interrogation left a lot to be desired. Sarah could only stare up at him in confusion while her senses still reeled from the impact of his hard body against hers.

'Why were you running like that?' Ravensdene looked past her, his eyes narrowing on the corner behind her, but when no one appeared, his gaze returned to pin hers with glittering intensity. 'Did someone accost you?'

'No! No.'

Clutching her bandboxes, Sarah tried to put her crazily whirling thoughts in some sort of order. It had been difficult before; it was impossible now. As well as Amy and the Beresfords, her mind had been so filled with her previous meetings with Ravensdene, with every instance of his gentleness, with that last heart-shaking smile, that the sudden re-emergence of the dangerous, cold-eyed predator was simply too much.

This was the man who had rendered her helpless in seconds, who had brought back her memories of Amy's screams, of harsh, laboured breathing, and the terrible silence that had followed.

'I didn't. . . I just remembered Lady Wribbonhall. . . and I was hurrying. . .'

'You just *remembered*? Miss Lynley, what possessed you to be so imprudent as to leave Lady Wribbonhall's protection in the first place? Why are you wandering around in here? Are you lost to all sense of propriety?'

She winced as the questions were hurled at her like thunderbolts.

'No, of course not. I—'

'Lady Wribbonhall is beside herself with worry. You have used her very badly.'

'I'm sorry. I didn't mean. . . I wasn't thinking. . .at least I *was*. That was why—'

'Thinking! Obviously not with any noticeable degree of reason.'

Sarah began to lose her temper. 'I don't know why I am standing here trying to justify myself to you, sir,' she declared, drawing herself up to her full height. It was all of ten inches below Ravensdene's but she was too incensed to care. 'If you will let me pass, I shall return to Lady Wribbonhall and make my apology to one who will accept it in the manner in which it is offered.'

Sarah didn't flatter herself that this speech went any way towards mollifying her rescuer, although why he should be so furious was beyond her, but it did put an end to his lecturing.

'By all means, Miss Lynley,' he said with more than a suggestion of gritted teeth. 'Let us go.'

'I don't recall asking for your escort,' Sarah informed him. 'Kindly stand aside, sir.'

She might as well have been talking to a rhododendron bush. Ravensdene took her arm in a grip just short of punishing, turned about and began marching her down the path. 'Don't be an idiot,' he muttered. 'And give me those bandboxes.'

'I said I don't need your—'

'And *I* said give me the damned bandboxes!' The

bandboxes were yanked out of her grasp with a force
that nearly took her hand with them.

Sarah ground her own teeth. Insufferable, arrogant
male! How could she ever have thought him kind merely
because of one or two peculiar instances when he had
obviously been acting completely out of character?

'There is no need to use such deplorable language,'
she stated, nose in the air. She was about to continue
along the same lines when he interrupted her.

'Be grateful it's only my language that's deplorable.
At the moment it's either that or I strangle you. Little
fool! I'm beginning to think you need a keeper.'

'A keeper! How dare—?'

'What in Hades did you think you were about? There
are soldiers all over this town. What if you had been
accosted?' His mouth twisted into a mocking line. 'Or
have you armed yourself with another pistol?'

Sarah glared up at him with heavy meaning. 'Unfortunately, no.'

A muscle clenched in his jaw but he didn't answer.
Which was just as well, Sarah reflected, because those
two words were about all she had breath for.
Ravensdene was hauling her through the gardens so fast
she would not have been surprised to find herself
achieving the miracle of flight.

They reached the gate by which she had entered and
she was bundled through it with scant ceremony. Knowing her face was unbecomingly flushed, and conscious of
an uncomfortable twinge in her side that presaged pain
if she had to walk much farther, she was somewhat
relieved to see a curricle and pair waiting near the
corner.

Then dismay engulfed her. Surely Lady Wribbonhall
had not abandoned her to Ravensdene's mercy? Would
she have to endure his disapproving company all the
way back to Wribbonhall Lacy?

'I am not getting into that curricle until I know

where—' she began, only to swallow the rest on a startled squeak as Ravensdene tossed her bandboxes into the curricle, then picked her up and tossed her in after them as if she weighed no more than their contents.

Sarah landed on the padded seat and bounced. Grabbing hold of the hood to steady herself, she sat up and glared at him. It didn't seem to have much effect. Impervious to the mental daggers being hurled his way, he walked around the curricle, climbed in beside her and flicked a coin to the urchin who was holding the heads of the two black horses in the traces.

For some reason the sight of the glossy pair annoyed her intensely. Why couldn't he have had grey horses, or chestnuts, or even bays?

'I suppose all your horses are black,' she accused irrationally. 'I'm not surprised. I daresay it comes in handy when you have to kidnap ladies at night. However, this is broad daylight, my lord, and if you think I am going to tamely sit here while you—'

'Don't put yourself to the trouble of screaming for help,' he advised, guiding his pair into a neat U-turn and setting off up the street at a smart pace. 'Lady Wribbonhall is waiting for you at the Lamb Inn, so you will have to endure being kidnapped for only five minutes. But you're right, Miss Lynley. All my horses are black.'

Sarah was too incensed to notice the calmer tone in which this last remark was delivered. 'Just what I would have expected,' she retorted, as if owning black horses was a crime worthy of the highest condemnation. 'And how, pray, did you come to be in those gardens at that particular moment, my lord?'

He followed this abrupt turn in the conversation without a blink.

'Lord Devenham and I met Lady Wribbonhall and Miss Wribbonhall as we drove into the yard at the Lamb. They had just discovered that you had not

returned to the inn after you had apparently become
separated, and both were extremely worried. Naturally
I offered to search for you while Devenham remained to
allay their anxiety.'

'Naturally,' Sarah muttered.

'And while we're on the subject of that particular
moment,' he continued with grim purpose, 'what was it
you were running from, Miss Lynley? And don't give
me any more whiskers about suddenly remembering
Lady Wribbonhall, or even forgetting her in the first
place.'

'But I did!' she exclaimed indignantly. Then subsided
abruptly into silence as she recalled what had caused her
most uncharacteristic lapse in memory. She could never
explain *that*. Nor could she tell him she had been fleeing
from something unseen, but sensed. It was entirely too
much like Averilla Smisby's invisible footpads. Goodness knew what he would make of such a weak story.

'I told you. I was thinking,' she said at last with more
than a touch of defiance.

This response remained unanswered for a few seconds while he was forced to negotiate a tricky path
through several other vehicles. Sarah glanced down and
could have sworn there was less than an inch of space
between her side of the curricle and a barouche drawn
up at the side of the road.

She had a strong urge to shut her eyes until they were
safely past, then inspiration dawned. Here was a
heaven-sent opportunity to lead the conversation into
less nerve-racking channels. Compared to that,
Ravensdene's terrifying style of driving was a mere
bagatelle.

'A neat piece of driving, my lord,' she remarked with
hideous brightness. She winced inwardly and tried to
paste a suitably admiring expression on her face. Either
she wasn't very talented at dissimulation, or

Ravensdene had been complimented too many times before on his handling of the reins.

'Thank you, Miss Lynley,' he said dryly. Then before she could rally for another attempt at casual conversation, his voice dropped to the soft, dangerous purr that set her insides quivering. 'Now, tell me what you were thinking about.'

Sarah swallowed. Her mind went completely blank. It was quite a shock, because a second ago it had been busily preparing a lecture on horses she had driven. 'I. . . my sister,' she blurted out, and felt her heart stand still.

He sent her a quick, rapier-sharp glance. 'Your sister? I didn't know you had one.'

'No,' she whispered. 'I don't. Not any more.'

She felt him glance at her again before he had to return his attention to the busy street. She was grateful he didn't speak. Expressions of sympathy or, worse, questions from him under the present circumstances would have dangerously threatened her control, already teetering on the brink. What on earth had possessed her to come out with such an ill-considered statement?

She was still trying to find the answer to that puzzle when Ravensdene turned the curricle into the yard at the Lamb Inn.

Sarah went limp with relief. The Lamb was often reputed to be the haunt of smugglers—indeed, there were even rumours that a secret tunnel led from the inn to St Mary's Church for the convenience of these ruthless persons—but Sarah wouldn't have cared if a deputation of murderous free-traders was waiting for them in the yard. She had never been so glad to reach her destination in her life.

Unfortunately, her relief was premature. As an ostler came running to take the horses, Ravensdene sprang down from the curricle and walked around to assist her to alight. Not with a politely outstretched hand, Sarah saw to her dismay. He meant to lift her down.

And in that same nerve-racking moment, as she gazed down into those crystalline green eyes, she found herself remembering in minute and accurate detail how it had felt to be held against him when they had collided; the crushing strength of his arms, the size and warmth of him.

Like being enveloped by heat and steel.

Sarah's mouth went dry as she got shakily to her feet. For some unfathomable reason her legs seemed to have turned to jelly. Various methods of leaping to the ground without his assistance darted through her brain, but before she could act on one he took the decision out of her hands.

Grasping her firmly by the waist, he swung her down and released her the moment her feet touched the ground.

Eyes wide, Sarah looked up at him, shaken to find that she had instinctively gripped his arms for support and now couldn't seem to let go.

Her gaze fell to her tightly clinging hands. She ordered herself to loosen her grip, to step back, but the command seemed to be lost beneath a haze of sensation that began in her palms, tingling against the feel of hard, muscled strength, and flowed all the way to her toes. Quite suddenly, she couldn't even breathe.

'You see how simple things can be if you would only trust yourself to me, Miss Lynley,' he murmured.

The words succeeded in snapping Sarah out of her daze. She gasped, snatched her hands away, and fled into the inn before he could enlarge on the theme.

She found Lady Wribbonhall alone in a private parlour and at once launched into a breathless, incoherent apology. It was several seconds before she realised that her explanation, in which Lydia Beresford, her little boy and the gardens had become quite incomprehensibly muddled, was totally unnecessary. Far from being beside herself with worry, Lady Wribbonhall merely looked up from her contemplation of their purchases with an expression of pleased, if weary, satisfaction.

Sarah halted in mid-sentence, her already disordered mind seething with wild conjecture, as a small commotion behind her heralded the arrival of Julia in company with Lord Devenham. Ravensdene followed them through the doorway in time to hear Julia's bright greeting.

'There you are, Sarah. Mama said she had seen you leave the haberdashery with another lady. We thought you must have met up with an acquaintance, but we were too far away to call out to you. Wasn't it a frightful crush?'

'Well, I don't wonder at you escaping, Sarah, dear,' Lady Wribbonhall added indulgently. 'I know how you dislike crowds, but it was very naughty of you to desert us like that. However, there is no harm done, and I see Lord Ravensdene has brought you safely back.'

'Yes, ma'am. And I am very sorry to have deserted you, but Mrs Beresford was not well and. . .'

Sarah let the sentence trail into the mists of oblivion while she wondered what in the world was going on. Where was the distraught chaperon of Ravensdene's description? Lady Wribbonhall looked perfectly happy, and was now launched on a lively discussion with her daughter and Lord Devenham. Sarah's brain reeled anew. Was *nothing* what it seemed today?

'Oh, Sarah, you will be delighted with the scheme we have hatched.' Julia, bright-eyed with excitement, broke into her chaotic thoughts. 'You, too, my lord. At least—' she hesitated, flushing, as she caught sight of Ravensdene's expression '—I hope you will join us.'

'Of course he will,' Devenham said, coming swiftly to Julia's rescue. 'Won't you, Nick?'

'Delighted,' Ravensdene agreed dryly. 'Where, precisely, am I to join you?'

'Why, at the ruins of the old Priory,' Julia informed

him, all animation again. 'Oh, do say we may go, Mama.
You see, Lord Devenham and I met Eliza Langdon and
her brother, and Harry and Sophie, when we went to
buy Sarah's bonnet, and Eliza suggested we have a
picnic. Everyone says the weather will hold and the
ruins are the perfect place. There are reputed to be
several ghosts haunting it, you know. Think of the fun
we'll have hunting for them.'

Sarah thought of it and shuddered. She had had
enough of invisible spectres to last her a lifetime. But
she was not proof against Julia's pleading eyes when
they were turned on her. She summoned up a smile of
agreement and was rewarded with an impulsive hug.

'Well, as the party will be a large one, I daresay it will
be quite acceptable,' Lady Wribbonhall approved. 'How
will you get there, my love?'

'Oh, there is not the least difficulty,' Julia assured her.
'Everyone will meet at Wribbonhall Lacy on Thursday
morning, and we ladies shall travel by carriage while the
gentlemen ride. I know you would rather go on horseback, Sarah, but you know what Sophie Sherington is
like. She would insist on riding also and her horse plods
along at such a pace it would take us forever to get
there. The carriage will be much easier, and I shall
drive.'

Lady Wribbonhall and Devenham spoke as one.

'No!'

'But—'

'If Miss Lynley would prefer to ride,' Devenham
added with the smooth address for which he was noted,
'I shall take her place in the carriage and handle the
ribbons. Miss Sherington will not be in riding gear so
there will be no argument from that quarter. How will
that suit you, Miss Wribbonhall? I can show you how to
feather-edge a corner.'

Julia had no fault to find with this adjustment to the
plan, and the innkeeper appearing at that moment to

inform Lady Wribbonhall that her horses had been put to, they all adjourned to the yard.

It was unfortunate that Ravensdene and Lord Devenham felt obliged to accompany them outside, Sarah thought. Until then she had considered herself to be coping with the situation quite well, avoiding Ravensdene's gaze by assiduously helping with the bandboxes, staying in the background, and in short trying to behave as if she wasn't there.

That was before Ravensdene stepped forward as she was about to mount into Lady Wribbonhall's barouche. Desperate to get away from him, she placed her foot on the step before she had lifted her skirt sufficiently and promptly tripped on the hem of her carriage dress. Only Ravensdene's swift action in catching her elbow prevented Sarah from landing face-down on the floor of the carriage.

'Thank you, my lord,' she gasped in an unnaturally high voice. She felt ready to sink into the ground.

He immediately took advantage of the situation to lean closer.

'Do I really alarm you so very much, Miss Lynley?' he murmured.

The hint of amusement in his tone had her spine stiffening. 'No, you do not!' she declared, looking him in the eye for precisely one second. 'Consider my clumsiness merely another example of a female losing her wits over you. Good day, sir.'

He laughed, a soft sound that sent shivers rippling through every limb, and taking her hand, raised it to his lips for the most fleeting of caresses. 'I'll remember that,' he said. 'Good day, Miss Lynley.'

Sarah's heart gave a violent leap. At the same time heat broke out all over her body. Really! Kissing her hand! What did Ravensdene think he was about? Didn't he recognise sarcasm when he heard it? Did he think she had *meant*—?

Her thoughts disintegrating into a maelstrom of shock, outrage and a shivery feeling that she told herself was fear, Sarah scrambled into the carriage and sat back against the squabs. She was not going to say another word. *Not one more word!* Until she was sure her brain was in control of her mouth.

And she was *not* going to look at him! Not this time. Never mind that he was watching her. Oh, yes, she could feel the touch of those glittering eyes, like emerald fire burning through her defences, could feel him waiting, compelling her to look at him.

When had it become so difficult to control her own senses, she wondered hysterically. Why was it so difficult to resist him? It should be easy. *Easy!*

Except. . .the resolve that had been forged into unbreakable steel in a sudden conflagration of brutality eight years ago was in danger of crumbling like so much dust. Everything around her had taken on a strange, frighteningly new face.

There was Julia, blushing at something Lord Devenham was saying to her as he held her hand for far too long. There had been Lydia Beresford, not only accepting her husband's touch, Sarah recalled, stunned anew by the knowledge, but actively, lovingly, seeking it.

Was that what Julia wanted of life, she wondered, painfully aware of the shy glow on her friend's countenance? She had known, of course, that Julia expected to marry one day, but she hadn't thought her friend would be so *eager*.

But then neither Julia nor Lydia had seen Amy lying broken and bloody and lifeless; they had not heard the dreadful sounds preceding her sister's death.

And as if to remind her, there was Ravensdene, dark and powerful and intense, standing by the barouche, positively *willing* her to look at him. She wished he would not watch her so. She wished she knew why he had exaggerated Lady Wribbonhall's concern for her.

She wished she knew which man he really was: the frightening stranger she had encountered in the woods, or the friend who had treated with gentle understanding what must have seemed to him to be very puzzling behaviour two days ago?

It would be easier if he was never kind, Sarah decided suddenly, as the barouche began to move. Because you could not reconcile brutality and tenderness. The two simply did not go together.

Nick eyed the besotted smile on his friend's face as the barouche turned out of the yard and disappeared down the road. 'Should I congratulate you, Dev?'

Devenham turned from waving farewell and grinned at him. 'Not yet,' he said. 'But I'm addressing the situation.'

'Ah. That explains why you're willing to indulge Miss Wribbonhall's quest for ghosts. The bonnet is a bit of a puzzle, however.'

'Bonnet? What the devil— Oh!' Devenham shook his head and laughed. 'You mean when I escorted Miss Wribbonhall to the milliner while we were waiting for you to find Miss Lynley. I tell you what, Nick. That shop was a nightmare. Ghost-hunting will be nothing to it. Never seen so many militant females in all my life. And it seemed to me that the less there was to the hats, the more the damned things cost.'

Nick's answering smile was a touch cynical. 'One of the pitfalls of the attached male,' he warned. 'Wives can be expensive.'

'Well, I daresay it depends on the wife,' Devenham remarked sapiently. 'And speaking of matters marital, you're not exactly being discreet yourself, old boy. Are you hoping to throw the local ladies off the scent by pretending an interest in Miss Lynley?'

'Hmm. An interesting thought. But to answer your question: no, not at all. It would be most unfair to her.'

'Oh, I don't know. Perhaps she wouldn't care. After all, she's the only female, apart from Miss Wribbonhall, who hasn't been hunting you.'

'Very true.' Nick narrowed his eyes thoughtfully at the now empty road. 'And I'm beginning to suspect why,' he added, more to himself than to Devenham.

'Good God! You're not piqued by her disinterest, are you, Nick?'

'I ought to stuff that remark down your throat, my friend.'

Neither voice nor expression had altered, but Devenham appeared gratifyingly alarmed. 'No, of course you're not,' he apologised hastily. 'Sorry, old fellow, but the way you said that. . .for a minute I thought. . . Well, it wouldn't be surprising if you did wonder why Miss Lynley seems to be immune. I mean, I know you've been out of England for twelve years, but you must know how eligible you are.'

'Good Lord.' Snapping out of his preoccupation, Nick seized the Viscount by the arm and began steering him down the street. 'You've been talking to my mother again.'

'Well, it's true,' argued Devenham, still apologetic but persistent. He began ticking off points on his fingers. 'There's the title, you're wealthy, you've been fighting in the Peninsula—'

'What the devil has that got to do with anything?'

'Gives you an air of glamour—or danger. Take your pick.'

'Bloody hell!'

'Actually—' Devenham ground to a halt with the air of a man who has just thought of something brilliant '—marrying Miss Lynley might not be such a bad idea after all. You'd be able to get on with the job of trapping your spy in peace.'

'I would certainly like to do so,' Nick said with heavy meaning.

A guilty look replaced the pleased smile on the
Viscount's face. 'Yes, I know. Sorry about setting you
up for this picnic on Thursday, Nick, but I couldn't
disappoint Miss Wribbonhall. She had her heart set on it
and. . . Well, you know how it is.'

'Only too well,' Nick murmured. For an instant his
eyes were cold with memories, then he shrugged them
off. He'd been young. Young and ignorant and blind.
But not any more. Now he knew precisely what he
wanted. Had known the instant he'd been informed that
Sarah was missing.

His eyes narrowed again as he remembered the rapid
succession of emotions that had jolted through him at
that moment. The quite irrational thought that she had
no business getting lost without him. The chilling fear
that, alone in a town full of soldiers, she might be afraid
or in danger. And overriding all, the sudden blinding
knowledge that he might lose something incomparable
if he didn't make her his.

His frown deepened. Obviously tightly leashed physical desire was affecting his cool, logical brain. There was
no need to think in such melodramatic terms. It had
been quite natural to worry about Sarah's safety, but all
he had to do was make it very clear to her that she was
to restrain her somewhat reckless tendency to place
herself in potentially hazardous situations. He did not
foresee a problem in the matter. He had seen enough of
Sarah to form a fairly accurate opinion of her nature and
character. When she forgot to be afraid of him—and he
was going to get to the bottom of that before he was
much older—she was a responsible, sensible young
woman. Exactly as the Reverend Butterlow had
described her, in fact.

And if he had to marry for expediency, exactly what
he wanted.

'Uh. . . Nick?'

Devenham's voice pulled him out of his reverie. He

wondered briefly what had been in his eyes to make his
friend sound so unusually tentative, before he recalled
where the conversation had left off.

'Don't worry about it,' he advised the Viscount.
'Unless there's something waiting for me at the receiving-office today, we might as well kick our heels at a
picnic as anywhere.'

'You're expecting a message from London?'

'Or closer to home.' He smiled slightly at the
Viscount's startled expression. 'I'm not entirely alone in
this,' he said as they started off again. 'Figgins is helping
me, of course, but I have one or two other contacts
along the coast.'

'Well, that's a relief,' retorted Devenham. 'Considering there's several miles of beach to watch. But what if
nothing happens? You said something about a trap
being laid, but if you think it's some local bigwig. . .' He
paused, brows drawn together in puzzlement. 'Can you
be sure of that?'

'Beyond reasonable doubt. God knows, in cases like
this anything can happen, but no one from that particular department of the Foreign Office has ever travelled
down this way, so the information has to be passed to
someone living nearby, and I can't see our traitor in
town forwarding it to a village tapkeeper or an illiterate
fisherman.'

'Forwarding. . . Good God! Don't tell me they use the
penny-post?'

Nick sent him an amused glance. 'Why not? Nothing
safer. Or more unobtrusive.'

'I suppose not, but. . .' Devenham apparently decided
to take his word for that. 'What about the French side of
things? You said your agent there discovered where the
information entered France. From the real French agent
whose place he has taken, I presume.'

'You presume correctly.'

'Hmm. And is this Frenchman now languishing in prison?'

'He's been eliminated.'

Devenham grimaced. 'I won't ask how. By the by, how does the information travel to France?'

'As far as we can ascertain,' Nick said slowly, 'a message is sent to France via fishermen who clearly have few scruples, that a certain cargo will be ready for shipment in a week or so. The French agent then crosses the Channel himself to take personal delivery.'

'Dangerous.'

'Yes, but necessary, I think. The people we're looking for on this side wouldn't have been able to travel to France regularly without their absence being remarked.'

'You're convinced they have to be persons in such notable positions?'

A wry smile curved Nick's mouth. 'I'm afraid so, Dev. The information that's been stolen in the past was available at only the highest level. It stands to reason it would be passed to someone similarly placed, who then, we assume, meets with the French agent somewhere near the beach.'

'Quite a chain.'

'And effective. The only weak link would be whoever runs the boat, and I daresay the fellow could be easily replaced should his conscience ever get the better of him.'

'My God! Murder?'

Nick shrugged. 'This might not be a battlefield, Dev, but it's the same war.'

'I know, but one doesn't realise— Hell, Nick, and here I've been ribbing you about all the distractions you've had to put up with lately. Damn it, there's the Assembly tomorrow night, too, and now Thursday...' Devenham shook his head. 'I hope you know that if you have to cry-off, I'll smooth things over for you.'

'Thank you, but I fully intend to be present at the

Assembly, and on Thursday. Our ghost-hunt may give
me an opportunity to retrieve my position.' He
grimaced, remembering Sarah in full retreat. 'Such as it
was.'

'Eh?' said Devenham, startled. 'What have ghosts to
do with catching your spy?'

'Nothing. I'm talking about catching a wife.'

The Viscount's jaw dropped. He stopped dead once
again—this time outside the receiving office. '*Wife*?
What in the— Do you mean. . . *Miss Lynley*?'

'Why are you surprised? It was your suggestion that I
marry her.'

'But you objected to it!'

'No. I said it would be unfair to *pretend* an interest.'

Devenham was struck speechless.

Nick grinned at his friend's dumbfounded countenance and turned into the receiving-office.

He ascertained that there were no messages awaiting
him and returned to the street to find the Viscount
standing exactly where he had left him two minutes ago.
A quite unaccountable flash of irritation went through
him.

'You know, Dev, you are giving an excellent imitation
of a stuffed and mounted trophy. I should think you'd
approve. Apart from my task here, weren't you enumer-
ating all the reasons why I should remarry the other
day?'

The Viscount came to life with a start. 'Well, yes, but
I didn't mean. . . I thought you'd choose. . .'

Nick turned his friend's footsteps in the direction of
the Lamb. 'I seem to be spending a great deal of time
today steering people in the direction in which I want
them to go,' he muttered, marching the Viscount along
rather forcibly.

'It's the direction you're going in that worries me,'
Devenham retorted, undeterred.

'You don't consider Miss Lynley to be a suitable match?'

'Damn it, there's no need to go all quiet and danger-ous on me, Nick. I daresay Miss Lynley is perfectly eligible. It's just that after Marianne... Well, surely some degree of attachment...' He looked at his friend and encountered a politely raised eyebrow.

'Oh, devil take it, I'm sure Miss Lynley is a very good sort of girl, but I find it hard to believe she's your sort. She's so timid for one thing. Take the last half-hour— she scarcely opened her mouth. And she practically has a fit of the vapours every time you go near her.'

'Oh, not every time,' Nick said thoughtfully. In fact, he mused, until that moment when Sarah had almost measured her length on the floor of Lady Wribbonhall's carriage, she hadn't seemed afraid of him at all this morning.

Of course, when they'd collided and he'd found his arms full of soft, fragrant Sarah, she might have reacted rather differently if he hadn't managed to put her away from him before she'd felt the effect on his body of her nearness. He had remembered just in time that it seemed to be the potential threat in a man's physical touch that frightened her.

On the other hand, she hadn't objected to his touch when he'd marched her out of his library the other day. Obviously he'd had her too confused to notice. Perhaps there was a lesson to be learned in that.

'Well, you're the only one who knows what will suit you,' Devenham observed at last. He sounded extremely doubtful. 'I just hope you're not doing this because of some misguided notion of protecting Miss Lynley in case her uncle turns out to be your traitor.'

'I gave up such idiotic notions of romantic chivalry years ago,' Nick said very dryly. 'Don't worry, Dev, I know precisely what I'm doing.'

'If you say so,' Devenham muttered, still uncon-

vinced. 'But I'll tell you one thing, Nick. If you really do
intend to marry Miss Lynley, the tabbies will have a
field-day comparing her to Marianne. They're so
entirely different.'

This prospect merely elicited a faint smile.

'Yes,' Nick said very softly as the Lamb Inn came into
view. 'She's as unlike Marianne as a single candle is
from a blazing chandelier. That's why I'm going to
marry her.'

of the first gentleman to ask for the honour of dancing
with her.

It had been a mistake. She was now imprisoned in a
set with a partner who was appallingly anxious to assure
her that now that the ——— ———— had reached
Bath, he would personally see to it that something was
of her ————.

CHAPTER SEVEN

WEDNESDAY evening's assembly had scarcely begun
when Sarah realised it was going to be an evening of
unmitigated disaster. She should have known.

The first intimation of what lay in store for her had
occurred when Lady Wribbonhall had introduced her to
the Master of Ceremonies. A very proper individual, he
had no sooner provided her and Julia with cards and
gold-tasselled pencils when both he and Lord
Devenham, who was escorting their little party, had
been nearly sent flying by a stampede of military
gentlemen wishing to pencil their names in for as many
dances as would be permitted.

Since Lord Devenham had taken the precaution of
soliciting Julia's hand for the waltz and the first country
dance, and Sarah's for the second, he had good-
naturedly stepped aside to wait for the crowd to subside.

It hadn't. Anyone who could claim the slightest
acquaintance with Lady Wribbonhall had done so, and
in the process had reminded Sarah of how much she
disliked being surrounded by large males. Or even
average-sized males.

She shuddered as she recalled the scene. She had
begun to feel slightly hysterical. Either that or the crush
of people, the chatter, the constant requests for dances
had been playing tricks with her mind, because she had
suddenly found herself entertaining a wild fantasy
wherein the Earl of Ravensdene appeared and whisked
her out of the crowd.

This incredible flight of fancy had stunned her so
much that, as one in a trance, she had accepted the hand

121

of the first gentleman to ask for the honour of dancing with her.

It had been a mistake. She was now imprisoned in a set with a partner who was apparently anxious to assure her that now that 'that fellow Bonaparte' had reached Paris, he would personally see to it that something was done. This heroic pose was rather diminished, however, by his unfortunate trick of tangling the gauze overskirt of her rose silk ballgown on his dress-sword whenever they went through the figures of the dance.

Sarah wondered why it was that military men felt obliged to wear weapons of violence to a ball. Perhaps he thought Bonaparte might decide to pop over from Paris for the evening. Perhaps she should have brought her pistol along. Either event would at least have given the conversation a decidedly new turn.

The absurd thoughts got her through the dance. Then, as the music ended, she happened to glance towards the doorway. That was when she knew beyond any doubt that the entire evening was destined for disaster.

Standing just inside the room, watching her, a slight smile playing about his hard mouth, was the Earl of Ravensdene. And not two paces behind him, being greeted by the Master of Ceremonies, were the Beresfords.

Sarah closed her eyes and tried to tell herself she was seeing things. She also tried to tell herself that the sudden leap her heart had given at the sight of Ravensdene was because he made her nervous.

Especially when he was smiling like that.

'I say, Miss Lynley, shall we have another go-around?' Her youthful partner looked at her hopefully.

'Thank you, Lieutenant, er, Millingham,' she responded, groping hastily for the right name among all the others swimming about in her head. 'But my card is already full.'

He appeared downcast but unsurprised by this mendacious piece of information, and restoring her to Lady Wribbonhall, went off in search of another partner, seriously endangering the gowns of several ladies in his path, not to mention his own feet.

'Good heavens, my dear, I believe you have made quite a conquest,' Lady Wribbonhall said placidly. 'Ineligible, of course, and he seems to be incapable of walking without stumbling every few steps. Can he have been *imbibing*, do you suppose? That is the disadvantage of these country Assemblies. Almost anyone can attend. Oh, Lord Ravensdene, how very gratifying. . . I mean, how very pleasant to see you here, after all.'

'Good evening, ma'am. Miss Lynley. I trust Lord Devenham made my apologies for my lateness. I was unavoidably detained.'

After the briefest of greetings, Sarah became very busy straightening her overskirt.

'Dear me, we are only too happy to see you here at all,' Lady Wribbonhall fluted. 'I am sure this sort of gathering where country dances rather than waltzes are predominant is not. . . Oh, look, Sarah, is that the lady I saw you with yesterday? Yes, she is waving. She appears a most charming young woman. You must introduce us, my love.'

Sarah groaned inwardly and looked up. Her gaze skittered nervously past Ravensdene without actually meeting the intent green eyes focused on her face, to see Lydia Beresford waving to her from across the room.

It was impossible to tell herself she was seeing things this time. She was trapped. There was nothing for it. As a martyr being led to the scaffold, she summoned up a brave smile and beckoned.

Mrs Beresford answered the summons with alacrity, crossing the room on her husband's arm.

'Miss Lynley,' she said with her warm smile. 'I am so glad to see you here tonight. May I present my husband?

He most particularly wishes to thank you for your kindness yesterday.'

'Truly, I did very little,' Sarah disclaimed, exchanging a handshake and smile with Major Beresford.

Close to, he was seen to be several years older than his wife and of serious mien. Although perhaps it was his illness that made him appear so, Sarah thought, as his expression lightened into a charming smile and she saw again the man who had gazed at Lydia with such tenderness. Conscious that Ravensdene was watching them and listening to every word, she felt a guilty blush heat her cheeks.

However, the Major's quiet thanks, without fuss or exaggeration, soon restored some of her poise. Sending up a fervent prayer that the meeting would go off without anyone discovering that she had stooped to following people unbeknownst to them, she turned and was about to introduce the Beresfords to Lady Wribbonhall when Lord Devenham's voice smote her ears.

'Good God, Will! Is that you? My dear fellow! Where did you spring from? The last I heard—'

What Devenham had heard was destined to remain a mystery. Sarah ceased to listen, her hopes of the parties separating before anyone happened to mention that she had managed to lose herself yesterday, and precisely where Ravensdene had found her, dwindling alarmingly.

Fortunately for her jangling nerves, Lord Devenham then redeemed himself by making introductions all round. Under cover of the general conversation that ensued, Ravensdene contrived to draw her a little apart. She could only be thankful that he kept his voice down.

'Why didn't you tell me you had been with Mrs Beresford yesterday?' he demanded. 'Instead of letting me think you were wandering around alone.'

Sarah tried to pull herself together. It was no use

falling apart at this point. She needed all her wits about her.

'Since I was alone when we met, would it have made any difference?' she retorted, the memory of his anger in her eyes.

He acknowledged the challenge with a rueful grin. '*Touché*, Miss Lynley.' Then as her heartbeat began to slow to a more normal pace, he added in a low growl, 'Just don't let it happen again.'

'Don't— I *beg* your—'

'Hush,' he interrupted. 'Your friend is preparing to go off to the cardroom.'

Sarah bit off her indignant protest with an almost audible snap of her teeth. He was right. With the innate good breeding that precluded them from joining a group of persons whom they had only recently met, the Beresfords were taking their leave.

'Lady Wribbonhall has invited me to bring Giles to visit her next week,' Lydia told Sarah as her husband shook hands with Ravensdene. 'What a very kind person she is. It will be such a delightful outing for him.'

'Yes, indeed,' Sarah responded warmly. 'I shall look forward to seeing you there, Mrs Beresford.'

'A most delightful couple,' pronounced Lady Wribbonhall to no one in particular as the Beresfords made their way through the crowd to the cardroom. 'Not pushing in the least. And so comforting to know that Lord Devenham is acquainted with the Major. Where did you say you met them, Sarah dear?'

Alarm screeching once more along her nerves, Sarah tried to think. Her brain seemed singularly uncooperative, but fortunately rescue was at hand. The music began for the next dance, and, as Lord Devenham turned to her to make his claim, it was easy to pretend that Lady Wribbonhall's question had gone unheard.

'I do believe this is our dance, Miss Lynley,' Devenham began. 'Shall we—?'

'You must be mistaken, Dev,' Ravensdene murmured. 'As it happens, Miss Lynley is promised to me.' He exchanged one brief glance with the Viscount who, to Sarah's horror, very basely surrendered the field without a whimper.

She stared after his retreating form for an incredulous second, wondering what else was going to befall her that night, then, refusing to submit so tamely, ostentatiously whipped out her card and studied it.

'As it happens,' she mimicked sarcastically. 'It is you who are mistaken, my lord. You will just have to—'

He reached out, plucked the card from her fingers and coolly crossed out Devenham's name and replaced it with his own.

While Sarah was still gasping with shock at this outrageous behaviour, he then proceeded to write his name against the waltz and the supper dance.

'Are you *mad*?' she squeaked, finally getting her breath back. Abandoning any pretence at good manners, she snatched the card off him and crossed his name out with wildly agitated strokes. Her pencil promptly snapped in two.

'I do not waltz, my lord,' she informed him, continuing to wield the useless stub with enough energy to demolish that as well.

'Good,' he purred, and a slow smile lit his eyes. 'Then, since Dev has very kindly taken himself off, we can stand up for the next country dance, after all. I want to talk to you.'

'You want to— *You* want—'

Sarah's breath deserted her again. She glanced around for deliverance. There was none, of course. Her unwanted crowd of admirers had deserted her, as well, just when she needed them. Probably scared off by the predatory panther standing before her, as poor Lord Devenham had been.

'Well, *I* do not wish to talk to you, my lord,' she finally got out. 'Of all the arrogant, ill-considered actions. As if I would even dance *three* times with you! You must be—'

He took her hand without any warning and tugged her gently towards him.

'For goodness sake, my lord! What do you think you are about?'

'We don't want to miss a place in the set, Miss Lynley,' he said very politely, while dragging her most impolitely out to the centre of the room.

Sarah tried to dig her heels in and found herself skating across the floor instead. By the time she found some purchase they were at the end of the set and the music had started.

'This is intolerable,' she hissed in a furious undertone. 'It is the longest set in the room. We shall be here forever.'

'I'm afraid so,' he agreed, his eyes gleaming. 'But the alternative was to join the other set which contains all three Miss Smisbys. I know you would not wish such a fate on a hapless male.'

'*Hapless male*? You, sir, are the most *un*hapless male I have ever encountered!'

He grinned at her. 'When faced with three ladies all decked out in brilliant orange, Miss Lynley, any male is hapless.'

'Oh, my goodness!' Sarah glanced around before she could stop herself.

The three damsels behind her were indeed the Smisby sisters. And they were indeed wearing identical gowns of a glaring shade somewhere between orange and scarlet. At close range such a blast of colour was positively painful.

'That particular shade is known as "sunset red",' was all Sarah could say in weak accents. 'It is very fashionable at present.'

Ravensdene cast a quick glance beyond her shoulder

and winced. 'I will take your word for it. However, I
much prefer your style, Miss Lynley. You look deli. . .
delightful.'

'Oh.' Feeling quite unnecessarily flustered by such a
mild compliment, Sarah felt herself blush a similar hue
to the garish spectacle behind her. 'Thank you, my lord.'

'But I am curious,' he went on. 'I'm sure you told me,
Miss Lynley, that you neither dance nor go into society.
Yet, here you are doing both.'

Sarah forgot about compliments. 'I was press-ganged
into this dance if you will recall, sir,' she retorted, glaring
at him. 'So if you have any complaints—'

'Oh, I'm not complaining. I merely wondered what
had changed your mind.'

Hardly surprising, she allowed silently, given their
previous acquaintance. She began to calm down somewhat, reminding herself that she still had the rest of the
evening to get through. Really, she'd had no idea how
exhausting it was maintaining an outraged demeanour.

'Lady Wribbonhall thought it would be good practice
for me,' she admitted gloomily.

'Good practice?' The smile that had been lurking in
his eyes all through the conversation vanished on the
instant. 'For what? Have you decided to sample the
pleasures of a London Season, after all?'

'Not if I have anything to say on the subject,' she
muttered.

He continued to study her through slightly narrowed
eyes, and Sarah felt annoyance flicker to life again. 'In
fact, sir, I have as much desire for a London Season as I
have to be in my present situation, which is to say none
at all. I would rather be at home reading a book or
playing chess with Uncle Jasper than at this stupid
Assembly dancing with—'

Their arrival at the top of the set put an end to this
comprehensive setdown. Nor did it seem to have the
desired effect. Those ice-green eyes that could take on a

dangerous glitter capable of chilling the blood in her veins were warming again with silent laughter.

'I am in entire agreement with you about the occasion, Miss Lynley,' he said as he turned into the first figure. 'But since we are here, I would much rather be waltzing with you.'

Sarah went down the set with her feet moving in one direction while her brain whirled off in quite another. She could have sworn that Ravensdene had said 'Good' when she'd informed him she didn't waltz. What was he talking about now? Was he trying to drive her insane?

And why did the thought of his arm about her waist as he guided her into the steps of the waltz make her feel so very warm and shivery all at the same time?

It was all very unnerving. So was the slow smile he gave her as they met again at the end of the dance.

'You said you wished to talk to me, my lord,' she reminded him, taking the plunge on the general principle that attack was the best form of defence against that smile. 'I presume it was not to discuss whether or not I intend to go to London.'

He raised his brows slightly. 'No, Miss Lynley, it was not.' He offered her his arm. 'In fact, I wanted to beg your assistance in one or two small matters.'

She blinked at him. 'Beg my assistance?'

'Yes. You may have been aware that I played chess with your uncle two days ago?'

Sarah nodded before laying a cautious hand on his arm. As they began to walk around the perimeter of the room she wondered if Ravensdene suspected that she had deliberately absented herself that afternoon.

A rueful smile curved his mouth. 'You were quite correct in your estimation of your uncle, Miss Lynley. Sir Jasper routed me in no short order. I am afraid he must have been extremely disappointed at such a poor challenge as I presented.'

'Well, you did warn him that you were out of

practice,' she recalled. She peered up at him warily. Something didn't feel quite right here. For one thing, that look of wry appeal Ravensdene was aiming at her did not really match the watchful gleam in his eyes, nor the dark, predatory grace with which he moved.

'That's what Sir Jasper said,' he agreed. 'However, the two of us might give him a match, Miss Lynley.'

Sarah stopped dead, frowning at him. 'You and me?' she clarified with deep suspicion.

He smiled. 'You did offer your assistance the other day.'

'I did?' She thought frantically. 'I did not!'

'It would not be such a hardship, you know. I am very quick to learn. Will next Monday be convenient?'

'Well, I—' Aware that the situation was again hurtling out of her control, she looked wildly around for rescue.

There was none. Lady Wribbonhall was still some distance away, and in any event had fallen into conversation with another matron. And although she could see Devenham making his way towards them, she knew whose side *he* was on.

Then as her gaze swept around the room in her search for Julia, Ravensdene's iniquities vanished beneath a wave of horrified disbelief. For there, standing in the entrance, resplendent in a bottle-green coat and matching pantaloons, was a sight that put the crowning touch on a series of increasingly hideous encounters.

'Oh, no!' she groaned, momentarily forgetting who she was with. 'Not the Frog.'

'Frog?'

The sharp question cut through Sarah's dismay like a sword slicing through silk. Startled, she glanced up at Ravensdene in time to intercept an extremely hard look before he switched his attention to the newcomer.

'Frog?' he repeated.

It was all too much. Even the reappearance of the Beresfords would have been preferable. Sarah began to wish for a quiet room where she could have hysterics in peace. She tried to do an abrupt about-face and immediately discovered another unpalatable fact. Ravensdene was utterly immovable. In fact, her impulsive movement nearly landed her in his arms.

'It is of no consequence, my lord,' she said, hurriedly backing away. 'Merely someone I met recently. Shall we—?'

'Too late,' he interrupted softly. 'Brace yourself, Miss Lynley. You are about to meet him again.'

Sending him a glare that she hoped plainly conveyed her opinion of this unhelpful advice, Sarah turned to confront her admirer from Tunbridge Wells.

She shuddered inwardly as he hurried towards her on short, bandy legs. A few weeks had not improved the gentleman's appearance. He was still almost as wide as he was tall, and his countenance, dominated by a pair of bulging blue eyes, still bore an unfortunate resemblance to one of the amphibian species.

These faults of person could have been forgiven, however. After all, the man couldn't help his looks, Sarah reflected, trying to be charitable. What caused her to shiver with distaste was his air of self-importance, which she knew was well-nigh impregnable and which made it impossible for him to believe his suit could be unwelcome to any lady he chose to favour with it. And this time there was no doting, possessive mama to stand in his way.

Suddenly Ravensdene's presence was elevated in her mind from disaster to godsend.

'My lord. . .'

'Don't concern yourself,' he bit out very softly. 'I have no intention of leaving you.'

There was no time to wonder at the grimness in his tone. The green-clad one was upon them. Before Sarah could prevent it, he had taken her hand and was bowing over it to the accompaniment of creaking corsets.

'Miss Lynley!' he uttered in throbbing accents, straightening and pressing her hand clammily between both of his. 'At last! I have found you!'

She tugged unsuccessfully at her hand. 'How do you do, Sir Ponsonby?' she responded coolly, suppressing an impulse to inform him that she would rather have stayed lost.

Ravensdene had no such scruples.

'You may restore Miss Lynley's hand to her, sir, unless you wish to part with your own,' he growled.

Even forewarned as she was, Sarah nearly jumped at the menace in the low threat.

Sir Ponsonby, on the other hand, had obviously never met a panther before. He obeyed, but only so he could raise his quizzing glass to one eye in haughty enquiry. 'I don't believe I know you, sir,' he began in the pompous tones that Sarah remembered only too well.

'Ravensdene,' stated the Earl with a bluntness that bordered on incivility. He appeared singularly unintimidated by an eye thus repulsively magnified.

Sarah hurried to avert the anticipated slaughter she could see gathering in his own icy-green gaze. 'Lord Ravensdene has only recently returned to England,' she explained. 'My lord, may I present Sir Ponsonby Freem?'

'If you must,' drawled Ravensdene.

Sir Ponsonby made a noise even more reminiscent of a pond denizen than his appearance. 'Miss Lynley,' he produced after an apoplectic moment. 'I have a matter of great import to discuss with you. A very personal matter,' he elucidated, glaring at Ravensdene. 'Shall I find you at home tomorrow?'

'No, you won't, Freem,' Ravensdene stated before Sarah could answer. 'And any personal matters you wish to discuss concerning Miss Lynley may be addressed to her uncle.'

'Oh, no. . .'

'When he is improved enough in health to be receiving visitors,' Ravensdene continued as if her faint protest had not been uttered.

'I am acquainted with Sir Jasper, my lord,' snapped Sir Ponsonby, rapidly turning red. It was not a hue that suited him. 'I would not incommode him in the least, as I am sure Miss Lynley is aware. And I must say, sir, that you might let her speak for herself. Unless you have some formal claim on the lady,' he tacked on rather nastily.

'Oh, please, Sir Ponsonby, we are beginning to attract attention,' Sarah begged. She was starting to tremble. The prospect of being the cause of an unpleasant public scene, especially a scene involving angry males, made her quail.

But even as her tremors increased, Ravensdene took her hand and tucked it securely beneath his arm.

'Tell Sir Ponsonby that you are unavailable to gentlemen callers, Miss Lynley,' he instructed softly, the barest hint of a smile in his eyes as he glanced down at her. 'I fear he will be satisfied with nothing less.'

'It is perfectly true, sir,' Sarah confirmed, trying not to cling to the reassuring strength of the arm that was all but supporting her. 'Besides, I am extremely busy just now what with shopping and assemblies and picnics and one thing and another and. . .'

'You know how it is, Freem,' Ravensdene confided as Sarah's explanation faltered in a morass of unnecessary detail. 'One social whirl after another.'

'So I see.' Sir Ponsonby looked around pointedly. 'I marvel, Miss Lynley, that you would leave your—'

'Not only that,' Ravensdene interposed ruthlessly, 'but Miss Lynley is teaching me to play chess. I'm afraid the project is going to take all her spare time in the foreseeable future. Now if you will excuse us, I must restore my partner to her chaperon. Don't think it hasn't been a pleasure.'

Sir Ponsonby opened his mouth but his victims were already walking away, one of them now shaking with a mixture of relief and suppressed mirth.

'I am not going to teach you to play chess,' Sarah whispered, laughter bubbling forth as she glanced back in time to see her vanquished swain storming towards the door. 'Oh, dear, he's leaving. How could you be so rude, my lord?'

'How can you say that, Miss Lynley?' he countered. 'I was being excessively polite. And I don't want you to teach me to play chess, merely to assist me against a merciless foe.'

She giggled again. 'I doubt you need any assistance at all, sir, but what can I say? I am in your debt. Thank you. Sir Ponsonby is the most odious little man imaginable, and simply impossible to get rid of.'

He raised a brow.

'I should say impossible to get rid of using civil means,' she amended hastily. Then seeing a certain sardonic gleam in his eyes, added, 'And don't you dare say I need a keeper, sir!'

'Would I be so tactless?'

'Yes,' she said without hesitation.

He laughed. 'I'm afraid you are quite correct, Miss Lynley. But whenever I cast my mind back over our rather memorable meetings, not to mention the fact that you are still trembling like a leaf, I am forced to the conclusion that you do need a keeper. Tell me, what qualifications would you require for such a position? Would civility be necessary all the time?'

Sarah didn't know whether to laugh, scold or scream in frustration. Trembling like a leaf? So much for taking charge of her own life. She couldn't even get through a country assembly without help. This was what came of socialising with males. She should have known better.

'*All* the time,' she asserted, trying to suppress the faint tremors still rippling through her. 'Which definitely puts you out of the running, sir.'

'That's rather unfortunate,' he murmured. 'Since it is when my incivility stirs you to anger that you forget to be afraid of me.'

Sarah felt as if he had just delivered a blow to her mid-section. Her smile vanished. Her breath left her lungs in a rush. Her legs felt as if they would no longer support her.

Afraid of him?

Well, yes, sometimes he *did* frighten her, but. . .

Surely he didn't want. . .?

'You. . .you would rather have me angry with you?' she ventured on a note barely above a whisper.

He regarded her thoughtfully for a moment. 'Rather than afraid, yes. I find I have developed a considerable aversion to seeing fear in your eyes whenever you look at me, Miss Lynley.'

'Oh! I don't. . . That is. . . It isn't. . .' She faltered to a stop, shaken and confused by the overwhelming urge to reassure him that was sweeping over her. But not knowing what to say. Dear God, she could hardly *think*, let alone speak.

'Isn't it?' he pressed gravely.

'No! No, it—'

He raised his free hand to cover hers, sending heat flowing through her in a tide of sensation that made her feel shockingly weak, and yet warm, so very warm. And safe.

Their steps had slowed to a stop, but she barely noticed. A haze seemed to envelop her brain; it took several seconds before she realised he was speaking again, his voice soft and yet strangely urgent.

'Miss Lynley, I am going to ask you a question that may shock you. It will certainly startle you. Please believe that, although I may not divulge the reason for it in our present situation, I do not ask it lightly.'

When his words finally made sense, Sarah knew she had stopped breathing. The assembly rooms and their colourful, chattering occupants disappeared. She felt as if she was suspended over a precipice, unable either to retreat or step forward, the strength of Ravensdene's will the only bridge beneath her feet.

'What is it, sir?' she asked, and knew he could hear the husky, nervous quality of her voice.

He tightened his hold on her hand as if he would brace her for what was to come. 'Miss Lynley, have you ever been. . .frightened by a man?'

The obvious restraint in the question surprised her. She had expected him to be much more direct. And though she knew what he wanted to ask, somehow it seemed very important to be sure.

'Do you mean. . .?'

His eyes were grim. 'I mean,' he said roughly, 'has some man ever abused you, little one?'

The endearment shivered through her on a ripple of heat. Her lips parted, quivering, but the instinctive protest rising in her throat died unsaid.

'No,' she whispered. 'It was. . .it happened. . .to someone else.'

He studied her closely for a moment, then nodded. 'Your sister.'

It wasn't a question. He knew. Perhaps he had seen something in her face, heard something in her voice. Whatever it was, he knew.

'I'm sorry,' he said when she didn't answer. 'Come, I'll take you back to Lady Wribbonhall. I won't upset you anymore.'

'I'm not upset,' she murmured, startled to discover it was true. She was uneasy with the subject, unwilling to say more, but she was far from the overwrought female he'd had to cope with on several other conspicuous occasions.

For some reason that she did not want to examine too closely, she wanted him to know that.

'There is no need to treat me as if I'm about to fall into a swoon, my lord,' she murmured. Then, compelled by the same unknown force, added, 'Although after our previous encounters I can imagine what you must think of me.'

'No, Miss Lynley,' he said very quietly. 'You can't. I have been at considerable pains to make sure of that.'

CHAPTER EIGHT

IF ANYTHING was calculated to render her extremely nervous prior to their next encounter, it would have to be that last remark, Sarah reflected the next day as she gazed up at the fluffy white clouds sailing across the deep blue sky.

A soft spring breeze whispered through the ivy-clad stone arches of the ruined priory, ruffling the flounces of her new cambric dress and bringing a faint flush to her cheeks, but Sarah had no thoughts to spare for the dangers of exposing her complexion to the sun and spring breezes. She was too busy assuring herself that Ravensdene had not meant anything cryptic or alarming last night, and wondering why the assurance had little effect.

After all, his remark could as easily have meant that his opinion of her was far from flattering. It would hardly be surprising.

Letting the desultory snatches of conversation from her companions drift around her, she stole a glance at Ravensdene from beneath her lashes as if a surreptitious examination of the object of her disquiet might provide a few clues.

He sat beside her on one of the carriage rugs thoughtfully provided by Miss Sherington, leaning on one hand, his other arm propped across his raised knee. The position moulded his breeches to the long muscles of his thighs and pulled his coat taut across the breadth of his shoulders and back. He had opened the buttons for comfort, but the conservative waistcoat thus exposed merely emphasized the fact that there was not a single ounce of excess flesh anywhere on Ravensdene's powerful frame.

A succession of tiny tremors chased one another down her spine. Considering the nature of the outing, there was nothing improper in the way he was sitting. Indeed, everyone else had disposed themselves in similar casual poses in the sunny spot they had chosen beside the walls of the ruined priory. But the hand taking his weight was flat on the ground just behind her hip, and she felt rather... *surrounded*. Close proximity to so much raw masculine strength, even if discreetly displayed, was not conducive to rational thought.

She wondered if she was the only one who saw anything dangerous about that relaxed pose. Since no one else had seen beyond his cool, civilised exterior, it seemed safe to assume she was. Sophie Sherington and Eliza Langdon had certainly possessed no qualms about vying with each other all afternoon for his attention. For some reason, instead of amusing her, their combined antics were beginning to grate on her nerves.

Shaking off the disturbing notion, Sarah leaned away from Ravensdene under the guise of gathering up the remains of the picnic luncheon.

'Oh, Sarah, don't worry about all those baskets now.' Julia, sounding slightly sleepy, bestirred herself to protest. 'I am feeling far too lazy to help you.'

'Yes, indeed.' Miss Eliza Langdon, a blue-eyed brunette, whose soft brown tresses were quite cast in the shade when seen beside Miss Sherington's striking auburn curls, took a last sip of lemonade and set her glass down. 'Really, there is something rather decadent about lunching *al fresco*. I feel quite dreadfully lazy myself.'

Devenham's easy smile flashed out. 'Drinking lemonade while lounging about on rugs in the middle of the day,' he said, saluting Julia with his wineglass. 'That's decadent, all right. Also dashed uncomfortable when you've been sitting on a rock for the better part of an hour.'

Julia giggled. 'Well, we could have brought those stools Sophie had in her carriage, but they would have ruined the atmosphere. You can't expect ghosts to show themselves if the ruins are transformed into a dining-room.'

'What do you think, my lord?' Sophie Sherington turned a wide-eyed face of enquiry towards Ravensdene. At the sight of her auburn lashes fluttering like butterflies gone berserk, Sarah found herself stifling another intense twinge of annoyance. 'Is there not something very *abandoned* about dining outdoors on rugs?'

'No,' said Ravensdene with uncompromising brevity.

'Oh. Well,' continued Miss Sherington, faint but pursuing, 'I daresay for gentlemen such as yourself and Lord Devenham, who have experienced the excitements of battle, a picnic does seem rather tame. What heroic tales you must have to tell. I am sure we would hang upon your every word.'

Ravensdene's eyes narrowed.

'Speaking of tales, Sophie,' Sarah intervened before he could assault Miss Sherington's ears with a blistering set-down. 'Weren't you going to tell us about the gray lady who is supposed to haunt the priory?'

Out of the corner of her eye she saw Ravensdene's hard mouth relax into a faint smile, and knew he was aware of the reason for her intervention.

As well he might be, she thought, rather incensed. It wasn't the first time she'd had to rescue one of his potential victims. First it had been Harry Marsham at the Wribbonhalls' party, last night Sir Ponsonby Freem had come foolishly close to annihilation, and now Miss Sherington's bird-witted conversation was trying his patience. Couldn't any of these people see the danger they were courting in irritating a predator?

She just managed to stifle a startled gasp as another question occurred to her. Who was going to rescue her?

Sarah gave herself a mental shake. It was that wretched comment of his that had done this, she mused crossly. She didn't need rescuing from Ravensdene because she *knew* he was dangerous—even if she was beginning to think of him as a friend. All she had to do, therefore, was treat him with friendly caution. Or should that be cautious friendliness?

Oh, wonderful! Now she was thinking in circles.

'And you wake to find her staring at you from the side of the bed, her cold fingers resting on your face.'

James Langdon's sepulchral tones, followed by various squeals and gasps of horror, intruded on Sarah's mental contortions. Hoping no one had noticed her abstraction, she tried to appear interested in the discussion.

'Well, I don't know,' Devenham was saying sceptically. 'Something always puzzles me. How is it that these ladies are forever draped in gray or white? Why can't they get about in scarlet or green or—?'

'Because they're ghosts, silly.' Laughing, Julia interrupted him to start a spirited argument, but Sarah noticed that her friend had turned quite pale.

Devenham had seen it, too, she realised, and had asked the nonsensical question deliberately. He was so kind. No wonder Julia liked him. He was kind without making one feel there was more to it. Devenham's style was light; his smiling blue eyes didn't hold the disturbing depths she sensed behind Ravensdene's cool gaze.

Even when those light green eyes were gleaming with amusement, she felt it. A darkness. A locked place deep inside where he allowed no one to trespass. She knew because she had her own dark place. A place where light had not reached for eight years.

And yet, now. . . In the past few days. . .she had felt a chink of light touch that dark, secret corner of her mind.

One tiny chink of light. . .and it had turned everything upside down.

'You are very quiet, Miss Lynley.' Ravensdene smiled at her, then lifted a brow slightly when she jumped at the sound of his voice. 'Are you indifferent to ghostly fashions or have you also succumbed to the decadence of the moment?'

Sarah felt herself blush as everyone ceased arguing to look at her.

'I think Lord Devenham has a valid point,' she finally managed after a nerve-racking moment in which her brain seemed to be paralysed. She wisely left the subject of decadence alone. 'Spectres do appear to be rather limited in their choice of colours. The males are usually black-robed monks or white horsemen.'

'Oh, Sarah, don't.' Sophie shivered dramatically and glanced up at the crumbling arches above them as though expecting to see a dark figure in one of the apertures. 'I am sure I shall be afraid to look around any corners in case I come face to face with a monk.'

'I think the monks left long before the priory fell into ruin,' Sarah assured her.

'Besides, he wouldn't have a face,' Harry Marsham added in the mistaken belief that he was being helpful. 'Black-cowled monks usually don't, you know.'

More feminine shrieks and shudders ensued.

Ravensdene eyed them all with some amusement. 'Well, if you're going to seek out these fascinating spectres, you'd best be about it,' he suggested, indicating the shadows beginning to lengthen on the grass. 'The daylight will not remain forever.'

'No, indeed.' Miss Sherington jumped to her feet, permitting the interested a glimpse of a shapely ankle, and smiled at Ravensdene in blatant invitation. 'I cannot wait to begin. Shall we start where the crypt was said to be, my lord?'

'Perhaps we should pack everything away first,' Julia

suggested, eyeing the wreckage in the centre of their circle with some misgiving.

'Very true.' Devenham watched three ants march past his booted foot to retrieve a crumb. 'The wildlife is starting to arrive.'

'So are the curious.' Harry Marsham nodded towards a grassy slope some distance away where a lone rider was silhouetted against the skyline, apparently watching them. 'Dashed impolite to intrude on us like that.'

'He's probably wondering who we are,' James said, shading his eyes as he followed his friend's gaze. 'I don't recognise the horse. Do you, Eliza?'

'Oh, never mind him!' Sophie interrupted impatiently. 'It is public land, you know. Besides, he's riding away now. Sarah, dearest, you won't mind clearing up, will you? I know you are much too sensible and mature to believe in ghosts, so I daresay you will be more comfortable here in the sun.'

'Well, really, Sophie—'

'No, I don't mind at all,' Sarah responded, calmly overriding Julia's indignant protest. The last thing she wanted to do was go scrambling about in a dank crypt. 'Go and find your ghosts. I shall be only too happy to stay right here.'

'But—'

'Oh, I say—'

'Don't worry, Miss Wribbonhall.' Ravensdene's quiet tone instantly squelched the voices of protest rising on the breeze. 'I shall remain to keep Miss Lynley company and lend my assistance in clearing up. I am accounted quite good at it, you know.'

That calm air of authority was really quite marvellously effective, Sarah conceded. She could only watch in bemusement as the rest of the party meekly gathered themselves together and wandered off into the ruins. And it happened so quickly that for a minute she didn't even realise how neatly she had trapped herself. She was too occupied with the totally unexpected sense of satisfaction flowing through her that Sophie Sherington had spiked her own guns—to use one of Uncle Jasper's favourite sayings.

It was not unlike the feeling she had had last night when, after ignoring the Miss Smisbys' collective and individual attempts to attract his attention, Ravensdene had left the Assembly before supper was served and after dancing only with her.

'Tell me, Miss Lynley. Just how old are you?'

Sarah blinked at the unexpected question. 'Two-and-twenty, my lord. Why do you ask?'

His firm mouth twitched as he began collecting plates and glasses. 'The way Miss Sherington was speaking to you, one would have thought you in your dotage.'

She laughed and bent to help him. 'As Sophie is only turned seventeen, she probably considers me to be so,' she said, suddenly feeling unaccountably happy to be with him. All at once her vague fears seemed ridiculous. The others were still within earshot, and they could be seen by anyone who happened along the road.

She straightened, the thought bringing a faint frown to her brow as she remembered the lone watcher. He had been too far distant to be recognisable, but an image of Sir Ponsonby Freem's stubborn features flitted through her mind. Surely he wouldn't have called on her uncle, discovered her whereabouts and followed her.

Sarah dismissed the notion. Sir Ponsonby might be stubborn, but he also had a high opinion of his own sense of propriety. He would not stoop to skulking about at a distance. Nor was the rider connected to her in any other way. It was foolish to be so suspicious. The man had merely been a passing traveller, curious to see picnickers at the ruins, no threat to her.

Putting the stranger out of her mind, she closed her eyes and lifted her face to the warmth of the sun, a smile curving her lips as she heard an echo of the ghost hunters' voices. Nearer, the liquid notes of a thrush rose and fell on the soft breeze that was brushing her cheeks and she could smell the sharp tang of grass and earth as the horses grazed.

It was one of those rare moments in time when everything felt perfect. In harmony. *Right*.

She opened her eyes on the thought to find Ravensdene gazing down at her. And as if it was the most natural thing in the world, she smiled at him.

Something flickered in his eyes—something so powerfully intense that she felt her heart give an odd little leap and her smile faltered. Then the green flames were banked. He smiled back; the crooked, utterly appealing smile that made her feel all warm inside, and with the warmth, the strange quivering within her was calmed and she felt at ease again.

He was probably thinking of Sophie and her wiles, she decided as she turned away and began packing baskets. She was glad he didn't spoil the precious moment by speaking. It felt good to be working together like this. As friends.

Could Ravensdene think of her in that way, she wondered, vaguely aware of a faint wistfulness tugging at her heart? He had probably never considered that a woman could be a friend, someone with whom he could share laughter, or quietness. Someone who understood about dark, locked-away corners. Someone who wouldn't expect anything more from him than friendship. She would like to be that person.

'Miss Sherington should count herself fortunate to possess your friendship, Miss Lynley,' he observed with an uncanny prescience that made Sarah wonder for a minute if he could read minds. He stowed the last of the baskets under the seat of Lady Wribbonhall's barouche and turned to indicate her dress. 'I expect it was to spare her disappointment that you elected to ride in the carriage rather than on horseback as was originally planned.'

'Oh. . .' Sarah felt herself flushing. 'Yes. Something like that.'

It hadn't been anything like that, but she would have gone to the stake before she admitted that she had worn her new cambric dress with its fashionable flounces and smartly striped Spencer because she had not wanted to appear at a disadvantage in her plain old riding habit.

'My remark was not meant as a criticism,' he murmured. 'Although when Dev allowed Miss Wribbonhall to take the reins on that sharp bend I did wonder if your decision had been rather precipitate.'

A more natural laugh escaped her. 'I must confess it took great fortitude not to grab hold of the door at that precise moment, my lord,' she confessed, dimpling up at him. 'And I hope you noticed that I did not scream, which is more than can be said for Sophie and Eliza.'

'Yes, those two young ladies do have a marked tendency to give full rein to their lungs,' he said dryly, running an eye over the chestnut pair who had kept the barouche on all four wheels despite their over-eager driver. 'I am only grateful that you did not feel obliged to follow their example, Miss Lynley, or even as placid a pair as this may have bolted. Remind me to strangle Dev when he returns. Better yet, let us go in search of him now and I can do it immediately.'

Sarah laughed, but obediently laid a hand lightly on his proffered arm. He promptly tucked it more firmly into the crook of his elbow as they began strolling towards the priory.

'I expect Lord Devenham would have taken control without any mishap had it been necessary,' she remarked, trying to do some controlling of her own. For some reason her heartbeat had become rather uneven, and though she was again conscious of feeling very small and defenceless this close to Ravensdene, the faintly thrilling sensations aroused by his size and strength now seemed more pleasurable than alarming.

Which was, she mused, vaguely alarming in itself.

'I commend your equanimity, Miss Lynley.' He glanced down at her, his eyes warm with amusement. 'Your calm good sense gives me great hope that we shall be able to defeat your uncle next Monday. I am looking forward to the encounter.'

'Next Monday. Oh, yes. To be sure.'

'You had not forgotten, I trust.'

'Well. . .'

Forgotten? Of course she had. How could she be expected to think of the future when the present was causing her such puzzlement?

'You mean you were going to abandon me to your uncle's merciless play without compunction?' he went on, casting her a reproachful look. 'Miss Lynley, I had not thought it of you.'

'It is no use trying to look pathetic, my lord,' she said, rallying under this blatant provocation. 'I have to tell you it simply does not work.'

'Ah. What a disadvantage we males are at when dealing with an intelligent woman.'

Surprised, she looked up at him.

'What is it?' he asked at once. 'Do you find it so astounding that I consider you intelligent?'

'Well, yes, I do,' she said frankly. 'When I know you consider me to be incapable of taking care of myself.'

His gaze softened. 'Intelligence does not make you any less vulnerable, Miss Lynley. In fact, some men would see your combination of intelligence and innocence as more of a challenge.'

'Oh. Well. . .' Not sure whether or not she had just received a compliment, and valiantly trying to lighten the suddenly serious atmosphere, Sarah brandished her reticule. 'That is why I carry a pistol, sir.'

His stunned expression was quite wonderfully satisfying.

'Don't tell me you are still walking around armed?' he demanded somewhat wrathfully.

She shook her reticule more menacingly. 'The first ghost I see, I shoot.'

After a moment of startled silence, he threw back his head and laughed aloud. Sarah decided she rather liked the sound.

'Miss Lynley,' he said when he had recovered. 'You are a darling. Every ghost haunting the place must now be shivering in its shroud.'

Sarah nearly tripped over a rock half-hidden in the long grass. Good heavens! A *darling*?

She ordered herself to object at once to Ravensdene's shocking familiarity in using such an endearment, but it was difficult to protest when one was trying not to giggle at the picture of ghosts shivering in their shrouds.

Nor did it help that her heart was fluttering madly somewhere in her throat. He had managed to throw her completely off-balance again, she thought dazedly. The man was beginning to make quite a habit of it.

'Well, you will be happy to know that you are safe from my pistol today, sir,' she began in a praiseworthy attempt to rally her disordered wits. 'But though I would expect Uncle Jasper to be rather old-fashioned in his views about females and firearms, you should have less antiquated notions of what is proper.'

'Not when it comes to my—' He stopped dead.

'Your what?'

He clenched his jaw. 'Never mind. Just don't let me catch you brandishing that pistol about. In fact, I expressly forbid you to even carry the thing.'

Sarah's own jaw dropped. 'Are you out of your mind?' she demanded at last. 'The only person who has the right to issue such a veto is my uncle, and I can assure you—'

'Or your husband,' he cut in, watching her.

Sarah stopped walking so abruptly that every bone in her body felt jarred. Like an animal sensing danger but unsure of its direction, she stared at Ravensdene, aware only of the intent expression in his eyes and her own racing pulse. The breath she drew in trembled audibly in the sudden stillness.

'Since I don't have a husband and do not intend to acquire one, my lord, that statement is completely irrelevant.'

He shifted his gaze from her face to the walls that now surrounded them, but Sarah did not make the mistake of assuming that her reply had brought the conversation to an end. Far from lightening, the atmosphere now seemed filled with a strange, brooding tension that made her feel as if the ruins themselves were waiting. When Ravensdene looked back at her, her heart began to beat so hard and so fast she thought it must surely be visible.

'You know, Miss Lynley, I had quite a long conversation with your uncle during our match the other day and—'

'Then I am not surprised you lost the encounter, my lord,' she interrupted quickly, desperate to forestall whatever was coming. 'Chess is a game that requires all one's concentration.'

'It does indeed,' he murmured. 'But it was actually your uncle who seemed rather distracted when we first began to play, and when I asked if he felt well enough to continue, he saw fit to confide the cause of his preoccupation to me.'

She was watching him now with the wariness of a small, cornered creature and for an instant Nick hesitated. Only for an instant. He was driven. Driven by the instinct to pursue that goaded him every time Sarah retreated. Driven by the need to make her his in the eyes of the world. Somehow he had to prepare her mind to be more receptive to the idea of marriage. Their marriage. And light-hearted, friendly banter seemed to be getting him nowhere.

'Sir Jasper told me,' he continued as softly and unthreateningly as possible, 'that your decision never to marry was greatly influenced by your sister's tragic death when you were only fourteen. Miss Lynley—' he removed her hand from his arm and held it in a firm clasp '—I know, none better, what it is to make decisions like that when one is very young, before maturity brings more reasoned counsel. But don't you think that your persistence in refusing to even consider marriage is contributing to your uncle's ill-health? He is extremely worried about your future.'

The sudden flash of terror in her eyes stunned him. She snatched her hand from his grasp and backed away.

'Uncle Jasper would never force me to marry to ensure my future. Never!'

'We're not living in the dark ages, you know,' he said gently. 'No one mentioned force.' All at once he felt a gut-wrenching need to move cautiously, as though any careless word or action on his part would hurt her unbearably. He took a step towards her and held out his hand. 'What frightens you so, little one?'

She drew back as if his touch might burn her. 'Nothing! Nothing frightens me!'

'If that is true, then you must surely realise that what befell your sister is not likely to—'

'Stop!' she cried. 'Stop it!' Shaking her head, retreating so quickly she almost cannoned into the wall a few paces at her back, she stared at him as if he was a spectre from the blackest pit, her eyes so anguished he barely suppressed an involuntary sound of protest. 'Whether I marry or not is none of your concern. I won't— Don't ever speak of this to me again. Not ever! Do you understand me? Not ever!'

Her voice breaking on the last word, she whirled, fled through an adjacent archway and vanished from sight.

Nick just managed to stop himself putting his fist through the crumbling stones beside him. He cursed long and comprehensively. God, he'd really made a mull of that. Like a fool he'd thought he could appeal to Sarah's good sense and concern for her uncle's health, without even considering that the mysterious circumstances apparently surrounding her sister's death had affected her more than he knew. What the devil had made him persist when a fool could have seen how uneasy the subject made her?

But even as he asked the question, he knew what had made him act so precipitously. Her smile. That sweet, faintly wistful, innocently enquiring smile that had hit him with all the force of a fist to the solar plexus. He'd literally been unable to move.

Vaguely he recalled that he'd managed to return her smile before Sarah had turned back to the task of packing away the picnic baskets. It was as well she had, before he'd forgotten all need for restraint and given in to the fierce urge to take her in his arms and taste every sweet curve of that delectably soft mouth.

Nick's mouth compressed as the heavy throb low in his body increased. He was a long way from giving Sarah the deeply sensual, possessive kiss he was beginning to crave. Somehow he had to win her tentative trust back. It wouldn't be easy, but —

He frowned, considering possibilities. Perhaps it would not be as difficult as he anticipated. If he knew Sarah at all, she would probably stop before she had gone too far into the ruins and rally her courage in order to face the rest of the party without arousing comment.

Yes, he was on the right track, he decided, with a grim sense of purpose born of sheer necessity. When Sarah calmed down she would find the others and, using them as a shield, treat him with polite indifference until she could retreat into her home. Then she would invent an excuse to absent herself from Monday's chess match.

'Not if I can help it,' Nick muttered between his teeth. He had reinforcements that Sarah had yet to encounter; plenty of troops ranged on his side who would be willing to gently prod her towards matrimony. All *he* had to do was assure her that she had nothing to fear from him.

But first, he told himself grimly, he needed a few hard facts. He had been assuming that Sarah's sister had been seduced and abandoned by an undesirable suitor and had subsequently died, that she might even have taken her own life, but those assumptions were possibly wide of the mark. Clearly another talk with Sir Jasper Lynley was in order.

And a word with Lady Wribbonhall might not go amiss either.

Sarah stopped where a sheltered cloister adjoining the ancient scriptorium shielded her from view, a prey to so many tempestuous emotions that she felt utterly battered by the turmoil going on inside her.

Foremost among them was a sense almost of betrayal. Even the pangs of guilt reanimated by Ravensdene's mention of her uncle's anxiety paled in comparison. Betrayal that Uncle Jasper had discussed his worry over her single state with Ravensdene, but, even more devastating, the fact that Ravensdene had overstepped the bounds by probing into that dark corner of her mind. All her happy expectations of a friendship between them had been shattered on the instant.

Which was ridiculous, she told herself a little forlornly. She had no right to feel that way. Ravensdene wasn't responsible for the workings of her mind. Because she chose to see him as a friend, did not mean he felt the same way.

This eminently practical point of view did not make her feel any better. To hurt, guilt and the terrified pounding of her heart was now added a distinct feeling of foolishness.

This was the second time she had fled from Ravensdene in complete disorder. And merely because he and Uncle Jasper had been discussing her in relation to marriage. As if the ceremony was about to be performed before she'd had any inkling of it.

Sarah pressed her cold hands to her burning face and slumped back against a convenient pillar. How *could* she have been so stupid? Ravensdene was right. They were not living in the dark ages. If he or any other man made an offer for her, all she had to do was decline.

Had she become so pampered, Sarah wondered, fighting back tears of savage self-chastisement, so spoilt by everyone's care and protection that she flew into hysterics at the first mention of the forbidden subject?

She let her hands fall and stared unseeingly down at them while she forced herself to contemplate that unpleasant possibility. Unless she wished to think of herself as possessing the sort of highly-strung, over-delicate sensibilities she despised, she had better pull herself together and brace herself to face Ravensdene again.

For a moment she quailed at the prospect. Then she remembered where she was. Brushing her cheeks quickly to erase any signs of tears, she straightened. First she would find the others. Courage was all very well, but sometimes one needed reinforcements.

In somewhat calmer fashion than the way she had dashed into the cloisters several minutes earlier, Sarah glanced around, trying to pinpoint her location in the ruins. She had been here before, but many years ago, and her memories of the place were vague.

Behind her, the colonnade opened onto a small quadrangle that allowed the afternoon light to pour into the stalls where the long-departed monks had once laboured over their illuminations and manuscripts. The westering sun cast her shadow before her in an elongated slant across the ancient flagstones. It was growing late.

Sarah turned her head to the right, the way she had come, listening over the faint breeze for the sound of voices that might lead her to the rest of the party. Several seconds passed before she realised that she was staring at another human shadow only a few yards away.

Her heart stopped. Shock sent ice flowing through her body until even her fingers and toes tingled. Like herself, whoever was standing there was hidden from direct view by the pillar beside him. Sarah had no doubt at all that it was a man who remained concealed so close to her, so motionless. She could see the clear outline of her bonnet in her own shadowy image, but the second image had no such distinction. He was bare-headed.

When her mind shuddered back into action a second later her first thought was that Ravensdene had followed her. It was more comforting than the possibility of an apparition, but she dismissed it instantly. The shadow was not much longer than her own, and in any event Ravensdene would not lurk behind pillars—even if he knew she was upset. She had first-hand knowledge of how he dealt with hysterical females, and it involved warmth and strength and comfort, not tactics that were eerie in the extreme.

Nor did she think that Lord Devenham would indulge in such pranks. No. The shadow probably belonged to James or Harry. One of them was lying in wait to convince the ladies that the place was haunted. It would be just like them.

So why didn't she call out and unmask the would-be ghost, Sarah asked herself, shivering? Why, at this inauspicious moment, were images of the unknown horseman flitting through her mind? And why was she experiencing the same chilling awareness that had over-come her in the gardens the other day?

One thing was certain. She was not going in *that* direction.

For a moment it looked as if she was not going in any direction. Her legs felt like tissue and her feet refused to move. Then, finally unglueing her feet from the ground, she began to make her way very quietly down the cloister.

She had not gone more than a few paces when an ear-splitting scream rent the air.

CHAPTER NINE

SARAH did not wait to see if the owner of the shadow reacted to the scream as she did. She gathered up her skirts and tore down the colonnade to emerge into the open at the entrance to what had once been the priory herb garden.

The cause of the commotion was not hard to find. Everyone was clustered about Sophie Sherington who was lying in a crumpled heap on the grass, nursing her ankle.

Everyone, that was, except Julia and Devenham.

But even as she registered their absence, Sarah saw the pair hurrying towards the small crowd from the direction of the crypt. Ravensdene was there also. He must have appeared about the same time as herself, Sarah thought, but from the opposite side of the garden, not far from where she had left him.

All were present and accounted for, and she alone had come from the cloisters.

She glanced back, half-expecting to see a concerned or startled stranger emerge from the corridor. The archway behind her remained empty.

Puzzled and still a little shivery inside, she joined the group, avoiding the long, searching look Ravensdene gave her by kneeling down beside Sophie, who was gasping out an explanation in which ghosts and hidden rocks figured largely.

'I tripped over this stupid stone,' she finished on a wail. 'When Eliza and I ran away.'

'Ran away from what?' Harry Marsham demanded with scant sympathy. He grinned. 'A ghost? *I* don't see one.'

Sophie glared at him. 'Something moved,' she insisted, pointing. 'Up there.'

Everyone turned to look at the partially ruined wall above them. As they did so, a bird flew into a crevice in the rough stone. It carried a twig in its beak. Clearly, domicilary construction was in progress.

'There's your ghost, Sophie,' Eliza said, laughing. 'I told you it was nothing.'

A chagrined frown crossed Miss Sherington's face, but Sarah noticed that her mouth was tight with real discomfort.

'Where does your leg pain you, Sophie?' she asked, taking the younger girl's hand.

Sophie's lip trembled. 'My ankle,' she quavered, reminded of her injury. 'I twisted it when I fell.'

Momentarily forgetting her altercation with Ravensdene, Sarah sent a fleeting glance up at him, fully expecting to see a hard look of disbelief on his face. Given Sophie's past performances, not to mention the activities of several other ladies, she would not have been surprised to find herself confronting a coldly furious male whose patience with female stratagems was at an end.

But confounding her again, he hunkered down on Sophie's other side, his expression conveying nothing more than grave concern.

'Then I suggest you do not walk on it on this uneven ground, Miss Sherington,' he said gently. 'If Lord Devenham brings the carriage around to this side of the ruins, would you permit Mr Langdon to carry you to it? You will be very much more comfortable there, I assure you.'

'Yes, thank you.' Obviously feeling more shaken than she appeared, Sophie turned from Ravensdene to the childhood friend who had always been there to mend her hurts. 'Oh, James, I'm so sorry. I've ruined every-one's day.'

'Nonsense,' he said at once. 'It is time we were
starting for home anyway. Don't worry, Sophie. I'm sure
you'll be all right and tight again for your waltzing party
next month.'

This sally drew a small, watery smile from her. Sarah
smiled, too, and gave him an approving look. 'To be
sure she will,' she agreed, taking a rather shaky breath.
'Sophie, while the gentlemen fetch the horses, why don't
you let me take your boot off? I am sure it must be
hurting you.'

The two younger gentlemen, taking this hint that they
were in the way, departed on their errand. Sarah glanced
up, every nerve quivering with apprehension when
Ravensdene did not immediately follow their example.

Their eyes met. He smiled faintly, rose to his feet, and
taking Devenham's arm, followed the others without a
word.

Sarah did not know what his silence forebode, but two
days later she was wishing Julia would follow his
example.

'But, Sarah, you can't refuse an invitation from Lady
Ravensdene. It would be most impolite when you have
no previous engagement.'

Setting her lips in a mutinous line, Sarah moved down
the garden path to select another bloom destined for her
uncle's library. 'How do you know I have no previous
engagement?' she asked, parting an early rosebud from
its bush with a rather agitated snip of her shears.

Julia frowned. 'Because I would be similarly engaged.
We do move in the same circles, you know.'

Sarah sent her a reproachful look which had absolutely no effect. Her friend returned to the attack with all
the uncompromising tenacity of a bull-terrier.

'As it happens, Mama and I have also been invited to
Comberford tomorrow, so you will not be alone. Lady
Ravensdene's note said that if the day is fine, we'll

partake of tea by the lake. Nothing could be more charming.'

Or more reminiscent of the picnic, Sarah thought, wincing inwardly. She still felt like hiding somewhere whenever she recalled her hysterical flight from Ravensdene. And then to have him treat Sophie with such kindness. . .

She had not been able to think of anything else all the way home or since. Not even the memory of the shadow in the cloisters had distracted her for long. No doubt the man had been an innocent visitor to the ruins, as startled by mysterious shadows and blood-curdling screams as she had been herself. He had probably exited at top speed in the other direction.

Having thus explained the matter to her satisfaction, Sarah had spent the past two days brooding over the thought that every time she decided that Ravensdene was best kept at a safe distance, he had turned around and behaved in a way that aroused the strangest feelings inside her. Wistful yearnings unlike anything she had ever known. And the only way she had been able to cope with them was to deny their existence.

Unfortunately, denial had not been effective. In fact she had been feeling quite inexplicably bereft, as if something of immeasurable value had been taken from her.

And as if that was not worrying enough, she was now wondering why Ravensdene's mother had sent her a very personally worded invitation. A large formal gathering she might have coped with, but her ladyship's note had sounded alarmingly friendly.

'Wait a minute,' she squeaked, abruptly jolted out of her reverie as Julia whisked her basket out of her hands and began propelling her towards the house. 'Where are we going? I haven't finished—'

'You are going to write a polite note of acceptance to Lady Ravensdene,' Julia responded with a steely-eyed determination that Sarah hadn't known her gentle friend possessed. 'And I am going to stand over you until you do it. My whole future is at stake.'

'What!' Sarah tried to halt and was dragged ruthlessly onward, through the hall and into the drawing-room.

'What do you mean, your whole future is at stake?' she demanded, finally catching her breath when Julia stopped beside a small writing table and indicated the quill reposing thereupon. She eyed her friend's flushed and agitated countenance and momentarily forgot her own problems. 'Julia, what are you talking about?'

Julia abandoned her terrier tactics and wrung her hands. 'Oh, Sarah, I haven't seen Bar—that is to say, Lord Devenham, since the picnic, even though he came to call on Papa yesterday, because Mama and I were out for hours visiting tenants and when we got back Papa had gone up to town on some stupid matter of business—as if he couldn't have waited. . . But never mind that. So I don't know what was said, but why would Bar—that is, Lord Devenham, call to see Papa and then not come to call today—although I've been here all afternoon—but, you see, if it's only me and Mama at Comberford tomorrow, Ravensdene might not feel obliged to stay in, and Bar—I mean, Lord Devenham, might go with Ravensdene to wherever it is gentlemen go when their mothers entertain ladies and I won't see him for *another* whole day and by then I will have died of anxiety!'

Her brain reeling from this spate of verbiage, Sarah fixed on the one word that seemed to have stayed in her head.

'Bar—?' she queried, fixing her friend with a look of heavy meaning.

Julia's flushed face took on an even rosier hue. 'Well, I did tell you that I had become quite well acquainted with Lord Devenham,' she said with an attempt at airy dismissal. 'His name is Barney.'

'Barney,' Sarah repeated. Several startlingly detailed

pictures suddenly sprang into her mind, racing through her memory with a speed that made her dizzy: Julia and Devenham hurrying from the crypt at the ruins, the slightly dazed expression in Julia's eyes, the soft rosiness of her mouth, the faint look of tension on Devenham's face.

'Good heavens!' she exclaimed, stunned into voicing the realisation aloud. 'At the ruins... You were... He was...'

'Yes, we were and he most definitely was,' Julia confirmed defiantly, clearly having no trouble in interpreting this stammered attempt at speech. Then, apparently overcome by her own memories, her hands clasped and such a glow came into her eyes that Sarah stared, hardly able to recognise her girlhood friend in the blushing, tremulous young woman standing before her.

'Oh, Sarah, when he kissed me...it was beyond anything.'

'Beyond anything,' echoed Sarah weakly.

'Yes. But there's more. When I said that, Barney just smiled at me and... Sarah, I swear to you, that smile positively turned my knees to water.'

'Knees to water.' She knew precisely what Julia meant. She seemed to have lost control of her own knees. An image of Ravensdene's hard, beautifully etched mouth had imprinted itself behind her eyes and would not be dismissed. She felt an abrupt need to sit down. It was almost beyond her control not to raise her hand and touch her own mouth, suddenly warm and soft and tingling.

'And I simply have to see him again as soon as possible, so you are going to pick up that pen and write to Lady Ravensdene.'

'Write to Lady Ravensdene.'

'Yes. Now!'

Oh, thank goodness. At last. An excuse to sit down.

* * *

She had been temporarily unhinged, of course. It was the only possible explanation.

'Another cup of tea, Miss Lynley?'

'Oh, no. . . That is, yes, thank you, my lord.'

Sarah winced at her incoherence, tore her gaze away from Ravensdene's mouth, and took cover behind her tea. Unfortunately her hinges didn't appear to have returned since her conversation with Julia yesterday. She still felt distinctly rattled. And all because her heart had given the strangest leap when she had seen Ravensdene and Lord Devenham coming across the lawn a few minutes ago to join the teaparty.

She had told herself it was uneasiness, or at least embarrassment at having to face him again, but when Ravensdene had greeted everyone without paying her any extraordinary degree of attention, her unruly heart had promptly plummeted straight to the pit of her stomach. She had been so distracted by the odd sensation that, since then, she had contributed not one word to the conversation.

Fortunately no one seemed to have noticed. Julia and Devenham were talking quietly together, while the two older ladies chattered away with all the comfortable familiarity of old friends. She hoped Ravensdene was equally oblivious to her inner turmoil, but when she risked a glance at him from beneath her lashes she saw him watching her intently.

'Have you heard how Miss Sherington does, Miss Lynley?' he asked at once, as if he had only been waiting for her attention before speaking.

Placing his cup on the table, he came to stand beside her chair. Beyond him the sun shimmered on the silvery waters of the lake, throwing his profile into sharp relief. Unable to see his face clearly, Sarah told herself he looked big and dangerous towering over her, but then he turned slightly as though wondering why she hadn't

answered, and the expression in his light green eyes held
nothing more threatening than polite enquiry.

Again that odd sense of loss tugged at her heart.

'I believe. . .yes. . .that is, I rode over to Sherington
Court the other day, my lord,' she stammered, wishing
she could stop sounding like a chit just out of the
schoolroom. 'Sophie had only twisted her ankle slightly.
Dr Salcott says a day or two of rest will set it to rights.'

'I am happy to hear,' he replied gravely, 'that an
epidemic of sprained ankles is not about to be unleashed
among us.'

Sarah's lips parted, confusion flitted across her face,
but the smile he had hoped to draw from her didn't
materialise. Instead, after a sidelong, half-wary glance at
him, she turned away as his mother addressed some
remark to her.

Nick gritted his teeth against a surge of impatience.
He would have liked to hurl tea-tray, plates and delicacies into the lake. Unfortunately he had to restrain his
natural instincts and accept the fact that he was not
going to have the opportunity today to recover the
ground he had lost.

But at least Sarah was here. He grimaced inwardly as
he recalled his visit to the Grange on the day after the
picnic. He already knew that Sarah had visited Sophie
Sherington that afternoon. Sir Jasper had let it fall that,
not five minutes after being informed of his imminent
arrival, Sarah had decided to pay the call and to drop in
on the Reverend Butterlow's ailing housekeeper on her
way home for good measure. Since he had seen said
housekeeper out and about, in perfect health, that very
morning, he had promptly returned home himself and
enlisted his mother's support. She had been positively
delighted to oblige.

Of course, now he had to make sure his matchmaking
parent didn't go too far in pursuit of the cause.

Shaking off the various schemes to get Sarah alone

that were floating about in his head, he pulled his attention back to the conversation going on over the tea cups. It was as well he did.

'Naturally I will move back to town when everything is settled,' his mother was saying to the company at large. 'Nothing is more tiresome than a parent on the premises when one is trying to establish—'

'What you mean, Mama, is that you are missing all your friends and cannot wait to hear the latest gossip,' Nick corrected her in quelling accents.

'Do I, dearest? Well, if you say so. Not that dear Papa was ever precisely interfering,' she went on, turning to Sarah with a charming smile. 'He was an exceptionally indulgent parent. And grandparent, too. Why, when Nicholas hit a cricket ball through the breakfast parlour window he roared for only five minutes. Of course, the window was closed at the time which—'

'Mama, I don't think Miss Lynley wishes to hear—'

'Unfortunately, his tolerance did seem to disappear as he grew older,' Lady Ravensdene continued with gentle inexorability. 'My mother was used to be the only person who could coax him into a better temper whenever anything tried his patience. From what Winwick tells me, you possessed the same talent, Miss Lynley. So useful.' She cast a glance at her scowling son and muttered cryptically, 'Two of a kind, you know.'

'Er, yes, ma'am. That is. . .' Sarah faltered, not quite sure what she was supposed to be responding to. It was difficult to attend to such a rambling conversation when her disordered mind was torn between her growing conviction that she had lost any chance of Ravensdene's friendship, and an awareness of him that was so acute she could practically feel him breathe. 'I have noticed that poor health does tend to irritate gentlemen somewhat.'

'Dear me, yes,' agreed her hostess. 'But I have every confidence in you. Such a pleasant part of the country, too. Nicholas always liked spending the summers at Comberford when he was a boy. An ideal location. So close to your uncle. So convenient.'

Sarah frowned. Had she missed something else in her distraction? She was already living with her uncle. How much closer did she need to be?

'I am sure dear Sir Jasper would agree,' Lady Ravensdene mused in her vague way. 'You have cared for him for some time, I take it?'

'Yes, ma'am.' Grateful that at last there was a definite question she could answer, Sarah found herself elaborating. 'My parents died when I was quite young, you see, and my sis. . .' She hesitated, took a deep breath and continued. 'My sister, Amy, and I came to live at the Grange.'

Lady Ravensdene nodded. 'Poor child,' she murmured. Although precisely which child she meant was rather obscure. 'Your devotion to your uncle does you credit, my dear. I daresay that is why I have not seen you in town any time these past few years.'

'Miss Lynley will tell you, Mama, that she has no taste for town life,' Ravensdene said before she could reply.

'Is that so?' Lady Ravensdene appeared inordinately thrilled by the news. She beamed. 'Excellent. And you play chess, too. Nothing could be more delightful.'

Sarah decided to abandon any attempt at keeping up with her hostess's conversational leaps and bounds. She suspected that such a feat was impossible. One needed one's wits about one, and hers had taken a leave of absence. Not only that, she had the uneasy feeling that Lady Ravensdene's style of conversation could not entirely be dismissed as the vagaries of a vague mind. The look in her ladyship's eye was unexpectedly shrewd.

She was just beginning to wonder when Lady Wribbonhall would put an end to the visit so she could go home and be miserable in peace, when a rather odd cacophony of noise sounded in the distance. Everyone else heard it at the same time. A shrill yapping, growing nearer, and rising above a chorus of high-pitched shrieks.

'What the deuce — ?' demanded Devenham, beginning to rise to his feet.

The answer burst onto the scene before he had finished. Around the corner of the house scampered a small puppy with three ladies in hot pursuit. Yelping with excitement, the puppy careered across the lawn, dashed straight between the legs of the light wooden table and vanished into the bushes growing at the side of the lake, leaving mayhem in his wake.

Cups, plates and macaroons went flying as the table teetered and fell. Lady Wribbonhall let out a faint scream as tea cascaded into her lap. Julia sprang out of her chair to avoid the same fate and promptly collided with the foremost puppy pursuer. Both ladies sat down rather abruptly on the grass just as the other two intruders reached them. One managed to stop in time. The other swerved wildly and, still shrieking, arms flailing, plunged headlong towards the lake. There was a loud splash.

Sarah, who had also leapt out of the way with perilous haste as the table crashed to the ground, suddenly found herself clasped securely against Ravensdene's side, held there by an arm that felt like iron about her waist. She didn't remember how she'd got there or seeing him move, but at her startled gasp he released her at once.

'Well,' he murmured for her ears alone. 'At least we know the puppy really exists. Now if only the footpads would put in an appearance. . .'

She didn't have time to reply to this frivolous utterance, or to wonder about her varied and shocking responses to his quick action. Everyone started talking at once as they sorted themselves out.

'My best maroon silk!' wailed Lady Wribbonhall,

tottering from her chair and flapping uselessly at the damage.

'Miss Wribbonhall! Are you hurt?' Devenham bent to help Julia to her feet, ignoring the other two damsels who were now gazing, eyes starting with horror, at the lake.

'Good heavens above!' Lady Ravensdene, still seated in solitary splendour, cup in hand, amid the wreckage, placed her tea carefully on Sarah's abandoned chair and raised her eyeglass. It was purely an affectation. She stared over it at the young lady who was extricating herself from the loving embrace of the reedy shallows.

It was Averilla Smisby, clad in a muslin gown that, wringing wet, did absolutely nothing to disguise the fact that she was wearing not a stitch of clothing underneath it.

'Oh, no!' she exclaimed, holding handfuls of dripping muslin away from her body. The material promptly clung to various other places. 'Oh, my! Oh—' with a sidelong glance at Ravensdene '—just look at me!'

Only the ladies obliged. Turning his back, Ravensdene gazed at the house as if suddenly struck by an architectural muse, while Devenham sank into a chair and put his head in his hands.

'Oh, good gracious me!' Lady Wribbonhall, clucking like a demented hen, rushed forward. 'Miss Smisby! You can't just stand there. Come out at once! Dear me! What is to be done? How could you be so *immodest*, so lost to all sense of decorum?'

As if her exhortations had released them from their shocked paralysis, the other Smisby girls hurried to their sister's aid. Sarah didn't dare catch Julia's eye as instructions and reproaches filled the air, rendering the scene more reminiscent of a hen-house in an uproar than before. She was already in dire straits trying to suppress the laughter threatening to overtake her.

Fortunately, Lady Ravensdene was made of sterner

stuff. She had been right, Sarah reflected, watching her ladyship's face as Averilla Smisby splashed towards the bank. Ravensdene's mother was no more vague than her son.

Rising majestically, her gaze still fixed in frigid disapproval on the apparition in the lake, she held out an imperious hand. 'Your coat, Ravensdene, if you please.'

He shrugged out of it and handed it over without a word.

Despite her struggle for composure, Sarah felt her eyes widen as she took in the solid proportions of his chest and shoulders, clad in fine white lawn. Before she could wrench her gaze away, he looked straight at her and winked.

She nearly choked. And he knew it, the wretch. It was all she could do to control herself long enough for Lady Ravensdene and Lady Wribbonhall to lead three very chastened Miss Smisbys away, one of them wrapped in Ravensdene's coat, her sandals squelching miserably with every step.

Only Euphemia looked back briefly. 'My puppy. . .' she began.

'Don't worry, Miss Smisby,' Lady Ravensdene interposed firmly. 'He shall be found and returned.'

'Is it safe to look?' Devenham got out in a strangled voice as the group reached the terrace and vanished into the house. He was still bent over, his head clutched between his hands.

But not for any reasons of discretion, Sarah discovered, studying him more closely. His lordship had been rendered utterly helpless with laughter.

She looked at Julia, then at Ravensdene. As one they all burst into similar paroxysms and collapsed onto the nearest chairs.

'Oh, dear,' said Julia when she could speak. 'How very dreadful it is to laugh at such a want of conduct, but how can one help it? When I think of Mama's face when

Averilla Smisby stood up in the water and asked everyone to look at her—' She broke off, overcome by another fit of giggles.

Sarah eyed her friend with mock solemnity. 'You would be amazed,' she said, 'at what some females will do.'

The abrupt cessation of mirth beside her made her turn her head. Ravensdene was regarding her, one midnight dark brow raised, a slightly quizzical look in his eyes. Sarah suddenly realised what she had said.

'Oh!' she exclaimed softly, but there was no real distress in the sound. In fact, distress was the furthest thing from her mind. On the contrary. She felt light, floating, as if a weight she had been dragging behind her had just been cut loose. It was the feeling of awkwardness that had plagued her in his presence, she thought. Her embarrassment at her idiotic behaviour the other day. In their shared hilarity it had vanished completely.

'You never said a truer word, Miss Lynley,' he murmured, and smiled at her.

'That's all very well,' said Devenham, distracting Sarah from the quick rush of happiness welling up inside her. 'But that young lady needs a good talking-to. Are you sure you're not hurt, Miss Wribbonhall?'

While Julia reassured him, Ravensdene rose to his feet, reaching out to set the table to rights in the same fluid movement. 'I think Miss Smisby will receive all the talking-to you would wish on her,' he observed. 'And if I know my mother, by the time she's finished with those three, they won't come near the Place again.'

'I should think not.' Julia giggled. 'But I suspect Leopoldina and Euphemia were as shocked as Mama. And Averilla could not have known you would be near the lake, my lord, so perhaps we should not be too harsh.'

'You are too generous, Miss Wribbonhall.' Ravensdene's tone was dry. 'Especially if, as I suspect,

that dog was deliberately turned loose inside the gates
and—'

'Good God! The puppy. I suppose we should go and
look for it.' Devenham sprang up and made a great show
of peering into the nearest bushes. 'Did you happen to
notice which way the little devil went, Nick?'

An amused smile crossed Ravensdene's face. 'No.
But feel free to search the place, by all means.'

'Least we can do, if it will get those harp—uh, females
off the premises betimes,' Devenham declared purpose-
fully. 'Miss Wribbonhall, you and I shall take the
woods.' He took Julia's hand in his before anyone could
suggest an alternative plan. 'Nick, why don't you and
Miss Lynley search the gardens?'

'An excellent idea,' Ravensdene murmured, manag-
ing not to grin.

Sarah, whose gaze had been going from one man to
the other all through the exchange, suddenly heard the
unspoken dialogue going on between them. She looked
at the lightly covered, powerful physique of her host and
felt a frisson of doubt slide down her spine. She might
be feeling more at ease with Ravensdene, but being
alone with him again was another thing entirely.

It was too late to protest, however. Devenham was
already leading an equally flummoxed but willing Julia
across the lawn towards the home wood. When they
disappeared into the leafy bower, Sarah swallowed
against the strange tightness in her throat.

'It is quite all right, Miss Lynley.' Ravensdene studied
her face for a moment, then said deliberately, 'Miss
Wribbonhall will be perfectly safe with Lord Devenham,
I assure you.'

'Oh. . .' Flustered, she clasped her hands. 'I am sure
she will be. That isn't what. . .'

'Is it your own safety that concerns you?'

'No! Good heavens, no. What could happen in a
garden? I—'

'Then shall we go?'

The calm question acted like a particularly effective dampener. Sarah ordered herself to stop babbling, unclenched her fingers and laid her hand on Ravensdene's proffered arm. The heat and hardness beneath her fingers immediately turned her limbs to water. The fine lawn of his shirt was no covering at all. She might as well have been touching his bare flesh.

She almost collapsed at the thought. The garden seemed miles away, but once they were enclosed by the tall, green hedges surrounding the formal arrangement of paths and flower beds, Ravensdene halted. It was a fortunate thing, Sarah reflected vaguely. She didn't think she could trust her legs to go any further.

'Miss Lynley,' he said gravely, covering her hand with his. 'May I speak plainly with you?'

Doubt and apprehension immediately suspended every faculty. He was going to mention her strange behaviour. She just knew it. Unable to speak herself, she gestured slightly with her free hand.

'I wanted to thank you for coming here today,' he began, his voice very deep and soft. 'After my unchivalrous insistence on raising an obviously delicate subject with you in such public surroundings the other day, I was not sure you would accept my mother's invitation. Thank you. You have made her very happy.'

Sarah could only stare at him while surprise continued to render her speechless. Having steeled herself for anything from reproaches to a demand for an explanation, the only response that sprang to her mind was a wild impulse to ask if her presence had made him happy, too. The highly improper question was so ready to tumble off her tongue that she was thoroughly distracted from her niggling sense that something was missing from Ravensdene's contrite speech.

'Please think nothing more of it, my lord,' she finally managed. 'My. . .my own behaviour was not precisely exemplary on that occasion. No doubt you have been wondering. . .that is. . .'

'I doubt if the reason is far to seek,' he said dryly. 'You've been nervous around me ever since our first meeting. I can hardly blame you. I was extremely rough with you; an action I now deeply regret. I can only assure you, Miss Lynley, that I will do everything within my power to erase such an appalling first impression, which is why I agreed to let Dev and Miss Wribbonhall search the woods while we tackle the garden. I hoped—'

He paused, looking down at her averted face, before adding in a voice so low she had to strain to hear the words, 'Please don't be afraid of me, Sarah.'

Oh, who could resist the sincerity in *that* plea? Certainly not she, Sarah thought, shaken unutterably by the knowledge that Ravensdene still regretted his violence in the woods and assumed she still feared him because of it.

'It is not precisely that I am afraid of you, my lord,' she whispered hesitantly. She kept her gaze lowered, almost unbearably conscious of the quietness of the garden, of how alone they were, of the growing intimacy of the moment. The chance to erase the impression she must have left him with at the picnic, to recapture that sweet sense of harmony, beckoned irresistibly, and yet she still felt a need to pull back, to protect herself in some way.

'There is no need to search for explanations, Miss Lynley.' He tipped her face up with a hand beneath her chin and met her troubled gaze. 'Given your usual good sense, I am sure you consider your reasons for avoiding marriage to be sound and sufficient.'

'Oh. Thank you.' Sarah returned his look doubtfully. 'I think.'

He smiled and, releasing her, began walking again, leading her towards a fountain that stood at the junction of several paths in the centre of the garden.

Sarah followed blindly, her thoughts quite uncharacteristically at sea. Having been told that an explanation was unnecessary, she now found herself overwhelmingly anxious to give him one. But what was she to say? The dreams that plagued her sleep were terrifying enough without reliving the nightmare during the day. Even the thought of relating the story behind her decision never to marry caused a roiling nausea to churn in the pit of her stomach. She couldn't do it. She needed something else. Something he would understand.

Sarah's eyes widened as an idea flashed into her mind. It would involve another discussion on the subject of matrimony, but what better way to eradicate the memory of her hysterical rantings of two days ago? And this time she was prepared. This time she could control the conversation.

'Marriage is, as you say, a delicate subject,' she remarked, feeling rather like a bather testing the waters, one cautious toe at a time. 'And one about which my views were fixed at quite a young age, my lord. While my parents were still alive, in fact.'

'Oh?' She felt him glance down at her as they strolled past a fragrant lavendar bush. 'From your tone, Miss Lynley, I deduce that theirs was not a felicitous match.'

'Far from it, sir. My father married late in life when he was extremely fixed in his ways and not inclined to tolerate the, er, flightiness of a much younger wife. Even though his own behaviour was far from acceptable.'

'Hmm. Let me tell you, Miss Lynley, that if flightiness is a euphemism for what I suspect, then a husband's age or behaviour has nothing whatever to do with it.'

Sarah blushed. 'Yes, I am fully aware that there are two sets of rules pertaining in society, my lord. A woman may look forward to comporting herself in an exemplary fashion while her husband does what he pleases, regardless of her feelings in the matter. Or she can seek a match in which the partners agree to lead separate lives once the wife has fulfilled her duty in producing an heir.

'Where no such agreement exists, however, constant arguments and acrimony are not very pleasant for the other members of a household, sir. In fact, it was during the course of one such altercation that my father was distracted from his driving, causing his curricle to swing wide on a bend and collide with a tree. Both my parents were killed instantly.'

'I'm sorry,' he murmured rather thoughtfully. 'It must have been most distressing for you. . .'

The silent 'but' hanging on the end of that sentence jangled loudly in Sarah's head.

'Yes, well, I daresay my reasons for avoiding either of those situations might be considered foolish, my lord, but I would rather remain single than—'

'Miss Lynley!' He halted with startling abruptness and turned her to face him, his hands resting lightly on her shoulders. 'I would *never* consider you foolish.' Both voice and expression gentled. 'Merely very sheltered and inexperienced.'

'Not so sheltered that I don't know what goes on in polite society,' Sarah retorted, feeling unaccountably annoyed by that remark. She promptly forgot how very big Ravensdene's hands felt wrapped around her more fragile frame. 'Just because your own marriage was an unusually happy one, does not mean—'

His grip tightened with a force that brought her awareness of danger rushing back with dizzying speed. Sarah gasped, fully expecting to hear her bones crack at any moment. 'I'm sorry,' she stammered. 'I—'

'Hush.' He released her immediately, silencing her by the simple expedient of brushing his fingers lightly across her lips. Then, taking her hand, he led her up to the fountain a few steps away and indicated the stone coping.

Sarah sank onto the makeshift seat with a willingness

that had nothing to do with compliance, her dazed mind grappling with the puzzle of how such a fleeting touch of Ravensdene's fingers could cause a shimmering ripple of sensation to flow from her lips to her throat, and from thence to spread a tingling heat across her breasts—and all this while her heart was pounding with alarm.

The puzzle was destined to remain unsolved. Ravensdene seated himself beside her and fixed her with an unnervingly steady regard.

'Who told you I'd once been married?' he asked.

His calm tone did absolutely nothing to soothe her frazzled nerves. 'Lady Wribbonhall,' she owned faintly. 'But it was not. . .not in any *gossiping* way, my lord.'

When he raised a brow in quizzical disbelief, Sarah felt a guilty blush suffuse her cheeks. Oh, why hadn't she been struck dumb before she'd come out with that statement about his marriage? So much for taking control of the conversation. It seemed to be drifting into rather perilous channels again, and far from being struck dumb, her tongue appeared to be taking on a will of its own, aided and abetted by a question that was suddenly dancing tantalisingly about in her brain. A question, she realised with a start of surprise, that had been hovering in the back of her mind for a very long time. Ever since Lady Wribbonhall had mentioned the subject, in fact.

'Yes,' she heard herself saying in earnest tones. 'Lady Wribbonhall quite understood why you might not wish to be pursued, my lord. Indeed, she seemed to have been greatly impressed by your wife's beauty and. . .and general demeanour. Angelic was the word she used, if I recall, and. . .'

Sheer disbelief at her own temerity at last had her clamping her lips shut on the rest. She looked into Ravensdene's frowning eyes and could not believe what she had done. Now it was she who was trespassing beyond the boundaries of friendship. As if some demon of curiosity had been released from the shackles of polite behaviour, and not even the memory of where curiosity had led her before had had the power to stop her.

Then as Ravensdene looked away, guilt and remorse swept over her in a swamping wave, the force of it almost drowning her. She had hurt him. She had behaved no better than Sophie Sherington. And now, when she needed to speak, to beg his forgiveness, her mind had ceased to function, her throat had seized up...

Oh, if only Julia and Devenham would return. The puppy appear. *Anything*.

'Yes, Marianne was incomparably beautiful.'

Sarah froze. Even her heart seemed to stand still. The words were spoken so quietly that for a minute she wasn't sure if she'd actually heard them. Hardly daring to breathe, she stared wide-eyed at Ravensdene, thankful that he continued to gaze down into the water hushing gently beside them.

'She was somewhat taller than you, Miss Lynley, and very fair. Her hair was that rare shade that shines almost silver in some lights; her face and figure were deemed to be perfection. Yes, an angel was exactly what she looked like.'

If someone had just dashed the chilly waters of the fountain over her, Sarah couldn't have felt more shattered. The shock made it almost impossible to breathe. It could not have been more obvious to her that Ravensdene's heart had been buried in the grave with his beautiful angel of a wife.

She found herself blinking back a sudden rush of tears and was horrified at her loss of control. What was happening to her lately? Why was she acting so unlike herself? Why did she *feel* so unlike herself? Panicked one moment, incredibly happy the next, only to be cast down into this trough of despondency. She should be grateful that Ravensdene was still conversing with her instead of delivering the set-down she deserved. The least she could do was respond with sympathy for his loss without embarrassing them both by turning into a watering-pot.

This stern, if silent, rebuke had her floundering under another tidal wave of guilt. She fought it back, determined that, this time, she would not leave Ravensdene thinking her prone to uncontrollable outbursts.

'I'm sorry,' she ventured, forcing a tentative smile. It wavered somewhat at the edges, but at least the exercise served to push her seesawing emotions to the back of her mind. 'I know what it's like to lose someone you love.'

He looked at her then, his eyes grave. 'Your sister?'

Sarah nodded, and in that moment she decided that whatever the cost to herself, Ravensdene deserved the truth. Or at least part of it. She had intruded, unforgivably, driven by her sudden incomprehensible curiosity about his wife, whereas he had demanded nothing. No explanations, no reasons, nothing. Because he thought she was afraid of him.

'Goodness!' she managed on a nervous little laugh. 'I do not know how we came to be so side-tracked, my lord, when I believe I was trying to explain that you do not frighten me.'

'Don't I?' he asked gently.

'Certainly not.' She sat up straighter, gaining confidence with her resolve to make amends. 'If I have seemed to you to have been dwelling on an episode to which I freely admit I contributed my share, sir, it is because those woods hold very disturbing memories for me. Memories that have nothing to do with what happened between you and I.' She hesitated, then finished baldly. 'My sister was assaulted and killed there.'

'I see.'

'Yes. And, unfortunately, the day we met was the first time I had ventured there alone.'

'Is that why you were armed that day?' he asked. 'Were you afraid something of the kind might occur again?'

Conscious of the searching quality of his gaze, Sarah glanced down and began trailing her fingers idly through the water. 'Not exactly,' she said slowly. 'It was not a. . . a random attack.'

When he didn't ask for clarification but just waited, she drew in a deep breath. 'Amy was murdered. By one of our grooms.'

Silence. She could almost hear his brain sifting through the scant information.

'What happened to the murderer?' he asked after a moment.

Sarah sighed and withdrew her fingers from the water. She folded her hands in her lap and contemplated the garden beds in front of her. 'He drowned. When his body was discovered washed up on the beach a day or so later, everyone thought he had been trying to escape by swimming out to one of the ships anchored in the Downs.'

This time the silence threatened to stretch into infinity. She wished she knew what Ravensdene was thinking, but a quick, sidelong glance at him revealed nothing more than a slight narrowing of his eyes as he, too, stared thoughtfully at the garden.

She did not need to read his mind, however, to know what the next logical question would be, and an explanation as to why a groom would want to attack and kill his employer's niece threatened to drag her down once more into the murky depths of her nightmares. She had said enough.

'Miss Lynley—'

'Dear me, we seem to have been sitting here talking forever, my lord!' She sprang to her feet, bracing knees that felt distinctly wobbly. 'Julia and Lord Devenham will be wondering what has become of us.'

'I doubt it,' he said very dryly, rising also. His unwavering gaze remained on her face a moment longer, causing her heart to beat uncomfortably fast as she waited to see if he would follow her lead. Then the unnervingly contemplative expression vanished from his eyes and he smiled at her.

'In fact Dev is probably proposing to Miss Wribbonhall even as we speak. I know he intended to do so at his first opportunity, and like any good strategist he seized it.' He grinned suddenly, the wicked, boyish grin she found so endearing. 'Why do you think he was so anxious to go hunting for that wretched hound?'

'Oh.' Sarah laughed at the memory of Devenham peering under bushes that clearly contained no recalcitrant puppies. A second later her brain rocked under the impact of Ravensdene's meaning.

'Good heavens! That means Julia will be betrothed. And then married. And then—' She stopped right there.

'Yes, we do seem to be forever running up against the institution of matrimony, don't we, Miss Lynley? However, I can assure you that Dev will handle the matter with a great deal more address than I did. Nor are all marriages like those you described earlier. You need have no fears for Miss Wribbonhall's future happiness.'

'Oh, I don't,' she stammered, thrown immediately back into confusion by this assurance. She wasn't sure if Ravensdene was referring to proposals or marriage. Either option held uncountable dangers as far as she was concerned. 'I am sure Lord Devenham is everything that is gentlemanly, but. . .'

The line of his mouth seemed to harden. 'Whereas I am not.'

'I did not say that, my lord.' *Well, not precisely*. Sarah blushed selfconsciously. 'And you *are* a gentleman.' She looked down and added after a painful pause, 'I, more than anyone, should know that.'

He reached out and took her hand, his long fingers

closing firmly about hers. 'Thank you, Miss Lynley,' he murmured, and waiting until she raised her eyes to his, he brought her hand to his lips and held it there.

Sarah felt her breath stop. Was this what she had feared? This liquid, melting warmth rushing through her. His lips were firm and yet gentle against her fingers. She thought once again of the lethal power beneath his civilised clothing, felt the heat emanating from his big body, and wanted only to step closer. In his shirt, breeches and topboots he was overwhelming in his masculinity, but she remembered how swiftly he had moved to stop her from falling, how securely he had held her, she remembered Lydia's trust in her husband and Julia's anxious wait for Devenham to declare himself, and for the first time in her adult life, she thought of safety, of protection, in the arms of a man.

The notion was enough to stun her into utter immobility, her gaze caught and held by the glittering green eyes that watched the myriad expressions flitting across her face with all the piercing intensity of a hunting cat.

Several excited yips from only a few feet away broke the spell.

Completely unnerved, trembling inside, Sarah jumped as though she'd been struck.

'I think we've discovered our quarry, Miss Lynley,' Ravensdene observed softly, releasing her hand. His deep voice was rougher than usual, the purr more of a low growl, but Sarah scarcely noticed. She was still trying to cope with the knowledge that, in the moments before the barrage of barking started, she hadn't wanted to flee, screaming, from the garden.

Shaking her head in an effort to restore her scrambled wits, she scurried around the fountain after Ravensdene, her speed due more to rattled nerves than any great desire to find the cause of the disturbance, and skidded to a halt beside her host, who was calmly surveying the scene in front of them.

A large ginger cat sat atop the stone wall at the end of the path, diligently washing one paw, while totally ignoring the hysterical antics of the puppy below.

'Heavens, what a fuss!' Thankful for the chance to hide her flushed countenance, Sarah hurried forward to scoop up the excited puppy. 'No, you are not another cat to be running up walls,' she informed her captive, who promptly started licking her face in a frenzy of affection. She cuddled the little creature closer, not at all disturbed by the enthusiastic greeting. 'Yes, I know it is all very exciting, but you have been a very naughty dog. Stop that, sir. I do not need a bath at this moment.'

'You will if you allow him to kiss you all over like that.'

Ravensdene strode up to her and plucked the squirming bundle of fur from Sarah's unresisting arms. Alarm bells jangled once more in her head. His voice still held that slightly rough note and he had sounded almost abrupt. As if...

She must be going mad. Surely he couldn't have meant that he wanted to...

Oh, if only there was not a regiment of butterflies dancing a quadrille in her stomach she would be able to *think*.

'Miss Lynley?'

'What? Oh, I beg your pardon, my lord. Were you saying something?'

His mouth curved in a wry smile as she glanced distractedly up at him, but behind the rueful amusement in his eyes was a hint of something so tender it made her breath catch.

'Merely that I'm glad you still consider me to be a gentleman. Your opinion means a great deal to me.'

'Oh.' Sarah focused her eyes on her feet. 'As does yours. To me, I mean.'

She shivered, suddenly conscious of a yielding sensation deep inside her. As though by saying the words, something, some part of herself that had once been very closely guarded, had softened, leaving her as vulnerable and trembling as a baby fawn gazing upon the world for the first time.

'What is it?' he asked quietly.

'I. . . I was just thinking. . .' She looked up, bewildered, only to have her gaze caught by the sight of the puppy, now peacefully asleep in the crook of Ravensdene's arm. She stared in wonder at the sight. The puppy, too, was frail and vulnerable, and yet there it lay, so tiny and trusting, in the hold of a man who could be either predator or protector. But which? How did the puppy know? How could she tell? 'I was thinking of trust.'

'A gift I would treasure always,' he said very softly.

There was a heartbeat of silence. He was waiting, Sarah realised. But for what? *Her* trust? She had not been speaking so particularly. And yet, he waited. It was like being poised on the brink of discovery, she thought, without knowing precisely what it was she was about to discover.

Then, as frissons of alarm began rippling along her nerves again, Ravensdene's free hand appeared in her line of vision. 'Friends, Miss Lynley?'

Oh-h-h. Every tightly wound muscle in Sarah's body went limp with relief. *Friends*. Oh, yes! She wanted that more than anything, and if Ravensdene did also. . .

Her spirits, so low only minutes ago, soared to dizzy heights. She raised her eyes to his. 'Yes, of course, my lord,' she breathed. And, a brilliant smile lighting her face, she put her hand in his.

'Friends.'

CHAPTER TEN

'ARE you quite certain, my lord, that Uncle Jasper was
the white?' Sarah levelled her brows at the chessboard
in front of her and contemplated the fast-approaching
conclusion to Monday's chess match and her imminent
defeat. 'It seems to me that since I took his place, I have
been losing pieces with unprecedented speed.'

As if to prove her point, Ravensdene removed a
bishop with a deceptively simple strategy that she
suspected had been planned at least three moves ago.
She glared at him. 'I thought you said you were out of
practice.'

He grinned unrepentantly. 'It's all coming back to
me.'

'Is it?' she muttered. 'It all seems to be leaving me.'

She bent over to examine the board more closely
before shifting a pawn a cautious square forward.

'At least you still have your queen, Miss Lynley.
Which is more than can be said for me.'

'Since it was not I who relieved you of it, sir, that is
poor comfort indeed. I could wish Uncle Jasper had not
felt the need to retire, and not merely for his own sake.'

A soft laugh was her only answer. Ravensdene leaned
back in his chair, one hand toying idly with her captured
bishop while he considered his next move.

Sarah found herself studying the strong, elegant
fingers curled around the carved ivory chess piece. The
two very different qualities intrigued her. Like the rest
of him, his hand was big, its strength obvious. Indeed,
she had felt the power in those long fingers herself. On
more than one occasion.

But there was a fascinating masculine elegance, also,

in the fine shape of his hands and the length of his fingers. An elegance that told of restraint, and a self-control that would not easily be surrendered. It made her wonder just how gentle those powerful hands could be.

'Your move, Miss Lynley.'

'Oh!' Blushing hotly, Sarah jumped and peered with what she hoped passed for intense concentration at her few remaining troops. What on earth had possessed her to entertain such a thought? No wonder she was being wiped from the board.

'Hmm. I see you have moved your king, my lord.' Now that was a truly intelligent observation. Especially since she was supposed to have been watching.

'He was in grave danger of being threatened, Miss Lynley. By your queen.'

'Permit me to tell you, sir, that you look to be in an invincible position,' Sarah contradicted, finally getting her colour back under control. She could do nothing about the odd little shiver travelling up and down her spine. The strange phenomenon still seemed to occur whenever Ravensdene's voice lowered to that soft, gentle purr.

'Not entirely invincible,' he murmured. 'Actually the king is relatively helpless. He can only wait for the queen to come close enough for him to capture her.'

'If she doesn't capture him first.' Sarah met his eyes for an infinitesimal second. Why did she feel so breathless all of a sudden when they were merely discussing chess strategies?

At least, she thought that was what they were discussing. With Ravensdene she wasn't always sure. Since yesterday she had recalled too many occasions when a commonplace remark on his part seemed to have held some deeper meaning.

'Ah, but that is one of the risks of the game,' he said, watching with great interest as she made a reckless diagonal dash across the board with the queen in question. 'Dear me. An unusual move, Miss Lynley. Did you happen to notice this knight lurking over here?'

'Oh, no!' Sarah squeaked in dismay as she watched an undefended rook carried off. 'How very unfriendly of you, sir.'

'Yes, I know,' he admitted without the least sign of compunction. 'And after our pact yesterday, too.' His green eyes glinted devilishly. 'What now, Miss Lynley?'

She had to laugh at his unabashed air of triumph. 'I'm afraid white will have to concede, my lord. That was my last major piece apart from the queen, and you will soon have that surrounded. Oh, dear. How will I ever break the news of such a rout to Uncle Jasper?'

The wicked laughter faded from his eyes as he carefully put the white queen down on the board next to his king. 'Perhaps you were playing under the disadvantage of worrying about your uncle,' he suggested. 'Is it uncommon for him to rest during the afternoon?'

'Not uncommon, no.' Sarah frowned as she considered the question. She was glad Ravensdene had put such an interpretation on her absent-minded play, but now that she came to think of it, her uncle had appeared to be in reasonably good point when he had claimed weariness after a disturbed night and had retired to his chamber an hour ago.

Her frown deepened as she took in Ravensdene's casual pose. He didn't appear to be in any hurry to leave, despite the absence of either host or female chaperon. And now that she came to think about something else, she recalled her belated discovery in the middle of the night, of what had puzzled her about their conversation yesterday. Ravensdene had certainly admitted to raising a delicate subject in public surroundings, but he hadn't actually apologised for mentioning the subject in the first place. Or for interfering in what was essentially none of his business.

He was rather good at that, Sarah mused, sending him a quick, covert glance. Seeming to say something without saying it at all. It was a talent that made her somewhat nervous, despite his avowal of friendship. After all, she might not have been friends with a man before, but it was safe to say that such a relationship would be rather different to the one she had with Julia, for instance. Perhaps a still greater degree of clarity on a certain subject was in order.

'Uncle Jasper often has disturbed nights,' she explained, gathering her thoughts. 'And I must confess, my lord, that until recently, it did not occur to me that my future might be one of the matters keeping him awake.' She shook her head, genuinely remorseful. 'I don't know why I didn't see. . .'

Ravensdene spoke slowly, as though choosing his words, his gaze on the black king and white queen standing side by side in front of him. 'Sometimes, Miss Lynley, when one has nurtured an idea in one's mind for a long time, one cannot see the wood for the trees, so to speak. Sometimes a. . .considerable jolt is necessary, to make one aware of the possible alternatives.'

A jolt? Well, she had certainly received several of those lately.

'Yes, well, it has recently been brought home to me, my lord, that Uncle Jasper needs reassuring.' She paused half-expectantly, but the only change in Ravensdene's expression was the faintly amused curve to his hard mouth.

So much for a more specific apology, Sarah reflected wryly. She resigned herself to the inevitable, and got the rest out in a little rush. 'So I think I had better confess the truth about my reasons for entering Society.'

'The truth?' He looked up at that, clearly startled.

Sarah felt a quite illogical burst of satisfaction when his black brows drew together. At least she wasn't the only one experiencing jolts.

'That would certainly be interesting,' he stated rather forcibly. 'What, pray, *is* your real motive in entering Society?'

'I intend to make as many contacts as possible in order to apply for a position as a governess or house-keeper when—' she faltered momentarily '—when the time comes.'

'A *governess*? A *housekeeper*?' Nick mentally ran through the more probable fates that awaited a house-keeper who looked like Sarah. The pictures forming in his mind were not reassuring. In fact, given time and his suddenly fertile imagination, they threatened to grow to nightmarish proportions.

He cast a lowering glance at Sarah's incensed expression. The trouble was, of course, that the little innocent had no idea of just how damned alluring she was. Even when she was scowling at him, as she was now, his body was tense and throbbing with the fierce male urge to drag her into his arms and change her scowl to soft female surrender. As for what happened to him whenever she smiled—

'Is there anything wrong with that?' she demanded, pulling his thoughts back to the present discussion. 'They are respectable professions, you know.'

'Believe me,' he stated with undiplomatic frankness, 'no woman in her right mind would hire you as a governess.' Her mouth fell open but he swept on regardless. 'And what would you do if your male employer turned out to be not so respectable? Pull a pistol on him?'

Sarah had managed to close her mouth, but this was too much. She rose from her chair and turned an intimidatingly haughty glare on him. Unfortunately, Ravensdene chose to remain annoyingly unintimidated. He stood up also.

'There would be no need for such an action,' she retorted, hurriedly backing away a few steps so he couldn't tower over her. 'If I were to seek a post where a man was my employer, naturally it would be an older gentleman. As your mother observed yesterday, I am well able to cope with such persons.'

A smile crept into his eyes, startling her. 'Sarah, you sweet little idiot, how very innocent you are if you think a man's age would ensure your safety.'

'O-h-h!' Flushed and floundering, she didn't know which statement to attack first. 'I am *not*.... How... Well, if you have a better idea, my lord, I would be more than happy to hear it!'

He eyed her heightened colour for a moment, then strolled across the library to prop himself negligently against her uncle's desk. His hands curled around the edge on either side of his thighs.

'As a matter of fact, I do,' he said quietly. 'A better idea that will benefit all of us. It is, in fact, the second matter in which I was going to beg your assistance.'

Sarah took in the distance between them and the careless way he was leaning against the desk, and began to calm down. Perhaps he had a companion for his mother in mind; in which case it would not hurt to listen. She took a deep breath and resumed her seat, folding her hands primly in her lap. This time she would behave with dignity — no matter what he said.

'I am listening, my lord.'

He decided to ignore the exaggerated sweetness in her tone. 'It would involve a position much like the one you mentioned, Miss Lynley. You would be in charge of several establishments, you would be a most suitable companion to their owner, and your presence would also ensure the gentleman's, er, protection.'

'Protection?' she repeated, startled. 'I am not some sort of guard, sir.'

'That was not precisely what I meant.' He thought about it, then added with a grin, 'Pistols wouldn't be necessary. At least, I hope not.'

She ground her teeth. 'My lord, I believe you are making game of me. It is not at all—'

'Oh, *hell*!'

The exclamation was so explosive that Sarah broke off to stare. Ravensdene straightened and took a couple of steps towards the window, raking his fingers through his dark hair. Stunned at such uncharacteristic behaviour on his part, she was totally unprepared when he swung about, crossed the room in three quick strides and hunkered down before her, covering her hands with one of his.

'I'm making the most awful mull of this,' he murmured, a rueful smile in his eyes. 'Miss Lynley— Sarah. . .' His voice went deep and soft on her name. 'I am asking you to do me the very great honour of becoming my wife.'

Everything in the room went still. Including her heart. She couldn't answer, couldn't think. Her voice, her mind, her every faculty remained suspended in the moment when Ravensdene had asked her to marry him. Then tiny tremors began coursing through her, making her shiver imperceptibly.

His hand tightened over hers. 'I know you have set your mind against marriage,' he continued very gently. 'But would you consider it just for a moment? There are several advantages to both of us.'

'S. . .sev. . .'

'Yes.' He went on as if she had asked a perfectly intelligible question. 'I have already mentioned the benefits to me. For yourself, you would have the comfort of securing your uncle's peace of mind, and I can assure you that *you* would be a great deal more comfortable and secure as my wife than as a housekeeper or a governess.'

'What you say is perfectly true, my lord.' Her voice sounded terrifyingly faint but at least it was working again. If only her brain would do likewise. It was like groping about in a thick, swirling fog, Sarah thought. She couldn't see properly, couldn't reason, couldn't marshal any arguments to refute his logic. She wondered vaguely why she didn't just say no. No arguments. No reason. Thank you for the honour, my lord, but no.

The words floated about in her dazed mind, but somehow they couldn't seem to get past the locked muscles of her throat. It was very strange, because several other words were having no trouble whatsoever.

'You mentioned that I would be in charge of several establishments, that I would be a companion... To you?' she clarified.

He nodded, smiling faintly.

Not his mother. Sarah dismissed the notion and tried to complete the list he had given her, but her mind boggled anew at the notion of Ravensdene needing protection. If he did, then she was Prinny and the entire Carlton House Set rolled into one.

'What you have described, my lord, sounds rather like a marriage of convenience,' she ventured at last, conscious of a need to tread very warily.

'Yes, Miss Lynley, what I have described does sound rather like a marriage of convenience.'

She considered the statement, frowning slightly. As if sensing that his touch might be adding to her confusion, Ravensdene removed his hand, rose to his feet and sat down opposite her. His watchful gaze never left her face.

'A marriage of convenience, sir, usually means that a wife...or...or husband, of course...is not required to meet certain... That is to say, there are, I believe, certain marital—' she searched frantically for the right term '—*obligations*, that...'

'Miss Lynley,' he interposed softly. 'If you accept my offer, I promise you our marriage will have nothing to do with obligations.'

'Oh.' She blushed hotly and looked down. 'That is

very reassuring, of course, but have you considered fully? I mean, we discussed such arrangements yesterday, if you recall. You have a title and titled gentlemen usually require an heir or...or something.' Oh heavens, if a benign providence was listening, she would sink through the floor and vanish.

Benign providence was apparently short of hearing that day. She stayed where she was, aware that Ravensdene was watching every flow and ebb of colour, every nuance of expression that crossed her face.

'It's true that I haven't considered the need for an heir,' he agreed after a long silence. 'Probably because, being the second son, I never expected to inherit the title. However, the necessity still doesn't arise, Miss Lynley. Fortunately, I'm possessed of two younger brothers, one of whom is already married and the father of several offspring.'

The familiar gleam of amusement came into his eyes when Sarah risked a quick glance upwards. 'I can assure you that the line of Daltons is in no immediate danger of extinction.'

She had to smile at that, but she believed him. If Ravensdene's brothers were anything like him, they were probably exceptionally virile men. She blinked in startled reaction to a thought that was so utterly alien to her.

'Miss Lynley.' Ravensdene leaned forward, drawing her gaze back to him. He linked his fingers loosely on the chessboard between them and fixed her with a steady regard. 'Sarah, yesterday you denied you were afraid of me, but you still seem to have serious doubts. Please tell me how I may further reassure you that you will have nothing to fear from me.'

'Oh, it's not...' Searching her mind for a way to explain her hesitation, she thought again of Ravensdene's first wife. Why would a man who had once insisted on following his heart, now be equally determined on a marriage in name only?

Or perhaps that *was* why, Sarah reflected, conscious of a sharp little pang in the region of her heart. Because Marianne could not be replaced in quite the same way. After all, who could follow an angel?

The realisation was unexpectedly lowering.

'We have established your duties as chatelaine and companion,' he murmured, cutting through her confusion at the sudden direction of her thoughts. 'And disposed of my need for an heir. What else is there?'

Sarah could only look at him. His expression was polite, calm, almost remote, the brilliant intensity of his light green eyes shuttered by half-lowered lashes as he waited for her answer. At that moment she might have convinced herself that he posed not the slightest threat to her; but she had the very powerful impression of a hunter—waiting.

'I think you could be dangerous,' she blurted out.

'Not to you,' he denied at once. 'Never to you. Besides—' the wickedly boyish smile flashed out '—didn't you hear me say it was *I* who needed protection? How can you doubt it after yesterday's episode with the Smisbys?'

From a deep well of feminine pride that she had never suspected she possessed, Sarah managed to summon up a severe frown. It was no use trying to explain her misgivings. She would never be able to sort out such a jumbled mishmash of conflicting doubts and emotions, even if she could bring herself to mention Ravensdene's former marriage again, which was impossible.

Being made fun of, however, was a different matter.

'I daresay being pursued so relentlessly is vastly irritating, my lord,' she agreed tartly. 'But you are not exactly helpless. I cannot imagine why you would want to go to the trouble of marrying a female you don't—

In short, sir, I can think of no one in *less* need of protection—from anyone!'

She waited, half-prepared for an ironic or humorous rejoinder, but to her surprise Ravensdene studied her broodingly for a second, then rose and moved a few paces away to stand in front of the small fire burning in the fireplace beside the chess table. He leaned one hand on the mantlepiece and gazed down into the flames as if fascinated, but Sarah suspected his thoughts were quite divorced from firelight.

'If I'd come to Comberford merely to spend the summer,' he said, starting to speak so abruptly that she jumped, 'being pursued by ambitious females wouldn't matter. But—'

'But?' she prompted in a suspenseful whisper.

He turned to look at her. 'Sarah, whether or not you accept my offer, what I'm about to tell you must go no further than this room.'

'Of course not,' she breathed, eyes wide and fixed on his. 'But you don't have to. . .'

'I want to,' he said, and smiled fleetingly. 'You see, little one, I trust you.'

Was that supposed to mean he expected her trust in return?

She didn't have time to ponder the point. Ravensdene was speaking again, his gaze once more on the fire, his voice low.

'Did you ever hear anything of the Battle of Badajoz, Sarah?'

She frowned, not expecting such a seemingly unrelated question. 'Yes, a little. I read the reports in the papers at the time. There was a terrible loss of life.'

He nodded. 'Almost two thousand men fell in the first two hours in a space less than a hundred yards square. I saw it.'

He was seeing it now, Sarah thought. In his mind. Reliving that day almost three years ago. To her it had been printing on a page, tragic, but distant. He had been part of it, perhaps part of an unsuccessful attempt to prevent it.

Something throbbed again, sharp and painful near her heart. She wanted to go to him, to offer comfort, to relieve the memory somehow, but didn't know what to say. An experience like that would be years in the healing. She knew.

'But it needn't have happened like that if the men in charge hadn't received the wrong information,' he went on after a moment. 'Or rather, the correct information in time.'

'Information? You said something of the kind once before.'

'Yes.' He glanced at her briefly. 'The two incidents are years apart and unrelated, but I want you to understand that any sort of information in the wrong hands can make the difference between life and death for hundreds of men. And it's my job to make sure that military plans or correspondence between Wellington and the Foreign Office don't fall into those hands.'

'Your job?'

'Well, up until six months ago it was.' He gave a short laugh and looked directly at her, his eyes hard. 'I was very good at acquiring information as well. Perhaps you should know, Miss Lynley, that the gentleman whose offer you're contemplating was a spy.'

Did he think she would be repelled by the admission? On the contrary, Sarah realised with a small sense of shock. She already knew he was dangerous. Now she knew he had probably done things to get information from the other side that would likely give her nightmares, but she also knew, suddenly and without any doubt, that he had never indulged in any mindless, senseless violence. He was a man of honour, with a sense of integrity so deeply ingrained he would always be marked somewhere inside by what he had done, despite the lives he might have saved.

'That must have been very lonely,' she said softly. 'Dangerous, too.'

There was a flicker of surprise in his eyes before they went cool and watchful again. 'When you're young, danger has a seduction all its own,' he said evenly. 'But to return to the point, although Napoleon's capture last year put an end to the war, it didn't necessarily mean that other activities came to a halt. I was still on the continent myself until six months after my brother's death.'

Sarah nodded. 'And now that Napoleon has landed in France?'

'There's a possibility that someone who was passing information across the Channel from here will do so again.'

'A traitor,' she murmured, understanding instantly. 'That's what you meant the other day.' Then the rest sank in. 'Here! You're at Comberford to stop him?'

'Once I know who it is, yes.'

'O-h-h. No wonder you didn't want all the attention and. . .'

'Precisely. I have to admit, however, that some of the blame for it can be laid at my door. I shouldn't have brought my mother with me, but as I told Dev, I thought it would lend a touch of realism.'

'Lord Devenham knows?'

'Yes, and Figgins, my groom. And now you, Miss Lynley.'

She had a fleeting wish that he would call her Sarah again. 'Well, be assured, my lord, that I will not repeat anything of what you have told me. As for your offer. . .'

She thought he moved but wasn't sure. No, not movement, she amended. It was as if he was suddenly alert, every muscle taut as he waited for her answer. She realised her hands were gripped tightly together in her lap and tried to relax them. 'I have decided to accept.'

He watched her for an instant then said with a faintly harsh intonation, 'For England?'

'Isn't that why you offered for me?' she countered, unwilling to delve too deeply into her reasons for accepting his proposal.

'I can't deny that I had no thought of marriage before I came to Comberford,' he admitted. 'But there are other reasons, Sarah. My estates do need a mistress, but I don't look forward to the prospect of fending off matchmaking mamas or the like every time I have to set foot in town. A marriage between friends seems a much pleasanter solution to the problem.'

A marriage between friends.

Sarah waited for the quick rush of relief she had felt yesterday. It didn't come. Instead she was conscious of a sensation that felt perilously close to a let-down. She hurriedly told herself it was a normal reaction to the worry of making such a life-altering decision.

'Well, I, too, would never marry simply for reasons of patriotism,' she said, rallying herself to respond in kind. 'If you do truly wish for a chatelaine who is also a friend, sir, I would be happy to fill the position.' She looked up at him somewhat doubtfully. 'There is just. . .'

'Tell me.'

'I was thinking of Uncle Jasper, sir. I don't wish to leave him at this time, but I can see that your need for a wife is somewhat immediate. However, I suppose an *engagement*. . .if it was puffed off in the papers. . .'

'Sarah—' He broke off, a rueful smile curving his mouth as he came to sit at the table again. 'I have a confession to make,' he said, the smile reaching his eyes as he studied her increasingly wary expression. 'Your uncle gave me permission to address you some days ago and—'

'Oh! I knew it!' she exclaimed. 'I thought something

was going on when Uncle Jasper— But I interrupt you, my lord. I'm sorry. Please go on.' Sarah subsided in her chair and waited for the rest.

His green eyes were alight with devilment. 'I was going to say that Sir Jasper is eager for our marriage to take place once the banns are read. In three weeks, to be precise.'

'*Three weeks*!' Sarah's voice soared. Visions of announcements, visits, shopping, fittings and packing, all danced giddily about in her head. 'But I can't. . .'

'Nothing elaborate, of course,' Ravensdene went on as if this feeble protest had not been uttered. 'Our families and immediate friends only. The ceremony would take place in the village church, and we could then partake of a simple luncheon here before returning to Comberford. Naturally a honeymoon is out of the question, but under the circumstances it would not be a requirement in any case.'

'But—'

'And you need have no fear that I will remove you any great distance from your uncle. No matter how my task here falls out, I am quite content to spend the summer at the Place. If any business should arise at Ravensdene Hall that needs my attention, I would be gone for only a few days at a time.'

'That is very understanding of you, my lord,' Sarah managed in even fainter accents. 'But. . .three *weeks*!'

He looked at her, his eyes very clear and intent. 'Sarah, may I be frank?'

'You always are, my lord.'

A faint echo of his smile appeared then vanished. 'I find it saves time. But the fact is that time is something Sir Jasper may be short of, and he knows it. He is very anxious to see you wed, but in proper form, and without the comment that must arise if we were to procure a special licence.'

'I see.' Sarah mulled that over and knew he was right.

And though the blunt assessment of her uncle's health
could not but distress her, Ravensdene had given her
the means to make sure that Uncle Jasper's last months
would be free of worry. It all seemed very civilised and
efficient. No wild displays of emotion. No mad outbursts
of passion. No need, therefore, to fear an assault upon
her person.

She wondered why she still wasn't feeling any wild
outbursts of relief.

'Very well, my lord,' she agreed briskly, shaking off
her strange mood. 'Three weeks it is.'

'Good.' He smiled and held out his hand. 'That should
give you just enough time to practise calling me Nick.'

Sarah's lips parted. No sound emerged, however.
Instead she found herself suddenly short of breath. And
since she had put her hand in Ravensdene's before he
had finished, she suspected he knew as much.

She swallowed and tried again. 'Yes, of course, my
lord. I mean. . .that is. . . N. . . Nick.'

'Nearly perfect,' he growled softly, and, raising her
hand to his lips, he kissed her fingers.

CHAPTER ELEVEN

HER short engagement might have been considered by some to be enough time to practise calling her husband by his given name, Sarah reflected three weeks later as the door closed behind her maid, but it was difficult to practise when the person you were supposed to be practising on was hardly ever present.

Nor did it appear that the situation was likely to change, despite the wedding that had taken place only that morning. Ravensdene had certainly been attentive enough during the ceremony and the luncheon that had followed, but his gallantry had ended when they had arrived at Comberford Place some hours ago. After greeting the servants, lined up in a vast array to welcome their new mistress, the master of the house had retired to his library, only reappearing, briefly, to dine with her before wishing her a very polite goodnight.

Sarah had suddenly found herself feeling very much alone. She no longer had the daily care of her uncle; tomorrow Lord Devenham was escorting the Wribbonhalls and Julia to his ancestral home for a visit with his family; even the Dowager Lady Ravensdene had driven back to town that very afternoon.

And considering that Ravensdene wanted a companion, she found his behaviour rather odd and not a little disappointing. Her wedding night was not what she had expected.

On the other hand, since she had not wanted a wedding night in the first place, she could hardly complain that her husband was treating her with proper, if rather distant, courtesy. There was, in fact, no cause for complaint at all, she told herself as she turned to survey her new bedchamber.

The room, with its heavy, old-fashioned furniture, was too large to be described as cosy, but with a welcoming fire crackling in the grate and the wine-red velvet drapes curtaining the windows and high, four-poster bed, it looked warm and comfortable. The walls had recently been covered with an elegant rose and cream flowered paper, the design of which had been repeated in silk on the daybed and dressing-table stool. Branches of silver candelabra provided plenty of light and the bed was made up with a feather-down quilt and a small mountain of plump pillows.

Every consideration for her comfort had been provided. And given the circumstances, her wedding day had been all she had expected. She had been cosseted and fussed over as much as a bride could wish, surrounded by family and friends and familiar minions all day, and now the quiet of her bedchamber was exactly what she wanted. No doubt Ravensdene had assumed as much, except. . .

Frowning slightly, she crossed the room to stand before one of the windows that looked out over the woods and a corner of the lake. It was dark outside. Her reflection stared back at her, an ethereal, ghost-like figure in a negligee of shimmering pearl silk and lace.

She was feeling quite strange, Sarah thought broodingly. Slightly let down, and yet nervous, on edge—although she had no fears that Ravensdene would open the door connecting their rooms and demand his husbandly rights.

That was the problem.

The totally unexpected thought literally sent her reeling. Her legs tottered and she was leaning against the windowsill for support before she knew it. Good heavens! Had she run *mad*? What was she *thinking*? She didn't want to find herself fighting off unwanted advances from her new husband. Of course she didn't. It was just. . .

She had *missed* him.

Sarah shook her head and told herself not to be ridiculous. Just because she had rarely seen Ravensdene, except in company, during their brief engagement, did not mean she had any reason to feel so unaccountably low in spirits. No doubt he had been busy hunting for his traitor. She, herself, had been constantly occupied; it was probably exhaustion that was responsible for her odd mood.

In an effort to boost her spirits Sarah thought back over the past three weeks, reminding herself that she had coped exceedingly well with all the myriad tasks of arranging a wedding at such short notice. Why, she had even routed Sir Ponsonby Freem who, when news of the engagement had reached his ears, had had the objectionable gall to follow her home from the village, where he'd been staying at the inn, in order to object to a state of affairs of which he did not approve.

Sarah shivered slightly and wrapped her arms about herself as she recalled the unpleasant incident. After a lengthy consultation about the wedding ceremony with the Reverend Butterlow, she had steeled herself to take the shortcut home through the woods—without a pistol—only to become aware, before she had gone half a mile, that someone was following her. The very softest rustle of bushes behind her had been singularly unnerving, reminding her far too vividly of the two previous occasions when she had thought someone was watching her.

It had also, however, made her angry. Scowling furiously, she had wheeled about, hands on hips, one small foot tapping on the ground while she waited. A minute later Sir Ponsonby had plodded around the corner, mopping his brow with a large handkerchief, his bulk clearly not suited to hiking through woods.

She had had the fleeting thought that her shadow had sounded much closer, but had been so incensed by then that the notion was completely forgotten as she had launched into a diatribe that shredded Sir Ponsonby's character and morals beyond recognition, before concluding with a scathing condemnation of gentlemen who spied upon and harrassed ladies who had made it clear they wanted nothing whatever to do with them.

Sir Ponsonby had retired positively crushed, unable to get a word in edgewise to defend himself. And she had done it all herself, she recalled, suddenly more cheerful. Despite the fact that, when he had been informed of the encounter, Ravensdene had had several pithy words to say on the subject of her confronting importunate suitors while quite alone, the truth remained that she had rid herself of a nuisance male without any help from her panther.

Her pleased smile promptly vanished. When had she started thinking of Ravensdene as *her* panther? That sort of reasoning could become very dangerous indeed. She would do better to remind herself that panthers did not make particularly suitable domestic pets. One could not tame them.

The thought was depressing. Now she was back to feeling lonely again. Yes, that was it. She felt. . .lonely. She *had* missed Ravensdene's company. Had missed the sense of companionship they had shared, the gleam of amusement that could warm his eyes and soften the stern line of his mouth. Had even missed the way he issued her with orders and instructions.

A tiny sigh whispered past her lips. No doubt now that they were married that sense of companionship would return, but. . .

She wondered what he was doing right now; if he was alone, too, and thinking as she was.

* * *

She was finally alone. He heard the faint click as the outer door to Sarah's bedchamber closed behind her maid.

Nick stood at his window, staring out at the glimmer of moonlight that cut a swathe across one corner of the lake and tried to remind himself that more than a plaster wall separated him from Sarah. The reminder did nothing to alleviate the rigid tension invading every muscle in his body.

Just as well, he thought grimly. That tension was the only thing holding him in check. He didn't dare release it. Used to moving at blinding speed when his quarry was in sight, he now had to summon every ounce of patience he possessed so as not to frighten Sarah away.

He cursed softly, remembering that three weeks ago he had not anticipated any problem with control. Damn it, he'd never had a problem with control. But this afternoon, when it had finally struck him that Sarah was under his roof, within his reach, *his wife*, he'd had to lock himself in his library, prey to a totally unexpected, unrelenting, grinding *need*.

Not that a contemplation of his grandfather's collection of ancient tomes had done any good. Need had since coalesced into an equally unrelenting, agonising ache. God knew how he was going to get any sleep knowing Sarah was snuggled up in bed right next door.

A bitten-off groan escaped him at the image. He had to think of something else. It shouldn't be too difficult. After all, it wasn't as if Sarah was Marianne, and he was blindly in —

His thoughts skidded to an abrupt halt. Nick narrowed his eyes at the moonlit view in front of him. Funny where a man's mind could take him when he was strung out on a rack of frustration. He wanted Sarah. So badly he hadn't trusted himself to do more than dine with her tonight. He also felt a fierce need to protect her, to shield her from harm. But that was because she was his wife. A sweet, desirable, and very suitable wife. There was nothing else involved.

In fact, if he was going to stand here brooding, he would be more profitably engaged in pondering his spectacular lack of success in discovering more details about Amy Lynley's murder. His instincts told him there was more to the story than perhaps even Sarah realised, and he never ignored those instincts. However, Sir Jasper had been too distressed by the subject to discuss it at length, and when subtly questioned, Lady Wribbonhall had told him with unsubtle bluntness that the story would be better coming from Sarah if he would only be patient and gentle.

Patient and gentle. Right. He wondered what Sarah would say if he turned around this minute, strolled into the adjoining room and told her he'd come for a chat.

The idea had some merit—until he looked at the grim purpose in the hard face reflected in the window. She would never believe it. He didn't believe it himself. And if he didn't find a way of releasing some of his more primitive instincts, success would be as elusive as his sweet, desirable and very suitable wife.

'Good heavens, Winwick!' Sarah paused in the act of raising a slice of toast to her lips and stared towards the open window. After a night during which some very disturbing dreams had invaded her slumber, she had looked forward to a peaceful breakfast in company with her husband. Both husband and peace, however, were conspicuously absent. 'What on earth is that dreadful racket? It sounds like. . .'

'Shots,' supplied Winwick imperturbably, continuing to pour coffee as if hearing shots fired at the uncivilised hour of eight in the morning was a perfectly common-place occurrence. 'His lordship has been practising for some time.'

'Practising! Whatever for? A siege?'

'Not that I know of, my lady. His lordship likes to keep his eye in, so he says, but while her ladyship was staying here she banned the habit.'

'I can readily understand why.' Sarah put her toast down and rose, the purposeful light of battle in her eye. 'Obviously his lordship is unused to having gently bred females in the house.'

Winwick permitted himself a tiny, satisfied smile. 'You will find the target set up in the garden furthest from the stables, my lady,' he instructed as she marched out of the room. 'His lordship didn't want the horses upset.'

'Didn't want the horses upset,' Sarah muttered, stalking towards the garden where she and Ravensdene had found the puppy. 'Are horses supposed to be more delicately—?'

Two more blasts in quick succession drowned her out as she reached her destination, but it hardly mattered. The sight that met her eyes had temporarily deprived her of speech anyway.

A target had been set up against the wall at the end of the long path, and standing an impressive number of yards from it, his back to her, was Ravensdene, a pistol in each hand.

Sarah's eyes widened as he brought both weapons up and fired them almost simultaneously. She had often watched her uncle try his marksmanship with the guns in his collection, but in the way Ravensdene was standing there, methodically sending ball after ball into the centre of the target, she saw a cold, deadly efficiency that chilled her to the bone.

When silence fell again she couldn't think of a thing to say.

'I'm sorry if the noise disturbed you, little one,' he said, turning to face her. 'How are you this morning?'

The polite enquiry, coming after such a demonstration of lethal skill, was strangely shocking. Sarah had to struggle for a full minute to regain her sense of outrage, not to mention her voice. She didn't bother asking how he'd known she was there.

'What do you think you are doing, my lord?'

'Testing these new double-barrelled pistols,' he replied casually, squinting down the barrels of the gun in his left hand. 'You have to shift the aim slightly for the second shot or it tends to fire low.'

Her blood was still running cold and he was discussing the merits of double-barrelled pistols? She glared at him. 'How very inconvenient.'

'Yes, I knew you'd understand, being such a crack shot yourself.' He looked up and grinned. 'Come and try it. I'll reload for you.'

'Uh. . . I don't think. . .'

'We can move a bit closer to the target if you like. I wouldn't want to have you at a disadvantage.'

'Have me at— Give me the gun!' Sarah was marching forward before she thought better of it, but if her eyesight was keen enough to glue pieces of shell together, she reasoned defiantly, then she could hit a much larger target with a gun.

'Here you are. I've loaded only one barrel, but that should be enough for you.'

'Thank you, my lord. Good heavens, it weighs a ton!' The pistol dangling from her hand felt more like a cannon.

'They are heavier than your usual weapon,' Ravensdene observed, with what she considered to be a diabolical smile. A hideous suspicion began to dawn on her, but he spoke again before she could put it into words. 'Here, use both hands—like this.'

He moved to stand directly behind her, reaching around to put his hands under her wrists to brace them. Gritting her teeth, Sarah managed to raise the pistol to chest height.

'I'll take some of the weight,' he murmured in her ear. 'You just aim and pull the trigger.'

Just aim and pull the trigger? How had she ever managed to get herself into this situation? She couldn't even get her fingers to move; the muscles of her arms were too busy melting beneath the warmth of Ravensdene's hands. The rest of her was not faring any better. He felt huge behind her. Huge and solid, as unyielding as the high brick wall behind the target; and she was caged within his arms, surrounded, his sheer size alone enough to send all her senses into a turmoil.

'Do you need any help?' he asked.

Help? Of course she needed help! That dark purr, so close to her ear, turned every limb to water. If he wasn't virtually supporting her, she would collapse in a heap right there at his feet.

The image was positively humiliating. Bracing herself, Sarah squeezed her eyes shut and jerked her fingers convulsively on the trigger. There was a deafening roar, followed by a small startled shriek as she was sent staggering back by the recoil.

Dropping the pistol, she whirled and clutched at Ravensdene's coat in an effort to steady herself. And was immediately stunned by an intense longing to nestle closer as his arms came around her, to have him hold her more securely. There was strength here. Strength and safety. Here in his arms she was sheltered, protected.

'You missed,' he said.

Something in his satisfied tone got through the reverberations still ringing in her ears. Sarah stiffened as a blush rose from her toes to her brow. Here she was thinking about being cuddled by Ravensdene when all *he* was interested in was—

'Revenge!' she exclaimed, raising her head to glare up at him. 'Oh, you wretch! You knew I'd never fired a gun in my life, didn't you? Don't you dare laugh at me like that.'

His mouth twitched. 'You may have noticed, my sweet, that a laugh has not crossed my lips.'

'You're laughing with your eyes.'

He seemed to go very still, his eyes darkening even as she watched. Sarah stared, fascinated. She hadn't known a man's eyes could do that, go from glittering ice-green to a jade so dark it was almost black. His voice was darker, too. Deeper, rougher, it stroked over her heightened senses like a gentle hand, leaving a shivery kind of heat in its wake.

'Am I, Sarah?'

Sarah suddenly remembered how close they were, how she had wanted to be closer. But even as she felt her heart begin to flutter wildly, her colour fluctuate, Ravensdene released her and stepped back a pace.

'I'm afraid I couldn't resist seeing if you'd go through with it,' he confessed, turning away to retrieve his pistol. 'But I should have known. You don't lack for courage, Sarah.'

The words were uttered lightly, but she felt a distinct sensation of tension. As if the air surrounding him was vibrating slightly. Or perhaps it was her, still trembling.

'I don't?'

'No. It gives me great hope.'

'For what?'

He didn't answer or even glance her way, but his smile was slow, almost lazy, as he concentrated on pushing a ball into the chamber of the weapon he held. The sight of that smile caused something to stir deep inside her. Something that was not lazy at all.

'How. . .how did you know I had never fired a pistol, sir?' she stammered.

'It wasn't difficult. No experienced markswoman would take a pistol from someone and stuff it into her reticule without first checking to see if it was loaded.'

'Oh. Uncle Jasper's pistol.' She remembered the episode in his library. 'Very clever, my lord. Dear me, how long ago that seems.'

'An age.'

'Well, I wouldn't put it quite like that, but— What are you doing? I have to tell you, my lord, that if you are loading those pistols again with a view to firing them, I shall object most strongly. I do not intend to eat my breakfast to the accompaniment of shots. You will cease and desist at once.'

'I will?'

'Yes. I do not approve of violent pastimes.'

'Very wifely. But the exercise serves to release some rather, er, primitive instincts, you know.'

'Exercise? You were just standing there.' She shivered faintly at the remembered impression of a lethal, unstoppable force. 'If you feel the need for exercise, my lord, you will have to do something else.'

'Something else?' he murmured. The lazy smile came back. 'Do you have any suggestions, my love?'

'Winwick, from now on, when his lordship is practising his shots, we shall have the windows closed.'

'Yes, my lady.'

'No doubt we shall all grow accustomed to the noise.'

'If you say so, my lady.'

'Perhaps I could persuade him to take up cricket instead, if he feels the need to hit something.'

'I would not recommend it, my lady.'

'Well, I know his lordship once broke a window in here, but—'

'Worse, my lady. The ball also shattered his late lordship's coffee cup. He had been about to take a sip from it at the time.'

'Oh. No cricket.'

* * *

'I thought you said there were fish in this lake, my lord.'

'There are, but you have to cultivate a little patience. Stop complaining. It was you who wanted me to take up something quiet, remember? And you called me my lord again.'

'Oh. Well, sitting about in a boat for hours, while not being allowed to utter a word for fear of scaring the fish, is going to the other extreme, sir. . . I mean, Nick.'

'Hmm. There's definitely room for improvement.'

'No, Sarah. You have to hold the horseshoe like this.'

'But it feels so awkward.'

'Not as awkward as it's going to be if you hit me instead of the spike.'

'Really, Nicholas, how can I hit you when you're standing right behind me?'

'Don't call me Nicholas.'

'Your mother does.'

'Only when she wants to annoy me.'

'Oh. Well, Nick, then.'

'Better, but I think there's still a little way to go. Tell me, my love, have you ever driven a high-perch phaeton?'

'I don't think this is the proper way to drive a high-perch phaeton and pair, sir.'

'Probably not, but at least we won't end up in the ditch.'

'But what will people think if they see us driving about with your arms around me?'

'They'll think we're happily married.'

'Oh. Are you happy, Nick?'

'Yes, little one. That was excellent, by the way. I think we're ready to try a variation on the theme.'

'What? But I didn't do anything.'

'Patience, my love, patience.'

'Patience?'

'Trust me. These past few days I've become an expert
on the subject.'

'Nick, what *are* you talking about?'

'Later.'

But the trouble was, Nick decided the day after the
driving lesson, it was 'later' that was going to take his
self-control to the very edge.

He sat back in his corner of the carriage and watched
Sarah arrange the skirts of her antique-gold, braided
and frogged pelisse neatly about her ankles. A matching
antique-gold bonnet framed her face, its jaunty sable
plume curling forward to mingle with her curls. The
sight of the feather almost caressing her soft cheek made
him want to wrench the whole thing off and do some
mingling himself.

He managed to cage his instincts. By dint of long
midnight walks through the woods and cold, early
morning dips in the lake he had so far kept his desire for
Sarah under some semblance of control, and he wasn't
going to ruin everything now because of a provocative
feather. Unfortunately, his restraint, not to mention the
more physical exertions he had inflicted upon himself,
had also succeeded in honing his body to an even
harder, more painful edge. Before another week was
out he was probably going to be driven insane.

But he would do it, Nick swore silently. He had been
given a taste of success in the knowledge that Sarah no
longer retreated from his touch. The next step was to
awaken her to the possibility of a deeper intimacy than
friendship. To awaken her slowly, carefully, with all the
gentleness she needed before she could give herself to
him completely, no matter what it cost him in willpower.
Because this past week had shown him something else.

The marriage he now wanted with her had become
too necessary for him to even contemplate failure.

'Do you know something, Nick?' Sarah stopped

fussing with her skirts and bent a severe frown upon him. 'When you said "later" I thought you were going to teach me an exciting new skill such as taking a fly off the leader's ear with my whip, but instead we're driving sedately along in a closed carriage.'

'Mmm-hmm.'

'That is not an answer. Why could we not have ridden over to visit Uncle Jasper?'

'Have I told you that you make a very charming countess, Sarah? Dictatorial, of course, but charming.'

'Dictatorial! I wish you will not go off at a tangent when I am talking to you, my lord. It is most distracting.'

He grinned. He didn't even mind her calling him 'my lord' now, he realised, when she said it in that delight- fully disapproving tone. 'I am very sorry, my sweet, but to tell you the truth, I have a rather tricky question on my mind.'

Sarah was promptly distracted. She blinked at him in surprise, having no trouble, even in the muted light of the carriage, in seeing the devilish gleam in her husband's eyes. 'You do? Good heavens, whatever can it be?'

His grin became another of those slow, lazy smiles. 'I was trying to decide whether or not to kiss you. And if I do, whether that extremely fetching bonnet would be in danger of coming loose and striking me.'

Sarah was quite sure her mouth had fallen open. 'You were trying to decide. . .'

She could go no further. Her mind was quite unequal to the task of expressing the utter confusion of her thoughts.

'Yes.' Ravensdene reached out and took one of her hands in his. Still stunned, she let it lie limply in his grasp, even when he slipped his thumb beneath her glove and began stroking the inside of her wrist.

'It is quite permissable to kiss one's wife, you know. In a friendly, affectionate kind of way, of course.'

'Of. . .of course,' she echoed faintly. It was amazing how the light stroking of his thumb against her flesh could play such havoc with her thought processes. She should be feeling at least a little alarmed at the thought of Nick kissing her. Her heart was, indeed, beating rapidly somewhere in her throat, but all she could think of was the past week, in which she had known nothing but gentleness from him, and that sweet sense of companionship that drew her closer to him with every day they spent together.

And now he wanted to kiss her.

'Um. . .well, if you would like. . .that is to say, my bonnet is really quite secure, Nick.'

'In that case. . .' he murmured. And leaning closer, he brushed his lips over hers in a caress so light she barely felt it.

'Oh.' The tiny sound of disappointment escaped her before she realised he had moved back only a few inches. Blushing, tremulous, suddenly more uncertain than she had ever been in her life, she waited.

'Close your eyes,' he ordered huskily.

She obeyed. For an instant a feeling of defenceless-ness threatened to overwhelm her, but then she felt Nick's mouth on hers again and warmth banished the sudden attack of nerves. This time he lingered, letting her absorb the sensations of his lips pressed lightly to hers, the gentle caress of his breath across her mouth, the shimmering heat rippling upwards from the touch of his fingers on her wrist.

When he drew back again she was feeling quite inexplicably witless. Her eyes flew open to find him watching her.

'That was. . .very friendly,' she managed to utter in a voice completely unlike her own.

'Did you like it?'

'Well. . .yes. . .that is. . .'

'You don't sound very certain.'

'I suppose that is because I'm not used to such activities, my lord.'

'Oh, no,' he growled. 'You're not going to retreat behind "my lord" this time, sweet Sarah.' His glittering eyes, deepest emerald in the shadowy carriage, looked straight into hers. 'I see I shall have to kiss you again so you can make up your mind.'

Her gaze held by his, Sarah could only manage a small nod of agreement. 'That would be very helpful,' she whispered, just before his mouth covered hers.

His lips were slightly parted. She felt the difference immediately, and was as instantly shaken by an impulse to part her own. She trembled, torn between shyness and the delicious feeling of his mouth moving gently on hers. Somewhere in the back of her mind she doubted if any amount of kisses would clear the confused mists from her brain, because each kiss was so much more than the last. Sweeter. Warmer. Oh, the warmth, seeping through her bloodstream until she felt as if she might melt.

Then just before he drew back, she felt the tip of his tongue trace the line between her lips and the warmth became a sharp little explosion of heat striking deep inside her.

'I believe we have arrived,' Nick murmured, releasing her wrist and reaching for the door.

Sarah blinked. His voice held the intriguingly rough note she had heard once before, but the words were so commonplace that for several seconds her whirling mind could hardly make sense of them. 'Arrived?' She gazed blankly at the portico of the Grange. 'Oh dear, I do hope Uncle Jasper doesn't wish to play chess.'

Uncle Jasper did wish to play chess, but, to Sarah's relief, he was happy to challenge Ravensdene to a match. It was just as well, she reflected, watching them from her seat by the fire, because when she made an observation on the game that immediately caused her husband to grin and her uncle to stare at her as if he'd never seen her before, it became perfectly obvious that she was still in a fuzz-brained trance.

Matters had not improved two hours later when she mounted into the carriage for the ride home. Fortunately, her uncle had not seemed unduly worried by her distracted state. In fact, when she leaned forward to wave farewell, she decided he was looking particularly pleased with himself.

'Sir Jasper seemed quite well,' Nick observed, echoing her thoughts as the landau swept through the gates.

'Positively beaming,' Sarah agreed absently. She supposed she should feel rather more concerned that her voice still sounded as if she wasn't quite there, but she had just discovered something else even more astonishing. Being alone again with Nick in the close confines of the carriage was giving her some very unfamiliar, not to say shocking, ideas.

'Nick?'

'Hmm?'

She studied the reticule on her lap with rapt attention while twisting the ribbons around and around her fingers. 'Now that you have kissed me in a friendly, affectionate kind of way, do you suppose we shall exchange many more. . .um. . .?'

'Many more such kisses?' he concluded for her. She could feel his gaze on her face. 'Do you dislike the notion?'

'Oh, no! I would be very happy to. . . That is, such kisses do not have anything to do with. . .with those obligations we spoke of. Do they?'

He reached across the small space between them and covered her restless hands with one of his. 'Sarah, I made this promise to you once before. Nothing of what we share will have anything obligatory about it.'

'Oh.' She sent him a shy glance from beneath her bonnet. 'What we share. That sounds so very agreeable, Nick.'

'Does it, little one? Does that mean you would like to share another kiss before we arrive home?'

'Yes, I would,' she breathed, her gaze now locked with his. 'I would like that very much indeed.'

'So would I,' he murmured in a soft rasp that was like a cat's tongue stroking down her spine. Or a panther's tongue, she thought, quivering at the memory of his tongue lightly tracing the seam of her lips.

'But this time—' he moved closer, studying the elaborate gold bow holding the ribbons of her bonnet in place under one ear '—we'll dispense with this.'

Sarah couldn't stop the breathless little gasp that escaped her lips as his fingers brushed the side of her throat. Nick's expression didn't change, but she felt a hard tension invade the hand still covering hers, an almost violent restraint, as though he had been about to tighten his grip at the small sound and had stopped himself in time.

Was he so wary of frightening her, she wondered, awed by the notion? Then the question vanished from her mind when he removed her bonnet and placed it on the opposite seat.

'You won't need this either,' he said softly, taking the reticule from between her clenched fingers and tossing it after her bonnet.

She trembled, suddenly feeling defenceless again. As if a bonnet and a reticule were any sort of protection, she thought, raising eyes wide with uncertainty to his.

'It's all right, little one,' he murmured. He touched the side of her face, his fingers incredibly gentle as he traced the curve of her ear, the delicate line of her jaw, the sensitive flesh just beneath.

Sarah's eyes half-closed, her lips parting on a tiny sigh of pleasure. She felt as if she was melting, all her limbs turning to warm honey.

'Sarah,' he whispered, making her look up at him.

He nearly groaned aloud when he saw the first signs of awakening desire in her eyes. And she didn't even know it, he thought. Didn't know what she was doing to him. Didn't know what she herself was feeling.

'I'm barely touching you,' he ground out, shaken by

the sweet innocence of her response to the light caresses. 'Barely touching. . .'

'Nick?' It was a soft cry of nervousness and need.

'Yes,' he murmured against her lips. 'Like this, sweetheart.'

He brushed his mouth over hers again very gently, waiting for the tension to leave her body. Slowly her lashes closed, silky soft against his lips when he kissed them. He kissed her brows, her cheeks, the delicious curve of her upper lip and with every undemanding caress he felt her soften, felt her give more of her trust, until he drew her closer and she was in his arms, willingly, at last.

'You're so sweet,' he breathed. 'Sweet Sarah.'

'Nick?' she cried again. She sounded dazed, but the nervousness was gone. Her lashes fluttered open. 'You said you would kiss me.'

Despite the raging need pounding in his veins, he smiled down at her.

'I am kissing you.'

'No.' A faint blush tinted her cheeks. 'Like you did before.'

Good heavens, she thought weakly. What had he done to her? But she was too enthralled by the promise of feeling that exciting little sunburst of heat again to be shocked by her boldness.

He lowered his mouth until their lips were just touching. 'With my tongue?' he asked in the softest whisper.

She shivered convulsively, the words alone enough to cause tiny arrows of fire to dart about inside her, and without warning the pressure of his mouth increased as he tasted her lips with a gentle probing touch that made her limbs go weak. This time the tingling explosion of heat had her clinging to him. Her lips parted, seemingly of their own volition and he was inside her mouth, touching, stroking, possessing.

Sarah gave a muffled cry of shock, feeling the impact of the invasion with every part of her being.

He withdrew at once, soothing her with fleeting little kisses that feathered over her eyes and cheeks before returning to her mouth.

'It's all right, sweetheart,' he murmured. 'Don't be afraid. I'm only kissing you. Only kissing you, little one. You'll like it, I promise.'

'Nick, I—'

'Yes. Just like that. Let me taste you, Sarah. I won't hurt you. Let me—'

No, he wouldn't hurt her. She didn't know why she was so sure of that. He could be violent, deadly, but in the urgent, husky tone of his voice she heard a plea she responded to instinctively. A plea that reached everything that was intensely feminine in her.

She trembled as he drew back far enough to look down into her face. She raised dazed eyes to his, wondering what she would see there.

Darkness. His eyes were so dark, blazing with a green fire that in one searing second had touched her senses, reached into the closed place in her mind, awakened something so deeply buried she hadn't known it existed.

'Do you want me to stop?' he asked, his voice low and tense with restraint.

Yes, restraint, she thought wonderingly. He was in control. He hadn't hurt her. Had not even frightened her, apart from that one moment in which she had felt more startled than truly afraid.

'No.' Her lips framed the word. No sound came out, but he understood. The fire in his eyes seemed to flare higher, reaching out to enfold her as he bent to kiss her again.

And then she couldn't see his eyes at all, because her lashes fluttered down as his mouth closed gently over hers.

CHAPTER TWELVE

THOSE kisses on the way home had really been quite extraordinary, Sarah reflected two days later as she arranged her collection of shells on the window ledges in the library. Not only had they taken over a large portion of her mind, rendering her prone to fits of abstraction at rather inconvenient moments, but just thinking about them stirred faint echoes of the deliciously thrilling sensations they had aroused.

Unfortunately, echoes were all she had. Since the interesting excursion to the Grange the other day, Nick had kissed her several times. Light good-morning kisses when they met at the breakfast table. Friendly good-night kisses when she left him in his library on her way to bed. And brief, affectionate kisses at various times in between. They were not, however, anything like the kisses on the way home.

She was very much afraid that those particular kisses were addictive. She wanted more. But Nick hadn't given her more. Despite the fact that she had done everything possible to tempt him, from shifting subtly closer whenever they were together, to touching him with shy, fleeting little forays of her hands at every opportunity. Neither method had worked. As far as she could see, he hadn't even noticed her tentative encouragement.

On the other hand, she could hardly blame him. She, herself, didn't fully understand why she should want to encourage him in the first place.

Sarah stepped back to see the effect of two large spiralled shells on the ledge behind Nick's desk, while her mind continued along a path that was far removed from shells.

She should have felt threatened, afraid, uneasy at the very least, at the thought of further intimacy with her husband. After all, it was not as if she wasn't aware of the dangers inherent in the subtle change in their relationship.

But she was changing, too. Something was happening to her. Something that had started weeks ago when she had encountered a man of brutal strength and lethal speed, and even through her almost mindless terror, had believed him when he said he wouldn't hurt her.

Was that the difference? she wondered, struggling to follow her line of reasoning to some sort of logical conclusion. Was the relationship between a man and a woman a simple matter of trust? She thought of all the married women of her acquaintance, and realised with rather startled bewilderment at not having seen it before, that they all seemed to have survived the experience. And in the case of Lydia Beresford, whom she had met again during her engagement, rather more than survived.

But then what of Amy? Had her sister trusted and been betrayed? Or had Amy's flirtation with a man who was bigger and stronger than her been nothing more than the poor judgement of a wilful, headstrong girl; a moment of foolishness that had cost her her life?

'You are looking very solemn, my love. What has put such a frown on your brow?'

Sarah glanced up, her breath coming a little faster at the familiar deep tones, as Nick strode into the library, closed the door behind him and walked over to join her at the desk. His green eyes narrowed on the newly adorned ledge.

'Ah, I see you've found a home for more of your shells,' he observed blandly. 'What a good thing we have plenty of window ledges at the Place. I feared I would be obliged to resort to smashing some of the collection, accidentally of course, before we were overrun.'

Despite her unnervingly uneven pulse, Sarah had to laugh. Her amusement promptly vanished, however, when Nick bent to kiss the tip of her nose. A quick, friendly kiss. She had a sudden, insane impulse to demand to know why a man who was clearly at the peak of his masculine strength and power was content with a marriage of convenience.

Then she wasn't at all sure she wanted to hear the answer.

'There will be no more smashing of shells,' she said severely, taking refuge in raillery. 'Really, Nick, I had no idea that males were prey to such constant violent impulses. It must be extremely wear—'

She stopped dead, abruptly aware of what she had said.

He looked down at her, eyes narrowed again, searching. 'Indeed? I thought you were of the opinion that males were nothing else but violent.'

Sarah felt herself blush. She knew he was watching her with the waiting intensity that always reminded her of a big hunting cat, but she couldn't prevent her gaze going to his mouth. 'I know better now,' she whispered, conscious of her heart beating wildly in her breast. Something akin to panic fled down her spine. She hadn't intended to say that! At least not until she'd done a great deal more thinking. Those four little words could hold a myriad of meanings and she wasn't sure how Nick would take them. How could she be? She didn't know precisely how she had *meant* them.

Blushing more hotly than ever, she rushed into speech once more. 'I see you have some letters, my lord. Is there a note from Julia, or Lydia Beresford perhaps? She was going to write when they were all settled at Devenham Court. How very kind it was of Lord Devenham to invite the Beresfords to join his party. Especially as the purpose of the visit is for Julia and the Wribbonhalls to meet his mama and sisters.'

Nick didn't answer. He was too engrossed with the
delicate tide of colour sweeping from Sarah's brow to
the neckline of her dainty muslin dress, and in tormenting himself with images of his mouth following the same
path. He wondered if the blush went as far as her breasts
and nearly groaned aloud at the swift stab of desire that
tightened his loins.

He wasn't used to restraint, damn it. These past few
days had been sheer torture. He had forced himself to
respond only casually to Sarah's shy, innocent advances
in the hope of winning more of her trust, but he had
discovered a rather fatal flaw in his scheme. The feel of
her small hands on him played havoc with his already
over-strained senses. His self-control was shot to pieces.
Sarah now only had to brush past him and his entire
body would clench in a spasm of need. But if he allowed
himself to start making love to her in his present state
and she called a halt, which was all too likely in *her*
present state, he wasn't at all certain he would be able to
stop.

Then he looked down into her clear amber eyes, their
expression doubtful, half-wary, questioning his long
silence, and knew he would always stop if she wished it.
If it tore him apart he would stop.

'No, there's nothing from Devenham Court,' he
forced himself to say, dragging his reluctant gaze back
to the mail in his hand. The long-term picture, he
reminded himself again. He also had a job to do. He'd
never had any trouble concentrating on a job before.
Why was it so damned difficult now? 'Only a letter from
London, some correspondence from my agent at
Ravensdene Hall and a note from the Sheringtons
reminding us of their waltzing party later this week.'

'The Sheringtons' waltzing party?' she repeated,
sounding so dismayed that the urge to toss the mail
aside, take her in his arms and savour the sweet taste of
her deliciously soft mouth again before he went out of

his mind, was effectively doused. For the moment, at least.

'Nick, I think I should tell you—'

She broke off, overcome by a fit of coughing as Nick produced a heavily scented, gilt-edged invitation card and held it at arm's length. 'Here it is,' he murmured, grimacing. 'Reeks of jasmine.'

'Sophie's favourite perfume,' Sarah managed weakly, catching her breath at last. 'Nick, about the waltzing party—'

'We don't need to attend if you would truly dislike it. No one expects us to engage on a social whirl at this time. I'm sure Miss Sherington merely sent the reminder as a courtesy.'

'But you wish to go,' she murmured, seeing the truth in the faint frown drawing his brows together as he perused the note. And she knew he didn't wish to attend the party out of any desire to socialise; it was part of his job. The sudden intrusive reminder came as an unpleasant jolt. She was startled at the twinge of resentment she felt that his attention was so obviously elsewhere.

'Sherington Chase is the only estate of any size that I've yet to visit,' he explained almost absently. Then, as if suddenly recalling her presence, 'Not that I suspect Lord Sherington particularly, but they live near the coast and our presence will give Figgins an opportunity to listen to any stable talk that may prove useful.'

'Especially as all the coachmen and grooms on the neighbouring estates have families who make their living from the sea,' Sarah added, forcing herself to match his cool tone. 'But you misunderstood me, Nick. It is not that I don't wish to go, precisely, but. . .the problem is that I do not waltz.'

'Good God, is that all? Don't concern yourself over the matter. The only man you'll be permitted to waltz with will be me.'

This unexpected but comprehensive edict had the totally predictable effect of once more robbing Sarah of breath. Especially as it was issued while its instigator was now glancing through the accounts from Ravensdene Hall.

'Well, I do not know how I am supposed to take that, my lord, but you still do not—'

The glittering intensity of his eyes when he turned his gaze on her was enough to make her forget the rest. All at once she had his undivided, utterly focused attention.

'It's called possessiveness,' he growled very softly. 'Get accustomed to it.'

Sarah's jaw dropped. Her mind reeled. *Possessiveness*? From a man who had been treating her like a *sister* for the past two days? Her vague feeling of irritation exploded into fully fledged outrage.

'Please do not put yourself to the trouble of exerting so much emotion on my behalf, my lord,' she stated haughtily, turning on her heel and beginning to stalk out of the room. 'If you had let me finish a moment ago, you would have heard me say that I do not waltz because I have never learned the steps, not because I wish to reserve the dance for my husband. Now, if you will excuse me, I will— *Nick*!'

Her startled cry was drowned out by the slamming of the door she had just opened. Sarah blinked at the sight of her husband, his large hand flat on the oak panels, barring her way, when she had left him at the other end of the library. He must have moved like lightning, she thought dazedly.

For a second his eyes held an expression that sent shivers racing all the way down her spine. She knew she had nothing to fear from him, but she had a sudden chilling vision of what was likely to happen to the traitor when Nick caught up with him. Then his face relaxed into a crooked, rueful smile that held its own particular dangers.

'Oh, sweetheart, don't look at me as if I'm about to attack you. I'm sorry. I'm afraid I've been guilty of venting my frustrations on you.' He removed his hand from the door and cupped the side of her face. 'Sarah, don't you know by now that I wouldn't hurt you for the world?'

'Frustrations?' she queried cautiously, not committing herself to answering that last loaded question until she knew just what frustrations he was referring to.

'Yes.' He seemed to hesitate, then glanced past her, indicating his abandoned correspondence with a quick movement of his head. 'I've just had word from London that, so far, no one has taken the bait they so optimistically left dangling in the files at the Foreign Office.'

'Oh.'

'Yes, "oh" is about all one can say on the subject. And since none of the local inhabitants have behaved in a suspicious manner, things have ground to an extremely irritating halt. It's a poor excuse for growling at you, I know, but—' the fingers against her cheek curled inwards, stroking her before he let his hand fall '—will you forgive me?'

'Well. . .' Sarah watched the hand that had touched her so gently clench into a tight fist at his side, and felt her pulse start to race as a rather daring idea occurred to her. 'Perhaps we could make a bargain, my lord?'

One black brow went up. He tilted his head, the glance he slanted down at her full of amused speculation. 'Bargain away, little one.'

Sarah swallowed the sudden knot in her throat. 'I'll forgive you, if you teach me to waltz,' she said, feeling quite uncharacteristically reckless. The slow smile he gave her made her wonder if she had just lost her normally sensible wits.

'Done,' he murmured before she could retract the offer. He held out his hand and bowed.

'*Now*?' she squeaked.

'Why not? Will you do me the honour, my lady?'

Well, when he put it like that. . .

Sarah smiled quite brilliantly and, remembering her observations at the Assembly, extended her left hand to his right. 'I should be delighted, my lord.'

Her formal manner and brilliant smile were then immediately shattered when Nick passed his left arm around her waist, drew her close and raised their clasped hands above their heads. Since he was so much taller than her the position had her arm stretching quite high. A feeling of intense vulnerability swept over her. His hand was warm and large, curved against her waist. He would only have to move it a little higher, she thought, shivering inwardly, for his thumb to brush the underside of her breast. And she would be unable to do anything to stop him.

She wished she knew if her shivers were shivers of alarm or excitement.

'Do you wish to hum a refrain?' he asked, with what she considered to be quite heartless ignorance of the fraught state of her nerves. 'Or shall we just go through the steps?'

'I think. . .just the steps,' Sarah managed through dry lips. She knew she was blushing hotly, but whether it was the relative helplessness of her position, her embarrassingly heated thoughts, or the feel of his hard body pressed to her side, she wasn't sure.

'It will be easier if you relax and let me guide you,' he murmured. 'I won't lead you into anything you're not ready for.' Then before she could search for any deeper implications in that remark, his hand tightened on her waist. 'Ready?'

She didn't get a chance to answer. Which was a good thing, Sarah mused in the hazy corner of her mind that was still capable of thought. Before she had so much as taken a decent breath, she was whisked into a whirling, twirling series of manoeuvres that had her stumbling blindly through the first steps while she listened to a spate of instructions that made her dizzy.

Fortunately for her reeling senses, sheer necessity had her pulling herself together before she tripped over her own feet. Embarrassment spun away as the book-lined walls whipped past her bemused gaze. She discovered, in fact, that it was impossible to feel embarrassed when one was being whirled about the room by a husband issuing commands such as 'Two to the left!' 'Right!' 'Turn!' in the voice of a parade-ground sergeant.

When they came to a halt several minutes later, Sarah felt quite breathless and her head was still spinning, but the basic steps of the waltz were indelibly imprinted upon her brain.

'There, how did you like that?' Nick asked, sounding as if he had not exerted himself in the least. There was a smile in his voice, but Sarah didn't have enough energy left to take affront at it.

'Most. . .most exhilarating,' she gasped, unconsciously leaning against him while the library walls gradually returned to their proper places.

'Of course, that is only one way of dancing the waltz,' he went on. His arm tightened with a slow but inexorable pressure about her waist and he drew her around to face him. 'In Vienna, a few people are starting to waltz like this.'

Sarah looked up. There was less than an inch of space between them. Her hand, released from its position aloft, rested against his chest. Against her palm his heartbeat was strong and steady. He wasn't even breathing hard, she realised.

'How. . .how very shocking,' she whispered.

His wicked smile made something warm and tingling uncurl in the pit of her stomach. Suddenly the library felt far too small. She felt far too flushed. And Nick felt far too big, too strong, too close.

'Not for us,' he reminded her. 'We're married.' His

lashes lowered, half-shielding the intent expression in his eyes, and he murmured, 'How do you feel?'

Sarah swallowed and thought about it. 'Small,' she produced in a similar-sounding voice.

The curve of his mouth was inexpressibly tender as he gazed down at her. 'You are small,' he said, his tone the deepest, darkest purr she had ever heard it. 'Very small. Very soft. Very delicate.' He lifted his free hand to lightly trace the fullness of her lower lip with his thumb before lowering his mouth to hers. 'That's why I'm going to be very, very gentle with you.'

Every nerve in Sarah's body sprang into quivering life as Nick's mouth brushed hers. He was going to kiss her. Oh, at last. Already a heart-shaking excitement was racing through her, causing the echoes of his previous kisses to fade into insignificance. She gave a small yearning murmur, her lips parting beneath his in instinctive invitation, her hands clinging to the powerful breadth of his shoulders.

His arms closed around her, steel bands holding her tightly against him, so tightly that the low sound he made as his tongue stroked into her mouth vibrated through her entire body. She trembled uncontrollably, all the strength going out of her limbs as Nick took her mouth with a slow, deep possession that made her feel weak and languid and yet more intensely alive that she had ever felt before.

And she was kissing him back. Unknowing, unthinking, drowning in sensation, seduced by the intimate penetration and retreat of his tongue until she was kissing him as hotly, was holding him as tightly, until every hard muscled contour of his body was imprinted on her softer curves.

Every hard muscled contour. . .

The stunning awareness of rampant masculine desire hit her with a force that made her gasp. But even as she tensed, Nick broke the kiss, swung her up into his arms and strode across the room to sit down in an armchair large enough to accommodate both of them. He cradled her on his lap, pressing her head against his shoulder.

'Hush, little one.' His voice was soft and husky, in stark contrast to the coiled steel of muscles held under rigid control. 'Is that better?'

Sarah nodded. She couldn't stop shaking, but nor could she stop clinging to him. He was danger, safety, terror, excitement. The blatant evidence of his arousal brought all her doubts and fears rushing back, and yet she wanted. . .

Dear God, she didn't know what she wanted. She was being seduced all over again even as he held her. The violently leashed power beneath her hands was an enticement she couldn't resist when he cradled her so carefully. Her fingers were moving almost of their own accord, kneading iron-hard muscles, pressing closer to the heat burning through the layers of clothing he wore.

'It's all right, sweetheart. Don't tremble so. I know you felt what kissing you does to me.' He made a sound that was not quite a laugh and brushed his mouth across her curls. 'Impossible not to feel it. But you don't have to be afraid. I only want to kiss you. . .touch you. . . Will you let me do that, Sarah?'

'That's all?' she whispered, anticipation and apprehension all but stealing her voice. She should be saying no and running from the library. He would let her go. She knew it as surely as she could feel his heart thudding against her breast. Was it that knowledge alone that kept her there in his arms?

'That's all,' he echoed, holding her closer. 'It'll be better this way, you'll see. You won't feel— I won't frighten you.'

'Nick, I don't know if I am frightened. At least. . .' She gave a confused little laugh that was as ragged as his had been and hid her face against his shoulder. 'I don't know what I'm feeling anymore. I don't know *anything*.'

He touched her chin with the edge of his hand, gently raising her face to his. She trembled again at the heat blazing in his eyes when he looked at her mouth.

'Do you want to find out?' he asked very low.

Sarah tried to speak and couldn't. Nervousness held her utterly still, but awakening desire and something more, something she couldn't name, called to her on a deeper level. She lifted a hand to his face, letting her fingers touch his mouth as if the answer lay there. Perhaps it did, she thought vaguely, feeling him tense even more beneath her caress. Strength and gentleness. Brutality and tenderness. She had thought they could never merge in the one man, but now. . .

'Yes,' she whispered.

The sigh had scarcely passed her lips when she felt his arms flex. With a groan that sounded as if it had been torn from deep within him, he pulled her closer and touched his mouth to the soft flesh beneath her ear.

Surprise held Sarah motionless. Half-anticipating another deep possession of her mouth, the tender caress took her completely unawares. She softened against him, her eyes closing, as he trailed lingering kisses along the line of her jaw and down to her throat, warming her, tasting, cherishing. Her head fell back and she felt his muscles bunch and shift beneath her as he turned slightly so she lay back against the high curved arm of the chair.

Dimly she realised that the position made her more vulnerable to him, but the waves of heat flowing through her swept all rational thought aside. He touched his tongue to the pulse beating wildly at the base of her throat and she shuddered in helpless, sensuous response. He traced the delicate bones beneath her flesh while his mouth went lower, and weakness invaded her whole body. Every muscle softened, went limp. She whimpered and didn't know if it was in protest or pleasure.

'Yes,' he whispered, raising his head to look down at her. 'Just relax, my little Sarah. Let me love you.'

He began to kiss her again. Long, slow kisses that went on and on until she had no awareness of anything save his mouth on hers, the warmth of his fingers stroking her throat, and a need that was growing more urgent with every second.

She shifted, suddenly hot and restless. Her breasts felt full, the nipples tingling. In some distant part of her mind she thought she ought to be shocked at her own response. There was a reason why she shouldn't be doing this, but she couldn't think, couldn't remember it. Needs she had never known before were overwhelming her. She wanted Nick to touch her there, where the tingling was becoming a sweet torment, knew without knowing that he could satisfy the strange yearning within her. Oh, if he would only touch her. . .only touch her. . .

Then her breath unravelled in a broken cry of pleasure as he stroked his fingers across her breasts.

The sound of her own voice startled her. Her eyes flew open to find his gaze on her, narrowed, glittering, utterly focused.

'Nick?' she whispered, her voice shaking. She didn't know if he even heard her, so absorbed was he.

'Again,' he murmured, and it was not a question. His hand brushed the tips of her breasts once more, but lightly so that she arched, instinctively seeking a firmer touch.

'Is this what you want, little one?' He bent to kiss her, so swiftly that Sarah didn't have time to answer, even had she been capable of coherent speech. For a moment the kiss distracted her, then she tensed, gasping, as she felt Nick slide his hand beneath the neckline of her gown and chemise and cup the soft flesh he had been tormenting.

'It's all right,' he said hoarsely, the arm beneath her

back tightening as if he was afraid she might struggle. 'I only want to touch you. I have to. . . Oh, God, Sarah. . . Sarah. . .'

Her lips parted on his name but no sound came out. When had it become impossible to speak, to see, to breathe? She could only feel, feel the heavy warmth of his big hand surrounding her breast, the exquisite arrows of pleasure darting through her with every stroke of his thumb over her nipple.

'Am I hurting you, sweetheart?'

His voice, low and rough, penetrated the hazy clouds surrounding her consciousness, making Sarah aware of the tiny sounds coming from her throat. Shameless, she thought vaguely. She couldn't even remember when he had loosened her clothes. She should stop him, open her eyes and say something, but it was too much trouble, easier just to murmur, to let the pleasure and warmth enfold her.

'No,' she whispered, and shivered, wondering if that was really the truth. He wasn't hurting her, and yet the strangest ache pulsed deep inside her. The chair was suddenly too small, too confining. She felt an urgent need to lie down, to have him stretch out beside her, to have him touch the ache, satisfy it. . .*somehow*. 'Oh, Nick. . .'

'This?' he murmured, and, lowering his head, he took the rosy, pouting tip of her breast into his mouth and gently tasted her.

Sarah almost fainted beneath the onslaught of sensations. She cried out, her lower body moving in a helpless rhythm that echoed every hot caress of Nick's tongue on her sensitive flesh. She felt his arms tighten, felt him move against her, and suddenly he was touching her in a way that wrenched a very different cry from her. A high, panicked sound that held shock, pleasure and terrified memory in equal measure.

Nick heard the shock, and the fear, and her cry went through him like a dagger plunging straight to his heart.

He stopped instantly, cursing himself savagely for a fool while he held Sarah against him, murmuring words he didn't even hear. God, what was he doing? He hadn't meant to take her this far; had intended to arouse her only gently, to awaken her gradually to his touch. Not to drive her into panic-stricken flight because his blood was pounding in his veins, his entire body was one vicious, grinding ache and he'd been only seconds away from taking her right there on the library floor.

The library floor, for God's sake! He must have been mad to start anything here. He hadn't even locked the door.

'It's all right,' he groaned. 'It's all right. Don't be frightened, darling. It's finished, right here, right now. You're safe. You're safe with me, Sarah.' If he repeated it often enough, maybe he'd believe it. Maybe she would.

'I know,' she half-sobbed into his shoulder. 'I know I'm safe. I'm sorry. Nick, I didn't know. . . I couldn't. . . it felt. . .'

'Sshh,' he murmured, rocking her gently. 'It's all right.'

She shook her head almost fiercely and clung to him as if she wanted to crawl beneath his clothes to the underlying warmth of his body. 'I feel so strange. Scared, but. . .not really. . . Oh, I don't *know*!'

It took Nick a full minute to realise what she was saying. When his mind finally grasped the fact that, far from succumbing to panic-stricken flight, Sarah was being torn apart inside by a battle between fear and her own awakening senses, he had to clench his teeth against the torrent of desire that swept over him. He surfaced to find her struggling to right her clothing without exposing any more of herself to his gaze.

Too late, he thought, stifling a groan as she managed

to pull the lace-trimmed strap of her chemise over one shoulder, hiding the flushed curves of her breasts. The sweet, hot taste of her still lingered on his tongue, making him crave more, but this wasn't the place—or the time—to ease the turmoil inside her by finishing what he'd started.

'Here,' he said, grimacing at the low, hoarse sound that emerged from his throat. 'Let me.'

She flinched away from his hand, shaking her head, not looking at him. 'No. I can do it. Let me go, Nick. Please.'

One glance at her averted face had him complying, but as he set her on her feet he stood also, keeping a steadying arm about her waist. Her hands were shaking so much she had to abandon the attempt to tie the laces of her chemise; when she reached for the tiny buttons at the back of her gown, he couldn't stand it any longer.

'Damn it, let me help you,' he rasped, brushing her hands away and moving to stand behind her. He could tell by the way she was trembling that she was having to fight not to flinch away from him again.

And he couldn't think of one damned thing to say. He wanted to comfort her, but sensed that comfort would overset her precarious control. He wanted to snatch her up into his arms and carry her upstairs to bed, but that was out of the question. He wanted to put his fist through the nearest available object, but knew only too well what that would do to her.

In any event Sarah didn't give him a chance to do anything. As soon as the buttons of her gown were securely fastened she flew to the door and yanked it open.

'I have to go,' she stammered, looking everywhere but straight at him. 'Mrs Winwick. . .menus. . .'

The door slammed behind her as she fled.

'*God damn it to bloody hell!*'

Nick wheeled and lashed out with his clenched fist,

sweeping everything on the mantelpiece to the floor. Candelabra, vases and various small ornaments flew across the room and hit the side of his desk with a resounding crash. The action served to release a totally insignificant fraction of the emotions raging within him.

He slammed both fists down on the denuded ledge and stared at the floor. God in heaven, what had Sarah done to him? He had never lost control of himself like that. *Never!*

Behind him the door opened again.

Nick turned so swiftly that the newcomer froze in the doorway. Then his gaze went to the wreckage on the floor. He frowned in disapproval.

'Never mind that,' Nick snapped. 'What the devil do you want, Figgins?'

The groom stepped into the library with all the cautious approach of a deer who knows a predator is nearby. He closed the door carefully behind him, an action that immediately drew his master's brows together.

'Thought you might be interested in seeing some hoofprints, me lord,' he murmured. 'But if I've come at an inconvenient time...'

'No.' Nick walked over to a small table near the door and reached for the brandy decanter thereon, fully aware that he had never resorted to finding answers in a bottle of brandy in his life. Not even when—

He replaced the decanter with a thump and turned. He might as well be distracted by Figgins as anyone. Sarah needed some time. And so did he.

'What hoofprints?' he demanded. 'There are hoofprints all over the place. At least there should be if my grooms are doing their job exercising my horses.'

Figgins ignored this growled aside with magnificent disdain. 'Not those sort of hoofprints, me lord,' he said. 'Actually, 'twere young Peake who found 'em. As nice a set as you would like to see, in that marshy bit o' ground beyond the lake. Lucky for us he took it upon himself to show me the spot and explain that it ain't healthy to tether horses in that kind of place.'

'He must know you would not do so.'

'Well, *you* know it, sir, but there's no getting away from it. A horse stood there for some considerable time, I'd judge. There's a few old trees about that would give cover. Nice place to watch the house—if'n someone wanted to. O' course, Peake didn't think of that. Blind as a bat, poor lad.'

Knowing of the rivalry that existed between Figgins and the Peakes, father, son and grandson, who had ruled the stables for decades, Nick merely narrowed his eyes. 'Go on.'

'Well, it looked to me like whoever it was tried to brush the prints away, but you know how it is in that type of ground, me lord. Unless you do a good job of marks that deep, as soon as the moisture seeps up again there you have it. Four nice little horseshoe-shaped puddles.'

'Any tracks leading away?'

'Not so's you'd notice,' Figgins answered. 'The ground dries out again fairly close by and the rides are full of tracks, coming and going. I think he went south.' He frowned meaningfully. 'Towards the Grange.'

'Or the coast.'

Figgins shrugged.

'All right, Figgins, we'll take a ride along the coast and then backtrack. See what we can find. You've done well, although I can't see why anyone would be watching this place if the bait in London hasn't been taken.'

'Something from an old job?' Figgins suggested.

Nick considered then shook his head. 'I doubt it. Up until six months ago I hadn't been in England for twelve years. Only a very few highly placed men knew of me and—'

He stopped, remembering that he had said much the

same thing to Devenham some weeks ago. 'On the other hand, the men we're looking for *are* highly placed, and astute enough to smell a trap and leave it untouched while they remove any obstacles. I warned them of that possibility, but you might as well speak to a stone wall as government ministers. Let's go, Figgins.'

'Aye, sir, but are you sure it ain't inconvenient? I couldn't help but notice—'

'Figgins, shut up.'

'Aye, sir. But it ain't as if he's out there now in broad daylight, and the little lady looked a mite upset when I passed her in the hall and—'

'*Figgins*!'

'Eh? Oh, aye. I forgot. I *should* have said, her little ladyship. Sorry, me lord.'

Nick raised his eyes to the heavens and gave up.

Arms wrapped around her waist as though to hold herself together, Sarah paced across her bedchamber to the window, turned and paced back to the door. She repeated the sequence several more times, her feet moving faster and faster with each lap.

It didn't help. Her pacing was doing nothing for the heated restlessness quivering inside her and no amount of arm-gripping was banishing the feeling that she was about to fall apart.

How *could* she have behaved like that?

Abandoned. Shameless. In broad daylight! In the *library*! She was horrified!

At least, she amended with rather despairing honesty, her mind was properly horrified, but her traitorous body persisted in remembering the incredible sensations aroused by Nick's hands and mouth. Nervous, yes even frightened though she was, she hadn't wanted him to stop. She had *liked* it.

Sarah stopped pacing, sat down on the nearest chair and put her face in her hands. Unfortunately, her

fevered brain continued to roll pictures past her closed
eyes. He had looked at her half-naked body, touched
her, oh, heavens, kissed her. . .

She sprang up and resumed her pacing, back and
forth, back and forth, faster and faster, until her skirts
were flying out behind her. If their marriage had not
been one of convenience she thought she might not feel
so dreadful. But it was. At least. . .

She fetched up short beside the bed. Across the room
her startled reflection stared back at her from the
dressing-table mirror.

If their marriage was one of convenience, why had
Nick started kissing her in a manner that had about as
much resemblance to a friendly affectionate peck as a
mild summer breeze to a raging tempest? Why, for that
matter, had he continued to kiss her and touch her when
he knew her views on the subject?

Not that she'd been raising her voice in support of
those views at the time, Sarah reminded herself, trying
to be fair. But had Nick merely lost control for a
moment, or did he want to change the terms of their
marriage?

She continued to stare straight ahead as she considered the question, conscious that her heart was
beginning to race again. Had this past week shown him
that friendship was not enough? After all, he was
physically at the peak of his strength, and if Lady
Wribbonhall was to be believed, had once loved
passionately. Given that, did he truly want her? Could
he want a real marriage? Could he even. . .oh, was it
possible? Could he even be falling in love with her—as
she was with him?

Sarah gasped in shock. She staggered against the bed,
one hand grabbing for a bedpost as her knees gave way.
Clutching the polished oak, trembling as if she had a
fever, she lowered herself to the quilt, her stunned gaze
still fixed on her ashen-faced image in the mirror.

She loved him.

She watched her eyes widen in astonishment, saw her lips part as though she would say the words aloud. No sound emerged, but it didn't matter. Her love for Nick was *there*. Deep in her heart. Had been there for a long time, blossoming, growing, waiting to be acknowledged. If she hadn't been so afraid, so cowardly, she would have recognised what was happening to her weeks ago. She wasn't *falling* in love. She had fallen. She was helplessly, irrevocably, utterly in love with a man who might never want anything more than friendship from her, and who thought she wanted the same thing.

But then, if she had changed. . .

Could he?

The question crept into her mind, tentative, silent, terrifying in its tremulous hope. She did not have an answer. She thought Nick enjoyed her company, he was kind to her, gentle with her. . .

'Oh-h-h.' The soft exclamation whispered through the quiet room like a sigh. Sarah leaned her forehead against the bedpost and trembled anew. Yes, so gentle with her, as if he knew how afraid she was of male passions. How could she not have fallen in love with him?

And for a few brief, shockingly exciting minutes there in the library, he had at least desired her.

Until he had remembered who she was.

The thought came out of nowhere, threatening to bury her fragile hope beneath a pall of blackest gloom. Not even the reminder that Marianne had been dead for over ten years eased the painful fist squeezing her heart. One indisputable fact remained. Nick had stopped making love to her. She had all but thrown herself at him and he had stopped.

Sarah made a small sound of pain and bent over, rocking herself until the first sharp pangs abated. The moment of despair didn't last long. She didn't let it.

Didn't dare. Better to remind herself that she had suffered worse than this and survived—and not by languishing about on beds.

But what was she to do? How did one go about fighting the ghost of an angel?

She sat there for a while, thinking over the past several weeks, searching for clues that might give her some hint of her husband's feelings. That was one thing in her favour, she thought, a little cheered. Nick *was* her husband. And he was very much a man. Men had rather primitive impulses. It stood to reason, therefore, that even the most controlled male would sometimes yield to those impulses.

Sarah stared at the mirror, considering that logical point of view. A second later she blinked, startled to see a very thoughtful, determined expression come over her countenance. It was rather similar to the expression Julia had worn when she'd made her write that note to the dowager Lady Ravensdene.

Then her eyes went wide again with astonishment. Good heavens! Surely she wasn't contemplating. . .

It was impossible. She couldn't do it. She didn't know the first thing about tempting a man. At this moment the very thought of what had transpired in the library was enough to make her wonder how she was even going to face Nick again without blushing from her brow to the soles of her feet.

And she was still afraid. That hadn't changed. She loved Nick, she trusted him, but the images of Amy were still there in her mind, fainter perhaps by day, but ripping apart the veils of sleep at night so that she woke often, sobbing and shaking with a terror that never went away.

Sarah jumped to her feet and stood shaking, fiercely resisting the urge to pace again. Pacing would not help her escape from the nightmare that was always at her heels, that had sprung to her mind the instant she'd

considered a real marriage. Nor could she think ration-
ally while in the grip of fear. She needed to do something quiet, something that would keep her from reliving
those heated moments in Nick's arms and wondering if
it had been like that for Amy before everything had
been destroyed because she had pushed a man too far.

Sarah shuddered and tried to push the memories
aside. Her restless gaze caught the corner of a box
visible through the open door of her dressing room. It
was one of the many chests brought from the Grange,
and had yet to be unpacked, but she knew what it
contained.

Her gaze sharpened. Yes, the very thing. Her sketching equipment. She would take her table and stool and
sketchbook down to the lake and draw. She would
empty her mind of fiercely passionate, green-eyed panthers and fill it instead with images of trees and lake and
sky.

She suddenly realised that, until that instant of shock
when Nick had touched her so intimately, her mind had
not been filled with images of her sister.

The knowledge sent her scurrying for her pencils. She
wouldn't think about it. At least not right now. She was
too confused. There was too much she didn't know.
About Nick, his intentions, his feelings. . . And her own
love was too new, too painfully vulnerable; a butterfly
just emerged from its chrysallis, unable to fly, fragile and
defenceless.

She needed time. She needed to restore the calm
balance of her mind. And then she would be able to
think about marriages of convenience, and what exactly
Nick had meant when he'd offered for her, and what she
was going to do if the answer was not the one she
wanted.

There hadn't been anything unusual about the tracks
beyond the lake. Nothing that would make it easy to

recognise a particular horse or to follow it. The entire afternoon had been a waste of time, Nick concluded grimly as he and Figgins returned from an inspection of the woods to the north of Comberford.

They had ridden for some distance, circling the grounds without finding any further signs that a rider had been watching the house. Whoever it was had obviously done so under cover of darkness, and had been careful to go to ground some distance away where the appearance of a stranger would not occasion comment that might reach the wrong ears.

He frowned at the thought, unable to rid himself of the notion that he had missed something rather vital in his observations on the case. But foremost on his mind at that moment was finding Sarah and setting things to rights.

Patting his horse absently, Nick dismounted and with a quick word to Figgins, strode towards the house. He shouldn't have left Sarah alone. All afternoon he'd been haunted by her distress, her flushed, averted face, the way she had trembled and shrunk from him.

Damn it, she hadn't even been able to look at him. He should have followed her, taken her in his arms no matter how she protested, and admitted that he'd intended to seduce her from the start because he wanted their marriage to be real.

That was what he was going to do right now, Nick promised himself, bounding up the front steps. He flung open the door and strode down the hallway. Then when she forgave him for deceiving her—and he wouldn't let her go until she did—he was going to set out to seduce her all over again.

His plan received a slight set-back when he discovered a minute later that Sarah wasn't in her bedchamber. But she had been. An empty box lay in the middle of the room. It looked as if its contents had been removed in something of a hurry.

Nick strode to the window and glanced out. He saw Sarah immediately. She was seated on a low stool beside the lake, a folding drawing-table set up before her, and she was sketching.

Sketching! As if nothing untoward had happened!

A volatile mixture of rage, frustration and desire surged through him at the peaceful scene. He turned on his heel and retraced his steps, meeting Winwick half-way down the stairs. The butler took one look at his face and flattened himself against the stair-rail. Nick scarcely noticed him. He crossed the hall in two strides, slammed open the library door and stalked towards one of the french windows that opened onto the gardens.

He had just stepped onto the terrace when the shot rang out.

CHAPTER THIRTEEN

SARAH heard the explosion from the woods less than twenty yards away and half-rose from her seat. Her hand was outstretched, about to put down her pencil when she saw a blur of movement from the corner of her eye. Before she could turn her head she was hurled from her stool, through the air and onto the ground.

She landed, unhurt but winded, on top of her assailant. 'Nick!' she gasped, stunned recognition restoring her voice.

It was all she had time for. He rolled, covering her with his body. 'Are you all right?' he asked very softly.

'Well, I was until—'

'Shhh.' His hand covered her mouth lightly and he raised his head, seeming to listen.

His warning was unnecessary. Sarah had ceased to speak the moment she registered the overwhelming sensations aroused by the feel of his weight on her. There was no time to be afraid. Warmth and weakness invaded every limb. Then she heard someone running along the path from the stables and tensed again.

'It's all right,' Nick murmured, releasing her mouth. 'It's Figgins. Stay down. Stay right here and don't move until I come back for you.'

'But—'

His green eyes blazed down into hers. 'Don't move!' Each word was enunciated with a savage clarity that silenced her instantly, then he was gone.

Sarah contemplated the greyish, lowering sky above her and wondered if she had managed to fall off her stool by herself, hit her head and become delirious. Hurrying footsteps and anxious voices reassured her that she was awake and lying flat on the lawn while waiting for her husband to return from who knew where.

'My lady! Lawks a'mercy! What happened? We heard a shot and that there Figgins goes rushing off, though I told him 'twas only his lordship firing at the target he's got set up in the garden—'

'I'm all right, Peake. Oh, heavens! Why is everyone running out of the house? Winwick, too. Have you all gone as mad as— Ouch!' Sarah sat up gingerly, rubbing a bruised knee. She assumed that since she was now surrounded by loyal retainers, Nick would not object to her moving. It was a mistake.

'Damn it, Sarah—'

She glanced over her shoulder to see Nick striding from the woods towards her. His face was a mask of controlled fury and something else she didn't recognise, and in that precise instant, as their eyes met, the significance of the shot hit her with stunning force.

She sprang to her feet and ran to meet him, everything else forgotten in the terrible fear seizing her heart. Seconds later, sudden memory had her halting as if she had run headlong into a wall. Her voice was barely audible, as if all the air had been knocked out of her body.

'Nick.' She extended a hand, saw it shake, withdrew it. 'You're safe.'

He caught her by the shoulders. 'Of course I'm safe, you little idiot. I thought I told you to stay down.'

Her laugh was a ragged sound of shock and confusion. 'It upset the servants. I think they thought I was dead, just lying there.'

'Oh, God, don't—' Ignoring the crowd behind her, he pulled her into his arms. 'Come on, let's get you into the house.'

'But, Nick, what happened? Where did Figgins go? Who. . .?'

'Hush. Later.' He laid a finger over her lips, the gesture silencing her more surely than his words. Fear lanced through Sarah again, settling like a sickening, ice-cold lump in her stomach, as she thought of traps and traitors, and that while panthers were predators they could also be hunted.

She pushed the thought away in sheer self-defence, listening only vaguely as Nick questioned the servants and gave orders. Someone picked up her scattered pencils and the small wooden stool. Winwick, looking pale and worried, retrieved her sketchbook. Nick let her go long enough to fold her drawing-table. She saw him run a finger around one corner of the wood before he tucked it under his arm and reached for her.

'You're going straight upstairs to your room and have your maid prepare you a warm bath,' he said, as the little procession started for the house. 'Then you're having dinner on a tray in bed.'

'But—'

'No arguments. You've had a shock.' His eyes met hers. 'Several shocks.'

Sarah felt the blush she had anticipated earlier suffuse her face. She looked away, praying he wouldn't mention what had happened earlier, hoping desperately that he would.

'There's nothing to worry about,' he murmured. 'I'll join you upstairs after dinner and then we're going to talk.'

Talk? That should prove interesting, she thought, beginning to feel slightly light-headed. What would they talk about? His precise definition of a marriage of convenience? Her conviction that he had found it so easy to stop making love to her because she was not the woman he loved?

Perhaps a discussion on those two points would be helpful after all. She might then be able to put into better perspective the mind-shattering revelation that had just burst upon her. That she would do anything, risk anything, to hold onto whatever Nick had left to give her. Because the past few minutes had shown her, with devastating clarity, what it would do to her to lose him.

Nick stood in the quiet, dimly lit bedchamber, looking down at his sleeping wife.

She appeared very small and vulnerable, curled up beneath the covers of the big four-poster. Her hair was a swathe of sable silk spilling across the pillows, her lashes soft fans of the same hue against her cheeks. One little hand was tucked under her chin, the fingers curling inwards.

The muscles in his gut clenched hard as fierce desire and tender protectiveness surged through him on a tide of emotion that nearly brought him to his knees. She was so innocent, and so sweetly seductive in her innocence. And if that shot had been an inch closer he could have lost her.

The part of him that was sheer, primitive savagery stirred restlessly, but his mind was ice-cold and steady. Had been from the moment he had seen the damage done to Sarah's drawing-table and had known that the intended victim had not been himself, but her. Since then he had examined and discarded theories with grim, relentless logic, searching for the one fact that eluded him until he was left with the only thing that made sense.

There were still two questions hanging over his theory. He had sent Figgins off to London for one answer; the other. . .

He gazed down at Sarah again and for the first time in years felt more than fleeting regret for what he had to do. She stirred, as though sensing the bitter emotion within him, but didn't wake.

Stifling a rough sound, Nick took off his coat and tossed it over a chair near the fireplace, then pulled another chair closer to the bed and sat down. He yanked off his boots and stretched his legs out. He might as well make himself as comfortable as possible; it was going to be a long night. But he couldn't bring himself to waken Sarah just yet. Let her sleep before he had to force her into the dark memories that lay trapped inside her—and that without any certainty of success. Let her sleep before he had to tear her apart to keep her safe.

Savage rage stirred again when he thought of the man who had threatened her life, and this time he let it prowl closer to the surface. It was necessary. Because something else lay beyond the savagery. Something crouched, waiting, beneath the rage; something as powerful, as predatory and, he knew, as ultimately destructive. Rage was preferable. He could control rage, he could use it. He needed it if he was to keep Sarah alive.

The other was something he would not even acknowledge.

Sounds filled her head, beating, pounding, drowning out the terrified throbbing of her heart. Choked screams. Harsh curses. Ripping cloth. The sounds of beasts locked in a struggle that could have only one end.

And she couldn't stop them. Somewhere in the depths of her nightmare she was sobbing, screaming at them to stop, but they wouldn't listen to her. Then the sounds stopped. The dream changed. She was running into darkness that had no end. Behind her danger stalked, coming closer no matter how fast she ran, no matter how far. But she had to keep running. She had to get help. Had to save Amy... Amy...'*Amy*—'

Sarah came awake with the scream still filling her throat. She sat bolt upright in bed, gasping for the air that always eluded her in the dream.

Strong arms came around her immediately, holding her against a large male body that was powerful and warm and infinitely safe.

'It's all right, sweetheart. I'm here. You're safe. It was only a dream.'

For a moment she was a terrified fourteen-year-old girl again, being comforted by her uncle. Then she heard the dark velvet voice of her panther and knew she was safer than she'd ever been before in her life. She turned into his embrace with a shuddering little sigh.

'Nick. You're here.'

'Yes, little one. I'll always be here.'

For immeasurable precious minutes she was content to nestle in his arms, savouring the feeling of his fingers threading through her hair, stroking damp tendrils from her face while the shadows of terror receded.

But thought and reality intruded all too soon. He must have come to her room to talk and found her asleep, and since he'd been there to comfort her before the echoes of her scream had faded, he had clearly stayed.

She blinked, slowly taking in the sight of his discarded raiment, the chair close by, illuminated by a single candle, the fire still burning in the hearth. She didn't know how long she'd slept, but sensed the hour was now quite late. Why was he sitting here on her bed dressed only in shirt and breeches? Why had he stayed?

'Better now?' he asked, bending his head over hers.

She nodded and made a move to be free, remembering the turbulent see-saw of determination and uncertainty that had eventually driven her into an exhausted slumber. The feel of his arms around her was heaven, but was it only kindness? Oh, why had he stayed?

His arms tightened, stilling her. 'You were dreaming of your sister, weren't you, Sarah? Tell me about it.'

The gentle command stole her breath. 'I. . .can't.'

'Yes, you can.' His voice was so soft and persuasive that she almost believed him. 'Tell me about it and it will start to go away. While it's locked inside you, you can't be free to—' His hand flexed suddenly in her hair, then relaxed and resumed its stroking. 'You can't be free.'

After a moment's reflection, she looked up at him. 'I never thought of it like that. Everyone kept telling me to forget it, but. . .' Tears stung her eyes and she lowered her head quickly before he saw them. 'It didn't work.'

'Tell me what happened to Amy,' he said again. 'How did it start?'

'We had been to the beach.' The first words came hesitantly and she felt Nick tense.

'We?' he said sharply. 'You were with her?'

She nodded against his shoulder. 'Yes. There was a storm coming, like the day you and I met, so we were hurrying. I saw a man beside the path. If he hadn't moved I would have walked right past him because it was getting so dark. But he moved, and I saw him.'

'The groom?'

'No.' Sarah took a long, quivering breath. 'But he was there. Amy looked past me and I heard her cry out, "Hal, what are you doing?" I wondered what she meant, then something hit me and I fell.'

'That's all you remember?' he asked when she fell silent. 'The groom, another man and being hit?'

She started to shake. 'No. I. . . I. . .'

'It's all right, sweetheart. It's all right.' God, he hated this. He held her closer, his mouth pressed to the soft curls at her temple. 'You're safe. It happened a long time ago. They can't hurt you now, Sarah.'

'I know.' She clung to him, instinctively seeking his male heat to counteract the bone-deep chill of remembered horror. 'It was Amy.' Her voice cracked on the name. 'Crane hurt her.'

'Hal Crane? That was the groom?'

'Yes. I could hear her screaming that he'd killed me and he kept shouting at her to be quiet. Then. . .it got worse. There were sounds. . .awful sounds. . . He was cursing her, telling her she'd made a fool of him and he was going to take what she owed. I tried to help her, but I couldn't move. I couldn't see. It was so dark and I couldn't see.'

She raised her head, unaware of the tears pouring down her cheeks. 'It was like some sort of horrible dream. Sometimes I thought I *was* dreaming. I'd be asleep and then wake and hear terrible things. And then. . .it seemed a long time later. . . I woke up again and there was nothing, just silence except for him breathing.'

'The other man, the one you saw, did he do nothing while Amy was attacked?'

His deep, gentling tone brought her back from the brink of her nightmare. For the first time Sarah realised she couldn't see Nick's face through the haze of tears blurring her vision, but she could feel his thumb against her cheek, brushing the wetness away. He bent his head and kissed her lashes, catching more tears on his lips.

'I don't know.' Her voice was husky and she swallowed, looking away again to stare at the glowing log in the fireplace. 'I couldn't see. Whenever I tried to open my eyes everything got blacker. But I heard his voice. He was angry, but his voice was so precise, so cold. I've never forgotten it. He called Crane a lustful fool and ordered him to kill me. . .if he hadn't already done it—'

He made a hoarse sound and she stopped. 'What?'

'Nothing, little one. Go on.'

Sarah shook her head. 'That's all I remember until I heard Uncle Jasper calling my name. It was raining but there were lights, and so many people. I didn't understand why. Someone turned me over and. . . Oh, Nick, I saw her.' Her voice broke again, shattering into silent tears that made her shudder convulsively. 'I saw Amy. . .'

'God Almighty!'

He held her to him, rocking her gently as she struggled against the wave of memory. When she could speak, it was in a whisper. 'The next time I woke up I really was in bed, and it was daylight. A few days later Uncle Jasper told me that Crane's body had been found and I didn't have to worry about giving evidence to the magistrate, that I should forget everything. I tried to tell him, but...' She drew back a little, eyes wet and anguished. 'Nick, do you believe there was another man?'

He frowned down at her. 'Yes, of course. Didn't your uncle?'

'Everyone said I was confused. Dr Salcott told me I'd taken a brutal blow to the head and had lost so much blood that I must have fallen into a delirium. But I didn't. I *didn't*!' she whispered insistently. 'But there was no evidence to prove there had been a second man and they wouldn't listen. They wouldn't talk about it at all, except to say it was a miracle I'd survived.' She shook her head and stared into the fire again. 'I didn't think it was such a miracle when it was my fault that she died. I knew... I should have stopped it.'

No, Nick thought, not bothering to correct that last remark. He knew that sort of guilt could only be lessened when time and healing brought the realisation that she'd been physically unable to save her sister. The real miracle was that Sarah had survived with enough inner strength beneath her gentle innocence to trust a man as much as she had trusted him earlier that day.

He stifled a savage curse as he thought of what she had suffered. Violently assaulted, drifting helplessly in and out of consciousness, but not mercifully out of it enough to be spared the knowledge of her sister's rape and murder and the cold-blooded threat to her own life. And then to be disbelieved, to be told to forget it. No wonder she had nightmares. He could willingly have consigned all her well-meaning but misguided relatives and friends to a collective hell, except that by their unwitting interference he'd been able to justify his questions.

It didn't help much. He would have questioned her anyway, which would, he decided, have sent him into a hell of his own making.

She sighed and seemed to relax against him. 'You were right,' she murmured. 'I do feel better now.' She pressed her cheek closer, rubbing her head against his shirt in an unknowingly sensual gesture that tightened his body. 'How did you know?'

Ignoring the growing ache in his loins, he tipped her face up to his with a gentle finger beneath her chin. 'We all have nightmares, Sarah.'

Her lovely eyes, unshadowed now and soft in the candlelight, gazed into his. 'Yes,' she breathed. 'Even you.'

Nick looked down into her face, more shaken by her words than he wanted to admit. It seemed to him that she was seeing straight into the soul he thought he had lost. He remembered other faces, friends, enemies, places he'd known, dreams where he couldn't find himself, and knew that with her he was whole again.

He bent until their lips were less than an inch apart. 'Not any more,' he said.

The kiss was gentle, demanding nothing, giving comfort. He was being kind, Sarah told herself as her eyes fluttered closed. But the warm touch of Nick's mouth on hers sent the sweetest ripples coursing through her.

Her lips parted, her arms crept around his waist, and so slowly that she couldn't have said when it changed, their mouths fused in a joining so long and deep she had no memory of when they hadn't been kissing. When Nick drew back, his breathing ragged, his face taut with the desire she had seen in him that afternoon, hope flared inside her with a force that was frightening.

'Sarah, we have to stop. You're not ready. . .'

The hoarse tone of his voice brought her gaze up to

his as he put her away from him, his hands sliding from her shoulders to her wrists. The emerald flames in his eyes had been banked, but she could feel tension humming through him in the fine tremor of his hands as they lay over hers on the bed. Then he broke that slight contact also, and she knew suddenly that what happened between them from that moment on was to be her decision alone.

The realisation made something inside her tremble once, violently, as if she had been abruptly abandoned in the midst of a thick fog, unable to see which way to go. Dimly she was aware that there might be a terrible price to pay if their relationship changed. She knew that he'd loved another woman whose place she could never take. But *she* loved *him*, with every fibre of her being; with her heart, her mind, her soul. Given that, there really was no choice.

'Ready?' she asked with an uncertain little laugh. 'I'm not sure I know what you mean by ready. But. . .' She looked up at him, quivering wildly inside with nerves and trepidation. 'I know I don't want you to leave, Nick.'

His smile was infinitely tender. 'I don't intend to leave. You're going to sleep in my arms every night from now on.'

'I. . .am?'

'Yes,' he said very softly. 'And one night, when you trust me again, I'm going to touch you the way I did this afternoon.'

She thought about that. 'Those obligations we—'

'*No. God damn it!*'

She jumped, her eyes going wide and startled. Then as her gaze flashed to his, she saw his control shatter in an explosion of raw need that stunned every sense she possessed. His face went hard, his eyes fierce, blazing, almost savage in their passionate hunger. He looked primitive, as if polite society had barely touched him.

Fear, sheer primal female fear, streaked through her, urging flight, but at the same time she was paralysed, completely and helplessly fascinated.

'I don't want any damned *obligations*,' he ground out through clenched teeth. 'I want to touch you and have you touch me. I want to look at you lying naked in my arms, kiss you in places you haven't even dreamed about. I want to make love to you until we don't know where you end and I begin, until we can't damn well breathe without the other feeling it. And then I'll want to start all over again. *That*'s what I want, Sarah. It's what I've always wanted.'

She swallowed into a silence that was deafening. 'That,' she managed with an incredible effort, 'was quite a list.'

His eyes closed and he turned away, breathing deeply in an obvious effort at control. When he looked back at her it was like gazing into the fathomless depths of the sea. Tension had put a white line about his mouth and his big body was utterly still, as if he didn't dare move.

'Which scares the life out of you,' he said, and the aching regret in his voice made her cry out in protest.

'No, that's not true!'

He raised his brows in disbelief and she flushed. 'Well, not the life out of me,' she amended. 'But—' a shy smile curved her mouth and her lashes lowered, hiding her expression from him. 'I expect most brides are a little nervous.'

'Sarah. . .'

It was a raw whisper. She felt him watching her and trembled with anticipation and longing and love. He reached out and touched her cheek fleetingly with the tips of his fingers, but didn't make her look at him. She was glad of it. She wouldn't have been able to hide the desperate hope burning fiercely in her heart at his words.

'Sarah,' he murmured again. 'Will you be my wife in more than name?'

'Yes,' she whispered without hesitation.

He dragged in a shuddering breath, then reached for her and drew her into his arms as if she was made of the finest, most delicate porcelain.

'I won't hurt you,' he vowed, and though the words sounded as if they were engraved in solid rock, it was the shaking of his voice that brought her gaze up to his. His eyes had gone dark with desire but this time she could feel the fierce hold he had over himself in the tension of the muscles beneath her hands.

'I know,' she whispered. 'I trust you, Nick.'

He gazed down at her. 'Enough?'

'What do you mean?'

'I might shock you, frighten you.'

She thought of the way he'd startled her that afternoon and shivered with remembered pleasure.

'Yes, like that,' he murmured, watching the colour bloom beneath her skin. He bent and kissed her gently. 'If I do something that shocks you, little one, will you trust me enough not to stop me?'

What could she say? The decision had been made. Yes, she was unsure, nervous, still afraid of the unknown, but she had given her heart, would give her life for him if it was ever asked of her. How could she withhold the one gift he desired? Loving him, she would give whatever he asked, without demanding more than he could give in return.

She couldn't speak for the emotions tightening her throat, but she leaned closer and, hiding the love in her eyes beneath lowered lashes, touched her lips shyly to his.

It was enough. With a hoarse sound that was vow and plea combined, Nick wrapped his arms around her, parted her lips with the gentle pressure of his tongue, and took her mouth with his.

Weakness flowed through her instantly. She thought she had known what to expect of his kisses, but this was different. Deliciously slow. Deeply possessive. He kissed her as if they had all the time in the world, as if he was prepared to spend the entire night teaching her how heart-shakingly intimate a kiss could be.

And he touched her, stroking her through the shifting silk of her nightgown, tracing the delicate bones beneath her heated skin, cupping the aching fullness of her breasts, shaping his palms to the indentation of her waist and the gently rounded contours of her hips and thighs.

He was so gentle. The contrast between the gentleness of his touch and the size and power of his hands made her shiver in an uncontrollable response that could have been fear or excitement or both. She didn't know and no longer cared. All she wanted was for him to go on touching her, kissing her.

'Sweetheart, do you want me to blow out the candle?'

The husky question against her lips made her feel as if she was surfacing from some deep place where thought had vanished, leaving only sensation. She opened dazed eyes and felt heat wash over her in a searing tide at the burning, focused intensity of his gaze. His eyes were narrowed, glittering, watching his hand as, one by one, he undid the tiny buttons that fastened the bodice of her nightgown.

She gave a soundless gasp and went still, scarcely breathing.

'I don't. . . I don't want darkness.'

'I won't rush you,' he murmured. And held her close, understanding. 'I know you'll be shy.'

Still holding her, he smoothed the garment over her shoulders and down to her waist. For an instant her hands were trapped in the long sleeves, but her small sound of protest faded as he swiftly freed her. Sarah shivered as the cooler air in the room touched her naked flesh and instinctively brought her arms up to cover herself. He didn't try to stop her, didn't make any attempt to remove the frail shield. He could have, easily, she thought wonderingly. But he merely smiled into her eyes and released her.

'Wait,' he said, and, standing, he stripped off his shirt in one swift movement before sitting down on the bed again.

Sarah's mouth went dry. Her eyes widened as she looked at him. She forgot to be shy about the fact that she was sitting there half-naked, exposed to his gaze. Clothed, he looked big and immensely strong, but now she could see his strength in the sleek, beautifully defined muscles that rippled beneath his skin as he moved.

A panther, she thought, utterly captivated. Lean and dangerous and powerful, with a kind of masculine grace that was riveting.

'You're beautiful,' she breathed, reaching out a hand to touch him. The feel of the black pelt covering his chest startled her. It was soft against her palm, but with an intriguing abrasiveness that was very male and strangely exciting. She curled her fingers into its thickness, then straightened them again to test the underlying layer of muscle. There was no give in him at all.

'You're the beautiful one,' he said huskily. 'And you're playing absolute havoc with my good intentions, sweet Sarah.'

She scarcely heard him, so enthralled was she by his overwhelming masculinity, but when he circled her other wrist with his fingers and slowly drew her arm away from her body, she went still again as he looked at her.

'So beautiful,' he whispered. 'Dear God, Sarah, I have to hold you.'

The expression of naked desire on his face made her tremble, but before she had time to be afraid, Nick wrapped his arm around her waist and drew her up against him and all thought was suspended. She felt their flesh pressed together for the first time and cried out in wonder.

He murmured reassurance against her lips, but her shock had been one of intense pleasure and she pressed closer, her arms curling around his neck as he began kissing her. And so gently that she felt as if he was peeling away the layers of her uncertainty and fear one by one, he laid her back on the bed and led her into a world of sensation she had never dreamed existed, easing her into passion, pulling back when it became too overwhelming, calming her with soft words and slow, tender caresses before taking her higher.

It was like flying, Sarah thought in some distant part of her mind. Flying into the heart of the sun. Heat surrounded her. Heat from his mouth on hers, on her throat, her breasts. Heat from his hands, those strong, beautiful hands, touching her in places that made her melt and shiver, until he caressed her with such devastating intimacy that when he left her for the few seconds it took him to remove his remaining garments, Sarah whimpered softly in protest.

Then he was back, gathering her into his arms, parting her legs as he lowered himself over her. Sarah's breath caught; she gripped his shoulders. Her trembling body stilled as she felt his weight, felt the intimidating strength of him against her softest, most vulnerable flesh. Just for a moment she felt smothered, overwhelmed, his sheer size and the sudden dimming of the light as his body seemed to engulf hers bringing panic bubbling to the surface again.

He knew, sensed it at once, for he went still also, his heart thudding violently against her breast, shudders racking the powerful muscles beneath her hands. And those betraying shudders were enough to ease her own tense limbs. She moved slightly and found that their bodies aligned as if made especially for the other, that the feel of his weight on her was a delicious excitement, sheltering and warm.

She moved again and heard the harsh breath he drew in.

'Oh, God, Sarah, don't. Be still, little one. I can't. . . I've wanted you for so long. Don't let me frighten you.'

'I'm not afraid,' she whispered.

But in her shaking voice he thought he heard the last remnants of fear and it leashed the raging hunger inside him as nothing else could. She was so small and delicate beneath him, offering him the gift of her innocence, that to hurt or frighten her would be to destroy whatever he had left of tenderness.

'Sweetheart. . .' He cradled her face in one hand, tilting her chin up until he could see into her eyes. 'Look at me.'

She didn't know if she could. The stark intimacy of meeting his gaze as he eased into her body was almost more than she could bear. She gasped once at a tiny, stinging pain that was gone before she even thought to flinch, and he caught the small sound in his mouth.

Then she lost her breath entirely, lost all sense of self, as Nick became part of her in a joining so absolute, so perfect, she felt as if her very soul had merged with his.

'Mine.' He groaned the word against her lips. 'Mine. Until we don't know where you end and I begin.'

'Yes.' She could only breathe the word, clinging to him, flushed and feverish, wondering how he could make her feel so much, so intensely. All her senses seemed to go wild as he began to move with heart-shattering care. She could feel him everywhere. Inside her, over her, around her. Fear was vanquished. In the dark, heated passion of his embrace the nightmare of the past was a distant memory, stripped of its power over her future. Instincts older than time were guiding her, urging her to move with him until she could no longer be still.

She heard him say her name, his voice desperate, driven; felt his arms tighten with almost crushing force, and realised in vague wonder that he was as helpless in this moment of complete and utter unity as she, taking pleasure from her body even as he gave it.

And then a sweet, wild fire began suffusing every quivering nerve she possessed, sweeping her beyond thought into a maelstrom of exquisite sensation until, with a sob of mindless surrender, she gave herself into his keeping, trusting him to keep her safe, while the deep, secret pulses of ecstasy throbbed through her body with every shuddering beat of her heart, bonding her to him for all time.

CHAPTER FOURTEEN

SHE awoke to sunshine and an absence of shadows. Somewhere nearby she heard the sound of water being poured and then the quiet closing of a door. Nick must have ordered a bath for her, she thought drowsily. How had he known when she would wake?

Sarah turned her head on the pillow and sleepily surveyed the thoroughly rumpled bed in which she was lying. The bed wasn't the only object in that condition. She was feeling thoroughly rumpled herself. Deliciously rumpled. In fact, her state of rumpledness would have been quite complete except that she wasn't wearing anything.

A beatific smile spread across her face. She was alone but no longer lonely. Nick had become so much a part of her, had made her so completely his, that even without his presence she felt linked to him in some vital way.

She smiled again and hugged the pillow to herself as happiness welled in her heart. Oh, if she had ever let herself dream of such a night the reality would have far surpassed any maidenly imaginings. To fall asleep in her husband's arms after he had tenderly cared for her after her initiation into womanhood had been almost sweeter than what had gone before. He might not love her and yet she had felt loved; infinitely cherished, infinitely safe.

She had thought there couldn't be more, but he had woken her twice during the night, teaching her the joys of sharing as well as surrender, making love to her until nothing existed except the dark, tender world of physical intimacy that he created for them. And though each time had been as the first, as gentle, the pleasure he had given her became so intense that at the end she thought she might die of it.

And then just after dawn he had left her. She remembered stirring, a murmured protest on her lips when the warmth of his arms was withdrawn. He had hesitated, one hand clenching on the curve of her thigh. Then, with a gruff command to go back to sleep he had gone. She had obeyed, sinking back dreamlessly into slumber, both mind and body in a state of blissful satiation.

She laughed suddenly, feeling quite unaccountably giddy, and hugged the pillow again. The future beckoned, bright and full of promise. She would heal the pain in Nick's heart and then set about winning his love. In her euphoric state she had no doubt that such a feat was entirely possible. After all, he had healed her, and she loved him so much.

A sudden vision came to her, of a predator prowling through darkness, always in shadow, hunting by night. He had lived in the shadows of war and loss too long, but she would make sure his future was full of life and laughter and love. The way her own life had been before tragedy had overtaken her.

Sarah glanced towards her dressing-room as memory stirred—of one thing still remaining. Somewhere in her wardrobe there was a small bandbox containing a bundle of clothes. The clothes she had been wearing on that last day with Amy. She had never worn them again but, racked by grief and guilt had been unable to destroy them.

But now everything had changed. Her love for Nick had made her whole again. Before she left her room she would hunt out those old clothes and have them taken away. Then she would be free of the past, free to coax her panther into the light.

Flinging back the covers with a sudden burst of

energy, Sarah hurried into her dressing-room and rang
for her maid. The task of bathing and donning a
chemise, petticoat and figured muslin gown didn't take
long. As soon as her hair was pinned up in a simple knot
from which tendrils hung in natural curls, she dismissed
the girl, then, taking a deep breath, she opened her
wardrobe and rummaged for the bandbox.

Her hands shook slightly as she drew it forth and
knelt on the floor to open it. There was still a lingering
trace of fear, but it seemed different. She wasn't sure if
it was caused by the mystery surrounding yesterday's
shooting or because she was confronting her nightmares
alone. She frowned as she lifted out the reticule she had
been carrying that day, remembering that she hadn't
told Nick about the part of the dream that had not
actually happened—where she'd been running from
danger.

A shiver raised the flesh on her arms at the thought,
and deciding there was no need to go through every
article of clothing, she lay the reticule down again. As
she did so something rustled inside. Strange. She tilted
her head, trying to remember. Had she been collecting
shells that day?

Curious now, Sarah retrieved the small bag and pulled
at the drawstrings. A few grains of sand lay at the
bottom, along with a cambric handkerchief, a length of
sea-green ribbon and something that had definitely not
been there eight years ago. A crumpled ball of paper.
Extracting it, she smoothed out the creases.

A quick glance at the writing thereon did not immediately solve the mystery. The note was in French. Scrambling to her feet, she carried the paper into her
bedchamber and over to the window, and was about to
bend her mind to the task of translating the faded
missive when the door opened and Nick strode into the
room.

All Sarah's faculties immediately seized up. It was

ridiculous after the night they had shared, but suddenly she was overwhelmed by a wave of paralysing shyness. It didn't help that the expression in his eyes as he looked at her seemed to her rattled nerves to be rather guarded. All her plans and resolutions were abruptly shaken by a quite hideous tremor of doubt.

'Oh! Good. . .morning, my lord.'

She expected a chiding comment, a smile—even the flicker of a smile would have been reassuring—but though the guarded expression faded as he crossed the room towards her, the intent searching look that took its place was equally as unnerving. He stopped only a yard or two away, but made no move to touch her.

'Are you all right?' he asked, his voice very low.

Even in her flustered state, Sarah recognised concern when she heard it. Her disordered brain promptly swerved in another direction. Had he taken her helpless response for distress? She remembered almost sobbing with ecstasy at one stage, remembered how tightly he had held her, remembered that although his muttered words had been of reassurance, his voice had been ragged, as driven as the powerful movements of his body.

She blushed to the roots of her hair and forced her throat to unlock. 'Yes, of course. Why would I not be? That is. . .' Her hand clenched, crumpling the note still clutched between her fingers.

Nick glanced down at once. 'I didn't mean to make you nervous, little one,' he said quite gently. 'Let me rescue that before you crush it beyond recognition.'

'Oh! No!' Sarah whipped the letter out of reach. 'It is nothing, my lord, I assure you. Merely. . .' Oh, good heavens, merely what? She couldn't think. Her action had been prompted by sheer instinct, a silent warning that she should read the missive herself, try to comprehend how it had come to be secreted with her belongings, before Nick saw it.

She should have known, however, that he would not be fobbed off with incoherent stutterings. He reached out, removed the letter from her frozen fingers and straightened it with a sharp flick of his wrist.

It took him only a second to see that it was written in French. He sent her one hard, very penetrating stare, then turned away and walked over to the fireplace to read it.

Sarah stared at his rigid back and felt her stomach start to churn. The tension emanating from him was so great she could almost see it humming in the air between them.

'Nick?'

He wheeled at the sound of her voice, stunned incredulity in his eyes. '*You*, Sarah? *You*?'

Completely at sea, abruptly terrified and not knowing why, she could only stand there, struggling to meet his gaze. The effort took every ounce of resolution she possessed. Incredulity was giving way to rage barely suppressed, but, far more devastating, behind the anger in his eyes she saw a bitter mockery that sliced into her heart with the savagery of a double-edged sword.

'Nick, I don't understand. What does it say?'

'You don't know, of course.'

She paled at the harsh sarcasm, but, somehow, it was that bitterness that gave her the strength to draw a semblance of dignity about herself, to lift her chin, to answer him, her eyes steady.

'No, I don't know. I found it only a few minutes ago among. . .among some old clothes and I haven't had a chance to read it.'

'Indeed? Then permit me to enlighten you, madam. I have not as yet perused the whole, myself, but a cursory glance is quite sufficient to establish to the meanest intelligence that this is a communication between spies!'

Her lips parted in shock. 'Spies? But how. . .? Oh, dear God, you don't think that *I*. . .?' She gazed at him in horror, unable to believe he would contemplate such a thing even for a moment.

He hardly seemed to hear her faint protest. 'Who else has access to your clothes, Sarah? Who else ventures to the beach armed? Or is found alone in a public garden, no doubt after meeting your accomplice. Oh, yes, you gulled me so easily, didn't you, my lady? With your shy innocence, your maidenly reluctance, your—'

'It wasn't *maidenly!*' She was suddenly rocked by a surge of anger so great it made her tremble violently. 'You *know* I was innocent! You know that, Nick. And you know why!'

He looked shaken out of his rage for a moment and she hurried on. 'What I told you last night was *true*. You must believe me! I would never betray—' But there she stopped, appalled, unable to continue as a dreadful suspicion flashed through her mind.

'Then you're shielding someone close to you. Or helping him. Is that it, Sarah? Your uncle? Or was it your sister? Is that what you meant last night when you said you should have stopped it?' He gave a laugh, short and hard. 'By God, I thought I had learned my lesson years ago after Marianne— But apparently not.'

'I know I can never be like her,' she began, her voice low and shaking. 'But it is not right to condemn me without—'

'Oh, you are more like her than you know,' he interrupted savagely. 'More talented, in fact. Let it console you that you made me forget for a few weeks how devious a woman can be.'

'Devious? No.' Stunned by this new charge, she could only flounder in utter confusion and hurt. 'Your wife was...'

'An angel?' His harsh laughter flayed her senses, mercilessly mocking. 'Yes, she even managed to look like an angel while she sat sobbing out a tale of abduction and rape when I caught her at an inn with the first of her many lovers. It was unfortunate from her point of view that the room contained a cheval mirror.'

'A. . .mirror?'

'I could see her face, my lady. The expression she thought she had hidden from me behind her hand while she wept. The performance was flawless—until I saw her secret smile. But that does not concern us now. Tell me, Sarah, were your nightmares caused by guilt, because you turned a blind eye to your sister's activities?'

She flinched at that but the pain of his accusations was becoming blurred. It hurt her that he would so instantly misjudge her, but a strange numbness was creeping over her. She was trying to think. There was something else Nick was telling her, something deeper than his words, but it was buried beneath the tangled weight of fact and surmise and suspicion buffeting her mind.

'*Answer me damn it!*'

She started, so lost in thought she hadn't realised he had come closer.

'Was Amy working with Crane?' he snarled. His hand flashed out before she could move and he circled her throat with his fingers. 'Or were you both in it up to your pretty necks?'

'I was only fourteen,' she whispered. 'Amy had been. . .flirting with Crane. That's what I meant. I should have told Uncle Jasper so he could put a stop to it, but it had happened before and she had always tired. . . I didn't know Crane would consider her promised to him. Nick, I didn't know he would kill her.'

Her voice broke, unconsciously pleading, and he stepped back, letting his hand fall.

Sarah scarcely noticed the frowning look in his eyes. He had not been hurting her, indeed his hand had been warm on her throat, his touch light. He might be enraged beyond reason, but somehow that gentle clasp had kept her from outright panic. But now desperation gripped her, setting her thoughts to scurrying back and forth like terrified mice.

'I don't know what Crane might have been doing,' she cried. 'But I can't believe that Amy... Nick, she was foolish and heedless and...and...like our mother in many ways, but she would not have turned traitor.'

'Could Crane speak French?'

'I...' Bewildered, she shook her head. 'No, of course not. He could scarcely read or write English. I couldn't understand why Amy—'

'Then how the bloody hell could he have acted alone?' he roared. 'Damn it, Sarah, we're left with you and your uncle. The proof is here in a letter you admit was in your possession and in language no servant would use.' He gestured furiously with the paper and started to translate aloud, biting the words off one by one. "Imperative we know the precise strength of the forces commanded by Well—"'

He stopped, so abruptly that Sarah blinked. Eyes narrowed, he scanned the rest in silence and then he went utterly white.

The change was so rapid that she did not immediately comprehend what was happening. Indeed, she had scarcely heard him for her mind and senses had been so battered she couldn't cope with anything more. Her only thought now was to escape. To find somewhere quiet and still so that, like a small wounded animal, she could hide while she tried to protect a heart in danger of shattering beyond repair.

Her nervous gaze darted from Nick to the door and she took a trembling step in that direction.

'No! Sarah.... God, what have I done? Sarah, I didn't mean—'

A discreet tap on the door cut him off. Before he could stop her, Sarah darted forward and opened it. Winwick was standing on the other side, looking faintly outraged at having to intrude on the lady of the house before she had left her bedchamber.

'I beg your pardon, my lady, but his lordship wished to be informed immediately should anyone ask for him, and there is an individual below who—'

'Yes, thank you, Winwick.' Nick strode across the room and into the butler's line of vision. 'I'll see him in a minute.'

'Yes, my lord, but that is not all—'

Seeing Winwick determined to continue, Sarah seized her opportunity. She slipped through the open doorway, ignoring Nick's fierce command to stop, and sped along the passage to the main staircase. Halfway down the stairs, knowing she was out of sight, she halted, clutching the bannister with one hand while the other tried to prevent her heart from splintering against her ribs. There was a terrible ache in her chest and she couldn't see, couldn't seem to focus properly.

The agony was not so much for the hurt Nick had dealt her—the shocking truth about Marianne, bewildering though it was, had somehow brought a measure of understanding, an instinctive knowledge that his accusations had not been wholly rational. No, the ache was for the pain Nick had suffered, and the enormity, the sheer impossibility, of the task she had set herself. A man who had once loved could perhaps be taught to love again, but a man who had been betrayed? A man who had then deliberately chosen to live among shadows, where betrayal was constant and a way of life?

Sarah clutched the bannister more tightly as a crushing weight of despair threatened to descend on her. Even Nick's trust seemed as beyond her reach as the stars, and yet how could she not try to win it, no matter how long it took?

Dear God, *this* was love, she thought, almost staggering under the realisation. Not just the pleasure and closeness of the night, nor the giddy happiness of this morning, but this emotion that filled her entire being, that forgave, that understood, that was stronger than resentment or anguish or doubt. An emotion that could, she discovered, still cling to hope in the face of seemingly insurmountable odds.

Shaken and trembling, she continued down the stairs, driven by the need to find a place where she could think. There was so much to consider. Nick's accusations for a start, and the horrifying conclusion that since she was innocent, the next likely suspect was her uncle. And yet she could not believe Uncle Jasper had lied to her all these years. He was too kind, too honourable. Somehow she had to make Nick believe that. He had not meant those terrible things. If she could just stay calm and explain. . .

She reached the hall and remembering that Winwick had interrupted to announce a caller, turned towards the library. Whoever the 'individual' was, he was probably waiting in the small room where Nick conducted estate business. The library would be empty and quiet.

She opened the door and stepped into the room — and remembered an instant too late that Winwick had been about to say something else.

'Oh! Excuse me, I. . .'

The gentleman who had been standing before the fireplace, studying the portrait above him, turned at the sound of her voice. He was tall and lean, with pale brown hair and eyes that rather matched his buff-coloured coat. Sarah had the strangest feeling that she had seen him somewhere before, but then she looked again at his eyes and forgot the notion. They were very bright, almost expectant, as though their owner was anticipating some excitement.

She wasn't sure if this was the 'individual' or another visitor, but for some reason that avid stare made her uneasy.

'I beg your pardon, sir,' she murmured, reaching back

for the door knob. 'No doubt you're waiting for my husband. He will be down directly.'

The man turned more fully towards her. 'Oh, no need to run off, my dear Lady Ravensdene,' he said in a very precise, very polite tone. 'Your presence will save us all some considerable time and trouble. Do come in and sit down.'

Instead of complying, Sarah stood rooted to the spot. Every drop of blood drained from her face. There was a roaring in her ears. It drowned out his last words, but she had heard enough. She would never forget that voice. Never.

'*You!*' Her horrified whisper echoed through the room seconds before the door was slammed open with a force that propelled her forward in an automatic move to avoid being trampled.

Nick strode into the library, his gaze lighting on her immediately. 'Sarah? Oh, my darling, thank God you haven't left the house! I didn't mean it, sweetheart! I—'

'Dear me, how very touching. And most convenient, I do declare. Yes, Ravensdene, it is I. Please close and lock the door behind you. If you need an incentive, you may notice that this small pistol in my hand is pointed at your wife. A toy, but it fires quite accurately over short distances.'

Nick froze, his eyes going very light and narrow. For a moment as his gaze flashed to the man in front of him, Sarah thought he was going to attack, then he seemed to relax, to go still and watchful.

'You won't shoot anyone in here, Catsby,' he said calmly. But he closed the door nevertheless.

Sarah jolted as the key turned in the lock. She hadn't taken her eyes off Nick, as if the sight of his face, hard and alert, would hold the recurrence of her nightmare at bay. He had not looked at her after that first searing glance, but she sensed he was aware of every breath she drew.

'Nick.' She could barely whisper. 'He was there. . . that day. He was the other man.'

'Ah. You do recognise me,' Catsby said before Nick could answer. 'I wondered if you had seen me the day your sister died, my lady, but when there was no investigation I thought I was safe. All these years. Such a shame that you had to give up your retiring life, Sarah. Really, you know, I could not take the chance that our paths might cross after you were so ill-advised as to marry Wellington's top agent.'

'You know. . .' Her brain reeling, Sarah glanced from one man to the other. 'You know each other?'

'He's my contact's secretary,' Nick said without shifting his gaze from the man whose hand was clenched around the pistol. He moved slightly, drawing Catsby's attention away from Sarah. 'So you tried to kill her yesterday, Catsby. Why not me? I was the one set to catch you and your accomplice, as you clearly know.'

'Quite correct, Ravensdene. You see, our esteemed superior has a habit of mumbling to himself whenever he is worried. One can hardly blame him for such an indiscretion—who notices a mere secretary, after all? I knew all about his little trap, baited with false information, but I could hardly shoot you out of hand. Think of the fuss. I couldn't risk that while true information continues to net me a tidy sum.'

'Money?' Nick scorned. 'Is that all the war means to you, Catsby?'

'Easy to be contemptuous when you're not obliged to live on a meagre salary,' Catsby spat, an ugly look momentarily twisting his features. He seemed to regain control of himself with an effort. 'A gentleman's pleasures are expensive, as I'm sure you'll understand. As for yesterday, well I confess that bungled shot was the result of temper. Your wife must have as many lives as a cat.'

He turned to Sarah, a chilling smile on his lips. 'I

nearly had you in those gardens at Eastbourne, you know. But Ravensdene always did have a habit of being where one would most wish him not to be.'

'The man in the street,' Sarah murmured, remembering. 'You nearly collided with us.'

'Yes, a fortuitous coincidence, was it not? I was in Eastbourne ostensibly to check on Ravensdene's progress, but, having seen you, decided to follow you instead. What I heard of your conversation was enough to cause me grave concern. You hadn't appeared to recognise me, but I couldn't take any chances once I knew Ravensdene had made your acquaintance. I followed you to the ruins, also, and later in the woods. It was most annoying to be so constantly interrupted by a succession of fools.'

'You've been stalking her?'

Nick's voice was so gentle that for a moment Sarah wondered why she went so cold inside at the sound of it. Then she saw his eyes and knew instantly that, though she had never seen that look before, others had. It was the utterly emotionless, ice-cold deadly stare of the predator, waiting for the right moment to kill.

'Dear me, you seem to think this is personal, my lord. Please disabuse your mind of the notion. Violence is most abhorrent to me, but my creditors are becoming rather insistent. Quite threatening, in fact. If violence is to be done, therefore, I would rather—'

'Abhorrent!' Sarah stared at him, hardly aware of having spoken. 'How can you say that when you stood by and watched while Amy—?'

'Sarah. Don't, sweetheart.'

'Oh, it's quite all right, Ravensdene. No, no, my dear, you must acquit me of condoning the assault on your sister.'

'Acquit you! I saw—'

Catsby made a deprecating noise. 'You saw my French accomplice, Henri, my lady. And Crane, of course. He was our go-between. Yes, I can see you've already worked out that there were three of us, Ravensdene. Your mistake was in assuming that since no one from the Foreign Office travelled to this part of the coast regularly, the information was posted to an accomplice. A logical assumption, but erroneous. A go-between was necessary to let me know when Henri arrived, since I could not loiter about Comberford without being noticed. Much safer to stay at an inn several hours away. Whenever I rode out everyone assumed I was visiting a mistress somewhere nearby, an impression I was always careful to impart. Amazing what people will swallow if one follows a regular routine.'

'However, to return to my story: useful though he was, Crane was becoming a problem. Really, that entire afternoon was a series of the most irritating setbacks. I was delayed by my horse throwing a shoe, and Henri, no doubt in a Gallic frenzy at the thought of missing the tide, decided to write me a note and leave it with Crane. There was absolutely no need for Crane to accompany Henri back to the beach, and no need to panic when they chanced upon two heedless girls. Henri, of course, fled directly to the beach after Sarah was struck, but then that fool Crane argued with Miss Lynley and one thing led to another. *I* had no knowledge of what had occurred until I came upon the scene after Crane had, er, finished with Miss Lynley. She was almost insensible with shock, but naturally I had to kill her.'

'Naturally?' Sarah's voice trembled and she saw Nick move abruptly before going still again when Catsby shifted to aim the gun at him.

'She knew too much,' he went on, watching Nick but still addressing her. 'I assure you I did not enjoy the task. Murder is such an unpleasant business, and then there was Crane to dispose of as well.'

'A fool but also a convenient scapegoat,' Nick said dryly.

'Precisely. It took little persuasion to convince Crane that he was in grave danger of being hanged for rape and murder. We joined Henri on the beach where Crane was, er, permanently silenced. Unfortunately, we then discovered that he had mislaid the letter Henri had left for me—we assumed during his contretemps with the lady, since it was not on him when we searched his body. That gave me a few nasty moments, I can tell you, but the woods were full of Sir Jasper's men by then and we couldn't chance going back to look for it. We had already been forced to flee the scene before ascertaining whether Sarah was still alive.'

Sarah shuddered at this cold-blooded recitation of events, but her mind was now strangely clear and very calm. The spectre that had haunted her for years had finally materialised, and now that she faced the reality fear had gone, replaced by an grim determination to see him pay for his crimes.

'You killed Amy,' she said very softly as though making it clear.

She felt Nick glance at her. 'Easy, love. He won't get away with it.'

'Oh, you think not, Ravensdene?' Catsby's polite tone slipped a little. 'You may be rash enough to try disarming me on your own, but you won't risk Sarah's life. It didn't take me more than a minute to see you're besotted with the girl.'

Nick's eyes met hers for the merest second but Sarah felt her heart shake. 'Yes, I love her,' he said calmly. 'And I'm not prepared to see you or anyone else take her from me, Catsby.'

'Oh, Nick. . .'

'Yes, yes, very touching, as I observed before,' Catsby interposed testily. 'However, let me assure you, Ravensdene, that I intend you to go together.'

'Don't be an idiot, Catsby. Who do you think is going to be your scapegoat for murder this time? One of the servants? As soon as you fire a shot they'll be breaking down the door. You wouldn't get beyond the terrace.'

Catsby smiled coldly. 'I am not quite the fool you believe me to be, Ravensdene. We shall go out to the garden where your servants have heard you firing guns at targets for several days, and there you will have a most tragic lovers' quarrel.'

He turned to Sarah. 'Brought on, of course, by your husband's investigation into Sir Jasper's affairs, my dear Sarah. You see, it is all perfectly logical. Distraught, you plead with Ravensdene to desist, becoming quite hysterical in the process and taking no heed of the fact that he is armed. In the ensuing struggle, he is accidentally shot. What else is there to do but put a period to your own existence? By the time the servants realise something is amiss, I will have returned to Eastbourne, where I have been staying, quite innocently, under orders to assist Ravensdene. Brilliant, as I'm sure you'll agree.'

'Not quite, Catsby,' Nick contradicted, much to Sarah's relief. She had been racking her brains to find a flaw in Catsby's scheme, but short of refusing to be marched at gunpoint out to the garden, she could find none.

'You see, I sent Figgins to London last night to discover if anyone from the Foreign Office was in the habit of travelling to *any* location a few hours' ride from here. Once he knows where, it will be a simple matter to bring the innkeeper to London to identify you. It's over. I suggest you leave the country immediately.'

'What!' Sarah gaped at him. 'You're going to let him—'

'*No!*' It was Catsby who interrupted her, his eyes wild. 'I won't leave the country and live in squalor. Don't you understand, Ravensdene? I'm in debt. Facing complete ruin. I can't let you stop me.' He jerked the pistol at Sarah, his polite façade cracking. 'Get over to the window and open it!'

When she hesitated, he lifted the pistol and pointed it straight at her heart.

'Sarah! Do as he says!'

Nick's sharp command jolted her into moving. She cast him a pleading look over her shoulder and he smiled faintly, softening his tone. 'Don't be afraid, my darling. I won't let him hurt you.'

It wasn't herself she was worried about. Catsby was clearly beyond reason, desperate enough to kill them here if he was pushed too far. Trying frantically to think of a way out of their predicament, she walked over to one of the long windows and unlatched it. Her gaze fell on the large shell she had placed on the adjoining ledge. She went very still.

'Good.' Following her, Catsby motioned Nick closer, matching him step for step. 'Now, we'll go outside as if for a stroll. Push the window open, Sarah.'

She lifted her hand as if to obey, moving very slowly.

Her hesitation was too much for Catsby. He began to swing the pistol towards her again, and in the split second when it was pointing harmlessly at air, she bent, grabbed the shell and hurled it straight at him.

He cursed viciously, flinging up his hand to protect his face. The gun went off with a deafening roar at the same time that Nick went past her in a deadly lunge that took Catsby down to the floor with him. The two men rolled, sending a chair toppling, then Nick came up on one knee, his arm hooked around his enemy's throat. Sarah saw the muscles bunch beneath his coat an instant before a sharp crack rent the air.

Everything seemed to go very quiet. Letting Catsby slide to the floor, Nick got to his feet and looked at her.

Sarah could only stare back at him across the few feet that separated them, unable to believe it was over. 'Do you think you should search him?' she finally asked, trying to sound perfectly calm. 'He might have another pistol.'

'Sweetheart—' The cold, deadly glitter left his eyes, leaving something dark and hurting. 'He's dead, Sarah.'

'Dead? Oh. Yes, of course he is.' Somewhere in the distance she could hear the servants hammering on the door. The noise was vaguely annoying. 'For a minute I thought you were going to let him escape.'

'Only while you were in danger. Sarah. . .'

'It's quite all right, you know.' She smiled at him. At least she hoped it was a smile because Nick seemed rather worried about something, but her face felt so stiff it was difficult to be sure. 'Thank you,' she added in a very polite voice.

'*Thank you*?'

She nodded. And her control crumpled. With a strangled sob of relief and reaction she flung herself into his arms. 'Oh, Nick, I thought he had killed you. . .when the pistol went off.'

'No.' His arms closed about her at once, strong and protective. 'Oh, God, Sarah, I'm sorry. I'm so sorry!'

She raised brimming eyes to his face. 'For what?'

'Yes, there are quite a few things for which I have to beg your forgiveness,' he said grimly. The line of his mouth hardened. 'Not least of which is the way I endangered your life and then caused you to witness. . . Oh, Sarah, little one—' his hand came up to brush away her tears '—you've had to live with such violent memories. I didn't want you to see me kill someone, to know what I've been, what I am.'

'You're the man I love,' she sobbed, clinging closer. 'Of course you're capable of killing someone, but only to protect others, not for your own gain. I'm *glad* he's dead. Why do you think I threw that shell?'

His laugh was ragged, and laced with wonder. 'My brave little love. Fortunately your aim is better with shells than with pistols. Oh, sweetheart, say that again. About loving me.'

She tried to obey but found that she was crying too

hard. And Nick was holding her too tightly, her cheek pressed to his racing heart, his face buried in her curls. His arms were like steel about her, but he was shaking.

Abandoning the impossible task of trying to sound coherent, she let their embrace speak for her, drawing warmth and strength from him while giving of her own.

A minute passed before he gently tipped her face up and kissed her. There was still a faint tremor in his hands and she gazed up at him wonderingly, awed that this controlled, powerful man could be rendered so vulnerable. And for love of her. She was almost afraid to believe it.

Then he smiled at her, and the tender concern burning through the amusement in his eyes removed every shadow of doubt from her horizon.

'Can you be brave for a little while longer, my darling?' he murmured. 'I think Winwick has found another key to the door. And I know he is going to disapprove most vehemently of shots fired inside a gentleman's house.'

Two hours later, Sarah was precisely where she most wanted to be. Ensconced on her husband's lap in her bedchamber, secure in his embrace, and engaged in the agreeable task of reassuring him that she was perfectly recovered from the vissicitudes of the morning.

'Would the innkeeper's evidence really have been sufficient to convict Catsby of treason?' she asked, having been doubtful on that point ever since Figgins had returned with confirmation of Nick's theory.

'Probably not sufficient for a conviction,' he admitted. 'But the suspicion alone, had it come to the ears of the cents-per-cents, would have made his life extremely unpleasant. Besides, he was in no condition to reason with any clarity of intellect this morning. The mere knowledge that I had exposed his methods was enough to tip him over the edge into panic.'

He drew her closer, his head bent protectively over hers. 'And once I knew he was the cause of the nightmare you've lived with all these years, I never intended to let the matter go to court.'

Sarah nodded and decided not to mention the small fact that she would have liked to have known of his intention. She had already scolded him for omitting to inform her that he'd been armed all along—to which he had replied, unarguably, that they could hardly have conducted a conversation on the subject at the time. And her panther was still looking rather tense and dangerous. It was time to turn the discussion into more interesting channels. Such as when he had first come to love her.

'Hmm. I think it was that night at the Wribbonhalls' when you laughed at the notion of carrying a pistol to a party,' he mused, pretending to consider when she put this crucial question to him.

Then he added with a rueful smile, 'Not that I was admitting any such thing *then*. I knew I wanted you, my darling, and had done from the moment I had you pinned to that tree, but even last night when I realised how close you'd come to being killed, I wouldn't let myself think in terms of love. The fear of losing you was too great.'

Sarah nestled closer. 'You won't lose me, Nick. Not ever.'

'I don't deserve that,' he said, his voice husky. 'Not after this morning.' He brought his hands up to frame her face, gazing into her eyes, his own dark and anguished. 'God forgive me, Sarah, when I saw that letter I tried to tell myself it couldn't be love tearing me apart, but I was lying. I knew then that I loved you no matter what you might have done, that I'd do anything to keep you from prison or execution, and that knowledge made me blind with rage. It's no excuse, but that's why I lashed out at you, why I was so damned unreasonable.'

'It's all right,' she murmured. 'I knew, somewhere inside me, that you weren't really saying those things to me.'

'When I started reading that cursed letter aloud and saw that it referred to *Wellesley*, as the Duke was once known, everything you'd been saying suddenly made sense. Apart from your own honour, you would have been too young to have been involved. My God, if you knew what I felt then. I couldn't think beyond the fear that I had driven you away forever. Even now I don't know how you can forgive me. I don't deserve you, Sarah, but I swear to God I'll spend the rest of my life trying to.'

'Oh, Nick, hush. I can hardly blame you for suspecting me when *I* suspected poor Uncle Jasper for a few horrible minutes, and with even less evidence. I suppose that letter was shoved into my reticule by the servants who found me that day. Being unable to read French, they would have thought it was mine if it lay nearby. Later I directed one of the maids to pack everything away, never dreaming something so damning existed. If I hadn't known Uncle Jasper so well. . .'

'Yes, you've had years to build your faith in your uncle, whereas I. . .'

'Whereas your faith had been destroyed,' she finished softly. 'I understand, Nick. Truly I do. You must—' She faltered and glanced away, sitting up straighter so he held her only lightly. 'You must have loved her very much.'

'Is that what you've been thinking?' he asked. And when she only nodded, he drew her close again, turning her face up for his kiss. 'I thought it was only your fear of men, or, rather, of intimacy with a man.'

She blushed and shook her head. 'Not with you.'

'Oh, love, if ever I heard an invitation. . .'

Smiling, he let the sentence trail off, but as she shyly returned his smile his expression changed, turning fiercely intent. 'Sarah, you don't know how rare and precious you are. Your innocence, your sweetness, your truth and courage. Yes, twelve years ago I fell in love with a pretty face. A boy's love that couldn't see past the surface to the vanity and shallowness beyond. And Marianne's betrayal did hurt for a while, but by the time she'd conceived another man's child and died, I didn't love her at all. There was nothing there to love.'

'I'm sorry,' she whispered, aching for the boy whose heart must at least have been bruised, his illusions shattered.

He kissed her again. 'I'm not. Because when I did find the woman I could love, my heart knew her instantly— even if my mind took a while to catch up.'

'Oh, Nick. . .' She couldn't help but laugh, even through the tears of happiness filling her eyes. 'I would rather have a man's love than a boy's.'

'You have both,' he said very softly. 'You've given me back a part of myself I thought was lost forever, Sarah. You've given me back a belief in honour, in goodness.' He bent and kissed her with devastating gentleness. 'You've given me back tenderness.'

'I don't think it was ever truly lost,' she said, touching his cheek with loving fingers. 'Just buried for a while. So you could survive in the world you lived in.'

'Oh, Sarah. . .my own sweetheart. . .' His arms closed around her in fierce possession. Sarah felt the surge of power in his body as he lifted her and rose from the chair to carry her over to the bed.

'I shouldn't do this,' he muttered hoarsely, laying her down as if she might break. 'Not after last night. It's still new to you. But I need you, darling. I need you more than you'll ever know. I'll be so gentle with you, I swear it.'

'I know,' she whispered, drawing him down to her.

'I'm not afraid, Nick. I was before because of Amy, but also. . .it wasn't *finished*. I always sensed danger somewhere, waiting. I think that's why I started walking and riding alone. I had some vague notion of drawing the danger out so I could be free. But now you've taken it away, and. . . I want you, too.'

A sound of raw need tore from his throat as he took her in his arms, sweeping her beneath him with a barely restrained urgency that made her go weak all over. She quivered with excitement at the feel of his weight on her, loving his strength, feeling deliciously helpless, but safe. So incredibly safe.

Their lips met. Clothing fell away. Whispered words of love, of need, of desire, drifted in the warm, golden light filtering through the half-drawn bed curtains. And this time their love was given freely, openly. Nothing was held back. Love so ardent, pleasure so intense, they reached the heights of ecstasy together and hovered there, their souls touching for one rare, timeless moment, before they rested, entwined, still one, so close they could not tell one heartbeat from the other.

A long time passed before Sarah stirred and looked up at her husband. She melted all over again when she saw the expression in his glittering green eyes. No longer hard or cold or dangerous, but warm and tender, and filled with so much love she felt her lips tremble with the quick rush of emotion filling her heart.

'I never imagined a man could be so gentle,' she whispered.

He smiled lazily and glanced down at their entwined limbs. 'You're not ready for anything else yet, my little love, but when you're used to me, when you feel completely safe, sometimes it'll be so wild you'll think we're soaring. But I'll never hurt you, Sarah. Not ever.'

Sarah thought about that and felt a distinctly wicked, distinctly female smile curve her lips. She raised herself on one elbow, crossed her arms on Nick's chest and propped her chin on her hands. 'How long do you think it will take me to grow accustomed to you, my lord?'

He grinned. 'Well, you're already showing an unusual aptitude for driving me out of my mind, so...' He cupped her head in one large hand and drew her closer to take her lower lip lightly between his teeth. 'Not long at all,' he growled.

Sarah had a sudden thought that it might be dangerous to arouse a panther. The notion didn't bother her at all.

'Would tomorrow be too long?' she enquired innocently.

'Why hurry?' he murmured, and gave her another of those biting little kisses. She felt his body tense against hers. 'First I'm going to taste every inch of you, sweet Sarah, and I intend to take my time over the process.'

Her arms wreathed around his neck. 'You do?'

'Yes.' Holding her lambent gaze with his, he turned slowly until she was beneath him. His hand cradled her face, gently holding her still for a kiss that was not gentle at all, but deep and possessive. When he lifted his head a long time later and Sarah saw the intense glitter in his eyes, she shivered in tingling anticipation.

'Sarah,' he said very softly. 'You know, I once told Dev that Marianne was like a blazing chandelier; the flames burn so hotly they swiftly die. But you, my Sarah, are the single candle flame that will burn in my heart for evermore.'

'Oh, Nick, I love you so...'

He didn't let her finish, but it hardly mattered, Sarah mused happily as Nick swept her once more into their private world of love and desire. It had all been said anyway. Her panther would never be entirely tamed, but she had won his heart. He would walk by her side.

For evermore.

Historical Romance™

Coming next month

EMMA AND THE EARL
Paula Marshall
REGENCY ENGLAND

Miss Emma Lawrence was badly in need of a new job, and
had no choice about accepting the post of governess to
Lady Letitia Hastings, young daughter of Dominic
Hastings, the Earl of Chard. What unkind twist of fate had
brought her to this, working for the man she might have
married when she was the rich Miss Emilia Lincoln?
And—more worrying—would he recognise her? In ten
years they had both changed out of all recognition—but
what had not changed was Emma's abiding love for
Dominic…

SEAFIRE
Sarah Westleigh
REGENCY 1814/15

Having finished school, Miss Miranda Dawson was on her
way to Barbados to join her family. But the uncomfortable
relations between America and England landed her in
trouble when the American ship Seafire attacked. Taken
prisoner of war by the Captain, Adam York, Miranda was
determined not to be cowed, and her defiant attitude
earned the admiration of Adam. But with their two
countries virtually at war, what future did they have?

One to Another

A year's supply of Mills & Boon® novels— absolutely FREE!

Would you like to win a year's supply of heartwarming and passionate romances? Well, you can and they're FREE! Simply complete the missing word competition below and send it to us by 28th February 1997. The first 5 correct entries picked after the closing date will win a year's supply of Mills & Boon romance novels (six books every month—worth over £150). What could be easier?

PAPER	B A C K	WARDS
ARM		MAN
PAIN	F U L L	ON
SHOE	L A C E	TOP
FIRE		MAT
WAIST	C O A T	HANGER
BED		BOX
BACK		AGE
RAIN		FALL
CHOPPING		ROOM

Please turn over for details of how to enter 🖘

How to enter...

There are ten missing words in our grid overleaf.
Each of the missing words must connect up with the
words on either side to make a new word—e.g.
PAPER-BACK-WARDS. As you find each one, write it in
the space provided, we've done the first one for you!

When you have found all the words, don't forget to fill in
your name and address in the space provided below and
pop this page into an envelope (you don't even need a
stamp) and post it today. Hurry—competition ends
28th February 1997.

Mills & Boon® One to Another
FREEPOST
Croydon
Surrey
CR9 3WZ

Are you a Reader Service Subscriber?   Yes ❑   No ❑

Ms/Mrs/Miss/Mr _____

Address _____

_____

_____ Postcode _____

One application per household.

You may be mailed with other offers from other reputable companies as a
result of this application. If you would prefer not to receive such offers,
please tick box.   ❑

mps
MAILING
PREFERENCE
SERVICE

C496
A